WHISPERING WIND

THE LEGEND

CIN MEDLEY

MED'S PUB
PUBLISHING

Published by: Med Pub's Publishing
Copyright © 2015 C. J. Medley
All Rights Reserved
ISBN 10: 978-0-9974021-5-5
ISBN 13: 0997402156
Cover by: Amanda Walker PA & Design Services
Editing by: Kendra's editing and book services-Kendra Gaither
Formatted by: Med's Pub Publishing

For McKenna
My Lou
You will always be my Princess I love you, forever Nana

My Beautiful Britt, without knowing you and learning from you I would have never known the patience I needed to write this story. I love you.

For the man of my dreams David, thank you for always encouraging me to go with it, your hand is in this story more than you know. I love you.

My friend Veronica (Roni) Colvin, thank you for reading all the pages, taking my phone calls at all hours of the day and night and for your insights. Someday Incredible will hopefully see the light of day!!!

And to all the rest who have read this story, given me your thoughts and critiques. I am thankful that you loved it so much and helped me decide to go through with it. You know who you are!

CHAPTER ONE

The sky was the most magnificent shade of blue. The wind blew gently and silently. The swaying of the grass and wildflowers that surrounded me, hidden in the field of bliss, spoke for the breeze.

My thoughts were full of the adventure my heart longed for, when Father's voice eased into my mind, "She is just like you, a wild spirit."

Mother's sweet voice followed his, "She will grow out of it, just as I did."

My father's bellowing laughter followed. My brothers call me a banshee, and a smile pulled at my lips. "It is only because I can best you at swords," I said to my oldest brother, Ardes. I could feel it deep in my soul, deep in my heart, that I would not grow out of this feeling, out of this desire, to live a great adventure. A heavy, happy, peaceful sigh escaped me, just as the low murmur of thunder moved across the land.

I hummed the lullaby Mother used to sing to me, smiling at the thought in my mind, as I rolled on my side and rested my head on my hand. The thunder came again, this time louder. The ground felt like it had a beating heart, like a sleeping giant had been roused into an awakened state. I did not remember ever feeling the ground move with such vibration.

It did not make sense, this thunder; the sky was clear, the sun high in the sky at midday. Pushing myself into a sitting position and turning my head away from the village to gaze out at the horizon, I saw the cloud. It was so low to the ground, it seemed to be touching it. Turning my head toward the village and wondering if I could make it home before the rain soaked me, I could not help but smile as I remembered the race from this very spot with my brothers, Ardes, Simon, and Westin. It had been a day just like this.

We were up on this hill practicing our swords. The boys always let me tag along. Ardes thought it best I learn to defend myself. When we heard the trumpets, we looked out at the horizon and could see the dust from the carriages.

"Jenna!" Ardes yelled.

Jenna lived in a neighboring kingdom, one in which Father worked very hard to maintain peace. The agreement was to meld the two families, to bond them by marriage. Ardes was to inherit our kingdom when Father was no longer able to rule. By joining our families, our kingdoms would ensure the treaty and keep peace throughout the land.

Ardes had met Jenna a few times on his solitaire rides through the countryside, so when Father told him of the marriage arrangement, he could not have been happier. This was the day that Jenna and her family were to come to prepare for the wedding. I love Jenna and knew she was going to be a wonderful sister and a valued addition to our family. I needed an ally in this family of boys.

"I will race you, Ardes, and if I win, I get to spend the entire day tomorrow with Jenna, with no interruptions from you."

"You are on, little sister."

Off we went, all four of us, running.

"If I win," Ardes yelled, "then I get the whole day with Jenna, without you."

This only made me run faster. There was no way he was going to spend the whole day alone with her. I needed a sister. I needed another female mind in the halls of Whispering Wind. Mother always agreed with Father, and his word was not to be negotiated. My legs were starting to burn as they carried me down the hill, my long red hair flying out behind me, the wind on my face, and the air rushing in and out of my lungs. Simon and Westin were on my heels, and Ardes was close enough in front of me that I could have reached out and grabbed him. Being the little sister was not an easy thing, especially when your brothers excelled at everything they did.

I made it to the edge of the village first, but Ardes, Westin, and Simon knew the village better than I did with all its twists and turns. They knew the shortest distances between here and the great gates that led to the castle. Father always forbade me from wandering the village alone, but as long as I stayed on the main road, I could come and go without guards. Having the guards follow me around when my brothers were not with me always made me feel like no one saw me for me; they just saw the king's daughter. The villagers treated me differently when the guards were with me, and I did not like that, so I knew there was nothing I could do but run as fast as my legs would move. I glanced over my shoulder to see how quickly they were gaining on me, but they were scattering in three different directions, each one more determined than the next to win. We all had our own reasons for wanting to win, and we all enjoyed besting one another. For me especially, victory was the greatest; the little sister being better than her brothers. The boys knew the shortest distances to the gates, but I had the straight path. I did not need to slow my speed to move around things in my way.

My legs pumped, and my chest screamed as I ran, but there was no way they were going to beat me. I heard Westin laughing as he ran. He never cared who won at any of our games. He just loved playing. Simon yelled as I passed him, "You will not best me, little sister," just before he tripped over something and screamed in pain as he fell to the ground. The laughter surprised me as it came so easily. "I do not think so, big brother," I managed to yell out. Just then, the gates came into view. My heart was pounding with the sweet smell of victory.

I could hear them yelling as I ran down the road. I had no idea where they were, so I ran faster. It was not about winning the bet anymore, but about besting them. The gates grew closer; ten more strides and I would be through them. Victory will be mine.

Being smaller than my brothers, I was able to bound around the corners faster than they could. They would need to slow down to keep from falling.

"Oh no, little sister. I got this one," Ardes yelled out, winded and smiling *as he pushed harder to pass me. But I made it through the gate just before him. Victory is mine! Ardes was closer to me than I cared. If he had wanted, he could have reached out, grabbed my shoulder, and sent me tumbling to the ground, but he did not. I was around the first corner, and then all I had to do was fly into the courtyard, across the wooden bridge, and hit the wooden doors. It was easy to do.*

"I will get there before you." It sounded like he was talking directly into my ear. That was how close he was.

"Never!" I yelled as my feet dug into the earth to propel me across the courtyard.

The sound of my feet on the wooden bridge before his was sweet. Over the sound of my pounding heart, heavy breathing, and stomping feet, another sound seemed louder, Ardes screaming. My hands hit the doors, and my body collapsed in a heap, gasping for air as I sat there laughing; well, trying to laugh at Ardes. His boot had caught somehow, and he had tumbled to his knees, slamming him into a giant pillar of wood. The guards were running up to see what the ruckus was about. They were used to our competitions, so they were not very concerned until they helped Ardes up. My laughter turned into screams as I saw my oldest brother covered in blood. He had gashed his head. My victory seemed unimportant.

My smile now was well earned, as I had still won. I bested him. I had bested them all. It was the thunder and the vibration of the ground that brought me back from my memory of victory. My smile was quickly removed as I turned toward the horizon only to realize it was not thunder at all, but horses. I was frozen, just like that kitten I saw as a child in the cold season. It had fallen into the water and could not get out. It was frozen half in and half out of the lake. I felt so bad for the poor little thing. It looked like a statue, just like me; frozen in fear.

The cloud stretched across the horizon. It was dense and a deep ash grey in color, the thunder growing. The sound of the trumpets forced my head to turn toward the village. Fear gripped my heart as the sound was replaced with screams of terror, screams I had never heard before, and screams I would not soon forget. My eyes followed the villagers to the great gates.

"Father," I whispered. "MOTHER!" I screamed.

I was on my feet, and my head jolted back to the cloud, noticing it was closer; so much closer. I was staring down at the village, thinking I can make this run. I did it before. Only this time, there was much more at stake than an afternoon of giggling in the garden with Jenna.

Before I could think, my feet were moving. The thunder grew louder and louder, drowning out the screams from the village. The wind whipped against my face as I flew down the hill heading to my family; my beautiful family. Fear is what was driving me forward, moving my legs and pulsing through my body. The horses were closer than ever, and the thundering of the hooves was deafening. I just needed to get to the bottom of the hill, then across the small field to the village. The run through the village would be easy. Faster! My mind screamed, and then a blinding pain, then blackness, and then silence.

CHAPTER TWO

The sounds of the night were faint. The pain in my head overpowered me before blackness came again.

CHAPTER THREE

The light of the day was warm on my face, and I could taste blood in my mouth and smell an over powering odor. *What is that smell?* I could sense the light through my closed eyes as I struggled to open them. They fluttered, causing me to wince at the brightness of the day. There was movement close to me. I heard something rustle across the ground. *Where am I?* Something or someone touched my hand, I tried to pull away, but my body would not react. The fear was building. *'Where am I? What happened? Who is with me? WHAT is that smell?'*

"Sabine."

Did I just hear my name?

"Sabine."

My eyes fluttered again. The light of the day was blocked by the figure leaning over me.

"Sabine?"

That voice, do I know it?

As the fog started to lift from my mind, the memories became clear; the thunder, the cloud, and the screams. The screaming I was hearing in my head was me; I knew that, somehow, without ever opening my eyes. I knew my family was gone.

"Sabine? Sabine, we are safe. Sabine?"

I forced my eyes open, but it, was very difficult to focus. My head was screaming from the pain, and the fear of what I was seeing in front of me made me scream again. His clothes were filthy, torn in a few spots and spattered with blood. His face was smudged with dirt and soot, and his eyes were full of fear and tears.

"Sabine," he said in a shaky whispered voice.

"Westin?"

My once beautiful vibrant brother with his childlike personality, always laughing and playing jokes, was kneeling beside me now as a terrified and broken man.

"The horses, the village, Mother and Father... I was running to get home." The thoughts came out in whispers, more so for me than for Westin. "Westin," I asked cautiously, "what happened? Where is everyone?"

He sat down with a thump, his head cast downward as if he was unable to look at me, and he whispered just one word through his tears, "Dead"

My heart stopped. My ears were ringing, and my head was pounding as loud as my heart was slamming in my chest. *Did I hear him right?* Before I knew what I was doing, my hands were on Westin, and I was shaking him, screaming in his face. "What do you mean dead? Who is dead, Westin? Why are you here? Why am I here? Why are we not dead?"

He spoke in the smallest of voices, but hearing his words made no sense to me. "I saved us, Sabine. I saved us."

Before I could gain control of myself, I let go of him and was on my feet. I wanted to see. I needed to see them, but my head did not agree, and, just as quickly as I stood, I fell. Westin scooted closer to me, wrapping his arm around my shoulders. I leaned my head on his arm, and that is when I saw it. The pillars of black smoke floated up from behind the hill in the direction of my home. The scream came from deep inside me at the realization of what I was seeing. It just did not seem real. Westin was crying. We sat there in the light of the day, holding one another, fearing for our futures, and fearing for what laid just beyond the hill. The sun had moved across the sky, and the light of the day was fading.

Westin sighed. "I am so sorry, Sabine."

"What are you sorry for, Westin? I am the one who is sorry. I am the one who scared you. There is no reason to scare you more than you already are. Westin, would you please tell me how I got here, and what in the world is that, awful smell?" I smiled as best I could.

With a small voice and wide eyes, Westin began to tell what he knew. "I was out riding when I heard the thunder, so I started for home, riding fast through the forest. As I neared the edge, I saw them. There were so many horses, Sabine, more than I could count. I hid and waited for them to pass, then I started racing through the forest to the village. I heard the trumpets, and as I got closer, I could hear the screams. I was so scared."

My hand reached out to his. "I know. I was very scared, myself."

"That is when I saw you running down the hill. I knew they were going to see you, Sabine, so instead of heading to the village, I rode faster to stop you. I did not get it right, and you ran right into my horse. You went flying through the air and hit your head on a rock," he said, whispering through tears. "I thought you were dead."

He was in my arms instantly. "I am not dead. I am right here with you."

Westin stopped sobbing and continued on with his story. "I picked you up and put you on my horse, then rode back into the forest." As he turned to face me, I could see the horror in his eyes. "I could hear the screams, Sabine. They would not stop. I wanted them to stop, so I rode until I could not hear them anymore. I rode to here." He pointed to the ground where we were sitting. "I was so scared you were dead, but I listened to your chest, and it was thumping. I laid you here, and I sat there." He pointed, to a space a few feet away. "I did not know what to do, so I just sat here and waited and waited. I could see the fires in the sky, and it made the dark of the night glow. Then I heard the thunder again. I was so afraid they would come this way, but they did not." My breath was caught in my chest. What Westin was saying made no sense to me.

Who would do this? Who would burn Whispering Wind? The tears fell from my eyes as Westin continued. "I waited for the dark of the night to come and go two times, Sabine, and then I went to look. There is nothing left but bricks and ash. Where the ground is not black from the fires, it is red from…" he hesitated, but I knew what he was going to say. *Blood.* "I left my horse in the woods and snuck into the village, just in case they were still there. No one was there, Sabine. No one. They are all dead."

Dead? Everyone in the village was dead? My mind was searching for the truth in what Westin was saying.

"Father is dead?" I whispered, not wanting, to hear the answer. "Mother?"

Westin nodded his head. "They are all dead… Father, Mother, Ardes, Simon, Jenna."

The words did not seem real as I heard them. "Who would do this to our family, Westin?" He did not have an answer. There was not a rational answer for it; for any of this.

"I buried our family, Sabine. I think Father would not want you to see them like that, especially him."

"What do you mean, especially him?"

"Father, I found him nailed to the great gate. It was horrible. Our family was slaughtered." He could not control himself any longer. I held my brother while he cried, and I cried with him. From the horrors he saw, his mind must be shattered. We were all each other had. There was no one else left.

His sobs seemed to lighten, and he pulled away. "When the light of the day comes, I will take you there to see, but Sabine, everything is covered in blood. What was not covered in blood was this." He touched the smelly blanket I was covered with. "It was the only thing that was not. I found it on the ground when I was leaving to come back here to you."

"How many days was I sleeping?"

"It has been five nights and six days. I was afraid you were never going to wake up. You have a very big bump on your head." He reached up to touch my temple. "I was afraid I killed you trying to save you."

My mind was whirling around, spinning out of control, just like the spinning top Ardes had made for Juliana that she loved so much.

"Who did this, Westin? Do you know?"

"No, Sabine. I did not see the faces of those who killed our family. I took you and ran. I was afraid to look back or to go back to help."

"You did the right thing. If you had not stopped me, I would be dead as well." My head was pounding. My mouth was dry and tasted like blood. "Do we have any water?" Westin handed me a skin sack. The water felt cool running down my throat. I wanted to drink it all, but I did not know how much we had or where we would get more, so I only took enough to wash the taste of blood from my mouth. "Westin, will you take me now instead of waiting? I want to see our home."

Westin needed to help me up. I was dizzy at first, and my vision kept blurring, but I managed to get on his horse. We walked most of the way to the hill. As we climbed, little by little, the towers of the castle came closer. I hoped it was not all destroyed. When we reached the top, we sat there looking down at the village, and our home, so still and lifeless. It changed me. Six days ago, my life was filled with love, laughter, and happiness. Our family was loved by all. My father's kindness was known throughout the land. The great love of Jenna and Ardes was legendary. I closed my eyes as if it would make all the horrors of what laid below disappear. The tears came without effort. My heart hardened in that moment. Nothing would ever be the same. Our once happy life would live in our memories from then on. That is where my love had gone. I could feel it in my chest, slowly dying and turning to stone.

I could not stop myself. It did not matter how much my head hurt. I slammed my heels into the sides of Westin's horse, and like a shot, we were racing, down the hill toward the village. When we reached the road, Westin slowed his horse, and we walked the rest of the way. As we drew closer, he pointed out where he found the smelly blanket. It was where we stopped just before we entered the village.

Sliding off the horse, standing there on the road, looking into what used to be our village and seeing the buildings lying in ruin, piles of smoldering rubble and ash, was a sight that would never leave me. The ground was black, soaked with the blood of our people. Men and women alike were strewn about like a pile of Juliana's rag dolls, burned and bloody. The smell was of burning and rotting flesh and made me gag. Westin tore part of my gown off and handed it to me, so I could wrap it around my face.

Standing there with the only member of my family left, I vowed to myself to find who killed my family and destroyed my home. If it took me the rest of my life, I would not stop until vengeance was mine.

"Sabine, what should we do? The dark of night is upon us."

"We need to move forward," I whispered. "I need to see our home. I need to see…" The words would not come out. As we walked further into the village, we saw that there were bodies everywhere. Slowly, I walked with Westin a few steps behind me, and the great gates got closer with every step. I did not want to believe that my family was dead. Maybe Westin made a mistake, and when we reached the castle, they would be there hiding, waiting for me, for us to come home.

The closer we got to the gates, the faster and louder my heart pounded. Nothing was moving in the village. Looking around, I could see in my mind the places I used to go. The blacksmith, Julliard Porter, made my first sword for me. His voice in my mind, 'Now, you mustn't tell your father I have made this for you. It is not proper for a young Princess to be fighting with swords.' I thought it was a huge secret, and I hid my sword from Father for the longest time, unbeknownst to me that it was Father's idea to have Mr. Porter make the sword for me and for Mr. Porter to make it a secret. I could not help but smile. The memory left as quickly as it came when I thought I saw a boot in the rubble. It seems so surreal to me. Perhaps my mind was playing tricks on me. This could not be the truth of what life was for us now. A few more strides from the gate, and my feet just stopped moving. In the glow of the near dusk of the night, I could see it. I could see the stains of blood on the gate, and in my heart, I knew it was Father's. Never again would I hear his bellowing laughter. Never again would I feel his strong arms hold me.

"Father," I said in a whisper as I moved closer, reaching up to touch it and running my fingers along the stains on the charred wood. This was where my father drew his last breath, on the gates of his kingdom, Whispering Wind. His life began here, and it ended here. In my entire life, there had not been bloodshed in our kingdom before this. We were a peaceful people, helping nearby kingdoms. Father always sent wood and food where it was needed. Our soil was the richest in all the known lands.

None of it made any sense. I could feel the tears welling in my eyes. I closed them, took a deep breath, and forced my feet to move past the gate. "I love you, Father." I was terrified to turn the corner. Beyond the wall was my home, but now it was just bricks; empty, with no life at all inside the walls. My body turned to face the inevitable, to face what would be my future.

The courtyard was the same as the village, with bodies and horses everywhere. The fight that took place here was incredible. It did not feel like I was walking, but more like floating, the way you do in your dreams, only this was not a dream like any I had ever had. This was a nightmare. The water in the brick pond in the center of the courtyard was red from blood.

The doors to the castle were no longer standing, but lay on the floor just inside the great hall. I forced myself to move forward. There were dark stains of blood everywhere; the walls, the floors, on what little furniture that was left. In my head, I could hear the screams of Mother, Jenna and Juliana echoing off the walls. My poor little Juliana; how scared she must have been. Ardes, fighting to protect his love, to protect Mother, died an honorable death. I heard my voice, but I was not sure where the words came from as I asked, "Where did you find them?"

Westin cleared his throat. I looked up, and tears were streaming down his face. He pointed to my right, and as I turned, I saw the dark spots on the floor. "That is where I found Simon."

I had no real control over my body at that stage. It just moved without effort to the dark spot. I stooped to touch the blood, but it was dry. I could not help but wonder how he fought. Simon was good with a sword, better than Ardes, he died with honor protecting our family, our home. My eyes began to search the floor. I could not see his sword but as I pivoted on my heels, I saw something across the room. With the light of the day fading, it was difficult to see what it was. My feet were moving toward the object lying just next to the giant fireplace, and I noticed it was Simon's sword. The distance between Simon and his sword was great. He must have been hit hard. As I bent to picked it up, I could not imagine the fear he must have felt.

"May you be with God, my brother. I love you." With Simon's sword in my hand, I turned to face Westin and asked, "Where were the rest?"

Westin was trying to light some candles he had found on the floor. He approached me encircled in a low glow of amber light. "Mother was there." He pointed to the great staircase in the center of the house. As we walked, I could see what looked like blood all along the floor. We approached the stairs and started to ascend them. About halfway up, Westin stopped. "This is where Mother was." He sat down next to the spot where she drew her last breath, where her life ended in what had to have been the greatest fear she had ever known. Sitting down across from Westin, the dark spot on the floor was hard to make out, but, I knew it was blood. It was Mother's blood, spilled in our home, in her home.

As we sat there in silence, I remembered one of the stories she used to tell us as children of how her marriage to father was arranged, just as Ardes and Jenna's. I could hear her voice like she was sitting next to me on the stairs.

"I was horrified when my father told me that I was to marry a stranger, a man I had never seen. I screamed at him, 'What if he is a fat, bald monster?'" We all giggled. Father was tall, strong and nowhere near fat, and he was a very handsome man. "I ran away from home that day. I was very stubborn, just like you, Sabine."

Her hand touched my face. I closed my eyes. I could feel her hand there... Tears welled in my eyes.

"I jumped on my horse, and off I went into the forest. I was determined not to be sold like a possession. I rode and rode, not paying attention to where

14

I was going or in which direction I was riding. I was so furious with my father. With being angry and not paying attention, I was knocked off my horse by a low-lying branch on a tree, of all things. I tumbled to the ground, which startled my horse, who in turn ran off. So there I was, sitting on my bottom in the middle of the forest, angry, dirty, and with no horse."

We all giggled, thinking of our mother sitting on the ground and dirty. She was always dressed in her best gowns, her hair never out of place, and her manners were perfect. She was a lady of the grandest kind.

"So I stomped my feet and let out a howl that I think scared the woodland creatures, for it grew very silent after that." She smiled a beautiful smile with big indents in her cheeks, just like Westin's.

"What did you do?" Simon asked. We all wanted to hear more.

"Well, I got up, dusted myself off, and started to walk. It was terrible. Tree branches were catching in my hair, and a few tore at my gown. My hands were filthy, and from brushing my hair from my face, my face was smudged with dirt. I walked for what seemed like half the day when I heard what sounded like thunder. I thought, 'Oh great, rain on top of all this.' I was looking up to the sky for signs of rain when I stumbled over a rock and tumbled to the ground. When I composed myself and got to my feet, I realized I was on a road of sorts, a path through the forest. I could not be sure of where I was, so I picked a direction and started walking." She chuckled and grew flush in the face. I remember her cheeks turned a rose red color.

"What is it mother?" I asked.

"Oh, I was just remembering the beautiful gentleman who came upon me on the road that afternoon. He must have been shocked at the sight of me."

"I was anything but shocked," Fathers voice came from the doorway.

Mother looked up and smiled at him. The love they had for one another was obvious to everyone who knew them.

"Yes, well that is what you say now, but you did not see your face." She turned toward us as she continued. "I heard the horses coming. I thought that my father had sent guards to retrieve me and drag me back home, so I could be sold into slavery to a man I did not know. I squared my shoulders, ready to fight them, ready to show them that I was no fragile woman, that I could and would best them. As the horses drew closer, I could see that they were not my father's guards at all. These men were strangers."

"Were you scared?" I whispered.

"Of course, my love, I was terrified, but I was not going to let them see that."

The bellowing laughter coming from the doorway startled each of us. Mother jumped and turned to look at Father. She was quickly on her feet and across the room and in his arms. "You should have seen her standing in the middle of the road like a great warrior, her gown in tatters, her beautiful long hair all messed up," Father paused to reach up and stroke Mother's hair, "her smudged face. She was a sight, all right. If I had not been so taken by the beauty standing in front of me, I would have laughed so hard, I would have fallen off my horse. But standing there in the road just as she was, a mess, was the most beautiful woman I had ever seen." Father looked into Mother's eyes and kissed her lightly on the lips.

"Sabine?" Westin was looking at me with a strange look on his face. "Are you all right?"

I tried to muster a smile to reassure him that I was. How I loved my Mother. I only wish she was there right then. I needed to feel the warmth of her embrace; a feeling I would only know in my memories from that point on. "I am fine, Westin. I was just thinking about Mother. Will you show me where you found the others?" Westin rose to his feet and turned to ascend the great staircase.

Following him silently, I remembered when we would race up the stairs. My brothers would always beat me, their legs much longer than my own allowing them to take the stairs two at a time. I looked up at my brother to see his outline in the glowing amber light of the candles. He was a simple man, and he was my only family. We reached the landing, and then turned to go down the hall toward Ardes and Jenna's room, but Westin stopped a few paces from the door and stared at the floor.

"This is where I found Ardes." He knelt down and put his hand on the floor. Westin and Ardes were closer than most brothers. He worshipped him, and the pain in his eyes, even in the low light of the candle, was obvious.

I knelt beside him and could see the dark spots on the floor. I reached down to touch the space, but it was cold and hard. I do not know what I expected to feel. Perhaps it was to feel the blood that ran from his body, or perhaps it was to feel Ardes, my oldest brother, my best friend. His laughter was present in my mind. Although he was a serious man, he loved to laugh. It hurt my heart to know that on this day he was not laughing, but crying as he died, knowing he had failed, knowing the fate of his beautiful Jenna and his precious Juliana. A great man Ardes was, an honorable man. "You will always be with me brother," I whispered into the darkness.

Westin stood, and through the amber glow shining on his face, the tears on his cheeks were hard to miss.

"You stay here, Westin. I will go the rest of the way alone."

He handed me the candle as I moved away from him. The door was in splinters and strewn about the room. Jenna must have barricaded the door to protect Juliana. As I moved, the amber light moved across the room. I saw their bed, and alongside that, the cot in which Juliana slept. My pace was slow, and halfway through the room, I nearly tripped over something on the floor. I bent to pick it up, and saw that it was Jenna's gown, or at least what was left of her gown. It was a gown I knew well. I drew it close to my chest and closed my eyes. I could hear Jenna's voice in my head.

"This one," she said as she held up the beautiful golden gown. I had never seen a gown shimmer in the light like that. "Father had it made for my mother, but when it was finished, she was plump with my sister, Eloise. It did not fit her, and she gave it to me. I am going to wear it to dinner tonight."

"It is so beautiful," I said as I touched the gown.

"Here." She thrust the gown into my arms. "Try it on."

"Really?" I could not get my gown off fast enough. Never in all my life had I felt anything so soft.

I looked down at the shimmering golden cloth in my hands. "Oh, Jenna, I am so sorry I was not here to help. Always my friend, always my sister." I moved to the bed. The coverings were white, but even in the dark of the night I could see the splattering of blood, and next to the bed, the cot where Juliana slept, I saw the darkness that engulfed the floor. She fought hard to save her precious baby, and she took her last breath trying to protect her. The sight was too much to bear; the rage, the blood pumping louder and, faster through my body, and the pounding in my head was so loud that I did not hear Westin when he called my name. He reached out and touched my shoulder. He scared me, and as I turned, I struck him in the face. He went flying to the hard, stone floor screaming. I ran to his side to comfort him, but he scurried away from me.

"You hit me, Sabine. Why did you hit me?"

"Oh, Westin, I am so sorry. You scared me. Are you all right?

He just sat there with his hand on his face, staring at me. "What got you so scared, Sabine, so scared that you would hit me?"

"I was thinking about Jenna and Juliana and how scared they must have been. Whoever did this to our family, are the kind of monsters that are far worse than any scary story, and far worse than any bad dream. We must find them and make them pay for what they have done." I reached out my hand to him, and he took it. "I am tired. Will you come to my room with me?" Westin nodded. I helped him up, and we walked out of the room. I turned to look again at the place my sister and her baby were brutally murdered. "Vengeance will be mine, sister," I whispered to the darkness.

We walked silently through the halls, the only sound being our footsteps. It never seemed to take this long to get to my room from Ardes and Jenna's. We finally stopped moving down the hall. Westin led me into my room. Looking around, I noticed nothing had been touched, nothing disturbed. The door was even intact, and it puzzled me. My bed was made as if nothing had happened. I climbed into my bed and sleep came instantly. It was the warmth from the light of the day shining in my window and coming to rest on my face that woke me. I opened my eyes. Westin was sleeping in the chair at the foot of my bed. Poor thing; this must be so hard for him. I have to think of a way to get him to safety, but what was safe? Where was it safe? Then it dawned on me. This happened to our kingdom, but what about the others? How many more were dead? What of Jenna's parents? They had to be told. I could send Westin, and then he would be safe. He knew the way through the forest to Jenna's homeland. He could make it in a few days. That is what I would do. They needed to be told.

I stretched and rose out of bed. I looked for something clean to put on. I must have made more noise than I thought because when I came out from behind my changing screen, Westin was awake. "Good morning," I said to him and forced a smile on my face. "Thank you for staying with me last night, for watching over me."

Westin smiled at me. "You are welcome, Sabine, but I think it was more for me than it was for you. I was scared. It is scary here now. I hear noises."

I smiled at him. "Let us see if there is any food here." Out the door I went with Westin following behind me. I took the hidden back stairs to the kitchen. I was not so sure I could stand the sights we encountered last night in the dusk of the day.

As we stepped into the kitchen, we were faced with a sight I would not soon forget. The servants were all dead, their bodies lying on the floor, and the cook on the sideboard. The smell was horrific. I gagged and ran out the door into the fresh air. I could not stop myself from shaking. I sat down on the steps, and Westin was soon beside me. He had some stale bread and some fresh water. I smiled at him and took the bread from him. "I think you should go to Jenna's home and find her father. Tell him what has happened. Bring him back here to see what was done to our home and to his daughter."

"But Sabine, I cannot leave you here alone."

"I will be fine, big brother. I will wait for you to return. Perhaps we can stay with Jenna's father for a bit, until we get stronger and can find out who did this. I will salvage all that I can, and I will take what has not been taken already. We will need to have things to trade. There is no one else but us. We will need to find a new home, and perhaps Jenna's father can help us. Your horse will move faster with just one on his back. You can be there and back in three days, two if you do not stop to sleep." I could see it on his face as he contemplated what I had just said to him. He knew I was right. He would have to leave me behind. "I will be safe. I will hear if someone comes, and I can hide. I will take all of the valuables and hide them until you return."

"What will you eat, sister?"

"I can go to the fields and pick the vegetables that hang on the vines. I can get fruit from the orchards, and the stream will provide water. I will be fine, Westin. You need to go now. If you stay to help me, we will only be wasting time. You know I am right."

Westin nodded his head. He gathered up some things and off he went. I stood at what was left of the gates and watched him ride through the village. He stopped short of the road and turned to look at me. It was as if he expected to never see me again. "I love you, Sabine. I will return." His arm rose, and he waved. Turning his horse, he disappeared. I stood there wondering if I would ever see my brother again.

As I turned and I was faced with the gate where my father had taken his last breath. I could not imagine it was easy for those who hung him there. Father was a strong man. I reached up to run my fingers along the charred wood. My fingertips touched a hole in the wood. I stood there looking in wonderment. "What in the world?" I searched the wood with my other hand, and my fingers found another hole. I stood there on the tips of my toes with my arms stretched out. "Father, oh Father, what did they do to you?" I whispered. Westin had said that Father was hung on the gate, but what he did not say was how. They nailed him to it. "I will avenge you, Father. I will not stop until I find them all."

CHAPTER FOUR

As I stood at the gate thinking of my family and how happy we all were. I could only hope that they were happy in death. My heart would miss them until we could be together again. I could not change what had happened. I needed to think rationally. "Goodbye, Father," I whispered to the wind as I started across the courtyard. I walked the great hall, and my eyes were searching the room for anything of value, gathering everything that was worth anything. Simon's sword was becoming a hindrance, so I took it off. It actually looked silly hanging off my gown, and I leaned it against the stone fireplace. After I was finished searching the first floor, I stood there looking at the small yet big pile of Mother's cherished things, and it saddened me. Where to hide them was my question. A smile came to my face as I remembered the perfect place. "Our fort," I said. Spinning around, I took off running toward the kitchen, focusing on the door leading out to the back not wanting to see the deaths that surrounded me. Once out into the sunshine and onto the lawn, I stopped moving. I saw the hedge across the great expanse of lawn, and thought aloud, "When did they get so big?" If I went through the hedge, it would be noticed, so I ran to the edge and worked my way along the wall behind it until I found what I was looking for; the opening to the cave which was our fort, our secret place.

Back out onto the lawn, I searched the grounds for the groundskeeper's wagon and found it leaning against the wall right where he left it. Grabbing the handles, I took off running, not sure why, but perhaps because the smoldering fires still produced smoke that rose above the wall and trees and could be seen across the lands. That and I was terrified. I did not know if anyone would come to investigate. I did not know if they would come back. Then it hit me; it had been days, so why had no one come at all? I could not cloud my mind. I had work to do. I began taking load after load to the cave. The cart just fit behind the hedge. It was nice to see all the things we had brought here as children, but there would be time to reminisce later. I needed to get upstairs and go through Mother and Jenna's things. When I was halfway up the grand staircase, a noise in the courtyard caused me to freeze in fear. I stood there searching the grand space in front of me for something to defend myself with. "Simon's sword," I whispered to myself. *Where was it?* Searching, I saw the sun reflect off of it as a shadow passed in front of the window. *Could I make it there?* Off I went, down the stairs and over the railing. I landed like a feather and bolted across the room. As I picked up the sword, another shadow passed behind me. I spun around, sword in hand ready to fight to the death. I would not allow them to take me alive. I crept toward the doors silently. I did not know I could move with such stealth and agility. I was amazing, and if I was not so scared, I would have laughed. I could just hear Ardes, bellowing laughter at the way I must have looked.

I stood against the wall, waiting. The shadow passed again, and I knew it was time to move. I flew out the door and charged, but to my surprise, there was no one there. *What was the shadow?* I wondered, and then he appeared from the bushes. It was Raiden, Father's horse. He was pacing the courtyard. This was about the time of day that Father took his daily ride. "Hey, boy," I said to him. He bobbed his head up and down and walked over toward me.

I reached for him but he backed away. "I know, boy. I am scared too." It was as if he knew what I was saying as he stepped forward. I reached for him again, and this time he did not back away, but let me embrace him. I hugged him like he was the only thing left in this world. To me, at that moment, he was. He was to become my best friend.

Raiden followed me back into the castle. "You cannot come in here," I scolded him. He stomped his hoof on the stone floor and snorted at me, so I laughed. It was a strange situation to laugh at, but I laughed anyway. "Fine, but I am going up there!" I said and pointed to the stairs. He followed me up the stairs and down the halls. I put a blanket on the floor and began to fill it with the things I had found. I dragged it from room to room, down one hall and then the other. Finally, I worked my way to Mother and Father's room. This room, Westin and I did not go into. I walked to the door and hesitated. Raiden sensed my hesitation and pushed me in the back with his nose. "I am going!" I reached up to rub his nose. The room was a mess; gowns thrown here and there, the bed tossed over, the curtains torn from the windows, the tapestries ripped from the walls. This room was a room filled with love and laughter. I could remember racing down the halls with my brothers when we were children to wake Father, so we could practice swords with him before breakfast. We would run through the door and fly onto the oversized bed. Father had told us once, that they needed such a large bed so we could all fit in it. There were many nights when the rains would come that we would all crawl into bed with them. We all had our own excuses, but the underlying reason was the same. We were all frightened, but Father would just laugh. I could hear his deep, raspy laugh echoing off the walls. God, how I missed that sound. It broke my heart to know that I would never hear it again. I would never hear his voice, hear his praise. I would never feel the warmth of his embrace. I would never see him kiss Mother in the courtyard again. "Father, I will miss you greatly." Raiden snorted, causing me to jump, and I screamed, "You really need to stop doing that! You scared me!" and then I giggled.

There was not much there. Apparently, whoever killed my family took what they could. I did not suspect that there would be much of anything in Ardes and Jenna's room either. As I went to leave the room, Raiden blocked the doorway. He stood at least sixteen hands tall and about six hands across his chest. "Come on, boy. Let us go." He would not budge. *What was he doing?* I turned and surveyed the room. *What did he want me to see?* He pushed me further in the room with his nose. "What is it, boy?" I walked around the room picking things up. I took Mother's gowns and went to put them in the chest. It was turned upside down. I sat the gowns on the floor and tried to flip the chest. It was huge and very heavy. I struggled to no end, but I just could not get it to flip. Raiden had come into the room. "What? Are you going to help me?" I said to him, and then laughed at myself. "I am talking to a horse." Just then, Raiden put his head down, nudging the chest, and he actually moved it a bit. "Ok, I get it. You are going to help me, right?" I reached down and slipped my fingers under the lid. I lifted it up high enough for Raiden to push with his nose.

Higher and higher it came. Then with all that I had, I gave it one last shove, and it finally flipped. The crash was loud. I could not imagine what it was that this chest was made of. It looked like wood to me. There were steel bands that held the wood together, but they could not weigh this much. Perhaps it is just because I am weak from not eating. I rubbed Raiden on the nose and thanked him. Picking up a gown from the floor, I began to fold it. As I bent over to place it in the chest so carefully, I saw something. There was a chip of wood missing from the inside on the bottom of the chest. "What is this?" I said out loud. Raiden responded with a neigh and a snort. I looked up at him. Was I losing my mind, or did the horse actually understand what I was saying?

I reached into the chest and slipped my fingers under the wood. I pulled but nothing happened. I thought that maybe I needed better leverage, so I climbed in. As I was doing so, the toe of my boot hit the lock. I heard a click and froze. "Did you hear that?" I said to the horse. I stepped out of the chest and looked at Raiden, then back into the chest. Nothing had changed. I slipped my fingers under the wood and lifted. The bottom of the chest swung up, and I gasped. Standing up, I looked down in wonder at what was so cleverly hidden in the bottom of my mother's chest. All those years I had played in this chest as a child, I hid here from my brothers. I played with my mother's clothes that were stored in this chest, and I never knew. *Did Mother know? How clever Father was.* I looked at Raiden. "Did you know about this?" He just put his head down and walked back to the door.

I stooped down and reached in. One by one, I picked them up, holding each one up to the light. There were brilliant colors of amber, red, green, white. Were these what they were looking for, I wondered, but that was impossible. Who would even know they were here? There were hundreds of gems. I could not even imagine the worth of them all. I needed to hide them, so I grabbed one of Mother's gowns and laid it on the floor. Handful after handful of jewels I pulled from the bottom of that chest. There were so many stones, big and small. When the last one was in the gown, I looked at them, sighed deeply, and gathered up the corners of the gown. I pushed the board back into the bottom of the chest, and then folded Mother's gowns and placed each one in the chest. Then I picked up the gown with the jewels in it and flung it over my shoulder and left the room. I went down the secret back steps, out the door, and walked to the edge of the hedge. Raiden followed like a little puppy as I squeezed behind the hedge and felt my way along the stones. "You are going to get all scratched up. You need to go back," I told him, but he just continued to follow me. When I got to the entrance to the cave, I pushed through the bushes. The cave was not big. It certainly was not big enough for a horse, but he would not and did not seem to want to leave my side.

I found a box I had brought from the great hall and started to put the gems in it. When it was full, I looked for another container, and another and another, until finally it was done. I decided to bury them, just in case someone was to find this place. So I spent the rest of the light of the day digging holes and burying the gems. When I finished, I left the cave and went to the stream to wash up. "Will you give me a ride to the fields to get some food?" Raiden stood still while I attempted to throw myself on his back. It was quite comical to watch, I was sure. Finally, he bowed, allowing me to climb up.

We walked through the village, him snorting at the stench, and I trying not to see the dead bodies or the blood-soaked ground around them. We finally made it to the edge of the village when Raiden's ears started twitching. He was pacing a second later. "What is it, boy?" I whispered as I leaned in and pressed against his neck. Just as I was sitting up, I heard them. The growling was immense; wolves. They must be here because of the dead bodies, the smell. One by one, they appeared at the edge of the forest. I counted eight in all. Surely, they would want the fresh meat, me and Raiden, before they would want the rotten meat. I had no idea what to do. The only weapon I had was Simon's sword, and there was no way I could take on eight wolves. They slinked toward us, teeth bared and growling a low terrifying growl. Raiden reared up, and I slid off his back and landed on the ground with a thud. His legs were flying out of control as the first wolf, probably the leader, lunged at him. I screamed, but the wolf screamed louder when Raiden hit him in the head. The wolf fell to the ground in a heap, not moving. Did he kill it, I wondered? I was sure he did not, so I jumped to my feet. I was very impressed with myself. I ran to where the wolf lay and pulled Simon's sword, then with shaking hands, slammed it deep into its chest. It was dead now. I stood there with my sword held high next to Raiden, waiting, almost daring, the rest of them to come. They all just stood there, baring teeth and growling, but they did not attack. In fact, they backed away.

The leader was dead, and if my memory served me right, I knew a pack would not attack without a leader. They turned and ran back into the forest. I must have looked very silly, standing there with my arm raised and holding my sword high, defending my village filled with dead people.

Dead people; that was the reason they had come, and they would be back. I turned to face the village. I could not let all those people just lie there and rot. I could not defend against another pack of wolves. Food would have to wait.

Raiden stood there watching me. I tore a piece of cloth from my gown and tied it around my face. The stench was unbearable. I walked up to the first body I found, grabbed it by the feet, and dragged it to the middle of the road. Then I went to the next body, and the next, and I continued until there were about twenty bodies. I was proud of myself. I only retched twice. I moved on down the road and piled another twenty or so, and I continued until the light of the day was just about gone. I had not eaten in days, and I was feeling it. I rummaged around in the rubble of what was once a very busy village. There had to be something left there somewhere. I finally found some fruit that had not rotted or been taken. I sat down and stuffed my mouth. I probably looked like a savage sitting there. I did not realize how hungry I was until I bit into the first apple. Raiden stood there looking at me. He must have been just as hungry. I picked up an apple and tossed it on the ground in front of him. It was gone in a second, so I tossed another and another. We sat there eating until we could not eat anymore.

"Now, what do I do with the bodies?" I asked out loud. The logical thing would be to burn them, but if I did that, the glow of light in the dark of night would be visible. There was not anything else I could do. I was not strong enough to dig graves for all the people, and there were still so many more. "We can hide in the cave, just in case someone sees and comes to investigate." Raiden neighed at me. I searched around, looking for wood or straw that was not already burnt. It was very much the dark of night by then and difficult to see. I needed a torch of some kind. I found a glowing ember of wood, tore the bottom of my gown off, and wrapped it around the ember. It took a few minutes for it to catch fire, and it did not last long. By the time I found all the wood to help with the six piles I had, I would be naked. I found enough wood to start one pile on fire, so that is what I did. I used the light from that to move on to the next, and then the next, until all six piles were blazing. Raiden bowed, and I climbed onto his back. We did not walk through the village. We ran. The fires were high, and the smell, I thought, was worse than the stench of the decaying bodies. Raiden rode us to the edge of the hedge. It was as if he knew this was going to be our home for a while. I slid off of him and worked my way along the rocks to the cave. Once inside, I did the only thing I had enough energy to do. I lay down and slept.

The light of the day slowly worked its way through the branches and the leaves of the hedge, creeping across the floor of the cave and onto my face, waking me. My eyes flickered open to see Raiden standing vigilant over me. "Morning, boy," I said to him. I swear it was almost like he was smiling at me. I stretched and stood up. My gown was tattered and torn to shreds. "I think I need some different clothing."

I made my way along the rocks behind the hedge, slowly so I did not make much noise. I did not know if the fires last night had brought people to investigate, if it had, I did not want them to know I was here, let alone see where I came from. I stopped and peered out. It did not look like there was anyone around, and just then Raiden nudged me with his head, as if he was telling me it was safe to go. I chuckled in my head. The stupid horse he thinks he is a dog. So I went, no one had been there. No one came to see what was burning here. No one came when my family was slaughtered. No one came when my village burned. Why would anyone come now?

As I climbed the stairs to go to my room, it dawned on me that doing all that work in a gown was ridiculous. I needed trousers, so instead of my room, I went to Simon's. His room was intact like mine. I walked over to his chest and flipped the lid. Inside were plenty of clothes, so I took off my gown and my undergarments and put on Simon's. I turned to leave, and then turned back to look at the chest. Just for fun, I kicked the lock, there was no clicking sound. I chuckled to myself and walked out of the room with Raiden following. I could have sworn he chuckled as well.

I was not sure where to start. I supposed the courtyard was a good place, but then again, the village had so many people in it, and the wolves would be back, so this was probably the best place to start. Back to work I go, and the task at hand was arduous. When I could not get to a body, Raiden would help. By the time the sun hit the center of the sky, we had managed to get eight piles of bodies. I started the fires, and Raiden and I went back to the cave. I fell asleep again almost immediately. This time, I had visions of my family laughing and smiling, when all of a sudden, they were engulfed in flames. I woke myself with a scream and startled

Raiden. "Easy, boy. Just some bad things happening." I told him and got to my feet. I grabbed a few apples and the skin of water Westin had left with me. "Westin," I whispered. I hoped he had made it to Jenna's father's land. He should have made it there already. It would take him two days to return. I had a lot to do, so the time would pass quickly. I started out of the cave, when Raiden grabbed my hair in his mouth, stopping me. On any other day, in any other time, I would have been scared and angry that Father's horse hurt me, but for the rest of my days, I would not look this gifted creature in the mouth. He was protecting me. I was not even sure how this horse could be so smart, so human like. I looked at him and thought, ok Sabine, you really are losing it. If you think this horse has some kind of magical powers, you are out of your mind. "What is it?" Now I was talking to him like he was a person. Raiden moved in front of me, nearly knocking me to the ground. I wondered how this horse was going to protect me from a man with a sword, so I pushed past him and moved slowly and silently along the rocks behind the hedge.

There were places in the hedge that allowed limited visual of the grounds leading to the castle. I could not see anything or anyone, so I continued to the end of the hedge. While standing there, peering out and looking for the intruder, I thought about the time when I was much smaller and hiding from Ardes.

He was searching all over. He went in the storage house, but then came running out looking like he had seen a ghost, calling my name, "Sabine!" I giggled, and he turned in my direction. I crouched lower. The hedge was just a baby like me. It was just high enough to protect me. He ran toward me but did not see me. "I know you are out here, Sabine. You are scaring me, and I cannot find you. Show yourself!" Ardes yelled. I sat very still and did not move as he ran off in another direction. I must have fallen asleep because when I woke, it was dark out, and I could hear everyone calling my name.

Mother's voice was panicked, almost tearful, as she called my name. Father was getting his horse ready to ride, as well as Ardes and some of the guards. I could hear Father giving orders, "Check the fields first, then the orchards. The rest of you, search the village."

Mother ran to Father. "Please, find our baby and bring her home. I do not know what I will do if she is gone."

I can still see the love in Father's eyes as he took Mother in his arms and touched her face. "I will not return until I have found her. You have my word." Then he kissed her. I crawled out from behind the hedge. As I was getting up, I heard my Mother scream my name, and before I knew what was happening, Father scooped me up off the ground and into his arms. I could still remember how hard he hugged me because it hurt to breathe. Then Mother was at my side, hugging me and kissing me.

I sighed at the memory, and then I heard it. There was a cracking sound like someone had stepped on a branch. I did not move. I did not breathe. Peering out from the hedge, I saw him. A man but not nearly a man, he was carrying something in his arms. I gripped the handle of Simon's sword and prepared myself to lunge. A few more steps closer he came toward me, and I counted in my head; one, two, three. Before he could blink, I was on him. We went tumbling to the ground with a thud, and Raiden was right behind me. We struggled and rolled in the dirt, ending with me perched on top of him with the sword resting on his neck. "Give me a reason not to slit your throat, intruder," I said in the toughest voice I could muster. The face looking back at me looked familiar. Those eyes, I had seen them before. The man laughed, and he laughed hard. I pressed on the sword, stopping his air flow. "Who are you, and what do you want?" I yelled at him. I had his arms pinned under my legs, and he pointed to the sword, so I eased up again.

"I am Jared of Wellington, Jenna's younger brother. And you must be Sabine."

I could not believe what I was hearing. There was no way Westin could be back already. "Liar," I screamed at him. "You are nothing but a thief, and a thief should be put to death." I pressed harder on the sword. He tried to point away from him, so I followed his gaze to see what he was carrying. Lying on the ground was the body of one of Father's hounds. I eased up on the sword, and he continued to talk.

"I am returning home from a long journey, and last night, I saw the glow of the fire in the distant horizon, so I rode all night. I got here just before dawn to see the devastation. What happened, and where is my sister?"

I eased up the sword and sat back on his stomach. "Dead. They are all dead," I said no louder than a whisper. I just could not bring myself to say it all out loud. To me, that made it final somehow. This man, Jared of Wellington, just lay there on the ground, looking up at me, and then I saw it. I saw that the words he said were true. A tear rolled down the side of his face. I slid off of him and sat on the ground. He sat up and turned to face me.

"Are you the only survivor?"

"No. My brother, Westin, too. I sent him to your father's kingdom to give them news of what has happened and to bring help. I am sorry for the loss of your sister."

"Oh, dear child, I am sorry for your loss. Your whole family, the whole village… How horrible of a thing to witness."

"I did not witness it, well, not all of it. I was knocked out, and Westin carried me away to safety. I did not return here until two nights ago. I have been trying to keep the wolves at bay by burning the bodies and anything with their blood on it." We sat there in silence for a while, and then it hit me what he had said. "You rode all night, and got here just before dawn?" I looked at Raiden and then at the sky. "I slept all day and night?" I asked Raiden. He actually hung his head down. Jared looked at me with what appeared to be a quizzical expression as he was watching me talk to the horse. He must have thought I had gone mad.

"Are you talking to that horse?"

I did not know what to say, so I did not say anything. I laughed and got up, dusting myself off. Jared stood as well. He was tall with broad shoulders. He was Jenna's younger brother, so he must be a few years older than me. I eyed him up and down, noticing he looked strong. He smiled at me and eyed me up and down as well.

"You do know that I let you tackle me?"

I smiled. "You can go right on believing that, sire," I replied and walked away.

He stumbled as he rushed to catch up with me. "May I inquire as to why you are dressed the way you are? I thought a lady was supposed to dress as a lady? You, my lady, are dressed like a man."

"Well, it is easier to move around in these clothes. I have work to do, and I do not have time to dress accordingly." I started walking faster then. He was making me uncomfortable. "As you can see, I am fine, so you can be on your way now. I am sure your father is waiting anxiously for your return."

"Oh, my father would never forgive me if I left a lady to fend for herself with no one to protect her," he chuckled.

I spun around so quickly that I almost fell. I guess the look on my face startled him, because he stopped. I could not stop the words from flying out of my mouth. It certainly was not lady like at all. "Excuse me, sire, but I did not ask for your assistance, nor do I care for your assistance. You may leave now, and it would be best if you did not return. It is not safe here, and I do not want to be responsible for the demise of yet another of your father's children. You know your way home. I suggest, sire, that you go there." I turned and walked away. Jared just stood there with his mouth hung open. I did not turn to look, but I think Raiden did the same. It was moments before I heard him coming up behind me, and he reached out and grabbed my arm. My first reaction was to swing as he spun me around. I connected with his jaw, and he went down. I did not realize the tone of my voice as I said, "Please, sire, do not touch me again, or I will have to show you just how good I am with a sword." Jared sat there on the ground with what appeared to be fear in his eyes. I was so shocked at my reaction that I just turned and walked away. As I walked, I could not help but smile.

Through the gates I went and out into the village. I put my rag across my face and proceeded to gather more dead bodies. Jared came and worked with me in silence. For the better part of the day, we were silent to one another. We managed to gather enough bodies to make twelve piles.

I stood there in disbelief at the death that was before me, every single man and woman that lived here in this village, in my father's kingdom, and had done so their whole lives, were gone. There was something wrong, though, but I just could not get it clear in my head. What was missing? Something was missing, and it did not make sense to me. I looked at Jared, and he seemed to have the same puzzled look on his face. All these bodies and all this death, but something was missing. I think it hit us both at the same time. The horror of what we were doing seemed to fade, and a feeling greater than that, if there was one, filled its space. "The children," we said in unison.

"There are no children here," I said to him. "Where are the children? What happened to them?" It did not make sense. *Were they taken? Were they hiding?*

Jared came running up. "What do you think happened to them? Do you think they were taken? Could they be hiding in the forest?"

I had no answers for him, so I said nothing. It did not make sense to me. If they had taken the children, then why would they kill Juliana?

"I do not know," was all I could manage to say.

"When my father arrives, we will have to send out men to search the forests to see if they are out there somewhere, and Sabine, if they were taken, we will do everything we can to find them and to bring them home."

I could hear the truth in his voice. I just could not understand how we would find them when we had no idea who had done this. An army big enough to do this, to kill an entire village and castle guard, would not be easy to stop.

"Thank you for saying that, Jared. Can your father's army stop the army that did this?" I spread my arms out and turned in a circle.

"We will build the army if it is necessary." I just smiled and walked away from him to look for some wood and scraps to start the fires. That was all I could do to stop myself from going mad. Jared followed. Once we had the fires going, I slowly walked toward the castle while trying to think of what happened to all those children. *Did someone get them out?* I was seeing the faces of the villagers, the people who used to smile at me, old lady Mariam who would give me fresh baked cookies. Everyone I could remember was there in those piles of bodies. Everyone was dead, everyone except the children. "I think they were taken, Jared. I have been going over the faces in my mind, and everyone is accounted for. Whoever did this, took the children, but why? It does not make any sense. Why did they kill Juliana, who lay sleeping in her cot? Why did they not take her as well?"

"Did you see her body, Sabine?"

"No. I did not see any of them. Westin came here while I was out, and he buried them. I do not even know where he buried them. He just said that he did and that they were all dead."

The three of us walked in silence, and along the way, we gathered up the food we found while searching for bodies. I wondered if I should share the cave with Jared. I did not know him, so I could not really trust him. The jewels and the cave would stay mine and Raiden's secret.

We did not speak until we walked into the castle. "Westin should be back tomorrow, and he will be able to tell us what he did with the bodies and if Juliana was among them." We walked into the kitchen, and I noticed the bodies were gone. "Did you take the servants out of here?" Stupid question; I knew that he had. He smiled.

"Yes, I put them in the stable this morning. While I was out there, I noticed a saddle. Your horse does not have one, so when we go, I will put it on him." Raiden snorted, and I could not help but giggle. "You do know how odd it is that you talk to a horse?"

"To be honest, Jared, I was not concerned with putting a saddle on Raiden. My attention was more on keeping the wolves at bay." It came out sharper than I had intended.

"I saw the one on the road. Did you kill it?" It was more of a challenge question, a smart remark if you will.

Smiling, I told him, "Raiden and I killed it. I think it was the Alpha, because when we killed it, the others left. I am sure they will be back, and there will be more of them."

"Well, I will say this, Princess Sabine. You do impress me."

I do not know why that made me angry, but it did. "It is not my goal to impress you. It is my goal to survive, to pick up the pieces of what is left of my life, and try to move on. Seeing as my family has been brutally murdered, I have nowhere to go and no one to go there with, so I am sticking with surviving."

He chuckled. "Well then, would it be rude of me to suggest you take a bath on this quest of yours for survival? I am pretty sure the wolves will find you just as revolting as those dead bodies out there."

I threw an apple at him. A bath sounded lovely. I looked around the kitchen, finding the big pots sitting along the hearth of the fireplace, and I knew the water was brought up from the well, but who had the energy to do all that? There was also the stream just beyond the hedge, just beyond the rocks.

"Would you mind standing guard while I bathe in the stream just past the hedge? It is not that I am scared, but I just do not feel like fighting with wolves with no clothing on."

He smiled. He seemed to smile a great deal when he looked at me. "It would be my honor to watch over you, my lady."

I rolled my eyes and headed up the stairs. The light of the day was fading, so I ran to Simon's room to retrieve some of his clean clothes from his chest. Just for fun, I kicked the lock again, but nothing happened. I laughed as I ran out the door. Jared was waiting by the doorway with what looked like soap in his hand. "I found this today when I was cleaning up in here."

"Thank you."

I knew that Jared would not be rude and watch me, as his father would not approve. He was a man, though, and I had caught him looking at me a few times. It made me feel uncomfortable to have a man watch me the way he was, so I made sure that where I entered the stream was covered by foliage. If he was going to look, he was going to work for it. I quickly got out of Simon's clothes and into the water. It was cold, but it felt so good against my skin.

The days had been hot, and I knew that my scent was not pleasant. It has been days since I had taken a bath. After the smell from the fires, and the smell from that thing Westin covered me with, I needed one. I could hear Jared whistling, so I hurried, as a whistling man was one who was bored, and I did not wish for him to be so bored that he came to have a look at what was taking me so long. I washed my hair, and then dove into the stream to rinse it. As I was putting on Simon's clothes, I heard something in the brush. I froze, and before I knew it, Jared was standing next to me, his sword drawn. He actually pushed me behind him. Like I cannot defend myself I thought. To be honest, I was glad he was there. A rabbit appeared on the other side of the stream, and we both laughed.

"Are you ready," he said, trying not to look at me.

"I am, indeed, and thank you." We walked back to the castle. I could not stop thinking about the children and what may have happened to them. Neither of us said a word. I was not going to tell him about the cave. The ground was dug up, and it was obvious, and I did not want him to know about the jewels, so we would sleep in the castle that night. "You can sleep in Simon's room, and I will, of course, be in mine."

"And him?" Jared nodded to Raiden.

I smiled. "He will stay with me. I cannot seem to get him not to. He follows me everywhere, right boy?" Raiden snorted, and we laughed.

CHAPTER FIVE

The dark of the night came quickly, and I was tired. We had done a great deal that day, so sleep came easily. The visions, however, came and made my sleep restless. Before I knew it, Jared was knocking on my door, saying something. I could not understand him because he was talking so fast. "Come in," I yelled at him.

The door burst open. "There are horses coming, lots of horses." My heart nearly jumped out of my chest.

"Who is it?" Then I remembered that it should be Westin. I jumped out of bed and ran to the window. I had the best view of the village from here. I could see the horses on the road, and they were moving slowly. There must have been a hundred of them, maybe more. I turned to look at Jared and asked, "Is it your father?"

"I am not sure. Should we go and see, or should we wait?"

"Well, if you are not sure, then we should wait." So wait we did. When they got to the gate, all movement stopped. That is when I saw Westin. I could not contain myself. "Westin!" I yelled. He jerked his head up and smiled that beautiful smile of his, and out the door I went. I beat Raiden to the gate. He had a more difficult time climbing down the stairs. Westin jumped off his horse and scooped me up in his arms. "You made it! I was so worried about you." I kissed him on the cheek.

"I brought back an army, Sabine." He was so proud of himself, and I was proud of him.

"I see that. Thank you, Westin. I am so glad you are safe."

"Me too, Sabine. I mean, I am glad that you are safe. I did not stop to sleep. I was so worried about you. Now, we will never have to leave each other again."

"No, Westin, we will not, and I was fine."

"I saw a wolf, Sabine, on the road. Did you kill it?"

I laughed. "Well, Raiden and I killed him."

"Raiden? Father's horse?"

Just then, Raiden came up and nudged Westin in the back. Westin spun around and hugged the horse, saying, "Hey, boy, it is good to see you." Raiden neighed at him, and we both laughed.

Jared came walking out of the house and said, "Strange relationship you two have with that horse."

"Hey, Jared," Westin said around Raiden's head with a big smile on his face.

"Hey, Westin, good to see you made it safely."

"You two know one another?" I was confused.

"Jared and I have met several times in the forest when I was out riding. I know that he is Jenna's younger brother, well, only brother."

Jared's father dismounted his horse and embraced his son. "It is a sad day that you have returned home, my son."

"I know, Father. I would have been home days ago, but I saw the fires on the horizon, and I came to see what had happened. It was a sight not fit for anyone to see, and I could not leave these people here like this. I came into the castle to look for Jenna and the family, only to find Sabine hiding in the castle courtyard. She told me what had happened, well, what she knew had happened, and I have been here protecting Princess Sabine and helping her dispose of the bodies."

"Yes, I have seen the piles in the road. We are here now, and our soldiers will help. Sabine, my dear, I am so sorry for your loss, for all of this."

"As I am for yours, sire." I bowed my head, and then turned to Westin.

"When you came here, while I was asleep, Westin, and you buried everyone, where did you bury them, and was Juliana with them?"

"I buried them in the field, and no, Sabine, Juliana was not with them. She was not here."

I turned to look at Jared. He was shocked, just as I was. "Where is my granddaughter, then?" his father asked.

"We do not know. When we finished for the day yesterday, it came to my attention that there were not any children among the villagers. The children are all gone. Jenna was found in their bedroom. I assumed she went there to get Juliana, and there is blood in her cot, so I thought she was killed as well. But now, since Westin said she was not, I believe there was no one who took the children to safety. It was whoever did this that took them. They took all the children, even Juliana."

There was silence. No one moved. It was Jared's father who spoke, "I have sent men to all of the neighboring kingdoms, some as far as five days' travel. I sent them to see if anyone else has been attacked. We must clean this mess up, and then, Sabine and Westin, you will come home with us. You cannot stay here alone without protection. You are family, and we insist you live with us. I will protect you. If this was a deliberate attack, and done only to you, then no one must know that you have survived."

I did not say a word. *Deliberate?* I thought. *Who would do this to my family? Was there someone who hated my Father this much?*

We spent three days cleaning up the village and the castle. On the morning of the fourth day, Jared came out of the castle as I was dragging Raiden's saddle out of the stable. He had a sword in his hand, and as he approached me, I could see that it was my father's. He got on his knee, slid the sword down his hand, and presented it to me.

"I believe, my lady, that this now belongs to you."

I let go of the saddle and took the sword from him. It was heavy, very heavy, and it was more than half my length. My father carried this sword with him every time he left the castle. "Thank you, Jared."

A few of Jared's father's men had returned with reports from neighboring kingdoms, and no one else had been slaughtered. No one had seen this army, and no one had seen the fires or heard the thunder. It was looking like the attack was against Father and his kingdom. I could not imagine what my father had done to warrant such a horrific act of genocide. My heart was cold, and the only thing I could think of was revenge. The only things I had left were Westin and the possibility that Juliana was still alive. As Jared helped me put Raiden's saddle on, Westin walked up with some wild flowers.

"Happy Birthday, Sabine," he said as he handed me the flowers.

"Thank you, Westin. I actually forgot," I said as I kissed him on the cheek.

"Happy Birthday," Jared said softly. "May I inquire as to your age?"

"It is the seventeenth year of her birth," Westin boasted.

"Yes, it is, Westin. Thank you for reminding me."

"You are welcome, Sabine," he replied, and off he went to get ready to go.

Everyone was getting ready to leave, to leave my home forever; the place where I was born, the place where I was loved, filled with a lifetime, my lifetime of memories.

"Would you like to take a last look around before we depart, Sabine?" Jared's father's voice was soft and kind.

"Yes, I would. Westin, will you come with me?"

He reached out and took my hand as we walked toward our home for what would be a very long time. I could see in my mind all the things we loved here. As children, we played on the stairs, we hid in the nooks of darkness in the halls, we scared one another, we laughed, we lived, and most importantly, we loved. Room by room, the memories flooded my mind. A few times, I could almost hear the laughter of my brothers and myself. My parents' room was filled with so much love, an incredible love, a great love. Lastly was Ardes and Jenna's room. We stood there looking in with the blood-stained floor and sheets. Somehow, it did not feel right being such a mess. "Westin, help me." I walked over to the upturned chest on the floor. Together, we lifted the chest. "Gather up Jenna's gowns, please, and bring them to me." I wanted their room to look nice, as nice as it could look with blood all over it. I turned to pick up a gown that was lying on the floor, when Simon's sword hit the lock. There was that sound again. Click. I froze. Westin did not hear it. I turned around and I could see that the bottom of the chest was slightly raised. I reached in and slowly lifted the floor. It was my gasp that caused Westin to turn.

"What is it, Sabine?" he asked and came walking over. I could not say anything. He looked down into the chest and drew in a deep breath. "Sabine!" he whispered. "What are they?"

"Jewels."

"Whose are they, Sabine? Where did they come from, and why are they in Jenna's chest?"

"I do not know, Westin." I reached in and took one from the chest. Turning to Westin, I told him, "I need you to do something for me. You must go get Jared's father, and only Jared's father. No one else must know. Hurry. Be quick and be silent. Remember, no one must know, not even Jared."

"Okay, Sabine. No one but Jared's father. Got it." He turned and hurried out of the room.

What was going on here? I did not understand why these jewels, as well as the others, were hidden like this. *Where did they all come from? Was this the reason?* This had to be the reason why my family was slaughtered. Perhaps Jared's father would know. He and Father were the same age. They must have known one another growing up.

Westin ran up to Jared's father and whispered in his ear, "Sabine needs you upstairs in Ardes and Jenna's room. She said to tell no one but you. It is a secret."

Jared's father smiled and patted Westin on the shoulder. "Well then, we shall tell no one. Lead the way, my young friend. Wait here for me. I will return in a moment," he said to his men and shot Jared a look. Westin and Jared's father walked through the castle and into Ardes and Jenna's room. I was sitting in the chair at the far end of the room. Jared's father came in and sat in the chair next to me.

"Thank you, Westin. Would you be a love and go check on Raiden for me? Maybe find him a few apples?"

"Sure, Sabine. I will make sure he has some apples." Out the door he went. He liked to do things for me like that. It made him feel useful.

Jared's father was a bit nervous. It might have been the terrified look on my face. "What troubles you, young Sabine?"

"Can you tell me of my Father before he was my Father?"

With a quizzical look on his face, he said, "What do you mean, Sabine? What brings this about? Your father was a good, kind man and a great king."

I held out my hand, and he gasped, for I held in my hand four giant jewels: a red one, blue, green, and a clear one. "This is what I mean. Why would Father have these? Why were they hidden in the bottom of the trunk, and where did they come from?"

In a very low voice, almost a whisper, he said, "So the stories are true then?"

"What do you mean, sire? What stories?" I knew of no stories concerning my father. He was loved by all who knew him, just as Jared's father had said.

He sat there for a long period of time without, saying a word. I could not figure out if he was afraid to tell me or if he was trying to remember, but then he spoke.

"When we were children, your father excelled at everything he did, much like Ardes. He was the best swordsman in all the land. He was the smartest, the bravest of us all, and he was my friend. I am not sure if you know, or what you know about your great grandfather, but he was a brutal man, hated by everyone, and your grandfather was fashioned to be the same, but he had a kind heart, a good heart. He pretended to follow his father's rule, until his father died, and then your grandfather changed the rules. He did not want his people to fear him or to live in fear. He wanted a peaceful kingdom, especially with his wife growing plump with your father in her belly. With this change of rule came great opposition. Your great grandfather's captains fought your grandfather nearly to the death, trying to stop him. In the end, your grandfather won, and his captains, along with anyone else who felt or showed opposition to his change of rule, were banished from the kingdom forever. They were stripped of any official titles they had, and they were cast out, but not before they robbed your grandfather of all his wealth. They took everything, causing your grandfather's kingdom to become the poorest in the land. However, the soil of what is your kingdom now was the richest in the land, so your grandfather asked for help from my grandfather, who in return supplied him with seeds to grow the fields and orchards you know today. The people, along with your grandfather, saved themselves, and he gave back to them all that he could. Together they worked, side by side, hand in hand, and together this kingdom became what it is today. In this time, your father, along with myself were born, and we were raised to believe that the people make the kingdom, not the king. We grew up in peaceful times, in a time when harmony ruled the land, not by any one man, but by all the people." He paused.

"As we grew, and as I said, your father became a great man long before his time. He had grown up listening to the stories of what your grandfather had done and how he became such a great king. Your father, now this is what no one could prove, had listened to the stories and hated the men who stole all that his family had, and he took it upon himself to take it back. He disappeared shortly after your grandfather's death, and he took only his trusted captains with him. He was gone for just over a year, leaving his kingdom without a king. When he returned, he was different. He was more mature. He was stronger and even more powerful. He was still a kind man, but something that happened in the time that he was gone changed him, made him less trusting. Time went on, and rumors surfaced about a band of masked soldiers who went from kingdom to kingdom in search of a specific group of men. Eventually, as the stories go, they found who they were looking for. They discovered the men who stole from his father. Their numbers had become great, and their wealth was at the expense of others less fortunate. What your father happened upon was an army of destruction, an army of barbarians. Although we have all heard stories of such people, I do not know of anyone who has seen them. They were just stories to tell, but these stories we heard, of this band of masked soldiers, were that of a horrible and vicious slaughter, leaving no one alive except the children."

I did not know what to say. *Could this all be truth?*

"Years after your father's return, he met and married your mother, and the four of you were born. Although your father never spoke of what had happened that year he was gone, the wealth of the kingdom had returned, and the reputation of your kingdom became what it is, or was, to this day. No one ever challenged your father's power. They just all knew he was not to be messed with. Your father, Sabine, was the most powerful man and the most feared man in all the land."

"But he was loved, not feared." My voice was small, like that of a young child.

"I think the word you are looking for here is not loved. I think it is respected. I think instead of saying feared, we will say respected. He was a good man. There is no doubt about that. He never hurt anyone, and that is why I agreed to the marriage of Ardes and Jenna. My beautiful Jenna truly loved your brother, and who was I to stand in the way of my oldest daughter's happiness? These jewels you hold in your hand are proof that the stories of what your father did in that year he was gone are true. He slaughtered those who stole from his father, and I am fearful that this is why your village and your family were slaughtered as well. Vengeance for what was done to the fathers of those who had done what they did to your grandfather. It all makes sense that none of the children were killed. What puzzles me is why they were taken. Why were they not just left to fend for themselves, as your father left those behind?"

With that said, he reached down and took a jewel from my hand and held it up in the light. "These jewels have blood on them, Sabine... the blood of generations, and now the blood of your family."

"With my family gone, and my father's kingdom destroyed, you are the most powerful. You should have them," I stated and handed them to him.

"I will take these only to keep them for you. Your father's kingdom is now your kingdom, yours and Westin's. You will rebuild. You will rule this land. This is yours, and these jewels are yours, but we cannot leave them here. We will take them, and I will keep them for you until you are ready. You are still very young, and Westin is still young in his mind. I cannot leave you here to fend for yourselves, so you will come and live with us in Wellington. I will tell my people that you are my orphaned cousins, and I will keep you safe. If word gets out that there have been survivors, I fear for your safety. I fear for your lives. You and your brother, are not as visually known throughout the land as your brothers, Ardes and Simon, were. We can keep your identity secret, and only those whom I have brought with me will know the truth, and they are my trusted soldiers. Come." He stood and took my hand. "Let us gather up the jewels and get moving, for the light of day shall soon be gone from this place." We filled sacks with the jewels and carried them to the horses. Jared did not say a word to me. He just watched me move. He watched me look at my home, and he saw in my eyes that for me, this was not over.

As we rode slowly from the castle gates and through the village, I thought about what Jared's father had said to me. I thought about how I would avenge my family, and I realized that I did not have any idea who these people were or where they came from. Then I remembered, "Westin," I yelled. He came trotting up on his horse. "Westin, remember that thing you covered me with while I was sleeping? You said you found it on the road by the village."

"Yes, Sabine. It was lying next to that bush right there," he said and he pointed to a bush.

I got off of Raiden and walked over to the bush. I do not know what I was looking for, if anything. We did not bring that thing with us when we came here. I turned to Westin. "Can you remember how to get back to the place you took me to keep me safe?"

"Yes, I think I can. Why, Sabine?"

"Listen carefully. I need you to go back there and bring that smelly thing back to me. We are going to start the journey to Jenna's homeland now, and you know how to get there, so you can meet up with us on the way. Can you do that for me?"

His eyes widened. It would be another adventure for him, and he would not let me down. "I can, Sabine, and I will." With that, he shot off into the forest. A few minutes later, I saw him heading up the hill. He would find it and bring it to me.

Jared sat there on his horse, probably wondering what in the world I had sent my brother to do. I just smiled at him as I climbed back onto Raiden. It was much easier to get on him now with a saddle in place. He was a massive animal. With the day more than half over, we set out to the Kingdom of Wellington. It was a hot day, so we just walked with the horses. There was no real hurry, and there was nothing I had to look forward to, except people looking at me with sad apologetic faces, pitying me for my loss. The light of the day was leaving the sky, replaced with the dark of night. We made camp deep in the forest. I had never been this far from my home before. The sounds of the night were different in the forest. Every little sound caused me to jump and become squeamish and jittery. I felt like a scared little girl. How I wish I had Mother and Father's great big bed to climb into. I wanted nothing more than to be brave, but I feared that I was not even close to that.

I heard the horse first, and I wanted to run into the dark of the night and hide, but it was Westin. He had caught up with us, and he had that smelly thing with him. "I found it, Sabine. It was right where we left it." He handed it down to me from his horse. I took it, wanting nothing to do with the smelly thing, but it was my only clue. Whoever it belonged to was there. He had participated in the killing of my family. One day, when I was strong, I would find who owned the horrid thing somewhere. Someone would know that animal skin.

Jared's father was watching us as we exchanged chatter, and he watched the animal skin as if he knew it. I wanted to ask him about it, but I thought that it was not the right time. I feared he knew more of the story than he had revealed to me at the castle. The look in his eyes was more fear than it was interest. In time, the truth would be known. I would make sure of it.

I had a sack of Simon's clothing, so I emptied it out and put the smelly thing inside. I did not want anyone to see it close up, or those who were not here to know that I had it. When we reached Wellington, I would have Westin hide it someplace safe away from the castle. I was sure that the smell was not an easy thing to ignore, but no one said a word to me.

46

The light of the day came fast, probably because I had a very hard time falling asleep. I did not understand how anyone could sleep with all the noise the forest makes. We started out again as the light of the day lit up the sky, Westin and I in the middle of the soldiers, and Jared with his father at the lead. We traveled through the forest, across a river, and we were working our way up what seemed to be very high hills, mountains perhaps, but I think mountains are higher. When we finally reached the top, the light of the day was hanging low in the sky, but the expanse that unfolded in front of me was breathtaking. It was the land of Wellington; the fields, the orchards, the village, and then right in the center of it all was the castle, white as white could be.

There was what appeared to be a blue circle that went all the way around it. It was truly a magnificent sight to see. The entire valley was surrounded on all sides by beautiful green hills filled with wild flowers and trees. The sun was setting, and the sky had a beautiful pink and lavender color to it. It was like nothing I had ever seen before. A place anyone would love to spend their days. I heard a trumpet sound, and it was closer than I would have expected, so there must have been guards nearby. We started our decent into the valley. It would surely be nightfall by the time we reached the castle. Everyone was silent. It was silent the entire journey, but as we neared the village, I could feel the excitement. Even the soldiers were feeling alive. I am sure their families were glad they had returned unharmed.

Jared had left his father's side and came trotting up to Westin and me. He leaned into me, saying, "For your safety, my lady, my father thinks it best we do not enter the castle by way of the village, but that we go with some of the soldiers through the back entrance to the castle. Keeping you two safe is the only thing on his mind."

"Whatever he thinks best, we shall agree."

So Jared, I, Westin, and about forty soldiers separated from Jared's father and continued on in the dark in a different direction. I was glad not to have to ride through the village. I was tired and hungry, and I was sure we looked like orphans. I was dressed in my brother's clothes and wearing his boots, and there was no way of hiding my hair. It was unheard of for a lady to wear such attire. It was going to be difficult enough pretending to be someone else, but Jared's father was right. We needed to be invisible. I would not want what happened to my family and our people to happen here in this beautiful place. We actually got to the castle before his father did. He needed to ride through the village to assure his people that their king had returned and put to rest any fears.

We rode our horses into the stables and dismounted there. Jared carried my bags for me. I brought Simon's clothes, of course, and what I could carry of my things. The bag with the smelly blanket, I carried. When Jared was a few paces ahead of us, I put my hand on Westin's arm to slow him down.

"What is it, Sabine?"

"Tomorrow, Westin, after we have rested, I need for you to do something for me."

"I would do anything for you, Sabine. I love you."

I could not help but smile. I was so glad that Westin had not died with the others. "I need you to take this sack and find a safe, dry place for it to hide. I need for you to hide it until we can figure out who it belongs to. Can you do that, Westin?"

He reached down and took the sack from me, saying, "I will find a place, Sabine. You need not worry. I will keep it safe for you."

I kissed him on the cheek. "Thank you, brother. Now, let us go inside and get something to eat."

"Okay, Sabine. I am very hungry."

We followed Jared silently through the back courtyards into the castle. It was quiet, and there was no one in the kitchen, at least no one we could see. He led us down halls that twisted to a large room lined with bookcases filled with books. There were tapestries on the walls and colorful rugs on the floors. The furniture was plush and colorful. I did not think I had ever seen things such as those, but then again, my father did not like a lot of fancy things.

"I will take your things to your rooms. My father wishes for you to wait here for him. I will return with food and drink in just a short time, so please, make yourselves comfortable."

"I will keep this one, Jared." Westin hung on to the sack he took from me.

"That is fine, Westin." Jared smiled a strained smile, and then he was gone, closing the huge doors behind him.

Westin and I sat in a pair of chairs on the other side of the room next to a huge fireplace. The light from the fire was the only light in the room. We did not say anything to one another for a long time.

"Sabine, I am scared. Are we to live here now, with Jared and his family? Is this going to be our new home?"

I smiled at him. "Yes, Westin, we are. Jenna's father has invited us to live here with him forever. We have no home now, Westin. We have no people. Everyone is gone, and Jenna's father was gracious enough to ask us to live with them. Now, you must behave yourself, and no playing jokes on the family or anyone else for a bit. We need to just get comfortable here with them and them with us. Do you understand?"

Westin nodded his head. I could not tell if his large eyes were excitement for a new adventure or fear that he was never going home again. I was too tired and too distracted to try and figure it out. Just then, the door opened. It was Jared with a young girl who was carrying a large tray. On it was food, hot cooked food, something I had not tasted in days, and drinks. She sat it down on the small table between us. Westin looked at me, and I smiled and nodded. We must have looked like savages the way we attacked the food. There was nothing lady like about the way I ate, but I had not had anything but fruit for days.

Jared's father came into the room, took off his sword, and stood it up against a door. "I see you have gotten food. Thank you, Jared," he said in a dismissing manner. Jared nodded and left the room. "Westin, are you enjoying your dinner, son?"

Westin looked at me and then at Jared's father. "I am sorry, sire, but I am not your son. Jared is."

Jared's father smiled. I think he actually stifled a chuckle. "Yes, he is, Westin. Thank you for reminding me."

"You are welcome, sire."

"First of all, my name is Samuel of Wellington, and you can call me Sam if you like, Westin."

"Thank you, Sam. My belly is full, Sabine, and I am tired. Do you think it would be all right if I went to bed now?"

I looked at Jared's father, and he nodded and called out, "Camille, would you please show Westin his room?" The young girl who brought in the food nodded her head. "Good night, Sabine. Good night, Sam."

"Good night, Westin, and thank you for saving me."

"You are welcome, Sabine. I love you."

"I love you too."

"Good night, Westin. I hope you like your new accommodations." He chuckled, and Camille guided him out of the huge room.

Samuel and I sat there for a bit in silence, me stuffing my face and him watching. When it appeared I was about finished, he cleared his throat. "I shared a great deal with you back in Whispering Wind, and we have not said another word about it. Is there anything at all that you would like to know? Any questions or thoughts you might have? Please feel free to inquire or share. Our home is your home now. I have told my servants to treat you as they treat my own family, my own children. They are finding proper clothing for you for the days ahead, and the dress maker shall make you some new gowns and anything else you may need. You will have your own room with your own attendants. They are drawing you a bath as we speak. Whatever you wish or desire shall be yours with no hesitation."

I wanted to say something about the way he looked at the smelly thing that Westin had brought me, but my head was foggy, and I was tired, so I just took this as my opportunity. "I would like very much to learn the art of the sword, sire. My father's sword is great and heavy, and I would like to learn the skills to wield it. I would like to learn to ride better than your best rider. I would greatly appreciate it if you could teach me how to run a kingdom too, as my father was grooming Ardes. This would have been my time to be given in marriage, but I do not see that happening now. I am to rule a kingdom one day, and I think I should know how."

"Well now, it is not the custom for a young lady to learn such things, but considering all that you have been through and the threat that possibly lies ahead of you, I think it would be wise for you to learn these things. I will instruct my finest swordsman to teach you all that you desire to learn, and my finest rider to do the same, whenever you are ready. I think that by teaching you to be a leader of a kingdom, your father would have appreciated it. I know that, but Westin is the rightful heir. He will need guidance. Would it be wrong of me to say so?"

"Westin is to be king, but my heart tells me he would not want to be, so I will learn all that there is and take my place as the ruler of my father's kingdom, well, what is left of his kingdom, which is just Westin and myself."

"Sabine, the loss of your family is felt deeply within our own. We are in your debt for welcoming Jenna into your family. Anything at all that you desire is yours."

"Thank you, sire."

"Sam, please call me Sam."

"Thank you, Sam. Tomorrow will be good for me to begin the training I requested." I smiled a little as I reached for more meat.

"I would like, however, to discuss the jewels now rather than later."

"I would like for you to keep them, to pay for mine and Westin's way while we are here. They are of no use to me."

"You will need them later in your life. I have no need for them, so I shall do as I said and keep them for you until you are ready for them. It is, after all, your legacy."

"With all due respect, sire... Sam, they are the reason my family was slaughtered. They are not my legacy. I really want no part of them." Just then, there was a knock on the door.

"Yes," Sam said. The small girl who took Westin to his room walked in.

"Sire, my lady's bath is drawn," she said, and then backed out of the room.

"Sabine, we shall talk more as the days move forward. Go and clean yourself and sleep. Tomorrow is another day. You are safe here. I give you my word." With that, Sam rose and left the room.

I grabbed a handful of meat, picked up my swords, and walked out into the long twisting hall. The small girl appeared from the shadows. "This way, my lady," she said and led the way down the hall.

"Camille, right?"

"Yes, my lady."

"My name is Sabine. Would you please call me by my name?"

"Yes, my lady." We both kind of giggled.

Camille led me to the great hall and to the staircase, which was grander than the one at Whispering Wind. My body was starting to feel all the days of no sleep and physical labor. It seemed to take forever to reach the landing. She led me down hall after hall, finally appearing at the door to my new room.

The room itself was huge; a giant bed on one end, a sofa, two chairs, a few wardrobes, and two trunks. On the farthest side of the room was a changing screen, and behind that was the biggest tub I had ever seen. The water had steam coming off the top. My clothes seemed to fall off my body. It felt so good to get into the hot bath, to just soak all that was the past few days from my body, to dip down and clean my hair. I felt alive again when I got out, I put on a clean sleeping gown, crawled into that giant overstuffed bed, and just slept.

At first light, I was up and ready to go. There were several beautiful gowns arranged for me to wear, but somehow learning to wield a sword in a gown did not seem right, so I put on Simon's clothes instead. I looked around the room for a leather strap. I discovered one in a pair of lace up boots, so I plaited my hair, and grabbed both Simon's and Father's swords, and headed down to the kitchen for breakfast. To my surprise, breakfast was served in the dining room, along with all the meals of the day. I found my way there with the help of Camille.

I walked into the room with my swords in hand. It was Jared's sisters' gasps that caused me to look up and come to a halt. Everyone sitting at the table was dressed for the meal; Jared, Sam, Jared's three sisters, and his mother. Westin was even dressed. I saw Jared's little smile as I was gazed upon with total and utter disgust at my attire. "I am sorry, Samuel. I was not aware it was so formal. I will go change."

"No, no, Sabine. It is all right. I just did not think you literally meant this morning when you asked me last night. I thought perhaps you would like a day or two to get settled in, and maybe take some time for yourself, but it is fine. I already spoke to my best swordsman, and he is willing to train you just as soon as he finishes his morning meal."

I took the open seat at the table, and with my best manners, began to eat my meal. I was introduced to the rest of Jared's family. His mother was Katherine. One sister, who was a year or two older than me, was Francine. His next littlest sister, who was a year or two younger than me, was Kaitlin, and then the baby, who was perhaps five or six years old, was Eloise.

"Sabine, I am so sorry for your loss and for all that you have endured these past days. My heart goes out to you and your brother. We want you to know that this is your home now, and you are our family. Jenna spoke so highly of you. She was so excited to have you as a sister, and she felt so secure coming to live with you." Katherine could not stop the tears. "Excuse me," she said as she got up and left the table.

I felt so bad for her. She had lost a daughter as well. She must be frantic with worry about Juliana. I ate in silence after that, as did the rest of the family. When I finished, I decided to take Samuel's advice and take some time before I began training.

"Samuel, I thank you for your words, and I think you are right. I will begin my training in a few days. Please extend my apologies to your swordsman, and my appreciation for his time."

"You are most welcome, Sabine, and I will be ready whenever you wish to begin," Jared said.

I looked at Jared. "You are going to teach me?"

"At your service, my lady."

I just smiled. I excused myself and took my swords back to my room. I thought it best to change my clothes as well, so I slipped one of the gowns on that were laid out for me, took my hair down, and then I went in search of Katherine. I felt we had a great deal to talk about.

CHAPTER SIX

Camille was a very helpful young girl. She guided me to the garden without effort. I was sure that one day, and hopefully soon, I would be able to navigate through the halls and grounds without any help. She took me to where Katherine was sitting on a bench alone. It was obvious that she was sad in her heart, and I knew just how she felt. I approached her as gently as I could, saying, "May I sit with you, my lady?"

"Why, of course you may, my dear." She patted the bench next to her. "I am sorry for being so rude at the morning meal."

"Please, my lady, do not give it another thought. I know the sadness you feel in your heart, for my family is gone as well, and you must know that I loved Jenna like she was my own blood sister. I was so happy when she agreed to marry Ardes. It was wonderful having a sister for the years she lived with us."

"Oh, she was so thrilled to be with you all. As much as it hurt to let my daughter go, she loved your brother so much that it saddened her when I disagreed with Samuel on the marriage arrangement. I did not want an arranged marriage for her. I wanted her to fall in love and make her own choice. Unlike me, I did not know Samuel when I married him. In fact, I had not ever seen him until the day we were joined. It was difficult for a long time. We needed to get to know one another. I cried a great deal back then. I felt as if my parents just sold me off like I was livestock. I thought it a very barbaric act, but as you can see, eventually we fell in love, and now I could not imagine my life without him. I did not want my daughters to feel the way I did, so when Jenna came to me and told me that she knew Ardes, and that she knew she already loved him, I agreed."

"My mother would tell us of how she reacted when her father told her she was to marry my father. I guess I lucked out in a sense. There is no one to force me into a marriage any longer. I do not know if I would want to be married now. Eventually, I am going to have to get married. I cannot rule a kingdom alone." I chuckled a little. "Me, ruling a kingdom? I am sure my father would have a good laugh at that one."

We sat there in the garden for a long time, not saying anything, just holding hands. I missed my mother so much my heart hurt. I would never have these conversations with her. She would never give me advice. I would never hear her stories anymore, and I would never hear her laughter as my father told his stories. I supposed Katherine felt my saddened heart, as she squeezed my hand.

"May I inquire, Sabine, why you want to learn to fight?"

"I am not sure, my lady. I just feel the need. I am so angry at what happened to my family. If it was not for Westin, I would be gone as well. I think I feel the need to protect him the way he protected me. I know that it is unheard of for a lady to do such things, and I understand if you object, but please understand that I need to do this."

"Oh, I understand more than you know, Sabine. I am amazed at your courage and your strength. Samuel has told me what you have been through these past days. I cannot imagine how you survived that. You will be a great inspiration to my daughters, and you have already impressed Jared." She smiled at me.

I chuckled. "I do not think he was impressed when I slammed him to the ground and put a blade across his throat."

Katherine laughed and squeezed my hand. "No, I am sure he was not."

We sat in the garden chatting for the rest of the morning. I could tell that Katherine and I were going to be friends. This transition into this new life was going to be easy. These people, this family, already felt like my own. The next few days were lazy days. I dressed appropriately and got to know my new family.

I had a seamstress measuring me for new gowns, day after day. I really did not need more than five, but she said she was to make me at least twenty. "Twenty gowns? Where in the world will I wear twenty gowns?"

"His Majesty likes to entertain, so I am sure you will have many opportunities to wear these beautiful gowns, my lady."

"Well, I am not one for such parties. I prefer to just sit in my room and read a book." The seamstress just laughed.

I had asked Jared if his tailor would make trousers and shirts for me, so when we practiced I would at least have clothing that fit me. Although I liked wearing Simon's clothing, because I somehow felt closer to him, they were rather large for me. I had the shoemaker making me shoes to match the gowns and boots to wear with my trousers. It continued on for days, as if our life before this did not exist. I supposed it was a good distraction and an easy way to adjust to our new life. Time did seem to move forward with ease, although, at night, when I closed my eyes and welcomed sleep, it was never peaceful. I had visions of the fear my family must have endured. My only hope was that their deaths were swift. My Father's I believe was not. I am sure he was the last to die, tortured by the screams of his family, of his people. The death of a king should be an honorable one, but not this king.

It was days before my clothing was finished, and when it was, I was ready. I had no intention on being the princess for the rest of my life. I would always be a princess, but one without a home or a kingdom. I went to Samuel one evening and spoke with him about the lessons I wanted him to teach me. We agreed to begin the following day.

"When the time suits you, Sabine," is what he said to me.

I nodded, thanked him, and went to my room. I could not sleep, so

I stood by my window and looked out over Wellington. It was a most impressive kingdom, and was quiet in the dark of the night, almost too quiet. I remembered that time when Mother and Father went to a ball.

Mother looked so beautiful in her gown. The servants were all asleep, and we waited in my room for them to return. My room had the best view of the gate. The house was scary that night. It was always the presence of Father that made me feel safe. We all sat on the ledge of the windows looking out over the kingdom, just like this night. There were lights glowing in some of the village shops, and we could hear a dog barking in the distance. I think we were waiting to hear the carriage come into the village. It was Ardes who broke the silence. He let out a giant roar, like a great lion. We all screamed, and Simon nearly fell out of the window, but Westin grabbed him just in time. Ardes started laughing and chasing us around my room. I was screaming and laughing, we all were, right up until Father came crashing into the room, sword drawn, with guards behind him to find us rolling around the bed giggling.

He was so angry. "What in the world is going on in here? You scared me half to death. You are supposed to be in your beds. Now, I suggest you all get there before I find a strap." Westin, Simon, and even Ardes took off running out the door. I did not think I had ever seen Father so angry with us, nor did I ever see my brothers so frightened of him.

I could not help but smile at the memory. I would give anything to hear his voice that angry right now. "Oh, Father, I miss you." I heard footsteps and looked down into the courtyard. It was Jared, he was out walking late into the night. We had not had a chance to speak alone since we had been at my home. I grabbed a dressing gown from the bed, slipped on my shoes, and made my way down into the court-yard. I was getting better at navigating the halls, but it still took me longer than I thought it would. I hoped that he would still be there when I arrived.

Jared was sitting on the bench in the center of the small garden. I walked up and sat beside him. "I cannot sleep either."

He turned and smiled at me. "Well, my lady, I have not slept since we met. I must say that I have never run across a lady such as you in all of my journeys."

"What, a lady who was a mess, homeless, wild, and untamed?"

He laughed out loud. "Oh, you are anything but those things. Try courageous, brave, daring, and let us not forget beautiful." He whispered the last part.

I must admit, that if the dark of night had not been upon us, Jared would have seen my cheeks glow red. "I do what I must to survive. Being the youngest of four, and being a girl at that, I have learned a great deal from my brothers. They were taken from me, however, before I could learn how to truly fight. That is why I am hoping you can teach me. I am grateful to you for agreeing to do so."

"I did not agree, Sabine. I requested. When you bested me out there in the courtyard that first day, I was stunned at your abilities, and most of all I was shocked by your nerve. Having nerves like that is a good quality in a swordsman. Having fear is not an option when you are fighting for your life."

"Jared, is something wrong?"

"I am not sure what you mean."

"Well, I thought we were friends, and now you seem so formal to me. Did I do something to offend you?"

"Oh, dear Sabine, no. You have not offended me. It is just that you are our guest, and you are a princess, and it would be rude of me to step out of place. I am just being polite. My father would have it no other way."

We sat there in silence for a long time. It was not until a guard cleared his throat that we moved. "It is not appropriate for us to sit here alone in the night. I shall walk you to the door, my lady, and then I will be on my way."

He stood and stuck out his arm for me to take. I did just that. We walked slowly to the door, and then he opened it and bowed to me as I walked in.

"Jared, can I ask you something?"

"You can ask me anything, Sabine."

"Why would you choose to be polite toward me over just being my friend?"

"Sabine," he paused, "I am not really sure. Can I get back to you on that?" He smiled.

"You can, sire. I will wait with anticipation for your response." With that, I turned and walked away. I heard him chuckle under his breath. I strolled up the massive staircase and wandered down the long halls to my room. I found myself at the window, looking out to see if he was still out there, and he was. He looked up, nodded his head, and then he was gone. I removed my dressing gown and climbed into the huge bed. Sleep was pleasant this night.

When the light of the day was upon the kingdom, I rose with an excitement in my chest. Today was the day I was to begin my training. I hurried and dressed and I made sure I dressed in a gown. Camille came in just as I was finishing and offered to tie my gown and comb my hair. I sat down at the dressing table Samuel had made for me and let her brush away. While I was at Whispering Wind, I really did not have the time to brush my hair, and I will not forget that first morning when she brushed it out before the morning meal. I swear she nearly tore half of my hair out, so I was not about to go without brushing my hair again.

When she finished, I rushed out of my room and headed down the hall. I was halfway when I realized I did not have any shoes on. *What is wrong with you, Sabine?* I said to myself and giggled. I ran back to my room where Camille stood with a smile on her face, holding my shoes. I slipped them on, and off I went. This time, my hurried walk was not a walk at all, but a run. I got to the top of the staircase and took a minute to catch my breath. I strolled down the stairs and into the dining room. Everyone was seated and talking, and as I walked to my chair, Jared stood and pulled it out for me. "My lady," he said and gestured with his hand for me to sit.

"Thank you, sire," I said as I sat down.

Breakfast seemed to take forever to finish, but I ate everything that I could. I would need my strength for the day. It was my first day of training, and I was excited. I stood and excused myself. "Where shall I meet you?" I asked Jared.

"In the back courtyard, and we can ride to the training ground from there."

"I will be but a minute." He nodded, and I walked as elegantly as I could out of the room. What I wanted to do was run, but I did not, not until I was up the stairs and around the corner. Camille was waiting in my room for me with my boy clothing. She giggled as I tore off the gown and proceeded to change. "Do you know how to plait hair, Camille?"

"Yes, my lady, I do."

"That is wonderful. Would you plait my hair for me? I am afraid I do not do it as tightly as I would like."

It did not take her long to finish, and it was tight. She had pulled at my head hard enough to make me wince a few times, but I assured her everything was fine. When she finished, I kissed her on the cheek, thanked her, and grabbed my swords from beside the door on my way out. I could not be sure if I was excited about learning, or if I was excited about spending the morning with Jared. *What are you thinking? Jared is only doing this because you asked Samuel to arrange it.* It did not matter. I was going to learn how to fight, and that was all that mattered to me. I needed to build my skill, so I could avenge my family. When I came out the rear doorway, I could see him standing in the back courtyard. He had already saddled up Raiden and was ready to go.

"Good morning again, my lady," he said as he slightly bowed to me.

"Good morning, Jared."

He held Raiden, so I could climb on him, and then he mounted his own horse. I had no idea where this training ground was. As we walked our horses along the stone path, I could not let the moment pass.

"I have something I would like to say to you."

"You can say anything you wish, Sabine."

"Listen, I understand that you are Prince Jared of Wellington, heir to the throne and groomed to be king, and I am Princess Sabine of

Whispering Wind, orphaned with an empty kingdom to rule. But while you are my teacher, I wish for us to be just Sabine the student and Jared the teacher. You do not need to call me my lady. It just would not feel right for either of us. You can continue your proper, cold, formal manners toward me everywhere else, except for the time you are my teacher, all right?"

"I am not sure you understand, Sabine."

"I really do not want to know, Jared. What I want is to learn how to wield a sword, and I want to learn how to fight. I want to learn how to kill a man who is three times the size of me, and I want to learn how not to be afraid. That is what I want, Jared. You offered to help me achieve that, so can we just concentrate on that and not all this proper, cold, behavior? There is a time and a place for it, and this just is not it."

"Agreed. As long as you are dressed like a man, I will not treat you as a lady."

"Thank you."

I could hear the joking tone in his voice, but I let it pass. It took longer than I expected for us to arrive at the training grounds. It was a huge oval shaped arena. There were battle dummies and huge circles with colored circles painted on them. "What are those for?" I asked as I pointed at the same time.

"Those are for the archers to practice. They shoot their arrows at them."

"Interesting," I said a bit louder than I had wanted. "Do you think that I might get you to teach me how to shoot an arrow?"

He laughed. "Oh, Sabine, you could get me to do just about anything."

I was a bit taken by that. What was he talking about? I decided it did not matter because I was about to take my first lesson. Father never let me go near our training grounds. I could not even sneak over there, because it was guarded on all sides. It was forbidden for a lady to see such things, at least to my father it was. He did not want anyone to be frightened, but here I am in my seventeenth year, a girl dressed in boy's clothing, standing in the middle of the training grounds.

"Now, the first thing we need to start with is movement. In order to not get killed or impaled, you need to be able to out maneuver your opponent. So first, let us just swing our swords and try not to hurt anyone." He smiled. We took our stances. I swung my sword first, and he protected. We went back and forth for a while. "Ok, you seem to have a grasp for movement. Now, I am going to get aggressive with you, and I mean aggressive, so keep on your toes, and I will do my best not to hurt you."

"Do not hold back just because I am a girl. I have bested my brothers before, and is pain not part of the learning process?"

He laughed a little. "Oh, I am not going to hold back. You can count on it, and yes, pain is one way, but Sabine, I am fearful that I could hurt you. My father would not be so forgiving if I injured his new found ward."

It began with force. I thought for sure when he swung that sword at me that he was going to knock me on my bottom, but I was not going down that easy. So we fought, and I fought hard against him. After some time, I had noticed that some of the guards had gathered to watch us. I think they were secretly wishing that I would best him. Round and round we went, and not once did he knock my sword out of my hands, nor did he knock me down, but my arms were hurting. He was forceful with his swings, and his sword hit mine hard, with my shoulders taking the blows. My hits, however, we not forceful at all, and that is what I needed to work on. A few times, I out maneuvered him, and he did not strike mine at all. We kept at it for hours, taking short breaks every now and again for a drink and for him to give me some instruction. When I could not hold the sword up any longer, I conceded, and that was the end of the lesson for the day. On our ride back to the stables, we talked about this move and that move and how I felt the force of his strikes.

"You are good at the maneuvers and the foot work. We need to teach you to hit harder, and we need to build up the strength in your arms. I want you to start working on that. Every day, I want you to carry two pails of water the length of the courtyard and back. Every other day, I want you to raise them higher and higher and higher, until you can carry them like this." He held out his arms fully.

"I can do that, and I will start after the midday meal. Thank you, Jared. I cannot wait until tomorrow when we can do it again."

"It is my pleasure, my lady," he responded and bowed on his horse.

When I got to my room to change for the midday meal, Camille was waiting for me. She took my hair out and brushed it for me. I did not think my arms were going to work for me to do it myself. "You know, my lady, you are the talk of the castle. No one can believe that His Majesty agreed to allow Prince Jared to teach you how to fight. It is unheard of for a woman of noble blood, a princess, to do such a thing."

Prince Jared... It had not occurred to me that he was in fact a prince. He was just Jared to me, although he was making it very difficult for me to view him as such. I suppose it was the same way that I did not think of myself as a princess. I never had. To me, I was just Sabine.

"I know, Camille, but I really do not fashion myself of noble blood. I am just a girl along with her brother that have been orphaned. I do not have my family to defend me, so I need to have the ability to do that for myself." I think she sensed the sadness in my voice.

"I am sorry, my lady. I know not of the circumstances in which you have come here, and I am sorry if I have made you sad."

"Oh no, Camille, you did not make me sad. There is nothing I can do that will bring my family back to me, and for the rest of my days, when I think of them, I will always be a bit sad." I reached up to squeeze her hand. "Thank you for taking care of me, Camille, and for doing my hair." I kissed her on the cheek and got up to go down for the midday meal. Everyone was in their usual spots at the table.

"Sabine, how was your training this morning," Samuel asked, looking at Jared.

"Oh, it was wonderful. Jared tried to knock me off my feet, but he did not prevail."

"Well, that is a good thing. I am not so sure I would appreciate my son knocking a young woman to the ground," he said with a crooked smile on his face.

"Can I come and watch you best him tomorrow, Sabine?" Westin was sitting on the edge of his seat.

Laughing, I said, "Oh, Westin, it will take a great deal of time before I can best Jared in swords. He is very good, you know, and of course you can come. We had a bit of an audience this morning. A few of the guards stopped by to watch."

I leaned toward him and whispered, "I think they were waiting to see if I could best him." Laughter erupted at the table, and we continued with our meal.

After the midday meal, I started my lessons with Jared's father. He would teach me how to run a kingdom, how to care for the people, how to manage the money, and how to grow the food. After the lesson, I asked Samuel if he had heard from his men who he had sent to the further kingdoms.

"Not all of them. Two of the six groups of scouts I sent out have returned with news of peace."

"I would appreciate it if you would please keep me informed of any news."

"Of course, Sabine. We will find who did this to your family and mine."

I could not help but wonder about the look on Samuel's face that night in the forest when Westin came with the smelly blanket. I thought he knew more than he was telling, but I would let it be for the time being.

CHAPTER SEVEN

For months, I trained with Jared and learned from Samuel. The scouts had all returned with news of peace, so I was no closer to finding out who had murdered my family. I would find them. I would avenge them.

My days were filled from the dawn of day to the dusk of night. Every day before the midday meal, I would walk the courtyard with my buckets full of water, and every day, Westin would cheer me on. Sometimes he would even do it with me. It was our time to share our thoughts, and his time to ask me questions about our future. He really liked it in Wellington. He would tell me stories of his secret adventures. Every once and again, we would hear someone scream from the castle when one of Westin's jokes came off without a hitch. I enjoyed this time, and Westin was right; it felt good to be here, but deep in my heart, I knew this was not my home.

It was not until I could walk the courtyard with my buckets filled with water and arms fully extended that Jared allowed the guards to fight with me. One by one, I bested them, and each time, they got bigger and bigger. It felt good to be able to best them all. A few times, Samuel came to watch. He would tell me in our lessons that I was growing into a very strong woman. "I have never seen a woman best any of my guards, especially Jared, but you, Sabine, have managed to do just that. I am proud of you and I am sure that your father would be proud as well."

"Thank you, sire," I said with a smile.

The seasons were changing, and it was getting colder out. The next day when I arrived at the stables to get Raiden, Jared was there waiting for me. "Today, my lady, I want to teach you some hand to hand combat. You never know when you will find yourself without a sword. I will use a wooden sword I carved just for the occasion. I would not want you to get cut or hurt," he said with worried eyes.

"I think that I have bested you plenty of times with a sword to have no need for worry now."

"Yes, you are getting better every day, Sabine, but there may come a time when an opponent knocks your sword from your hand and comes at you for a physical attack. You are quite small in size, and any one man could easily take you down, so I think I need to teach you how not to get thrown on the ground. As you can see, I had the guards lay straw on the ground, so when you fall you will not hurt yourself." He smiled at me.

"Oh, I would not be so sure of yourself, my lord. It might not be me that is on the ground."

Jared laughed hard and loud, which only made me more determined than ever to best him in hand to hand combat. Unfortunately for me, it did not happen that way. I did in fact find myself on the ground at every occasion. It was difficult at best, and I was sure it would take all of the cold season to achieve. Day after day we fought, and day after day I landed on the ground. On this day, I was to watch Jared and another guard named Charles do the fighting. Jared told me to watch and learn, so I did. For hours, I watched Jared throw Charles on the ground. Though Charles did best him a few times, it was mostly Charles who landed on the hay. On our way back to the castle, Jared gave me more exercises to do every day after the midday meal. I was to lie on the floor of my room, and with the help of Camille, I was to balance my two buckets of water on my feet. When I could hold them there without spilling a drop, I was to move my legs up and down. I needed to do this as well as walk the courtyard each day.

That very day after the midday meal, I was in the courtyard doing my walking, and then Westin helped me carry the buckets to my room. "What are we going to do with these, Sabine?"

"Well, I am to balance them on my feet without spilling any of the water."

Westin laughed his boyish laugh. "This is going to be fun."

Camille was there waiting for us with lengths of material to soak up any water I happened to spill. I was confident that I could do this without spilling any water, but I was wrong, and the laughter that echoed from my room and down the halls was heard throughout the castle. Time and time again, they fell off and soaked me, and Westin and Camille laughed. They were having so much fun, and all I could think of was Jared sitting somewhere laughing at me.

Days and days passed, but I could not get the buckets to balance, and I could not get Jared to budge. Time and time again, I was thrown to the ground. Time and time again, I was soaked with water. Weeks had passed, and my audience had left, so it was just Camille and I in my room. Finally, I began to achieve my goal. One day up went the buckets, and up they stayed. Camille screeched in joy, but I just laid there not moving.

"Well done," I heard from the doorway. I turned my head to see who it was, and the buckets fell, soaking me. Jared stood in the doorway, unable to move, his face and eyes glued to me. It was a look I had never seen before. He was mesmerized as if he was in a trance. When I stood up, he turned around in a jerking motion. "Excuse me, my lady," he said quickly, and then he was gone. I stood there looking at the door in disbelief, and then Camille giggled.

"He fancies you, my lady."

"What?"

"He fancies you. I saw it on his face, in his eyes, my lady. He fancies you."

"What do you mean by he, fancies me?" I had no idea what she meant. Camille just blushed and started to clean up the water. "No, just leave it. Let us do it again." Without another word about Jared, I continued, and each time they balanced. Not once did I spill the water. Over and over, Camille took them off my feet and then put them back on, and each time I held them there longer and longer. My legs hurt, like my arms hurt when I was carrying the buckets. Finally, I had enough, and I was tired. Camille took the buckets and left me in my room to change. I did change, but not into any clothing. I just dropped what I had on and climbed into bed. Sleep came quickly. I did not wake until the light of the day crossed over my eyes. When I woke, I realized that I had slept both the day and the night.

It was not until Camille came in my room to check on me, that I realized I was not wearing any clothing. She gasped when I sat up to greet her. I quickly gathered up the covers, and she excused herself and left the room. I dressed for breakfast and went down to the dining room. Everyone was there except for Jared.

"Jared wanted me to let you know that he will not be able to train you today. He has instructed Charles to take his place. He will return in a few days," Samuel said.

Charles? Where did Jared go? Why did he leave? "Thank you, sire, but where did he go?"

"I had some business in another land three days ride from here, and Jared went in my place. He will return when it is done."

I had to admit that I was sad he had to leave, and I was confused why he would leave. He never let anyone else fight with me. I ate in silence and went to change. I walked to the stables, and Charles was there waiting for me. It just did not feel right. I could not engage with him. "I'm sorry, Charles. This is not going to take place today. I cannot fight with you. Please, excuse me. Thank you for your time."

I walked back to the castle, got my buckets, and back and forth across the courtyard I walked. I was not feeling so excited about anything, and I did not understand why. Westin even seemed to be sad. We carried the buckets to my room and did my exercises there. That day, I managed to get them all the way up and down three times before the buckets tipped. I was done after the first soaking. I changed my clothes and decided that I was going to go for a ride on Raiden.

Samuel would not let me go alone, so Charles and another guard named Blake were to escort me. I wanted to go alone, but I understood why Samuel insisted. I asked Charles and Blake if they would either ride in front of me or behind me, and they agreed and chose behind me. I just wanted to be alone with my thoughts.

I let Raiden take me wherever it was he wanted to go. I was lost in my own thoughts. I could not understand why Jared would leave without saying something. Why would he want Charles to train me in hand to hand combat, when he would constantly tell the guards to be very careful with me? Things just did not make sense, and the way he left my room, the look on his face. I had made a decision. When he returned home, I would voice my thoughts and demand that he tell me what was going on. By this time, hours had passed, and I was furious. Without thinking, I slammed my heels into Raiden, and the next thing I knew, I was flying through the forest. Raiden was fast and very careful where he ran. I leaned down into his neck and flew. It felt so good, and I was so into my thoughts that I did not hear the guards yelling for me to stop.

"Faster, Raiden, faster," I said in his ear. I think he wanted to run as well. He had not been ridden properly since Father. He walked me around, but he had not run like this in a long time. I did not know how long we rode like that, but we burst out of the forest and onto a plain. It was vast and open and beautiful. The sun was still high enough in the sky to light up the day. I kicked him harder, and he just knew what I wanted, so off he went. The guards eventually stopped trying to catch me and waited at the forest edge. Raiden ran for a very long time. He made an arch in the plain, and eventually, we were headed back toward the guards. That was when I saw her golden yellow hair flowing out behind her, riding just as hard as me. Raiden slowed as we approached her, and then gradually came to a slow trot and then a walk. She flew past me. Her face was glowing with delight, and her smile was huge. I watched as she raced through the plain and then back, and she slowed as she approached me. With eyes wide and a smile wider and breathless, she said, "Hi, I am Rebecca of Blackmore, eldest daughter of King Gerald."

"I am Sabine of. I am Sabine, my lady."

"Hi, Sabine. Do you ride here much? I have never made your acquaintance, have I?"

"No, my lady. We have never met."

"Please call me Rebecca. Do you want to ride together for a bit? I need to get heading back soon. I ditched my guards, and I am sure they will be coming at any moment," she said with a giggle. We started out with just a walk, and of course Blake and Charles lingered in the back ground. We chatted about this and that; where did I live, where she lived, how far from one another we were. She asked if I would come again tomorrow for another ride. "This time we could race," she said, giggling.

I turned in my saddle and looked at Charles. "Could you bring me back here tomorrow?" He nodded.

"I shall meet you just after the midday meal. I am not sure how long it will take me to get here. I was just wandering around and decided to run Raiden, and I ended up here. Charles assures me that he will be able to return me to this place, though, so until tomorrow, Lady Rebecca." Just then, her guards came rushing through the forest with their swords drawn, and we broke out into heavy loud laughter.

"I shall see you then at midday." She flashed a brilliant smile and took off in full run across the plain.

Charles and Blake did not say a word about me running off, and as it turned out, we were not that far from Wellington. When we rode up, Samuel was outside waiting for me. He did not look happy at all. "Where have you been, Sabine? I have men out looking for you."

"I went for a ride. You sent Charles and Blake with me, sire. I have not been gone that long, have I?" I knew I was gone for most of the day.

"Yes, Sabine, you have. It is nearly the evening meal, and you left right after the midday meal. That is a great deal of time. Please, Sabine, limit your riding time to much less than that."

"Of course, sire. I did not mean to worry you." He smiled at me and held out his arm to walk me into the house.

The evening meal was huge, as it always was, but I was not very hungry. I ate a bit, and then excused myself. I wanted to be alone with my thoughts. I missed seeing Jared at the table. I went to my room where Camille had drawn me a bath. I climbed in without hesitation and sat in the hot water until it turned cold. Camille washed my hair and rinsed it with warm water right off the fire. After I put on my sleeping gown, and then my dressing gown, she combed my hair. I then told her good night, so she would leave me to my thoughts.

Well, my thoughts were not as persistent as my desire to sleep, and sleep won over.

CHAPTER EIGHT

The light of the day seemed to have come very fast. I wanted to sleep more, and I did not like that Jared was not here. I dressed and went down to have the morning meal with Samuel and his family. Westin seemed to be in a state of sadness, as his smile was gone, and his eyes were very sad. "What is wrong, Westin?"

"It does not seem right that Jared is not here. I miss him." He looked so melancholy. "He is very nice to me, and I am missing Ardes and Simon."

"I know, sweet boy," I said as I reached for his hand. "I miss them as well, very much so."

It was a somber start to the day. Jared surely kept us occupied and away from our thoughts of our family. "Samuel, I am going to ride again today. I have met a friend, and perhaps you know her. Rebecca of Blackmore?"

"I do indeed know Princess Rebecca of Blackmore, and I most assuredly approve of your new friendship with her."

I smiled. "I shall be leaving after the midday meal, and of course, Charles and Blake will accompany me. I will return accordingly."

"That is fine, Sabine, and thank you for telling me of your journey. Enjoy the ride and the countryside."

I finished my meal and went to change. I was not going to fight with Charles. I was not in the mood. I would postpone my training until Jared had returned. On this day, I would focus on my buckets until it was time to ride to meet Rebecca. I was getting better and better. I lifted and bent my legs eighteen times before I got soaked. I changed and went down for the midday meal, which I ate rather quickly. Westin's mood had lightened up. He played a trick on the cook, who was quite upset with him. He was lucky she did not thrash him with a willow whip.

I was excited to have a new friend, since my only real friend, well girlfriend, was Jenna. I had some good times with Francine and Kaitlin, but it just was not the same. I excused myself and walked elegantly out the door and up the stairs, but when I turned the corner, however, I ran. I changed into a less formal gown, and off I went. When I got to the stables, Charles and Blake were waiting with Raiden fully saddled.

"Charles, would you mind if we rode fast today? You lead, and I will follow?"

"Whatever you wish, my lady."

We rode, and we rode fast. It was not as fast as Raiden could run, but it was quick. It did not take us long to reach the plain. I looked for her, for my new friend, Lady Rebecca, but she was not here yet, so I asked Charles if it would be all right if I rode alone, and he agreed, saying, "As long as you stay within my sight, my lady."

I kicked Raiden in the sides, and off we went. Riding side saddle was not as much fun as sitting on a horse like a boy. I pulled on Raiden's reigns, and he came to a stop. I jumped off him, and then climbed back up. It was difficult to swing my leg over him with this gown on, so much so that I lost my balance and fell to the ground. I could just imagine how I must have looked. Before I knew what was happening, Charles was at my side. "My lady, are you hurt?"

I was so embarrassed I wanted to die. "I am fine, Charles, just a bit clumsy, I am afraid."

"Let me help you, my lady," he said and put his hand out. "If anything happens to you, Lord Jared will have my head."

Well, I did not expect to hear that. "What do you mean, Charles? Jared told you to keep me safe?"

"Yes, my lady. He instructed me before he left for his journey. He told me that he was putting his trust in me to keep you safe, that I was to protect you with my life if need be."

"Why in the world would he say something like that?" It was a bit snappier than I had intended.

"My lady, Lord Jared is not to be questioned. He was very intense about your safety. Now, what are you trying to do?"

"Well, I cannot ride the way I would like sitting side saddle, so I was trying to sit like a boy, but this gown got in the way. If you could hold onto me, so I do not fall again, I am sure that I can manage then."

I climbed back up, and with the support of Charles, I managed to sit comfortably on Raiden. "Thank you, Charles." I kicked Raiden, and off we went. Raiden ran like the wind. He did an arch again, and soon, we were traveling back toward the guards. As we grew nearer to them, I could see that there were three other people beside them. "Rebecca," I yelled. She waved from atop her horse. Raiden ran and pulled up to a halt in front of her.

"Now boys, I think I am safe here in this meadow with Sabine. There are four of you now, so stay here while I ride with my friend."

I could see their faces, and they were not happy, but they complied. I had to laugh to myself. I was sure that their job was to keep her safe at all costs.

We turned and rode for a while. Raiden, obviously being the bigger horse, took the lead. He would only run in an arch. Once in a while, we would ride past the guards. We slowed to a normal walking pace, so we could talk. We laughed, and Rebecca told me of her love for a man named Edward of Collingwood. He sounded so wonderful the way she described him; chiseled features, blue eyes, reddish brown hair. The way her face lit up when she spoke was enough to convince me that she was in love. "What does being in love mean to you, Rebecca?"

"Well, that is a strange query, Sabine. What does it mean to you?"

I honestly did not know what to say. "I do not know. I have never felt anything for a boy, except my brothers of course, and somehow, I do not think that is the same thing you are talking about. Your face lights up, and your eyes twinkle when you talk of Edward."

She giggled. "You do not have a boy you fancy, or one that fancies you?"

"What does that mean, fancy? My attendant said that to me about a young man at the manor, but to be honest, Rebecca, I really do not know what it means."

"Well, it is like he is always looking at you, and he cannot keep his eyes off of you. He is kinder to you than most boys, and he protects you and makes sure your honor stays intact. You know, he likes you."

"Well then, my answer to that is no. I do not know of anyone such as you describe." That was apparently not the truth, though. Charles had said that Jared ordered him to keep me safe, to guard me with his life, but I could not tell her that. I was supposed to keep my identity a secret, especially if we were to make people believe that I was Samuels's orphaned cousin. That would make me related to Jared.

"You will one day, Sabine, and when you do, you will know just how I am feeling. It is a wonderful feeling. Your heart races when you see him. You get excited when you know you get to spend time with him. You feel like you are floating on the clouds."

"It sounds wonderful."

Just then, we heard a whistle. It was the guards. "Can you meet me here again tomorrow, Sabine?"

"I am sure that I can."

We turned our horses around and started back toward the guards. "Want to race to the guards?" she asked, and then we were off. I let Rebecca win. I knew that Raiden could have beaten her horse without even breathing heavy, but she was my new friend, and I liked her a lot. We waved good bye to each other, and then she was gone. Just as quickly as she had appeared, she disappeared.

We rode back to Wellington in silence. I was lost in my thoughts. Rebecca had talked about feelings of love, and I had a few of those feelings toward Jared. I was excited when I was going to spend time with him; this I knew because fighting was just no fun without him.

He had sworn Charles to protect me with his life. Just the thought that Charles would die to keep me safe sent shivers down my back. I wondered if these feelings were something like the love Rebecca talked about. We reached Wellington sooner than I expected, so I put the thoughts of the afternoon away. I had a lesson with Samuel before our evening meal, so I went to go wash up and change for that.

The evening went by rather slowly. Having Jared absent really did make the days go by so slowly, but Westin's spirits had picked up immensely. He had pulled off yet another trick, one that left Samuel soaked from a bucket of water. As I sat around looking at my new family, a sense of peace came over me. I knew that Westin was going to be all right, though we would always miss our family. Each day for the next six days, Rebecca and I met in the field and talked, raced, and spent time together. It felt so good to have a friend. I missed Jenna so much, and Rebecca was a good distraction. On the afternoon of the sixth day, when we returned, I saw that Jared's horse was in the stable. My heart jumped knowing he was home. Now, I could confront him and find out why he would leave without telling me, and why he left Charles to teach me. I was walking from the stable when I could hear him yelling. *Why was he yelling?* I rounded the hedge and saw him, and it was Charles that he was angry with.

"I told you, no ordered you, to teach her, not take her running the country side where she could be a target. She was not to leave the castle grounds. How dare you disobey a direct order?"

I was shocked, and I was not about to let him talk to Charles that way. He did not do anything wrong. I walked quickly, more like ran, over to them. "Excuse me, Jared, but Charles has done nothing wrong. What gives you the right to speak to him this way? I am a full grown woman, and you have no right to assume you can treat me as if I were not."

Jared spun to look at me. "This does not concern you, my lady, so please excuse yourself from my business." he stated, and then turned back to Charles.

What? What did he just say? I could not stop myself. In a voice louder than I expected, and much louder than I cared for, I responded,

"You know, I have no idea who it is you think you are talking to, MY LORD, but I am not a servant of yours. You do not get to order people around to control my every move. I am a person with a mind, and I WILL do as I choose, and you or anyone else will not tell me any differently. If you cannot deal with that, then I shall be on my way. As for Charles and Blake, it was out of consideration to YOUR father, the KING, that I allowed, and yes I said allowed, them to tag along with me. You, SIRE, had nothing to do with it. Now, unless you want to go toe to toe with me in the stable, then I suggest you lower your tone. And keep in mind, MY LORD, you would be wise to watch your tongue when speaking to me, or you may find it lying on the ground." I turned and marched into the house, slamming the door behind me. I did not stop moving until I reached my room, and I slammed that door as well.

Jared and Charles just stood there stunned. Jared turned. "I am sorry, Charles. I do not know what came over me. That woman has gotten under my skin for some reason."

"It is not a worry, sire. Good night."

They shook hands, and Charles left. Jared stood there stunned with a smile on his face. In his heart, he knew he was a goner. I stood in my room furious. How dare he think it acceptable to speak to someone like that. Just because he was to be king did not give him the right to be so brutal. I was not about to stand by and let it happen. There was a knock on the door, so I walked over and opened it. Camille stood there with a big grin on her face, and in her hand was a piece of paper. "My lady, Lord Jared sent me with this," she said and handed the paper to me.

"Thank you, Camille." I took the paper and shut the door. I sat the paper on the table, walked to my bed, and got on it. I was not about to read his apology. He should have come himself, but he was obviously a coward. He would rather send a note than face me himself. Well, two could play that game. I would not face him. I would avoid him at all costs. That night, I would have the evening meal alone in my room. I got up and went to the door, as I knew Camille would be waiting outside, and she was. "Camille, would you please pass on my apologies for not coming down to dinner, and would you please bring my meal to me here instead?"

"Yes, my lady," she looked in the room and spied the note on the table. "Should I deliver a message to Lord Jared, my lady?"

"No, Camille. There is no message for Lord Jared."

I closed the door and returned to my bed. I could only hope that I was not being rude to the rest of the family, but that man was out of control. I decided to take my meals in my room for a while. I looked for some paper and a quill, and found they were on the table. I scribbled a note to Charles.

Please take this note to Lady Rebecca tomorrow on the plain. Thank you, Charles, and I am sorry for the way Lord Jared treated you. He should not have done that.

I folded it accordingly and wrote his name on the front. Then, I wrote one for Rebecca.

Lady Rebecca,

Please accept my apologies, for I will not be able to carry out our plans for a few days. If you could meet me in three days, that would be lovely. I will be there to explain then.

Sabine

I folded this one the same as the one to Charles, and I wrote her name on it, then I sealed both of them with my wax seal. It was one of the few personal things I brought with me from Whispering Wind. I set them on the table next to the one Jared had sent me and would give them to Camille when she returned with my evening meal.

Camille returned shortly after I had finished the notes. She set the tray on my table and proceeded to serve me. "That is not necessary, Camille, but I do need you to do a few things for me, if you would?"

Camille nodded." Anything at all, my lady."

I walked over to the table and picked up the two notes I had written. "I wish for you to deliver these two messages to Charles. Do you know who he is, Camille?"

"Yes, my lady. Charles is the guard who was assigned to protect you while Lord Jared was away. I know who he is."

"Thank you, Camille, and you must not tell anyone of this, not even Lord Jared. Tuck them in your skirt, so no one will see. You must keep this secret."

"I will tell no one, my lady." Out the door she went, and I sat and ate my evening meal alone. It was rather nice actually. After I finished, I decided to change and get myself ready for bed. Camille would come for the tray, and I would ask her then what Charles had said. I climbed into bed and under the covers. The bed was so soft and so big. I felt very small lying there. Then the knock came, so I climbed out and went to the door. It was Camille. "My lady, are you ill?"

"I suppose it must look that way, but no, Camille, I am just tired. Did you deliver my notes?"

"Yes, my lady. Charles said he would do just that tomorrow after the midday meal."

"Thank you, Camille. I would like it if you brought my morning meal to my room as well."

"As you wish, my lady."

I noticed her look at the note from Jared as she went out the door. I shut it behind her and climbed back into bed. The quiet was nice. The room was dark except for the glow from the fireplace. I could hear the guards laughing and talking. The courtyard had a way of carrying the sound from the grounds. I could hear the footsteps of those who were on guard for the evening, and then I heard him, whistling. Jared was outside in the courtyard whistling. He made me so angry. I got up and shut the shutters on my windows with a loud slamming noise. He would surely know that I was not happy. As I climbed back into bed, the whistling had stopped. I smiled. Good! He got my point!

CHAPTER NINE

My sleep was restless. I could hear nothing but the vicious tone in Jared's voice as he screamed at Charles. When Camille quietly came in my room with my morning meal, I woke instantly. I think it was out of relief that the night was over. When Camille brought the tray to place on my bed, I noticed the strain on her face.

"Camille, what is the matter? You look worried?"

"His Highness, King Samuel, has inquired if you are ill, my lady. He wants to know if he can come to your room and speak to you."

"Please inform him that I am not ill, and if he wishes to do so, he may come to see me."

"My lady, Lord Jared inquired if you had read his note or not."

"No, I have not, and I have no intention of doing so either. If you would like to deliver it back to him, you may do so. It is on the table by the door." The poor thing actually looked frightened. "Camille, Lord Jared has not raised his voice to you, has he? You are not frightened of him, are you?"

"No, my lady, and no." She backed away and left the room, leaving the note. Sitting there looking at the obviously huge portions of food on the tray, I was not as hungry as I should have been, so I just picked at some fruit and a few nibbles of bread. It was not long after Camille left that there was a knock on the door.

"Sabine, it is Samuel. May I come in?" I opened the door and allowed him to enter. He walked over to the big chair next to the fireplace and asked, "Is everything all right, my dear?"

"Yes, Samuel. I am fine, really. Please, do not worry."

"Is there a reason you are not participating in the meal times down stairs? Has someone offended you in any way?"

Offended me? I almost laughed, but Samuel was genuine, and he really was concerned. I tried hard to compose myself. "No, Samuel. Everyone is wonderful, and thank you again for allowing us to live here. I do not want to be a worry. My apologies. I just need some time alone that is all."

"I told you before, Sabine, that you and Westin are now our family. I cannot say you are my children, and with that, I worry about you just as I would worry and be concerned with my own children. I just want you to know that if you need to talk, or want to talk, I am always available to you, or Katherine would make herself available. Anything you need, my dear, anything at all." He smiled as he got up. "There are many books in my library, Sabine. Please, feel free to choose any one of them to read."

"I have already done so. Katherine extended the offer that first day, and thank you, Samuel, for the words of kindness and more so for the feelings of welcome you extend to Westin and me." He moved toward the door, and I followed. I saw him glance at the note. He reached for it, picked it up, and turned to face me. In the sincerest voice, he handed me the note and said, "I think it best you read this."

I did not take the note. "It would be greatly appreciated, sire, if you would return that note to Jared. I really want no part of it."

"May I inquire why, Sabine?"

"Yes, Samuel. You may inquire, but may I have your respect if I refuse to answer?"

"Of course, my dear. You will always have my respect." He smiled that gentle smile of his and left my room, taking the note with him.

I was not sure what to think of all of that. Did Jared go running to his father, telling him I refused to speak to him? It did not matter. I wanted no part of a tyrant. I should have told his father how he behaved, but it would have been silly to do so. He is, after all, a full grown man. I changed into my clothing and opened the shutters. I saw Jared flying out of the castle gates on his horse. Wherever he was going, he was going fast. I thought that would be a good time to go to the library to get another book. I was assured no accidental meetings with Jared.

The room was vast, as almost every room here was. The walls were lined from floor to ceiling with books. There were even shelves in the middle of the room. The windows were the same floor to ceiling, with dark heavy velvet draperies that hung on them, which kept the sun from fading the books, I supposed. I could not choose just one book, so I borrowed three. I hated to admit that I needed Camille to guide me back to my room. I climbed up on my bed and opened my first book. Page after page, I flipped through, but I could not tell what I had read. The only thing I could seem to think about was Jared and the way he rode out of here this morning. I shut the book with a popping sound, giggled, and lay my head down.

I spent the next two days in my room alone. Westin came to visit me often. He asked several times why I was so sad, and why I wanted to be alone. He asked me if he had done something to make me mad, and I assured him that he did not. I refused to acknowledge that it was Jared I did not want to see. I asked Westin to make me a map of all the important rooms, so I would not need Camille to guide me around. He was more than happy to do so.

On the fourth day, when Camille brought my morning meal, I had prepared another note for her to give to Charles. It simply asked for him to prepare Raiden and to tell no one that we were going. I made Camille give me her word that she would not tell a soul.

After the midday meal, I had Camille guide me to the stables through the house, so I would not run into Jared. I also wrote a note to Samuel, letting him know where I was going and to be discreet in not telling anyone where it was I had gone. I trusted his discretion and to honor my wishes. We reached the stables, and Raiden was ready. Charles and Blake led the way, and we went the back way as not to alarm anyone in the castle that we were leaving. It felt good to be out in the day. We rode hard, and we rode fast. I just wanted to see my friend. When we arrived, Rebecca was not there yet, and I hoped that she remembered. I asked Charles if it would be all right to ride, and he nodded as he always did, a man of few words. Raiden took me away from their peering eyes, and I climbed down and lay in the grass. It was such a beautiful day. How I loved it when the ground was new again after the rains had come. I could feel the thunder of the horses, and I sat up. Rebecca had come. She was on her way across the plain. "Hello, Sabine," she said as she dismounted her horse and lay in the grass beside me.

"Have you been ill?"

I giggled. "No, I have not been ill. I am, or was, very disturbed by the actions of another that forced me to avoid them, and the only way I knew how was to remove myself."

"Could this person be a boy?"

"I would not deem him a boy, nor would I consider him to be a man. He is a cruel and vicious person who thinks he can control the things I do and the places I choose to go."

"Wow, you should hear your voice. If I did not know any better, I would say you, my dear Sabine, fancy this boy, this man."

"I do no such thing. He is arrogant and infuriating. I wish not to discuss him. Tell me, Rebecca, of your Edward. Have you seen him?"

She laughed out loud. "Whatever you wish, my friend. Yes, I have seen him. We do not get to talk much, as my father discourages our meetings. He says that Edward is not of my station, and I should not allow him to believe that there is any kind of future for us, but I do not care what my father thinks or says. My heart belongs to Edward, and I will not marry anyone but him."

"Marry? Did he ask you?"

"No, he did not ask me, but I know if he could that he would. My father would not even consider it. He told me that I am to marry another when the time was right."

"Another? Do you know who it is?"

"No, but the day of my birth is coming. I am to begin my eighteenth year, which means I am to be married, to the highest bidder no doubt. I told my father that I will not be sold off into slavery just so he can look good."

I remembered my mother's story of how she did the same thing to her father, and how she did in fact marry the man her father had chosen for her, only my mother was already in love with him. I told Rebecca the story, and then I told her of my brother and Jenna. "So is there not a chance that you will love this man your father will choose for you?"

"No, Sabine. My heart belongs to Edward, and it always will."

We did not say much after that. I am not sure how long we laid there in the grass, but it was nice just to be with my friend. It was Charles' whistle that brought us back from wherever it was we were. I laughed, saying, "It is like I am a lost dog or something. He has to whistle so I will return." We both laughed.

As I climbed up on Raiden, Rebecca asked if I was to come again tomorrow, and I assured her that nothing would stop me. We parted ways, and back to the castle we went. Upon arriving, Jared was in the stables waiting for me. He did not say anything until we were outside and heading toward the courtyard.

"Why have you been avoiding me?" I ignored him and kept walking. "Sabine, I am talking to you," he said, his voice a bit firmer this time.

But I just kept on walking. It was not until he grabbed my arm that I stopped. "What? Are you to force me to listen to you?"

"If I must, yes. You need to hear what I have to say."

"Jared, there is nothing you have to say that I want to hear. You are a cruel man, and I want no part of you. I witnessed your anger toward an innocent man, a man whom you ordered to guard me, and because..." He pulled me close to him and kissed me. I could not believe the nerve he had.

I tried to get away from him, but I was in shock by his actions. Instinctively, I stomped on his foot, which caused him to yell and release me. Then, as he bent from the pain, I brought my knee up and smashed him in the face. He fell to the ground, and my first instinct was to help him and to apologize. I felt so bad. "You, sire, shall mind your manners. Do not ever touch me again without my permission." It was all I could say. I turned and proceeded into the castle. I heard scuffling behind me, and then Jared yelled.

"But you do not understand, Sabine!" I heard as I entered the doorway, but I proceeded up to my room and slammed the door behind me.

I paced back and forth while talking aloud to myself. "Who does he think he is, taking that liberty with me? How dare he think he could just grab me like that? And to kiss me..." I stopped moving, and put my fingers to my lips. "He kissed me. Why did he kiss me?"

Through my window, I could hear Charles in the courtyard helping Jared.

"My lord, are you all right? That one has a wild spirit," Charles said as he helped Jared get up.

"I will not disagree with you, Charles. She does, indeed. Why will she not listen to me? What does she say of me while on your rides?"

"She does not speak, my lord. She just merely rides."

"Where is it that you ride too, Charles?"

"If I beg your pardon, my lord, I choose not to answer. Princess Sabine has asked me to keep my word, and my lord, if I do not keep my word, then I am not worthy of the task set upon me to watch over her and keep her safe."

Jared just stood there, stunned and most intrigued. "I pardon you, Charles. You are indeed a man of your word. Would it matter if I ordered you to tell me?"

"No, sire. I am sorry, but it would not."

I heard Jared chuckle then say, "I must speak with her, and I must do it now rather than later."

"Good luck with that one, sire. May I suggest you keep your distance?"

"Distance has been the problem, I am afraid, Charles."

I looked out only to see Jared moving toward the castle, toward me. The knock on the door sounded like a cannon and startled me. I let out a yelp like an injured puppy. "My lady, it is I, Camille. Can I be of assistance?"

Strange that she would ask that of me. Camille never waited to come in; she would just knock and open the door. She was, after all, my attendant, and I had given her permission to do so. There must be something else behind her request.

"No, Camille. I am fine. Please, just leave me alone." There was silence, I paced my room thinking of that kiss, I could not tell how much time had passed, and then another knock. I rushed to the door, ready to scold her, but it was not Camille standing there when I opened the door. It was Jared. I did my best to slam it in his face, but he stopped me.

"I will not push my way into your chambers Sabine, but you will hear what I have to say."

"You fail to understand me, Jared, when I say to you that I have no interest in what you have to say to me. I know what I saw, and I know what I heard, and your actions this day, sire, leave very little for my desire to spend any time alone with you. Allow me the sense to know that I am correct. You are nothing but a tyrant, a cruel and horrible man that I wish to have nothing to do with." I stood my ground. I was not going to yield.

"No, Sabine, I am not. What I am is very concerned with your well-being, more concerned than I should be. You are but a waif of a child, and I cannot explain, nor do I understand, the hold you have on me."

"A child? You stand in my doorway calling me a child? Well, let me just remind you, sire, that I just bested you in the courtyard. Can a child best a man? I think not! Now, please, leave my presence, so I may get on with my day." With that, I attempted to slam the door again, which came with great resistance.

"I will do no such a thing. If you think me a tyrant for wanting to explain, and using any means in which to do so, then so be it, but you will listen to me." He actually pushed his way into my room, shut the door behind him, and bolted it. I was locked in a room with a man I feared, but I was in his father's house. He would not harm me. I stood ready for his advances. I bested him once. I would best him again.

He walked up to me, and I stepped back, but he kept coming and did not stop until I fell in the chair on the other side of the room. He put his hands on either side of me and brought his face very close to mine. I could feel his breath on my face as he spoke. In a very calm voice, he said, "You clearly do not understand."

I went to speak, and he silenced me with another kiss. My reaction was to slap his face, but he grabbed my hand. "You will not speak until I have finished. If you do not want me to kiss you, then I suggest you keep quiet until I am finished. For each time you speak or look like you will speak, I shall kiss you to stop you. Is that understood?"

I did not know what to say. Oh that is not true at all; I had plenty to say, but I had no desire to feel his lips on mine, so I nodded.

"Ever since that first day we met in the courtyard of your father's castle, I cannot seem to keep myself from protecting you. You were trembling the entire time you fought me. No one should ever feel that afraid. I admired you for being so brave, and I was taken by your beauty, Sabine. You are just but a child, and your beauty leaves me breathless."

I went to open my mouth to scream at him that I was not a child, and he kissed me again. I pulled away from him, and he smiled. He was enjoying it all far too much.

"I told you what I was going to do if you spoke. I can do this all day if you would like. I will have my say, and then I shall leave you, but I will have my say." Tyrant is what I was screaming in my head; arrogant tyrant. "When my father arrived and extended our home to you and Westin, I was beside myself. I was glad that he had done so, because then I could watch over you and make sure no one would bring you harm, and I was confused by the feelings that were growing inside of me. On our way back to Wellington, I spoke to my father of these feelings. He made very good observations. Firstly, you had just suffered a great tragedy and had lost your entire family. Second, you were just a child…"

I opened my mouth with every intention of screaming at him

again that I was not a child, but again, he silenced me with another kiss. "Now, we can do this all day long, or you can listen, and I can be on my way. The choice is yours." I said nothing.

He began again, "Second." he paused and looked at me with a sly smile. He was quite handsome; a tyrant, but a handsome tyrant. I felt something stir inside of me. "Second, you were just a child. I pointed out that you were in FACT of age. He also pointed out that I am four years, nearly five years, older than you, I have far more life experience than you, and that I am more mature. I argued the point with him, that you had seen and experienced things I have never. His words to me were sound and true. He told me, in no uncertain words, that you were not the chosen one for me to take as a wife. That has already been determined. He left me with a great deal to consider, hence the lack of conversation between us on our journey here. I had no idea what the feelings that were stirring inside of me meant. I just knew, as I still know, that you take my breath away. You are fierce when you need to be." He reached up and touched his nose, and I could see there was still a hint of blood. "You are unlike any woman I have ever encountered. I knew when we arrived here from Whispering Wind that the only thing I could feel for you was that of being a friend. That is why I agreed to teach you, but I know now that was the wrong thing to do."

I sat there in disbelief. *What was he saying to me?* I went to speak, and he covered my mouth with his. The resistance on my part was less than the first few times he kissed me. This time, I wanted to slap him less.

"I am not finished," he said, his voice a bit unsteady. "Training you in sword combat was fine. I was impressed by your sheer energy. I was impressed by your ability to wield a sword, and most of all, I was confident that we could be just that, friends. However, when we began hand to hand combat training, things changed for me. I looked forward to our daily training more than I did with our sword training. I could not wait to touch you. At first, I was afraid that I would hurt you, and I would never be able to forgive myself if I had, but touching you now makes my skin feel like it is on fire. That day here in your room, the day I left you, when I saw that water pour onto you and the way those loose clothes clung to your perfect body, I understood it all. I could not stay here and think rationally. I needed to leave and decipher my thoughts, to make myself understand that this was forbidden and that I am promised to another."

I got one word out, "What," before he covered my mouth with his. This time, I did not fight him. I did not pull away. I let him lead me, let him lift me out of the chair and wrap his arm around my waist. I let his hand come to my cheek and brush along my face. I let him kiss me. As he pulled away, I finished my thought, "are you saying, Jared?" Again, he kissed me, and God help me, I kissed him back.

We parted, and he said breathlessly, "I am saying, my beautiful Sabine, that I am in love with you. That is why I was screaming at Charles, I was worried with fear that you had been taken from me. I never want to be without you, Sabine." With that, he kissed me again. I had no idea how long we stood there in the light of the day coming in the window of my room, but when we parted, there were feelings stirring within me that I had no idea what they were about. I could not help but wonder if they were what Rebecca was talking about in the field, about how she felt toward Edward. It was Jared's voice that brought me back to the plain I was on. "I have said all that I needed to say. It is your turn."

I just stood there looking at him. My thoughts were not my own. My feelings were feelings I knew not.

He sensed my lack of anything, smiled his brilliant smile, and simply said, "I love you." I must have blushed because he smiled bigger, if that was possible. "I need to speak with my father. I must tell him of the events of this day. He instructed me to keep these feelings to myself, but I could not go another day thinking you hated me." He turned and left my room. He left me standing there unable to speak, unable to move, unable to breathe.

Jared walked out of the room breathless. He knew that he would love no other. He could still feel Sabine's sweet tender kiss on his lips. He also knew what his father was going to say; that it was forbidden. It did not matter to him what his father thought. Sabine was his match, and he knew it. He felt it in every part of his soul. On his way to his father's study, he could think of nothing but the way it felt to kiss and hold Sabine. He walked past countless servants, but did not see one of them. He passed his sister on the staircase, but did not see her, and he passed his mother in the great room, and did not hear her when she asked what was wrong with him. He did however, see or rather feel the door to his father's study when he slammed right into it.

"Come in."

Jared opened the door and entered his father's study. He knew what was going to happen before he closed the door behind him. "Ah, Jared, my son, come in and sit down. I think it is time we had a talk."

Jared turned to face his father, knowing well what he was about to say. Somehow, Samuel knew everything that took place in his kingdom. Sometimes, he knew them before they even happened, like today. "What happened to you?"

"I had a conversation with Sabine." He reached up and touched his nose.

Samuel laughed. "The girl has a spirit that I believe is not to be tamed by anyone."

"I will have to agree with you, Father."

"Here. Sit," Samuel said as he motioned to the chair.

Jared did as his father asked, but what Jared did not know was that his father already knew he was in love with Sabine. He had known it all along. It was not until Jared ran from the house that day he gazed upon her soaked body that Samuel had his confirmation, and he knew it was time to stop it before it had a chance to grow. What Samuel did not know was that Jared had just confessed his love to Sabine, and that he had come to inform him that he had done so.

"You are going to be twenty-two years of age soon, Jared, and I believe it is time for you to settle down."

"That is strange, Father. I was just coming in here to talk about this very thing."

"Well, good then. I have arranged for you and Princess Rebecca of Blackmore to be wed."

Jared thought he was hearing things. *Did his father just say Rebecca of Blackmore? Who was she?* "Father, I do not know this Rebecca, and she..." His father cut him off.

"Her father is King Gerald of Blackmore, and this marriage was arranged years ago. I gave him my word. It is a good match, and it will secure our lineage. After what happened in Whispering Wind, we need our allies, and we need strong allies, especially now that Sabine and Westin are living with us. If someone were to discover that they are alive, there is no telling what could happen."

"But, Father, I do not love this Rebecca. I am in love with Sabine."

"Nonsense, Jared. You are to marry Rebecca, and that is all there is to it. Sabine is not an available option. She is a remnant of a very horrible occurrence. It is most unfortunate for her, but she has no family. She has no kingdom, therefore, I am sorry to say, she has no promise of any noble marriage. I know that sounds harsh. I adore Sabine, but no woman has ever ruled a kingdom, and Westin is not the ruling kind."

"Father, you cannot be serious in your thinking. She is a human being. She comes from a strong line. She is a princess."

"A princess, yes, but she is a princess with no kingdom. Jared, please accept this. Your path was agreed upon when you reached the sixteenth year of your birth. This would have taken place then, but Rebecca was still a young child. It was necessary for her to be groomed and prepared for you."

"You make it sound so barbaric, Father, like she is cattle being held for sale. I cannot, in good conscience, marry someone I do not love."

"You will grow to love her as I grew to love your mother. This is the way I was given in marriage. It is the way, Jared."

"Well, Father, you are king. Change the way."

"Yes, Jared, I am the king, and you will be king one day when I am no longer here. You will have a bride of noble blood, and you will produce an heir to carry on after you."

"I mean no disrespect, Father, but I will not marry Rebecca of Blackmore. I will not."

"Jared, it was not a request."

"You cannot order me to wed, Father. I will not do it." With that, Jared stood and walked to the door.

"You will not marry Sabine, Jared. I will have her removed from our home, and you will never see her again, if you do not wed Rebecca."

The love Jared felt for his father stopped him from speaking. He opened the door and walked out, right past his mother who knew what had just happened. He ran up the stairs to Sabine's room, and without even knocking, he walked in and said, "We need to leave, and we need to leave now. This is not a safe place to talk."

I followed him out to the stable where we got our horses and rode into the forest. He did not say a word the entire way. I knew this was not going to be happy news. He was so distant and angry. We stopped by a stream, and he helped me down from Raiden. We walked for a little bit, and he took my hand. We just stood there looking at one another, when I realized he had remarkable blue eyes. They were kind eyes. They were Jenna's eyes.

The stirring in my stomach, and the way my heart pounded in my chest, was new to me. What was this feeling?

"Sabine, I have known for some time now how I feel about you. I just did not know how to say it, or even if I was supposed to say it or even feel it. At first, I tried to ignore it. I thought I was doing a great job of it until that day I came to your room. The feelings were too much for me to bear. I ran because I was afraid you would see it and laugh at me, and that, I am afraid, would have crushed me. When I returned and you were gone, and I discovered that you were gone all the days that I was, I became frantic. My father saw this in all of my actions. Today, I went to tell him that I love you, and before I could get the words out, he informed me that I was to marry another."

My heart hurt. My hands started to shake. He was to marry another? He saw the pain in my eyes and pulled me into his arms. It felt good to feel the warmth of his embrace. No one had held me since my father, and my father's embrace felt nothing like this. "I am so sorry, Sabine. I should have known this would happen. I never wanted to cause you any more pain than you have already experienced in your life. I should not have told you how I felt. I just could not stand that you hated me. I needed for you to understand what you saw. I told my father that I would not marry someone I did not love. He threatened me, Sabine. He told me that if I refused him, that he would send you away, and I would never see you again."

It was all so much to take in. I had no idea what he was saying to me or why. I did not know what I was feeling, but it felt like I was about to lose someone who was very important to me. Jared and I had spent just about every day together over the past year. I did not know what I would do if I could not see him again. I pulled from his embrace and walked along the stream.

"I think we should just be what we are, Jared... what we were before tonight. We have spent every day together for a year now, and there is no way I want to have a day without you in it. I cannot leave Wellington. Where would we go? I am not ready yet to be able to protect Westin. We cannot do this, Jared. Your father is right. You must do what is expected of you. It is your station in life to marry a bloodline and produce an heir. You are the only son to the king."

"I do not think that is possible, Sabine, at least not for me. I have had a bit longer to deal with my feelings than you have. I cannot ever feel this way about another woman, like I feel for you. I will never be happy. My father would never take my happiness away from me, and I cannot believe that my mother would allow him to."

"Jared, I did not even know I had feelings for you. I do not know what these feelings are that I have. Perhaps your father was right. I am just a child. I have no life experience. This past year I should have been groomed to become someone's wife, but instead, I spent it learning how to kill a man two times my size."

He turned me to face him again. His hand came to my face, and he kissed me. "Does that feel like we can just be friends?"

"Jared, when you kiss me, I become confused. I wish you would not do that. This is serious. Your father wants to send me away, and I do not want to go, so I think you should not kiss me again. You are my friend, and I do not want to be without you in my life. That much I do know. Tonight has been very confusing for me, and I wish to go home." I walked to Raiden and climbed atop him. "Will you please take me back?"

"Of course."

We did not say anything on the ride back. I could feel his eyes watching me, just as I watched him. He was quite handsome, and he was my friend. In the stable, while we were taking the saddles off our horses, he whispered, "I love you," to me. Then, just before we walked out the door, he pulled me into the shadows and kissed me.

"I might not ever get to do that again."

Samuel was leaning against the fence just outside the door when we walked out. "Sabine, dear, would you please wait for me in my study?"

I bowed my head to him and kept it bowed. I did not look back. I just walked to the house where Camille was waiting, of course. "My lady, where have you been? It is late, and His Highness is looking for you."

"He found me, Camille. Would you be a dear and show me to his study?"

She complied and led the way. I went in and sat in the chair I sat in one year ago.

In the courtyard, Samuel and Jared sat talking. "My son, I do not want to send the girl away, but I cannot have the gossip of your late night trysts. You are promised to another, and I will not have my authority challenged. I have made arrangements for Sabine and Westin. They will leave in the morning. Her father left behind a great deal of funds, so I have purchased them a small home to live out their days. I have assigned Charles and Blake to travel with them, and they will not return."

"Father, do not do this. We just went to talk. Sabine has decided that we should just be as we were. I will marry Rebecca of Blackmore. I will not dishonor you, but you must know that my love for Sabine shall never leave me. I will never act on it, but it will never leave me."

"We shall see about that, my son."

"So they can stay?"

"Yes, they can stay. I do know she is a strong young woman, but it was just one year ago today that her family was slaughtered. For me to send her away now would only be cruel. I will discuss this with Sabine, and I will give her the choice. They can stay if they like, or they can go. Now, good night, my son." Samuel walked to the door. He went into his study and sat next to Sabine. "I understand that Jared has expressed to you his feelings."

"Yes, sire, he has."

"And do you feel the same for him?"

"I do not know, sire. I do not know how I feel or what I feel. I just know that I cannot imagine not having him in my life. We are close, yes, but I am afraid that I know not these feelings he described to me. I know that he is promised to another."

"Yes, he is."

"I would not stand in the way of that, sire. Please, do not make me leave this home."

"Dear child, I do know what day this is, and I am not a monster. I will not make you leave this home, but I will extend to you and your brother the opportunity to leave Wellington. I have purchased a small cottage for you six days ride from here, and I will assign Charles and Blake to travel with you, and then they would stay with you until the end of your days. If you choose to stay, you must understand that Jared will marry another."

"I do, sire, and thank you. We choose to stay here. May I go now? I wish to retire to my room."

Samuel stood, so I stood. "I would like to continue my rides at midday."

"Of course, my child. You may resume your activities."

I smiled and left the study. Camille was at the end of the hall waiting for me. I did not say a word on my way to my room. I went in and shut and bolted the door. I did not want any visitors that night. I had much to think about. Most of all, I wanted to talk to Rebecca. She spoke of love, knew love, and maybe what I felt was love. I put on my sleeping gown and climbed into bed. The light from the fire left a soft amber glow on the walls. It was very peaceful, and sleep came easily.

CHAPTER TEN

The light of the day stretched across my room just as my eyes opened. I lay there wondering about all that took place the night before. Had Jared really professed his love for me? I could not help but smile at the thought of his sweet kisses on my lips. He was a man who thought I was beautiful, and he loved me.

I climbed out of my huge bed and put on my gown, I put on my shoes and walked to the door. Lying on the floor was a mysterious note with my name on it. I noticed, as I picked it up, that it was Jared's handwriting. I tore at the wax seal and opened it up.

My dearest Sabine,

Although I realize that we may never be together, I must reinforce to you that my love for you shall never falter. You are seared into my heart, and it belongs only to you. Today, I cannot meet you in the stables for our hand to hand combat lesson, for I am to ride with my father and mother to meet the parents of the woman I have been promised to marry.

Please do not be sad, for I do not love her. Our return is unknown, but Charles will tend to your safety, and we shall speak when I return.

I love only you

Always yours Jared

My heart felt sad at the thought of Jared with another, but I knew my place, and I also knew that I could never have him. I tucked the letter in the side of my chest, closed the lid, and went down for the morning meal. It was just Westin and I, for Kaitlin and Francine had taken the journey with Jared and his parents. It was strange to sit in this huge room at this table alone with Westin. I would have to get used to it. Samuel could still send us away. Jared would marry, and his bride would live here, so Westin and I would surely have to leave. I was not sure that I could live in the same house as him, but I did know that Samuel would find an excuse to have us depart. I had been taken off course, taken away from the real task, and that was to find who did this to my family and to find Juliana. I could not help but wonder why Samuel had not gone after her, since she was his only granddaughter. *Could that be why? Could it be because she was a girl, an orphan, like me?* I considered that perhaps leaving Wellington would be better for us, and I could definitely get more done under less watchful eyes. I could search for the barbarians who slaughtered a kingdom, and most of all, I needed to find Ardes and Jenna's daughter. I needed to make her safe. She would be nearly two years old now. *Would I even know her?* I would never forget her eyes. They were Jenna's eyes, and even more so, they were Jared's eyes. I would know her anywhere.

I finished my morning meal and went to the stables. I needed to get out and think. The following day would be the eighteenth year of my birth. I would have been given in marriage soon. I needed to take control of my life. I needed to think out a plan. I thought I would take Samuel up on his offer for me to leave with Charles and Blake. Westin would stay here. Father would never forgive me if I let anything happen to him. Charles and Blake were there in the stables as I began to prepare Raiden for a ride.

"My lady, may I do that for you please?" It was Charles.

"Charles, I do know how to saddle my own horse."

"I have no doubt, my lady, but His Highness Prince Jared was very specific that you were not to get hurt, not even a fingernail, or he would have my head." He smiled a crooked smile at me.

"Then, by all means, Charles, I would not want you to lose your head. I might need it." I climbed up on Raiden and leaned into him.

"You want to run today, my friend?" He answered with a stomp of his hoof. "Charles, I would like to go someplace I can ride fast, some place that is open and free of trees. Do you know of such a place?"

"I do indeed, my lady."

We took off, staying to the road for most of the journey, and then we cut off to the right. We usually went to the left when I was to see Rebecca. I really wished it was time to see her. I really needed to speak with her about all that had taken place. Just a while longer until midday.

"Your meadow awaits you, my lady," Charles said as he stretched his arm out in front of him.

I had not been paying attention to where he had taken me, but when I followed his hand and looked beyond his fingers, before me lay a meadow of mountainous size. I smiled, kicked Raiden in the sides, and we were off. Raiden ran, and he ran fast, the wind from his speed whipping past my ears. The feel of freedom was like no other I had felt. I could not help myself. "Faster boy," I screamed, and he obeyed. Thunder, his hooves sounded like thunder. The pounding of my heart took over my senses, and the air flowing over Raiden's head was incredible. He ran, and I rode him long and far.

All I could think about were Jared's kisses. I thought I wanted the wind to blow him out of my head. He was clouding my mind. I did not want to think about swords or hand to hand combat. The only thing that seemed to matter was him. I was so confused by it all that I really needed to talk to Rebecca. Raiden ran in his usual arch. It amazed me how smart he was, and this day, I had to believe that he knew exactly what I needed. Seared into his heart is what the note had said. He loved me, but what did I know of this love? I knew nothing of what was between a man and a woman. I just knew what I observed with Father and Mother and what was between Jenna and Ardes. I knew how their eyes sparkled when they saw one another, of how Jenna and Mother's voices would change when they spoke of Ardes and Father. I had always wanted to feel the way they looked. I supposed that was what I felt. I could not seem to stop smiling, although I was very confused. I felt very happy inside.

In the past year, I had felt nothing but rage and vengeance. I must not lose sight of that, I thought to myself. I must find who did this to my family. I pulled on Raiden's reigns, and he promptly came to a halt.

"I need to talk to Rebecca. I need to know what this is that I am feeling and if it will go away. I need to focus on finding those who did this to our family." I was not talking to anyone, just talking, but I think Raiden understood me, for he began trotting back to Charles and Blake. As we rode up, I said, "Charles, I would like for you to take me to see Lady Rebecca now."

He bowed his head and turned to begin the journey. The journey to the plain to meet Rebecca did not seem long, but perhaps it was because my mind was occupied.

"Charles, how long have we been riding?"

"I am not sure, my lady. It has been a while now. Would you care for a drink or some food?"

"You brought food with you?"

"Yes. Lord Jared had said that today you would probably want to ride all day, and if we went out, we should bring drink and food with us."

I stopped Raiden and just sat there looking at him in disbelief. *How would Jared know what I was thinking? Did he know me that well?* "Well, I am thirsty, and Raiden would probably like an apple. Do you have an apple, Charles?"

"Yes, my lady. I do."

We stayed in that spot in the forest for a few minutes. Raiden enjoyed his apple, and I had one as well. When we were finished, we continued on our journey.

Rebecca was riding full force when we arrived. It was as if Raiden knew what to do, and we set off to meet her somewhere in the middle. She was so beautiful, riding with her long golden hair flowing out behind her. Raiden came to a stop without me having to pull on the reigns, and Rebecca did the same.

"I am so furious with my father. I am almost tempted to run away," Rebecca said as she climbed off her horse, and we sat in the grass together.

"Why? What has happened?"

"Oh, he informed me, INFORMED me, that the man he chose for me to marry will be arriving at the end of the day. I told him I was not interested in meeting anyone that I loved Edward, and that was whom I wished to marry. He INFORMED me that would not be possible because I was to marry another. Can you believe him? I should run away and teach that old man a lesson!!" she finished with a giggle.

"Well, that is horrible, Rebecca. I am so sorry."

"Oh, do not be sorry, Sabine. I will not marry him. So how have you been? You look different."

I looked different? Did love make you look different? Did Mother look different before she met Father? Ardes did not look different when he fell in love with Jenna, although he did smile a great deal more, and he did not pay as close attention to things as he had before they met. "I am fearful that I am different, Rebecca. I am so glad that you are here. I have much to talk with you about."

Without telling her too much about my past or where I was staying, I managed not to tell any untruths. "Then, the next thing I know, he is telling me that he loves me, and he kissed me so many times. The last time was the time that I realized I was feeling different about him. He has such incredible blue eyes, and his smile is so charming. I just do not know what is happening to me, Rebecca. I cannot think straight."

She threw her arms around my neck and squealed with delight, "You are in LOVE, my dear sweet Sabine. Is it not great?"

"But how do you know I am in love?"

Her laughter was both infectious and aggravating. "Because that is what I feel for Edward, silly. It is the most wonderful feeling, is it not?"

"Well, I am not so sure that I care for it at all. I like having my wits about me. I have things I need to do, and these feelings are making my thoughts get all mixed up. I do not have time to be in love." I nearly shouted the last line.

"Sabine, you cannot stop love. When it happens, it is for life. It is not something you can control or ignore."

This frustrated me even more because I needed to train and get stronger. I would not be ready until I could best Jared. I stood up and started to walk away from Rebecca, and of course Raiden followed. Soon, Rebecca was at my side. We did not speak for a long time. It was the vibration of the earth and the sound of thunder that caused me to look up. Approaching were four guards, and they rode right up to us. "My lady, your father requests your presence at the castle immediately."

"Well, you can tell my father that I will be there when I am ready to be there."

"He told us you would say that, my lady, so he told me to tell you that if you do not come willingly, then we are to bring you by force."

Rebecca laughed. "Is that why he sent four of you? What, is he worried I will best you all?" The four guards just sat there on their horses, trying not to look worried.

"You tell my father I will return soon. I am speaking with my friend, and it would be rude to leave in the middle of our visit."

The guard bowed. "As you wish, my lady," he stated, and off they rode.

"Do you fight?" I could not resist.

Rebecca giggled. "I think my father wished he had sons, for he has taught me well, too well. I can best all of his guards."

"Can I tell you something?"

"Always."

"I can fight as well. Maybe tomorrow we can practice together."

"Really? That is wonderful. I knew I liked you for a reason, Sabine. I would love to fight with you. That is, if my father has not locked me in the dungeon." She poked me and laughed. "I must get going. Father is old and not well. I think I might have been too hard on him today. I will see you tomorrow, Sabine, and do not forget you cannot fight love."

That really was not what I wanted to hear. I needed to fight this love or whatever this feeling was. I could not have Jared, and that was that. I could, however, have my revenge. Charles was watching me linger on the plain and rode up to me.

"Is everything all right, my lady?"

"No, Charles, it is not. Can you tell me something? How much do you know of Samuel's plan to move me six days ride from here?"

"I only know that he has requested that Blake and I escort you and your brother and remain with you till the end of your days."

"And what if my days were longer than your own?"

"Oh, my lady, we would not be the only ones to go with you. There are several others as well. His Majesty was very clear on that. It was presented to us as a lifetime package, and only the guards who were not married were offered the opportunity to protect you."

"Opportunity? Why would leaving your homeland, your family and friends, be an opportunity, Charles?"

"My lady, we know who you are. We know who your father was. It is an honor to protect you, and it would be an honor to make it a life-long decision."

"Even if the risk is death itself? You would be willing to die to protect me?"

"Yes, my lady, it would be an honor."

I was having a difficult time understanding why he would say that. I was not anyone special. I was an accidental survivor of a brutal massacre in a kingdom two days ride from here. As far as I knew, he had never been to Whispering Wind, and he had never met my father. Why would this man, along with countless others, risk his life for mine?

"Why would you do that Charles? Why would you risk your life for mine? I do not understand this valiant and noble behavior."

"My lady, a very long time ago, before I was born, my grandfather was friends with your grandfather. Although my grandfather was just a guard, your grandfather was his friend. When the uprising occurred in your kingdom, and your grandfather's guard turned on him and nearly killed him, it was my grandfather who fought and risked his life to protect him. It was a friendship that lasted a lifetime. Together, as equals, they rebuilt your kingdom, along with all the villagers. I admire your family, and I will fight to the death to protect you and your brother."

"Why are you not a part of my father's guard?"

"When my mother married, she married a man who was a guard in this kingdom. This is where I was born, so this is where I serve, but now I have a chance to bring it full circle, to protect the grand-daughter of a man my family admired."

Blake cleared his throat. I had not even noticed that he had ridden up. "I feel the same way, my lady."

I could not help but smile. "Thank you both for taking care of me and volunteering to give your life for mine."

"You are more than welcome. We should get going back to Wellington, my lady. The light of the day is running short."

I looked up to the sky and noticed he was right. "We will need to ride swiftly if we are to make it back before the dark of night sets," and we did just that. When we reached the castle, Westin was waiting for me.

"Sabine, I was worried about you. You left after the morning meal. Where have you been?"

"Oh, Westin, I am sorry. I just needed to have some time to myself. I needed to clear my head and to think. Today has marked a year since our family left us. I think I was sad a little, and I just did not want to make you sad. Come on. Will you come with me to raid the kitchen?"

His eyes lit up. "Oh, I would love nothing more, Sabine."

"Charles, would you mind taking care of Raiden for me?"

"I will, my lady."

Off we went, hand in hand to the kitchen. I was so hungry I had eaten nothing but a few apples. We sat in the kitchen at the bench eating, laughing, and remembering our family. It was a day that started out badly and turned good. I loved my brother; he was the sweetest person I knew. It was going to be very hard to leave him behind, but he had grown to fit this family, and it would be the right choice to leave him here where he would be safe.

"Westin, will you walk me to my room? I am very tired and wish to sleep."

"Of course I will, Sabine."

Together, hand in hand, we climbed the massive staircase, hand in hand, we walked down the halls to my room. "I love you, Westin."

"I love you, Sabine. I will see you in the morning. Good night."

"Good night, Westin."

Camille was in my room sitting in the chair. She looked as if she had been crying. When I came in, she jumped up and ran over to hug me.

"I am so sorry, my lady. It was a horrible thing for His Majesty to take Jared away to marry another. He loves you so."

I could not stop from laughing. "Oh, Camille, it is all right. We all must do what is required of us. Jared will grow to love his new wife in time. We are friends, and that is all we will be, and I am all right with that. My path is different in this life than his. He is to rule the kingdom, and I am just an orphan. It will be fine, my dear. It will be fine. Now, I am very tired, Camille. You can go for the night and thank you for caring so much."

My sleep was surprisingly peaceful. I woke knowing that there was so much that I needed to do that day. Camille came in to help me dress, but I was not ready. I wanted to spend some time with Westin alone, behind closed doors. I did not want anyone to invade my conversation.

"Camille, would you be a dear and have Westin join me for our morning meal here please?"

"I am sorry, my lady, but your brother has left early this morning. But I will get your meal right away."

Westin left? I wondered where he was off to. Well, that would give me more time to think of the best way to tell him that I would be leaving Wellington when Jared married. I scooted out of bed and got dressed. I sat down at the desk and prepared my writing materials. I would need to write letters to Katherine, Samuel, Westin, Rebecca, and Jared. I could leave secretly and not tell them how I was feeling. There was a knock on my door. "Come in, Camille."

There was no response, so I went to the door and opened it. I was surprised to see Charles standing in the hall.

"Yes, Charles? Is there something I can do for you?"

"No, my lady. I have a message for you from Princess Rebecca of Blackmore. Her personal royal guard delivered it early this morning." He handed me a letter.

"Thank you, Charles. I will speak to you soon."

"My lady, her guard is still in the stables. He was ordered to wait for a response."

"Well then, I shall read this note and respond. Please, excuse me." I came back into my room and tore open the note:

My dearest friend,

I am appalled at my father's choice. I met him and his family last night, which is what all the fuss was about while we were on the plain. I need to see you as soon as you can get away. I will meet you on the plain. I will leave as soon as I get your note.

Yours

Rebecca

Bring your sword. I need to let some anger out.

I could not help but smile, although I had plans this day. It was, after all, my birthday, and I would have loved to spend it with someone instead of spending it alone. To fight with someone other than Jared would be nice. I giggled at the thought of Charles and Blake's faces, not to mention Rebecca's guards, as they stood by watching two women slamming it out with swords. I grabbed my quill and scribbled a simple note.

My dear friend,

I will meet you on the plain with sword in hand. I will leave right after my morning meal. Do not worry. All will work itself out. See you soon

Sabine

I folded it and sealed it with the wax seal. After opening the door to find Charles standing in his guard stance, I handed it to him and said, "Would you please get Raiden ready? We will leave after my morning meal."

He bowed his head and away he went. Camille was coming with my tray, so I left the door open for her. When she sat my tray on the table, I noticed a package on it.

"What is this, Camille?"

"Oh, His Highness Prince Jared asked me to give this to you today. What is it, my lady?"

"Well, Camille, I have no idea, but I do not have time for games today. I will be leaving after I finish my meal, so you can have the day to yourself. I would like to be alone now."

Camille could not have left fast enough. He remembered it was my birthday. My heart was racing as I lifted the package into my hand. Removing the cloth covering revealed a small wooden box with a paper wrapped around it. As I unwrapped the box, I noticed that the inside of the paper had writing on it; Jared's writing.

My beautiful Sabine,

Today is a special day, and for the woman who owns my heart, I thought a special gift was in order to celebrate your birth.

I love only you

Jared

My hands were shaking as I lifted the lid of the tiny box. Tears welled in my eyes as I reached in and removed the thin chain, lifting it out to reveal a locket. It was tiny, but I knew why; so that it could be hidden easily within my bodice. I put it on, and it was perfect and hid perfectly right next to my heart. I smoothed out the paper and put it with the last note he had left me. With my food gone, I grabbed my father's sword and went out to the stables.

Charles and Blake were waiting for me. I handed Charles my sword, and he took it with a concerned look on his face. He did not say a word and just slipped it into his saddle. We mounted our horses and began our journey to the plain. While we rode, I could feel the locket pressing against my chest. They were silly, these feelings I had for Jared. He was a man I would never be able to love openly. It did not matter either way because my plan was to leave Wellington and begin my journey to find who it was that murdered my family.

When we arrived on the plain, Rebecca was not there yet, so Raiden and I went riding. I needed to clear my head of the childish thoughts of 'happily ever after' with Jared. The wind felt good on my face, and I am sure that it was good for Raiden to run. I pulled on his reins to slow him down. I needed to talk this out.

"Hey, boy. What would you think about leaving Wellington?" I was not sure what I expected him to do, but I needed to talk it out, and I had no one I could talk to. "Samuel told me that he had purchased a cottage six days ride from here for me and Westin to live our days out. See, Jared has decided that he loves me, which I find silly since I do not know what love is. I do have feelings for him, but I do not know what they are. We need to go and find who slaughtered our family, and we need to find Juliana." Raiden snorted and hit his hoof on the ground a few times. "So, you are with me on this? I have a plan in mind. When Jared is married, then we shall leave. I cannot live in the same house as him and his new wife. Oh, Raiden, it is going to be hard to leave Westin."

"Is Westin the name of the man who has stolen your heart?"

It was Rebecca; she had arrived without my hearing her. I laughed. "No. Westin is my brother."

"Well, where is it that you are going, Sabine? Did your secret love offer to marry you?"

"Oh, God no. Never mind. So, what has happened?" We climbed off our horses and sat in the grass.

"Well, first of all, I met the ogre my father thinks I am to marry. He is so cold and proper, not to mention arrogant and sort of rude. I hate him, and his father is worse. He is a pig. He treats his wife like she is no one. I think he thinks of women as objects instead of people with feelings. I have heard stories of this man, of this king."

"What kind of stories?"

"Oh, things like he reveres his son as if he were some kind of God, and that his other children mean nothing to him but a way to forge kingdoms. His oldest daughter was sold off so he could one day take over the kingdom of her husband. He is a monster, Sabine, and I have told my father of this man's intentions, but my father will not listen to me. I will not marry this man's son. I will not do it."

"Oh, Rebecca, I am so sorry for you, but you do know that it is your duty to do as your father requires. It is your station in life as a princess to carry on the royal bloodline."

"I can tell you this, Sabine. I will not marry him. I have sent

Edward a note as well this morning, for him to meet us here as soon as he can, and then I will discuss this with him. Did you bring your sword?"

"I did." I stood up and raised my hand for Charles to come over. When he arrived, I asked him for my sword. With a panicked look on his face, he removed it from his saddle and handed it to me.

"Wow! That is some sword."

"Thank you. It was my father's."

Laughing, Rebecca managed to say, "Can you even lift it?"

I smiled back at her. "Oh, you better believe I can. Shall we, my lady?"

I raised my sword, and we began to fight. I thought Blake was going to have a major break down, as well as Rebecca's guards, but Charles reassured them all that we were fine. We swung our swords hard at one another. It seemed it was a draw at the end of every round. Rebecca was good, but she was not as good as me. I was, after all, trained by one of the best swordsmen in all the lands. We continued our fight for some time, until we heard horses. Rebecca dropped her sword, yelling, "Edward!"

I looked in the direction her head turned, and riding up with four other men was a young man with reddish colored hair. He was not what I had imagined in my mind. He jumped off his horse and ran to Rebecca, scooping her up in his arms and kissing her like Jared had kissed me that night at the river.

Edward released her and looked at me. "Well, you would have to be Sabine. Hello, my lady," he said, bowing. "It is wonderful to make your acquaintance. I am Edward."

For fun, I curtsied. "It is a pleasure to meet you, Edward. I am indeed Sabine."

Turning back to Rebecca, he asked, "What is the emergency, my love?"

"Well, my father has thrust upon me a monster of a man to marry. I will not do it, Edward. I will marry you."

His laughter was loud. "Oh, my love, I am sure that he is not a monster at all. He is just not me!" He kissed her on the forehead.

"He is a monster. That is why I have asked you here today. I have a plan. I will not marry him, and I want to leave before the wedding. I want to run away with you."

"Well, as much as I would love that, your father will hunt us down, and I would for sure spend the rest of my life in the stockades, while you would be dragged to the alter and married off. There is no place we would be able to hide."

Standing there listening to them, I thought of my own plan to leave. Would Rebecca's father put it together that she could be with me? Would Samuel know we were together if we ran off at the same time? Samuel did purchase the cottage, so he would know where it was, would he not? I would not say anything just yet.

Charles whistled, and I looked up. It was my signal to get ready to go. "Rebecca, I am sorry, but I need to go. Will you meet me here tomorrow?"

"I can meet you for another thirty days, for that is when the wedding is to take place, and I will not be here when it is time."

I reached over and kissed her on the cheek. "Be strong, my friend. Until tomorrow."

I climbed on, Raiden and Edward handed me my sword. "That is some sword you wield, Sabine."

"Thank you, Edward. The sword was my father's. Good bye, my friend, and it was lovely to make your acquaintance, Edward." On our ride back, I needed to talk to Charles. I trusted him more than I did Blake.

"Blake, would you mind riding ahead of us? I wish to speak to Charles alone."

"Of course, my lady." Off he rode.

When I was sure of his distance, I began with my query. "Charles, will you tell me what you know of this cottage?"

"Well, I know that it is a very generous cottage, with plenty of room. It has a bit of land with it, as well, and a stable."

"Does Samuel know where it is?"

"I am not sure, my lady. Why?"

"Who went and purchased this cottage, six days' ride from here? If it was not Samuel, who did so?"

"It was my brother, Joseph. He was sent on a secret mission just before the cold season last year."

"So you are saying that this cottage was purchased shortly after we arrived at Wellington?"

"Yes, and I do know that Joseph was sworn by the king himself to never reveal the exact location to anyone, and to never mention it again."

"Do you think your brother would talk to me about it?"

"My lady, I am sure he would, for he is one of the guards who would be accompanying you and Lord Westin, if you were to leave."

"I will need to speak to him before Samuel returns. Can you arrange that?"

"It would not be a problem, except that His Majesty has already returned."

"What do you mean, Charles?" That did not make any sense. Why would they have returned so soon? Jared said it would be days. I hoped that no one was ill.

"Well, word came this morning that they would be returning to prepare for the wedding."

"I thought the wedding was taking place now. I thought that is why the whole family went, to marry Jared off and return with his wife to the castle."

"No, my lady. They should have arrived by the time we return. That is why we left the plain."

"Well, Charles, perhaps you could arrange for Joseph to accompany us tomorrow in place of Blake?"

"Yes, my lady. I think Blake mentioned he was not feeling well today," he said as he smiled a huge smile. I realized that Charles was a very good looking man. I wondered why he did not have a wife. I supposed it was because he was still rather young.

CHAPTER ELEVEN

The rest of the way back to the castle was silent. As we rode in the back way, as we did each time we left and returned. I noticed there was a great deal of movement around the stables. The closer we got, the easier it was to hear what all the fuss was about. The guards were all talking about the return of the king. Apparently, he had returned with some new guards, who were from Jared's soon to be wife's kingdom, and they were here to exchange places with some of Samuel's guards. It was an exchange of good faith. They were here to keep tabs on Jared, and the guards who were to go were to keep tabs on his promised wife. I tried not to be so obvious in my listening as we rode into the stables. Charles excused himself and went outside. I climbed off Raiden and proceeded to take off his saddle. I whispered to him to keep our chat a secret, and he nudged me with his nose.

"What secret would that be, my love?" It was Jared.

I spun around, probably more excited than I should have been. "What are you doing in here? Hiding from your wife?"

"I have no wife, Sabine, and I have vowed to myself that the only wife I will have is you." He said this as he wrapped his arms around my waist and kissed me.

Flustered, I pulled away from him. "Jared, we agreed to be just friends. It is not proper to be kissing a man who is promised to another."

He smiled that beautiful smile of his. "Oh, my sweet Sabine, I did not agree to anything. I am merely pleasing my father until I can figure a way out of this mess. I met my, would be wife, and let me tell you. She is a woman I would not wish on my enemy. My father knows how I feel, Sabine, and there is nothing he can do to change my feelings for you. Oh, and Happy Birthday. Did you get my gift?"

I reached up, pulled it from my bodice, and dangled it in the air. "I did and thank you. I love it."

He smiled and kissed me again. "Tomorrow I wish to accompany you on your ride to wherever it is that you go every day."

"I am sorry, Jared, but I must decline your request. What I do and where I go is something that is for me. I wish not to share it with you or anyone else." I was thinking that, tomorrow, I was to speak to Charles' brother, Joseph.

He looked at me somewhat shocked. "If that is what you wish, my love."

"You really need to not call me that. You have been promised in marriage, and it is not proper for you to call me that, and it is not proper for us to be alone with one another. Now, if you will excuse me, I need to change and wash up for the evening meal." I walked out into the courtyard. The guards were still chatting about the exchange. I looked at Charles, and he had a strange look on his face. It was almost urgent. He nodded at me, and I nodded back. In my room with the door closed, I relaxed. The situation with Jared was becoming tense, and I needed to keep him at bay so that Samuel did not send me away before I was ready. I needed to make sure that Westin stayed here. He did not like change, and he was so comfortable here now. Just as I had that thought, Westin jumped out from behind my dressing screen.

"Surprise, Sabine!!"

"Oh, Westin, you frightened me. Where did you go this morning? I wished to have our morning meal together."

"I am sorry, Sabine, but I wanted to finish your present." He pulled from behind his back a long thin object wrapped in a cloth. "I made it myself."

"Oh, Westin, you did not need to do this," I said, reaching for the object. As I took the covering off it, I was shocked and amazed at the skill that went into making it.

"It is a sheath for Father's sword. The leatherworker in the village, his name is Gus, helped me make it for you. Do you like it, Sabine?"

"Yes, of course! I love it!" In my hand was a leather sheath all hand sewn, and engraved in the leather were the letters P S W W. "Westin, what do these letters stand for?"

"Princess Sabine of Whispering Wind, I could not put your name on it because Samuel said that we had to keep who we are a secret. I thought no one would know what they meant, so I put those on there, and see? It has pieces of our family crest all over it. They are not together, so no one will know what it is, except for me and you."

I could not stop the tears. It was the most beautiful gift I had ever gotten. "I love you so much, Westin. I love it and thank you." I hugged him more tightly than I should have. These were the things about Westin that I would miss the most when I left. "I need to get dressed for the evening meal, so would you please excuse me, and I will see you down stairs."

"Okay, Sabine, and I love you too."

As he closed the door, I could not stop the tears. Today had been a very emotional day. I took my time getting dressed, as there really was no hurry getting downstairs tonight. The talk at the table would be nothing but chatter of the coming wedding. Francine and Kaitlin would be all excited about getting new dresses and about planning the party, not something I wished to listen to, but I needed to show that it did not affect me.

I walked in the room to find that there was no one there seated at the table. It did not make sense. I was always the last to arrive. I sat in my chair and waited. Someone walked in behind me, and before I could turn to see who it was, their hands were on my eyes.

"Do not be afraid. It is me, Camille."

I could not help but smile, thinking, Westin. Just then, I heard everyone yell, "Happy Birthday, Sabine!" Camille took her hands off my eyes, and sitting on the table was a beautiful cake and presents. "Oh, you really should not have done this."

"Nonsense! Do you think we would have let your eighteenth birthday go by unnoticed?" Katherine said as she leaned in to kiss me on the cheek. "Happy Birthday, Sabine." Her hand squeezed my shoulder. I was sure that she was thinking of Jenna.

The meal seemed to take forever to finish. The gifts were lovely; a bracelet from Katherine and Samuel, a hair comb from Francine and Kaitlin. Honestly, I could not wait for it to be over. There was small talk and giggles, but not one mention of the wedding. Perhaps Katherine suggested it not be spoken of on my birthday. They all felt sorry for me, I was sure. This would be the year I was to wed. My plans were not of marriage, but of revenge and finding Juliana. It amazed me how no one ever talked of Juliana. It was as if she never existed, the same as it was with Jenna. The girls never speak of their sister. Her name was never mentioned.

"Excuse me," I said. "I would like to retire to my room, if that is acceptable. I have had a rather long day, and I would like to go to sleep." I stood, as did Jared and Westin. "Westin, will you walk with me please?"

"Of course I will, Sabine."

We left the dining room, and all was silent. We did not speak on our walk to my room. I just wanted to spend some time with him. I was fearful he would not care for me after I left him here. At my door, he kissed me on my cheek and bid me good night. I watched my big brother bounce down the hall and out of sight.

Movement in the hall startled me. It was Charles. In a low whisper, he said, "My lady, can you meet me in the stables after the house is asleep?"

"Of course I can. Is everything all right?"

"No, my lady. I am afraid it is not all right. Until then," he replied, and then he was gone.

Thinking it would be best if it looked like I was going to bed, I changed into my sleeping gown and climbed into bed with a book from Samuel's library. I did not read it. I was listening to the sounds in the house and waiting for the time when everyone was sleeping. When I was sure that no one was awake, I slid on my boy clothes and put my hair up, so that if I was seen, it would look as if I was a boy and not me. I crept silently down the back staircase and out the door. I stayed along the wall of the castle until I was sure I could not be seen out any of the windows that faced the stables. Moving silently from tree to tree, and looking up constantly toward the windows, I made my way to the stables. Raiden was surprised to see me, as I was to see Charles and Joseph.

"It is not safe to talk here. We need to find another place," Joseph whispered.

"Come with me. I know of a place," Charles whispered back, taking my hand.

We stayed close to the walls of the buildings until we were at the castle gate. Charles slid through a small opening, nearly getting stuck, and I followed and then Joseph. We walked for a few minutes into the woods, until Charles thought it was safe.

Joseph began talking in a whisper. "I am to leave in the morning to go on the exchange. We are to watch Prince Jared's promised wife. She has made it clear to her father that she will not marry him, as Jared has made it known to the king that he will not marry. Sabine, we do not know one another, but I am fearful that you are in danger. The King has decided that you are the reason this union will not take place."

"Charles said that you had secured a cottage for us six days ride from here."

"Yes, I have, but the king feels you will not go willingly. There has been talk that he is planning on kidnapping you and taking you there against your will."

I could not help but laugh. "When would he be planning this, Joseph?"

"The day of the wedding. That way, Prince Jared would not know what has happened to you until it is too late."

"Joseph, Charles said that you, and only you, know the where-abouts of this cottage. Is that true?"

"Yes, my lady, it is true. Not even the king knows. What I have heard is that on the day of the wedding, when we escort the bride here, I am to leave with twenty-five other guards, Charles included, to escort you to the cottage."

"Thank you, Joseph. You do what you need to do, and we will keep in contact. Charles, you swore to protect me, and I have a plan. All will be revealed in time, but I think the king shall have his wish. Joseph, when is this wedding?"

"Not for thirty days, my lady."

"Thank you. Now, we need to get back before someone notices that we are gone."

I managed to make it back to my room without being seen. I changed my clothes and got back into bed. Sleep would not come to me. My mind was too alert. Samuel was going to kidnap me and take me away against my will. *Who was this man? Why did I trust him?* I felt like an utter fool. I would not allow him to best me at wit. My brothers taught me well, and that man would not control me. I could not leave Westin at Wellington; that was obvious. I had thirty days until I was to be taken away. *Thirty days... Why does that sound familiar?* I had the support of Charles and Joseph and a few others. If Samuel truly did not know of the cottage or which land it sat on, he could only guess at where it was. It was six days' ride, and he knew not of which direction Joseph rode. It would be with a great deal of luck if he were to find us. Then that was it. I would actually allow Samuel to kidnap me. He would be giving me exactly what I wished for without even knowing he was doing it. The need to help Rebecca and Edward kept coming to the surface. If no one knew where this cottage was, then why not bring Rebecca and Edward? I did not want my friend to marry such a monster as her intended. Somehow, I was going to have to tell her of this diabolical plot of Samuel's to remove me from Jared's life by kidnapping me. I could not help but chuckle. It was his plan. He would think he had won. My room seemed lighter somehow.

Had the light of the day already begun to rise? I did not sleep, and yet I was not tired. I got up and went to the writing table.

My Dearest Friend

It is vital that we speak as soon as it is possible. Swords or not?

Sabine

I folded the paper and sealed it with a wax seal. I hurried and dressed, but the house was still sleeping. I needed for Blake to deliver this to Rebecca as soon as he was able. I moved as I did last night, not making a sound. I found my way to the guard's quarters and happened upon Joseph, who was packing his belongings into a satchel.

"Joseph, could you retrieve Blake for me please?"

"It would be my honor, Your Highness."

"Joseph, you must never call me that. Here I am just Sabine, an orphan."

"Yes, my lady. I just wanted to say it once. It is my honor to be in your trust."

He went into the barracks, and soon Blake appeared. I walked away from him to make sure we were not overheard.

"I need you to leave now, without saying a word, and get this note to Lady Rebecca, and then wait for a reply. Can you do that for me?"

"I can and I will, my lady."

"Thank you, Blake. You are fast becoming a trusted friend."

After he was gone, I wished Joseph well and made my way back to the castle. When I arrived in the kitchen, the servants were already awake and getting things prepared for the morning meal. There was very little chatter today, and Katherine seemed a bit off. Perhaps she knew what Samuel had planned for me. There was only one way to find out. I decided that later in the morning I would seek Katherine out. She was usually in the garden, so I would see if I could get her to talk a bit. I excused myself and wondered through the grounds, looking for the garden. Amazingly enough, I found it and Katherine as well.

"May I sit with you, my lady?"

"Please call me Katherine, and yes, of course, Sabine. You may sit with me any time you desire, my dear."

"I know that the past few days must have been difficult for you with it being a year now since Jenna's death." I could not find any other way to enter into this deceitful conversation. I needed to find out what she knew about Samuel's plan, if anything.

"Yes, it has, Sabine. I miss my daughter a great deal, unlike her father, who seems to have forgotten she even existed." Her voice trailed almost to a whisper as she continued, "He is like that with the other girls as well."

That was my chance. I needed to find out what Samuel was really like, and there was no one else who knew him better. "I do not understand what you mean. Does he not hold his daughters in the same regard as he does Jared?"

"Oh, Sabine, he holds no woman, myself included, in any sort of regard. He is a man who believes that men are the most important, and that women merely supply the world with the men who will in turn run it."

For a moment, I was speechless. I was not aware that it would be this easy to gain information from her. I felt so deceitful, but Samuel was planning on kidnapping me, and I was not so fond of that idea. I needed to be very careful how I spoke to her. She has to want to tell me.

"Yes, I have noticed that no one speaks of Jenna or Juliana. She has been missing for a year now, and I have heard of no rescue attempt."

"No, and I am afraid that there will not be any attempt to save my granddaughter. For Samuel, it is as if she is dead as well." She could not hold back her tears. I put my arm around her and just let her cry.

"Is this why no one speaks of them?"

"Samuel told us that they are both gone, and that there is nothing we can do about it, so we are never to speak their names. I am so afraid, Sabine, that I married a monster. He was such a loving and kind man, especially after Jared was born. When I continued to produce girls instead of boys, he lost interest in me as well. He was disappointed with each birth of our daughters. He has no interest in them, and he seems obsessed with marrying Jared off to produce an heir. It saddens me that he will not allow Jared to marry you, when it is so obvious that he is in love with you. The girls will be given in marriage to men they do not know, only to secure the kingdoms that surround ours, just as Jenna was. Jenna actually loved Ardes, however, and I was so happy for her."

This was interesting information she was giving me. Samuel wanted to secure the kingdoms that surrounded his. Was his plan all along to secure Whispering Wind? Is that why he did not care that Jenna was dead and Juliana was missing, because she did not produce a male?

"Well, I am a princess with a kingdom. Why would he not approve a match between us?"

"Sabine, you are indeed a princess, but you have no right to the kingdom. You are a woman, and it is unheard of for a woman to rule a kingdom. To Samuel, you are just not worthy."

"Then, why has he been teaching me how to rule?"

"I do not know. Perhaps it is to keep you busy and away from Jared. Samuel had told me when you first arrived that you were going to be nothing but trouble for us, and that he was unsure of bringing you here. He is up to something. Sabine, forgive me for saying this to you, and I wish not to frighten you, but I am fearful of what Samuel will do if this marriage does not happen. I have heard him threaten Jared on more than one occasion. Jared is a man of his own mind, and I am afraid that something terrible is going to happen. Samuel will force his hand and demand that Jared marry. I believe that you will be what he uses to do exactly that."

Shock was the only thing I felt in that moment. Those words she was saying to me were words that Joseph had said. I needed to be very careful of myself in the days ahead. I turned away from Katherine, so she would not see the shock on my face, and spied Blake off in the distance. He nodded his head and disappeared.

"Thank you, Katherine, for telling me these things. I know it was not easy. I hope that we can talk again soon. I am going to leave you now to your thoughts of Jenna and Juliana." I kissed her on the cheek and left.

Walking through the garden in the direction in which I saw Blake was difficult at best. I wanted to run. I needed to be away from here. I wanted to know what Rebecca had said. I found him at his post, and as I approached, he whispered one word to me, "Raiden", so I continued past him to the stables. Once inside, I needed to be careful. The new guards were in here as well as ones I did not know. They all watched with sharp eyes as I entered.

One said, "Excuse me, my lady. Can I help you with something?"

"No, I just thought I would come and see Raiden. Do you have any apples?"

"No, my lady. We do not feed apples to the horses." Smiling, I kept on walking. "Hey, boy." I reached up to rub his head. I swore he smiled at me. I searched his pen for a note, but did not see anything. I reached up to scratch his ears, and then I felt it; a note tucked into his bridal. I slipped it out and placed it in my bodice. No one noticed. I whispered to Raiden, "I will be back. We are going for a ride today." He snorted in response.

I needed to look casual as I walked back to my room. Blake nodded as I passed him, and I nodded back. When I finally reached my room, I closed the door and leaned against it. Opening the note, I read the two words Rebecca wrote:

Swords Now

Grabbing my sword, I left my room and went to find Samuel. "I am going for a ride with Charles and Blake. I did not want you to worry about me or where I have gone."

"Thank you, Sabine. I trust you are enjoying your freedoms here?"

I thought it strange he would say that to me. "Yes, Samuel, and I want to thank you for not putting restrictions on me." Two can play this game.

"Sabine, I just want you to be happy and comfortable here. I am pleased that you have a friend and that you enjoy riding. It is good that you leave the castle from time to time."

"Thank you, Samuel. I am not sure when I will return, so if I miss the afternoon meal, will you please make my apologies?"

"Of course, Sabine. Enjoy your ride." I left feeling as if he left something unsaid, and then I went to find Charles. He was in the stable, putting Raiden's saddle on him.

"How did you know I wanted to leave now, Charles?"

He just smiled at me and said, "I had a feeling when Blake left early this morning, my lady. We are ready when you are."

"Good, then let us leave. Could you please take care of this for me, Charles?" I handed him my sword covered in my new sheath Westin had made me.

Blake was the first to speak. "My lady, this morning when I left to deliver your note to Princess Rebecca, I could not help but notice that I was being followed, as we are now."

I did my best not to look around and said, "We are being followed now?"

"Yes, my lady. There are always eyes upon you and those of us who protect you."

"Do you know who these eyes belong to? Are they Jared's eyes, or are they Samuel's eyes?"

"It eludes me." He said.

We rode for a bit. "Charles, do you think it is safe for me to see Rebecca? I do not want to put her in danger."

"My lady, the king knows of your friendship, so I do not believe he will do her harm."

We came through the forest and onto the plain. Rebecca was already there, and she rode up to us. "Well, it took you long enough."

"I left as soon as I got your." Before I could finish, a group of guards, six of them, came riding up.

"Oh, these are my new keepers, some kind of trade agreement my father made with the monster's father," she said and laughed.

Riding up was Joseph and two other guards from Wellington, along with Rebecca's usual guards. I was stunned, so much so that I was unable to speak. The air had become electric with fear on all our parts. No one said a word. I was so confused as I stared at Rebecca, looking for some kind of an explanation, but Rebecca had no idea what was wrong. She did not know that the man I loved was the man she was being forced to marry. Samuel knew this, just as he knew of my friendship with Rebecca. Was this a joke?

"What are all the long faces about?" Rebecca said with a laugh, "Come on, Sabine. Let us ride." She turned her horse and away she went.

I looked at Joseph and then to Charles and Blake. Charles just nodded, and I took off on Raiden. Rebecca and I rode without saying a word for a long time. When we were the furthest from the guards, I pulled on Raiden's reins to stop him. Rebecca came riding up. "What is wrong, Sabine?"

"We need to talk. I am fearful that we are in serious danger, Rebecca, all of us you, me, Edward, my brother Westin, and." I was not sure I would be able to get his name out, but I had to say it.

"And who, Sabine?"

"Jared."

"Not Jared of Wellington? He is the monster my father wishes me to wed. Why would you bring him into..." she stopped. "He is the one you love." She whispered.

I put my head down and reached to touch the locket. "Yes." There was silence and then laughter. Rebecca was laughing. Why would she laugh?

"Oh, this is perfect. It all makes sense now. I did not put it all together until right this moment. The guard uniforms I knew they looked familiar. Your guards wear them as well."

"We have a great deal to discuss, Rebecca. I have a story I need to tell you. I was sworn to secrecy, and this must never leave this plain. Agreed?"

"Agreed."

We climbed off our horses and sat in the grass. I decided that the beginning was the best place to start. I told her everything, and when I was finished, I looked up at her face. I was surprised to see tears streaming down her cheeks, and then she threw her arms around me and hugged me.

"Oh, Sabine, I am so sorry for all that you have lost. You poor thing."

"Thank you, Rebecca, but you must never speak of this again. There is more to this than I have told you, and I am fearful that our very lives are in danger."

"I give you my word. I will never speak of this with anyone, but you are going to tell me of this pending danger, are you not?"

"Yes. As it turns out, Jared's father seems to have a plan, one greater than any of us are aware of. Katherine said something to me this morning in the garden. She had said that Samuel married off Jenna to my brother to secure my father's kingdom, and that he will marry his other three daughters off for the same reason, just as he is forcing you and Jared to marry, to secure your father's kingdom. My family was slaughtered, along with the entire village, and it frightens me to think that perhaps Samuel had something to do with it. Jenna did not produce a male child. She had a little girl. Katherine told me that Samuel has no use for women in life, except to gain access to other kingdoms. It makes sense to think that he may have had a hand in what happened to my family. Juliana was not murdered alongside of my family. She was taken along with all the other children in the village. There is more to this, and it seems that I have less than thirty days to discover the truth before all of our lives are destroyed. I have a plan. When I first arrived in Wellington a year ago, Samuel sent Joseph out to secure a cottage for me and Westin. It is six days ride from here. Samuel ordered Joseph to keep the location a secret. Joseph has confirmed that Samuel does not even know where it is. I think we can all find safety at this cottage, far from Samuel's reach."

"It all sounds wonderful. I can marry Edward, and you can be with Jared, but we will need help, Sabine, and lots of it."

I could not help but smile. "Rebecca, I have not told you all that there is to tell. The story will have to come in pieces, for it would take days to tell you everything there is. We will have our help, and it will come in abundance."

Charles whistled just then, and the guards started coming toward us. "Please remember, not a word to anyone, not even Edward."

"I give you my word, but I must say, Sabine, that I am fearful for you."

"Do not worry about me, Rebecca. Charles is in on this with me. He is the one who has made me see that I am indeed in danger. We will talk each day of our plan." Just then the guards arrived.

"I shall see you tomorrow, my friend, after the midday meal as always." I smiled and climbed on Raiden.

"Until tomorrow, Sabine."

On our ride back to Wellington, I could not help but think of the lengths that Samuel would go to keep me from Jared. He knew of my friendship with Rebecca, and had not said anything about it, knowing that she was Jared's promised wife. I was beginning to think this man was setting us all up for some horrible demise. I would outwit him. He would not win. I would have to go to him and play the part. After the evening meal, I planned to ask to speak with him in his study. I would tell him that I wished to leave Wellington, and that I wished to go sooner rather than later.

"Charles."

"Yes, my lady."

"Are there guards who would defy the king?"

"Yes, there are very many who would find it an honor to protect you and Lord Westin."

"Charles, do you know why they would choose death over the king they have been sworn to serve and protect?"

It was silent for a while. I watched Charles struggle within himself to find the correct words to speak. "Well, my lady,"

"Charles, please call me Sabine when we are together like this."

"Well, Sabine, King Samuel is a cruel man. He told you that he had sent groups of scouts to scurry the countryside for any word on what happened to your family. He did not do that. The total disregard he has for the fact that his only granddaughter is missing is unheard of. We are only privileged to certain pieces of information, but there is talk among the villagers and the guards. Have you ever noticed, Sabine, that you have never been allowed to go into the village, and that we leave and enter the castle through the back gates? There is a reason for that. There are traders in the village that have traded with people from your own kingdom. You are very well known in most lands. It is not every day a young princess can best a future king in swords. Westin is not known in this land, although he is special and not like most men, yet he has the freedom to wander around. The king has been very specific about your freedom. Although you think you have freedom, you do not. It is guided by the king. We have been given orders as to where we are allowed to take you on your rides."

"Why would he allow my friendship with Rebecca?"

"He told me that it was good that the two of you were friends, and that it would be easier for you to accept that your friend was going to marry Jared than someone you did not know."

"Do you think he choose Rebecca when he discovered that we were friends?"

"No, Sabine. The marriage was arranged when Rebecca began her thirteenth year, long before Jared even knew who you were."

We had arrived at the castle gates, and the new guards watched me with the eyes of hawks. I would otherwise find it strange and offensive, but I had to laugh to myself at how silly it was. If they only knew I was on to their purpose. Inside the stables, I put Raiden in his pen and proceeded to take off his saddle.

"Did you enjoy your ride, my love?"

"Jared, you really need to stop this. If your father finds out that you are secretly meeting me, he will have my head."

He laughed. "Oh, Sabine, my father is not that cruel," he said, and then he kissed me.

I needed to resist him at all costs. He could and would ruin my plans. "This cannot happen again," I scolded him, which in turn just made him laugh harder.

"Oh, my dear Sabine, there is nothing in this world that can stop me from wanting to be with you."

"Well, Jared, there has to be, or this will end badly. Now, I need to go and dress for the evening meal."

I managed to squirm away from him and leave the stables. When I arrived in my room, Samuel was waiting for me. It was odd that he always appeared when I had been with Jared. It was as if he knew every move I made. I could not help but wonder if it was his eyes that watched me.

"Sabine, I am sorry for intruding in your private room, but I think it is time you knew the truth of Jared's promised wife."

Oh, this was going to be good. He was going to set into motion a seed of doubt in my mind about my friendship with Rebecca. I sat down in the chair and tried to keep the smile off my face. I was going to beat him at his own game of wit.

"Samuel, I am glad that you are here. I was going to come to speak with you after the evening meal. I have considered your offer to leave Wellington. I believe it would be best if Westin and I left here. I am grateful for all that you have done for us, and I believe the jewels we discovered at Whispering Wind will be compensation enough for all that you have extended to Westin and myself. I do not think that it is best for us to stay on here after Jared marries." I had to make sure that I saw his face when I spoke the next words. "Rebecca of Blackmore."

He is a good mastermind. He did not even wrinkle a brow. "So you are aware of Jared's intended? That is good, Sabine, that you are not upset or angry that it is your friend."

"Samuel, I am old enough to know how this works. I know that it is Jared's station to carry on the bloodline. If my parents had not been murdered, this would be my time to argue with my father about marrying a man I do not know or love. I have told Rebecca the same thing, which is that it is her station to do as her father requests of her. You know I have feelings for Jared, and he for me, and I do understand and have accepted that nothing will ever come of it. For the sake of everyone involved, I believe now that it is best that Westin and I leave here. I am grateful, as I said before, for all that you have done for us, and I hope that when the time comes to part, we part as friends."

"Of course, Sabine. If you are ever in need for anything, you can get word to me, and I will provide you with all that you need. When would you like to leave?"

"Well, I would like to be the one to tell Jared, if that is acceptable, and I am going to need time to get Westin used to the idea. He loves it here, and you know he does not like change. I need to make it an adventure for him. I would like to tell Jared first, so if I could have some time with him alone, I would appreciate that. I would think that in seven to maybe ten days would be acceptable to leave."

"I will give you permission to explain to Jared, and I thank you for that. I will not say a word to anyone in the house. I will leave that to you."

"Thank you, Samuel. I appreciate that. One more thing, would it be asking too much if I were to request that Camille come with us? I have grown very fond of her."

"As I had said before, Sabine, whatever you require."

He rose from the chair and left my room. I could not help but smile when he left. I had just bested him. He was giving me exactly what I wished, and little did he know that he was giving me his son as well.

I dressed for the evening meal and made my way to the dining hall. Everyone was seated as usual. I supposed I was always late, and they were waiting for me. We ate our meal with the usual chatter from the girls, with Samuel pretending to respond and seem interested. I noticed that Katherine was watching me with fear in her eyes. I could not help but wonder why. I found a break in the conversation. It was my chance to engage Jared.

"Jared, I have gained permission from your father to speak with you in private. I was hoping that tomorrow after our morning meal, if you did not have any pressing matters, you would accompany me on a ride. Charles and Blake would come along, for it is not proper for us to be alone now that you are promised in marriage. Since our training has come to a completion, and circumstances have changed immensely, I think it is time for us to talk. Would that be acceptable to you?"

I thought for a minute that he and Katherine were going into shock by the look on their faces.

"Of course, Sabine. I am sure that whatever Father has for me to do, he will excuse me from it."

"I will indeed, Jared. It will be good for the two of you to finally put an end to this tension that is always between you two." Holding the smile from my lips was more difficult than pretending to show defeat to Samuel. The man had no idea what was going to happen in ten days' time, and I would be sorry to not be here to see it. I excused myself and went back to my room. It was going to be a very long night.

CHAPTER TWELVE

The light of the day had arrived. Today was my big day with Jared. I was going to have to reveal to him that I knew Rebecca, and that his father was a tyrant. This was going to be a very difficult day; that is a given. I dressed and made my way to the dining hall to share one of the few morning meals I would have left with Samuel and Katherine. That was part of the life here that I would miss, a sense of family, even if the head of the family was a tyrant.

Everyone was sitting as usual when I arrived, everyone except for Jared. I tried not to notice, but Samuel had to mention it.

"Sabine, my dear, Jared wished for me to extend his apologies for his absence this morning. He had some business that would not keep, and he wanted me to ask if you would please postpone your ride until he returns."

"Oh, that is fine, Samuel. I have plenty to do. I am going to visit with Rebecca this morning, if that is all right?"

"That is fine, my dear. You enjoy yourself."

"Thank you, Samuel. I will. Westin, when I return this afternoon, I would like to go riding with you, if you are not too busy?"

His face lit up. "I would love to ride with you, Sabine. I will be ready and waiting for you to return."

I smiled at him and excused myself from the table. I had plans to work out with Rebecca, and details to figure out about my leaving. I hurried to the stables, not bothering to return to my room to retrieve my sword. Game play would have to wait. I had asked one of the new guards to find Charles and Blake for me and tell them that I was in the stables. I went in and began to put Raiden's saddle on. They arrived, and we left promptly.

"I wish to ride fast today, Charles. There is much to do."

When we were far enough away from the castle gates, Charles said in a rather low voice, "Lord Jared is waiting for you, my lady, by the stream."

"But we have watchful eyes upon us, Charles."

"I took care of those eyes myself this morning," Blake added with a peculiar smile on his face.

"Oh, Blake, I am hoping you did not hurt anyone at my expense."

"No, my lady. I was under the orders of His Highness Prince Jared."

We took off into the forest, and before I knew it, I could see him standing next to the stream. The sun was shining through the trees onto his golden brown hair. He was beautiful. I could not get off of Raiden fast enough. We embraced, and the kiss was long and deep. I pulled away from him and began, "There is much to be said, Jared. We have not the time for this. I thought you were gone on business. At least, that is what your father had told me."

"Yes, he is a cunning man indeed. I am to be on a mission for him, one that will keep me gone for nearly three days. I could not leave while you needed to speak with me, so I arranged this meeting so you can tell me what is so urgent."

"I am concerned, Jared, that your father is more cunning than you believe him to be. He is a monster, a tyrant, and it is with hope that you are not your father's son, for the misbehaving's of your father are surely going to anger you."

He laughed. "Oh, my beautiful Sabine, what an imagination you have. My father is not what you say he is."

"Jared, I am going to tell you a story, and I wish for you not to interrupt me. When I am finished, then you can judge whether or not I am using my imagination with my concern of your father."

"I shall let you tell me your story, and then I will reassure you that you are wrong."

"First, let me answer a question you asked me that day in the stables. Where is it that I go every day? I go to meet my friend on a plain, a friend I met on accident, a friend who is in love with a man named Edward."

Jared raised his eyebrows and looked at Charles and Blake. "Her name is Rebecca of Blackmore. Yes, Jared, my friend is your intended bride, though neither of us knew until yesterday, but your father knew. Another fact, right after Westin and I came to Wellington, your father sent Joseph on a mission six days ride from here to purchase a cottage for Westin and me to live in. His plan was to send us away all along. Another fact, your father never sent any scouts out to look for those who slaughtered my family and stole your niece, his grand-daughter. Fact, your mother had told me that your father ordered her never to speak Jenna or Juliana's names again. Fact, your father has arranged to kidnap me the day of your wedding and take me six days ride from here, to a place you will never find me."

I stopped talking. From the look on his face, I thought I let out too much information at one time. I needed for him to absorb what was said.

"This is not truth you speak, Sabine. My father would not do these things."

"I have confirmation, Jared. Speak to your trusted guards," I told him and looked at Charles and Blake.

"Everything she says, sire, is truth."

"Why would he do this?"

"Your mother told me yesterday in the garden that your father will marry you all off to secure the kingdoms around yours. He married Jenna off to Ardes, and when she failed to produce a male heir, he disregarded her. Katherine also told me that after your birth, she continued to have daughters, and your father disregarded her. What you see is just a face he puts on for show.

"Jared, I think your father orchestrated the slaughter of Whispering Wind. I cannot prove it, but I believe that I am right. Do you remember when he came into the castle before we left? I had found in the bottom of Jenna's chest, secretly hidden, a fortune of jewels. Well, I gave them to your father, and he then told me a story of my family's history. Charles had confirmed this with his story of his grandfather. I know this is much to believe, but please trust me, Jared. I believe it to be truth. Your father sent you away today because I told him that I needed to tell you that I was leaving."

"You are not going anywhere."

"You must listen to me, Jared. I am leaving in ten days' time, and your father does not know the location of this cottage. Joseph was told to keep it a secret. He is the only one who knows. You must continue with this game your father has set into play until Westin and I are safe. I will not allow your father to use me against you, as your mother suspects that he will. She believes he is going to hurt me in order to make you marry Rebecca. If he thinks that I am leaving, and that you are going to marry Rebecca, he will let me leave. You and Rebecca must keep the lie going until we are safe. There will be plenty of time for you to leave Wellington and come to me. I need to do this, Jared. I need to find who slaughtered my family, and I need to find Juliana. She has been gone for a year now."

He just stood there looking at me. "This is a great deal to take in, Sabine."

"It is the entire truth, sire. We have known about your father's intentions for quite some time now," Charles interrupted.

"I know it is, Jared. You have had but a few moments, whereas, I have been living it for a few weeks. Now, you must go. I will know more when you return. If your father does not allow us to have our time together, then you must arrange for us to meet again before I go, so I can tell you the full plan."

"Be careful, Sabine, for if what you say is the truth, my father will not allow anything to get in his way. I will speak with my mother when I return. Charles, Blake, I am entrusting the life of the woman I love to you both. Please keep her safe."

"We will, sire. With our lives we will protect her."

"I love only you, Sabine." He kissed me and left.

Charles, Blake, and I continued on to meet Rebecca on the plain. She was already in a full run when we arrived. I saw Joseph riding toward Charles as I took off on Raiden to meet Rebecca. We met in the middle as we usually do and climbed off our horses to lie in the grass.

"So, tell me, Sabine, what is new with you? You look a bit flush in the face. Have you been meeting with my future husband?" She giggled wildly.

"I have indeed, my lady," I responded as I rolled over on my side. "There is much we need to share, and we have very little time. I have told Samuel that I want to leave. I told him that I could not stay in Wellington anymore. He agreed to let me go, so I have but ten days. You and Jared must continue with this wedding charade. If you do not, I am fearful that Samuel will use me against you both."

"But I am not going to marry him, Sabine."

"I know you are not, but you both have to continue the way you are. I will need for you to trust me with Edward, so we can get him to safety as well. When we are all safe and out of Samuel's reach, then and only then, will you and Jared join us. I will send Joseph to get you both. I still have not worked out all the details, but I will get them to you if we cannot meet up again. You are my friend, Rebecca, and I cannot let this mess I am in affect your very life. We will survive this. I give you my word."

She giggled, "Really, Sabine, we need not worry about the cloak and dagger stuff. My father and King Samuel are just men who want their own way. I am not fearful of either of them. I trust you with Edward. I know he loves me."

"Good, because I am trusting you with the man I love as well. Joseph will be our contact if we cannot meet, and he will let you know when to have Edward meet us. I think I should get going. I need to talk to Westin and let him know that we are leaving Wellington." I got up and mounted Raiden.

"Sabine, do you honestly believe this is going to work?"

"I do. I have trusted people who know far more than I. This man, King Samuel of Wellington, will not best me at wit. I will not allow him to stop me from avenging my family and finding my niece. I owe it to Ardes and Jenna to save their daughter. Until we meet again, my friend."

I rode back to Charles and Blake, and we began our journey back to Wellington.

"May I speak freely, my lady?"

"Of course, Charles."

"I spoke with my brother, Joseph, and he got word from the king concerning your pending departure. He was ordered back to the castle in five days' time. I instructed him to tell the king, if he asks, that the cottage is in a different direction than what it is. He has agreed to tell the tale. We are all in this with you, Sabine. We will help you escape and avenge your family."

"Thank you, Charles. I need for you to instruct Joseph to inform Rebecca's love, Edward, on where to go and where to meet us. He is coming with Westin and myself, so we need to keep him safe as well. Rebecca and Jared will join us when the time is right. For now, the wedding is still on, and our plan is coming together. King Samuel will not best me at wit. That man, I believe, is the reason my family is dead. He was definitely shocked when Westin and I turned up alive, and I am sure that if Jared had not been at Whispering Wind, Westin and I would have met up with my family sooner than anticipated."

"My lady, I am fearful that you are correct."

There was not another word said the entire ride back. As usual, I went to the midday meal. Westin was excited to be spending some time with me, as I was with him. I was not excited about telling him the untruth of why we were leaving. He would not be able to contain the truth if Samuel asked him. It was best for him to believe in the lie. I loved my brother, and I wanted nothing more than for him to live a long and healthy life.

We walked to the stables holding hands. It always made Westin feel calmer somehow when you held his hand. We mounted our horses, and I asked Charles to take me to the plain he took me to the day of

Jared's departure. Westin and I did not speak; we just rode side by side smiling at one another. Upon arrival at the plain, he said, "This is nice, Sabine, spending time with you."

"It is indeed, Westin, but we have much to talk about. Come. Let us go ride for a bit." Off we went. Raiden slowed as we came to a big tree, and so we dismounted. I took Westin by the hand, and we sat in the shade.

"Westin, how much do you like living in Wellington?"

"I like it a lot, Sabine, but I do not think that Samuel cares for us to be there."

"Well, that is very observant of you. It is not that he does not like us to be there, but rather it is just that there are some things I do not think you understand."

"I know that Jared loves you, and I know that you love him. I know that Jared has to marry another, a girl named Rebecca. I know that Samuel is not happy that Jared loves you and does not want to marry this Rebecca."

I could not help but laugh. "You are right on all those points, Westin."

"Well, then, why can you not marry Jared, Sabine? You are a princess."

"Yes, I am a princess, and you are a prince. You see, Westin, we are without a kingdom, and we have nothing to offer Samuel or Jared, and that is fine. Westin, Samuel has purchased a cottage for us, and I think it is time that we left Wellington and moved on with our lives."

"Just you and I, Sabine?"

"No, not really. Charles and Blake will come with us, along with some other guards, but yes, it will be just you and I. It is hard for me to love Jared, knowing he is going to marry Rebecca. I went to speak to Rebecca today. She is my friend. We did not know that Jared was her intended match. She understands that I need to leave. I wanted to speak with Jared this morning, but Samuel sent him on an errand, so when he returns, I will tell him thank you and that we must go. He will be angry and sad, but, Westin, it is the best for all of us."

"Does Samuel know we are to leave?"

"Yes, I spoke with him last night before the evening meal."

"Sabine, what will we do at this new cottage? We do not have any money. How will we eat? Who will cook for us?"

"Oh, Westin, do not worry. Remember all the jewels we found? Well, I gave them all to Samuel, and he has reassured me that we will want for nothing for the rest of our days." In my head, I was wondering just exactly how many days that was.

"Ok, Sabine. If you think it is what we should do, then I will go with you." He smiled that beautiful smile of his, and I could see Mother in his face. How I missed her.

We ran our horses all the way back to the castle, and I let Westin win. Raiden could have taken his horse by lengths if I had let him, but it made Westin feel good to win. He seemed excited to go on an adventure. I was just fearful for what lay ahead. Would Samuel try to kill us, or was he going to stay true to his word? Somehow, I doubted he would stay true.

As we were walking out of the stables, I noticed a guard from Rebecca's father's kingdom who was staring at me in a very odd manner. His eyes were cold, almost murderous. It sent shivers down my spine. I had no idea who he was, but he surely did not look like a guard; more like a monster.

"Come, Westin, I will race you." And I took off running. I wanted to be out of his line of sight. When we rounded the corner, I saw Blake walking from the castle. He did not look well, almost sick. I wanted to ask him if he was all right, but he shook his head at me, as if to warn me off. This did not feel right at all. Something was terribly wrong. I felt fear well up inside of me, the same fear I felt when I saw my home from a top that hill a year ago. Could something have happened to Jared, to Rebecca? I needed to get into the house. I needed to find Samuel or Katherine. I took the remaining distance as quickly as my legs would carry me, just as I ran through the village while racing my brothers. I passed Westin and hit the door long before him, but I did not stop running. I ran into the dining hall, and it was empty. I ran through the halls to Samuel's library, and it was also empty. I ran to his study, and there they were, the whole family all sitting in silence.

When I busted through the door without even knocking, they all jumped in surprise.

"What is it? What has happened?"

"Oh, Sabine," cried Katherine.

"No," was all I could say. It could not be Jared. He could not be gone. Katherine rose from her chair, but I backed away from her. I did not want to hear what she was going to say. "NO!" I yelled. Her eyes were huge. It was obvious she had been crying. I saw Samuel stand behind her. He had a very smug look on his face, almost as if he was enjoying this. I wanted to leap past Katherine and rip his heart out. I wanted to kill him.

"Sabine, my child," he said in a very dark tone.

I could not stop myself. I knew this man would murder his own child. I knew he murdered Jenna. Why would he not murder Jared to get what he wanted? He was a monster.

"DO NOT CALL ME YOUR CHILD! Samuel, you are not my father."

He actually smiled at me. "Sabine, I am afraid that you are in shock. Perhaps you should go retire to your room for some rest. As you have pointed out, you are not a member of this family, and this is indeed a family matter."

"Samuel, this concerns Sabine as well. Juliana was her niece as well as our granddaughter."

What did she say? Juliana was? "What?"

"My dear," Katherine started as she put her arm around my waist, "a man who is in Samuel's employ has come to Wellington, and with him he brought Juliana."

"What did you say? Juliana is here? Where is she? I must see her. She must be frightened to death."

That was when everyone froze, and that eerie silence came again.

"Sabine," Katherine said in a whisper that I almost did not hear. "Sabine." I turned to look at her. "Sabine, I am so sorry to tell you this, but the child is not alive."

It was that hill all over again; the ringing in my ears, the flash of light, and then darkness.

CHAPTER THIRTEEN

When my mind awoke, I could feel the presence of someone in the room with me. I could hear footsteps, breathing, and I could hear the sounds of the night. I heard a soft knock, whispers, but none of it made sense. My eyes would not open. Then I felt a cool hand on my mine, and I heard my name, "Sabine." I needed to open my eyes, but then the memories came rushing back; the man in the stable court-yard, his murderous eyes, Samuel's evil smile, and Katherine's tears.

"Sabine, my love," the voice whispered.

My eyes fluttered, and I heard his voice, "She is waking up."

There were footsteps, and I could feel people around me. The light in the room was low, and the figures were just shadows around me. "Juliana," was all I could get out.

"Sabine, please wake up. I am so scared." It was Westin's voice. He was crying.

"Westin?" I reached up to find him, and he grabbed my hand.

"Sabine, wake up. Please, wake up, Sabine."

"My head hurts."

"I did not hit you with my horse this time. You fell and hit your head on the floor."

I tried to smile. My eyes started to focus, as well as my hearing. I could hear sobs in the distance. Katherine was here, and so were Westin and Jared.

"What are you doing here?" I asked him. "You are supposed to be gone for three more days."

He chuckled. "Sabine, it has been three days."

Everything was so out of focus. "Juliana... Where is Juliana?"

"We were waiting for you to wake up, so we can bury her, Sabine," Westin said through his tears.

That was when it all came back to me, and my eyes were open, and my body was moving. "I need to see her."

Hands were on me, forcing me down. "Sabine you hit your head pretty hard when you fell. You have a very large bump on your head. You must not try to get up."

"Westin hit me with his horse at full gallop. I am fine. Where is she?" I looked at Jared. "Take me to my niece. I need to see her." I did not care any longer what Samuel might think of my relationship with Jared. He did not matter to me. He was a monster, and this was not right. Juliana was not dead.

"Westin, help me please," Jared asked.

The two of them helped me. I half walked and they half carried me to the chapel, which to be honest, I did not even know was here. There was her tiny little body, lying on the stone alter. She was covered in a white silk cloth.

"Please leave me."

"But, Sabine."

"Leave me." I was loud and firm.

They let go of me and left the chapel. I walked, with great effort, toward the tiny little girl's body. It was almost unnoticeable on top of the giant alter. I reached up to pull the silk cloth from her face. The child was dirty and wearing rags for clothing. Her hair was wild and full of dirt and leaves. She looked like a banshee. This could not be Juliana. My heart would know if this was her. I reached for her to hold her in my arms, to feel the little girl I once rocked to sleep. This child was much bigger than what Juliana would be. She would not even be two years old yet. She was just a baby when she was taken. I stroked her face and outlined her eyes, closing mine and pulling the memory from my mind. My hand traced the memory, and this face did not fit; the mouth, the eyes, the nose. This was not Juliana. "Poor baby girl, what did they do to you? I am so sorry," I whispered these words, for I knew deep down inside that there were eyes watching me, Samuel's eyes. I needed this to be convincing. He needed to believe that I believed this was indeed Juliana.

I sat there for a bit of time, holding this dead child and wanting not to believe that Samuel ordered the death of this poor thing just to convince me and his family that she was dead. But he did, and I knew in my heart that Juliana was still alive. I heard footsteps behind me, and I forced myself to cry for this child. It was so unfair that she had to die because of me, because Samuel is a monster. I felt his hand on my shoulder.

"I am so sorry, Sabine, for the loss of your brother's child." It was Samuel. *My brother's child, is he serious? What about his granddaughter?* "You had us worried, Sabine. You hit your head hard on the floor. You should be in bed, dear. We will bury Juliana in the morning." He actually choked when he said her name.

"Samuel, I must apologize for the way I treated you, and for the way I spoke to you in your study."

"It is fine, child. I understand that you thought it was Jared we were crying for. All is forgiven."

"Samuel, I would like to have my conversation with Jared now that he has returned. It should not take long, and I would like to leave the day after next please, if that is acceptable."

"Of course, Sabine. I understand that you want to start your new life, now that the last thread of your family is gone. It is just you and Westin now, and it is only fair that you move on from this travesty."

"Thank you," I said as I handed him the child. He was shocked that I did, but he did his best not to show it. He played his part and laid her gently on the altar, and then covered her with care with the silk cloth. I almost laughed at him. He helped me up, and we walked out of the chapel arm in arm to Jared and Westin.

"Jared, Sabine would like to have some words with you. I think the garden is empty."

I looked at Jared as he spoke, "Thank you, Father. The garden sounds lovely."

I could see that he was doing his best not to smile. Samuel handed my arm to Jared, and he took it just as any gentleman would. We walked in silence to the garden. I saw the bench that Katherine liked to sit on. It was in the middle of the garden, in the open. There would be no way anyone watching us would be able to hear what I was about to tell Jared. We sat, and I turned to face him.

"Please do not touch me, for I fear we are being watched. I have to speak quickly, and you must listen. You are going to have to react and play this part, Jared, for my very life depends on it. I am hopeful that by now you have figured out that your father is who I say he is."

"Yes, Sabine. I have spoken to my mother, and all that you have said is truth."

"That child in the chapel is not Juliana. I would know her, and that is not her. Your father had this child murdered to make me believe that it is Juliana. I saw a guard in the courtyard by the stables the day Samuel told me of Juliana. He was not a guard Jared, but he wore the tunic of Rebecca's father's guard. He looked at me and Westin with murder in his eyes. I believe your father plans on having us murdered when we leave here. I am hoping that Charles, Joseph, and Blake do not allow it."

"I will tell them, and yes, Sabine, I have seen him as well."

"I have asked your father to allow us to leave the day after we bury that poor child. I will not get to see Rebecca again, so you must go to her and tell her of the change of plans. I know that you two do not like one another, but, Jared, she is my friend, and you two are in just as much danger."

"I will do as you ask."

"The cottage is six day's ride from here. When we get there, I will send Blake back with instructions. He will wait for you and Rebecca to be ready, and then he will bring you to join me. I need for you to get word to Charles and Joseph. Have them tell Rebecca to tell

Edward where to meet us along the road we will be traveling. I am going to make Charles take me back to Whispering Wind. There is something there I need to get before I leave here."

"Sabine, Charles will protect you with his life. I do not like that you are going on this journey without me. I wish you would wait for me to accompany you."

"We cannot go together, Jared. Your father wants me dead. I am sure of it, and so is Charles. Have you not taught me well? Are you unsure of the skills you have embedded in my mind?" I could not help but smile. "You need to react now. Throw a fit or scream at me. We are being watched, and it would not look good if you did not play along."

I was actually shocked when he jumped up and started screaming at me.

"There is no way, Sabine. You are not leaving Wellington. I will not allow it."

"Jared, you do not own me. I am free to do as I choose, and I choose not to interfere with your life. I am leaving, and Westin is going with me."

"I will follow you. My father cannot do this."

"It is not your father who is doing this, Jared. It is my decision. I have been here far too long. You have gained feelings for me that you should not have. We are not each other's match. I will not allow you to bully me."

"Bully you? We shall see about that, my lady." And he turned and left me standing in the garden alone. I followed him into the castle, but he was much faster than I. He went straight for his father. I could hear him screaming all the way down the hall.

"I will not allow you to remove her from my life, Father."

"Jared, it is of her own accord that she leaves."

"No, Father. You have made her feel unwelcome by forcing me to marry Rebecca when I do not love her."

"It is your station in life, Jared, to marry and produce an heir, and that is what you will do."

I walked in just as Samuel was speaking. "Jared, your father has been gracious enough allowing us to stay here. We are not going to be a hindrance to your life any longer," I said in a bit softer voice. "Jared, we need to leave. We need to move on. The reminders of the past will stay with me for the rest of my days, but we need to move on with our lives. Westin needs to not live with these memories." I threw this in for effect, and I actually had to choke back the laughter. "Now that Juliana has been found, there is nothing to keep us here." Jared was facing me and smiled. "Samuel, I apologize for Jared's anger. It is my fault. I am going to retire to my room. Thank you again for your support. Good night."

"Good night, Sabine, and you are welcome."

I walked out of the room slowly. Camille, to my surprise, was in the hallway with tears streaming down her cheeks.

"What is it, dear?"

"Oh, my lady, so much has happened. First the baby, then you fell and hit your head. You were sleeping for days. I was so frightened, and now I hear you are leaving."

"Well, about that, would you like to come with me, Camille? I have grown very fond of you. I asked Samuel if I could bring you along, and he has agreed."

"Oh, my lady," was all she got out before she flung herself at me, sobbing. She nearly knocked me over. We stood in the hall holding one another. When she finished sobbing, she looked up at me and said in a whisper, "I would love to go with you. I would be honored, Your Highness."

"Shhhhh, I am just an orphan, Camille, just an orphan."

We walked back to my room where Westin waited. I bid her good night and closed my door. Westin just sat there in the chair with his head down.

"What is the matter, Westin?" I asked, walking over to him.

"I am sad because of Juliana, Sabine. I did not want her to die."

"I know, Westin. I am very sad as well, but it is all right. She is with Jenna and Ardes now, and we still have each other. We are leaving for our new home in a day, so that should be fun."

"I do not think I am going to like this new home, Sabine. I am used to this home."

"I know, Westin. I am too, but we have stayed here long enough, and this is not really our home."

"Then why can we not go back to our home, back to Whispering Wind?"

"Because, Westin, some very bad people killed our family, and if we go back there to live, they will know that they did not kill all of us. We would be in danger. Enough time has passed that whoever did that has been satisfied that we are all gone. We will be safer in our new home. I promise."

"Okay, Sabine. I will go with you. I am tired now. Can I go to my room?"

"Of course you can, my love."

"I love you, Sabine."

"I love you too, Westin."

Poor thing, he was so confused. I hated Samuel for doing this to my family. I was sure now that he was the one behind this, behind it all. By now, he will have gotten his report of what took place in the garden, and hopefully he has been convinced that I meant what he thinks I said. I needed to trust Jared that he would take care of things. I wanted to write Rebecca, but I could not take the chance that something would go wrong. I needed to sleep. That is what I needed.

The light of the day came quickly, and my head still throbbed. I dressed and made my way to the dining hall. When I arrived, I was stunned at what I saw. Sitting at the table were Rebecca and her family. She rose and ran to me, throwing her arms around my neck. "Sabine, what are you doing here? Is this where you live?"

"Rebecca, what are you doing here?" I said for Samuel

She played the part well. "This will be my family when I marry him." She jolted her head toward Jared and smiled, but no one saw. "It is my place to be at his side when he buries his niece. Is she your niece as well?"

"Yes, Rebecca. I am sad to say Juliana was my niece. I am sorry that

I have not told you anything of this part of my life. I feel as if I have deceived you."

"You, my dear, are my friend, and I do not feel deceived. I am pleased that I can be here for you as well."

"Well, thank you, Rebecca. It means a great deal to me to have you as my friend. I will surely miss you when I depart tomorrow."

"What? You are leaving? Why would you leave?"

"You know I cannot stay here any longer. You and Jared will marry and have a happy life, and that is what I wish for you both. Westin and I need to move along with our lives. We have nothing to hold us here, now that Juliana is…"

"Oh, you poor thing," Katherine said as she moved us toward the table. "Come and let us eat."

I was thankful for Katherine's interruption. I could not be sure how much longer I could do this. Waiting until the light of the day came again would be too long for me. I needed to get away from Samuel. We ate our morning meal with Rebecca seated next to Jared, and it was obvious to everyone at the table that neither of them wanted to be next to the other. I supposed this was the way it would look if I were in the same position as Rebecca, being forced into a marriage by my father. I would give anything to have that argument with him. Instead, I am sitting at the table of the man who had my family and his eldest daughter murdered. Samuel of Wellington has met his match in me. He has not won, and it will be my greatest delight when he finally realizes that I will be the one to destroy him.

The ceremony for the murdered child was simple and sweet. I cried for her little life that was taken from her by this madman. I cried for my brother, Westin, who believes that this is Ardes and Jenna's baby. But in the end, we would find her together, and we would come back here and end this with Samuel.

When it was done, I spoke briefly to Rebecca. I met her mother, and I spoke to Katherine. She wished me well in my travels and smiled at me. I hoped that she knew what we are planning. I hoped that she knew that Jared and I would be together. It made me happy to believe that she did. I excused myself and went to my room. I was not surprised to find Camille there packing my things. I tried to tell her that the fancy gowns were not necessary, but she insisted on bringing at least one. I kept my boy clothes out for travel. I thought it best I looked like a boy instead of a girl, and I suggested to Camille that she borrow some from one of the house boys. I would have loaned her a set of my own, but I thought it would be best if she was dressed as a servant.

"Camille, I need to go to sleep. We have a big day tomorrow, and a long journey ahead of us. We can finish in the morning. I really do not need all these things. Just my regular gowns are fine."

"Okay, my lady. You sleep, and I will go finish my packing."

"Good night, Camille."

She closed the door, and I bolted it. I did not want anyone to disturb me. I wanted to be alone with my thoughts. Morning came fast, as I knew it would. Before I could dress, Camille was at my door. As I walked to unbolt it, I noticed a note on the floor. I picked it up and asked Camille to wait a moment. I tore the note open. It was from Jared.

My love,

I will not be here when you depart. I cannot bear to see you go. It rips at my heart to know that you will be out there on your own. I will be frantic with worry until I hear that you have arrived safely.

Please keep the only woman I will ever love safe. You are right, I have taught you all that I know, and I must trust in you to defend yourself if need be.

Until I see you again, take my heart and my love with you. Stay safe.

I love only you

Jared

I tucked the note into my bodice and unbolted the door. Camille came bouncing in the room. She was obviously excited about the adventure that lay ahead of her. I could not tell her that her very life was probably in danger. I let her go about packing my things and worked my way to the dining hall. As usual, I was the last to be seated. Rebecca and her family had gone, and apparently Jared had accompanied them, as any man who was to wed would. I was proud of them for playing their parts. There were just twenty days until the wedding, and I was sure that Samuel was thrilled that this would be the last time he would see my face at his table. I could guarantee him that it would not be the last time he saw my face.

The girls cried when we went into the courtyard, as did Katherine. Samuel was his charming self and pulled me aside.

"I gathered these up for you, just in case you run into trouble and need to trade." He handed me a small satchel. I knew what was inside. I did not need to look. What bothered me was that he had told me that I would want for nothing, so why would I need these jewels? It was a set up. What he just handed me was payment for whoever he hired to murder us.

"Samuel, I do not want these. I told you I have no desire to take them. Westin and I will be fine. We will manage." I handed the satchel back to him. "Thank you again for all that you have done for us." I turned and walked away. He was not going to give in, so I counted in my head. One, Two, Three, Four, Five.

"Sabine." I knew he was going to do it. He had to make sure those jewels were with me. Otherwise, his murderer would not do his job.

I turned. "Yes, Samuel?" Looking past, him I could see the disbelief and horror on Katherine's face. She just realized what was happening. She just realized that her husband, the King of Wellington, was a tyrant, a horrible murderous tyrant, who would stop at nothing to get what he wanted. I felt a bit of satisfaction in seeing her face.

"I insist that you take these. They were your father's, and therefore, they should be yours."

"Samuel, as I said before, I do not want them. Please, abide by my wish not to take them from here. They will do nothing but remind me of what I have lost." There, he could not argue that point, and he did not.

"As you wish, Sabine. Have a safe journey."

"Thank you, Samuel."

I was amazed at how many guards were coming with us. I found it a bit odd, considering Samuel planned on having us murdered, that he would send to their deaths thirty or more of his own troops. I happened to see Charles' face as I mounted Raiden, and it was filled with worry. I did not see Joseph, however. Perhaps we were meeting up with him. I would ask Charles when we were away from the castle. Westin was ready, as was Camille. I waved to Katherine, and off we went. We were well into the forest before I spoke to Charles.

"Where is Joseph? I thought he was the only one who knew the way."

"He will be meeting us on the plain where you and Princess Rebecca used to ride."

"Charles, something has you worried. Is everything all right?"

"No, my lady, things are not all right. We were sent with enough food for just ten days. We should be bringing much more than that, but His Majesty ordered us to just bring ten days'. It has me bothered."

"Well, I think I can clear that up for you. Samuel has arranged for our murder."

"Are you sure?"

"Oh, I did not want to believe that he would actually do it, but the encounter we had in the courtyard secured that fear. It is a long story that I will tell you in time, but for now, the satchel he tried to give to me."

"Yes, I saw that."

"Well, inside the satchel was the payment for our murder. Inside the satchel were jewels, jewels that I discovered at Whispering Wind while I was there after my family was murdered. I gave them to Samuel as payment for allowing us to live with him. I had no need for them, and he is, after all, the king. Charles, I am afraid that I am going to have to trust you and depend on you to keep me alive. Do you trust all of these men?"

"I handpicked every one of them. They are all loyal to me."

"And you would be willing to bet your life on it?"

"I would indeed. I want you to know that I will keep you safe, and I will protect you for the rest of your life. You are safe with me."

"I trust you, Charles, but we need to be very alert about what lies ahead of us. If you have ten days' worth of food, then it is logical to think that in the next five days, someone will make an attempt on my life. I would suspect that it will come in the dark of the night when no one can see, while we sleep."

"Sabine, I give you my word that I will not let anything happen to you, that we will get to the safety of the cottage, and that we will get Jared and Rebecca to you."

"Thank you. I think we should have a few men lag in the back or go off on their own to see if we are being followed. I am fearful that Samuel's eyes are upon us as we speak."

"I will talk to my men this evening when we make camp."

We came out of the forest onto the plain where Joseph was with about twenty more guards. I was taken aback at the sight of them. The majority of them were Rebecca's father's guards. Joseph rode up.

"Well, Joseph, it looks as if you have been busy." I smiled at him.

"Your Highness," he bowed his head toward me. "These men are true to the cause of saving you and stopping King Samuel. The stories that have been milling around the land of what happened to your family has caused wonder in the minds of those who serve to protect our kings. The problem is that the king I serve to protect is the mastermind to what we believe to be an uprising."

Another guard rode up, one from Rebecca's father's land. "Your Highness," he bowed his head as well. "It would be our honor to escort you to safety and to protect you and your brother. We know that we face treason if we are caught, but right is right."

"I thank you all for putting our lives before your own, but I must warn you before we go any further. King Samuel is planning on murdering me and my brother on this journey. He tried to send the payment for this act along with us, but I refused to take it. Our journey is a treacherous one. I am sure we are being followed as we speak, and I will understand if you choose not to go, but you must understand that you may very well lose your life."

Just then, another group of guards rode up. Encircled in them were three riders, one of which was the guard I saw that day coming out of the stables. My heart was pounding as they drew closer. Charles and Blake, along with Joseph, positioned themselves in front of me as they approached.

Speaking to Joseph, one of the guards said, "We did as you suggested and positioned ourselves just outside of Wellington. We followed the caravan, and as you suspected, we discovered these three." He pointed to the three men.

I moved Raiden from behind Charles. "What is your purpose, sir, in following us?"

The men just looked at me, saying nothing.

"Well then, the decision remains as to whether we allow you to live or die on this plain today. Let me tell you this, though. Your payment has been left behind in Wellington with your master, King Samuel."

One of them turned and looked at the man who was in the courtyard. Nothing was said.

"I know who you are, for you wear the same cloth of those who murdered my family," I continued as I reached for the satchel on the back of Raiden and pulled out the cloth that Westin had found in Whispering Wind. "By being so careless in your pursuit of me, you have managed to show us all who your master is." That sparked a fear in them. "You will not leave our company alive, and whoever follows after you shall meet the same fate as you. I am curious as to what has driven you to slaughter an entire village and destroy a kingdom. Could it be the promise of wealth? Could it be a deceitful story which provoked revenge? I am gathering that it is the latter. You were unsuccessful in the promise of wealth. King Samuel now holds that wealth. I know this because I discovered it and then gave it to him, so your pursuit should end with me and be taken up with him."

The man from the courtyard spoke. "The story you tell is a lie. There was no wealth in that kingdom."

I laughed, which shocked them all. "Then what would possess you to follow us and make an attempt on my life? An empty promise of wealth again? Samuel will not allow you to live after you have finished the task of murdering me and my brother. It does not matter how many of you there are. His guards are the best men in all the lands, as you can see by your very own capture. They are more cunning than you. They are more trained than you. They are far more loyal to me than to Samuel, and I am afraid it is you who is wrong. You had your hands on it all at one time. It was hidden in the bottom of two trunks. You emptied them and flipped them over. I discovered what really was hidden in them."

"Your father destroyed our land, destroyed our kingdom, and took all that we had. What happened to him was justice."

"You know not of justice, sir. You know only the story you were told as a child. If my father was such a monster, then why are you alive now? Why did you not kill the children in our village? Because my father took what was taken from his father, he returned the kindness of leaving you all alive. It was Samuel who bred the lie into your hearts. It was Samuel who told you an untruth. These men who stand with me today, on this plain, it was their grandfathers who fought against yours in a rebellion."

"You spin the lies. You are just a child, and you do not deserve to live. You do not deserve to draw another breath."

It happened so fast that all of us were in shock. Joseph drew his sword and ran it through the man's chest. Westin let out a gasp, and Camille screamed. I just sat there looking at Joseph. "Now, would either of you like to join your companion?" he said to the other men. Not a word was said as the man fell off his horse to the ground. Joseph calmly said, "Dispose of this body. We do not wish to leave a trail for King Samuel. Shall we go, Your Highness?"

I nodded, and we began the journey of six days ride to our new home. I was positioned just behind Blake and Charles, while our guests were in the back of our little caravan. Westin and Camille were just behind me, and Joseph was in the lead. Once we were on our way, Joseph came back to me.

"Your Highness."

"Joseph, my name is Sabine, and I would like for you to call me that please."

"Thank you, Sabine. I carry with me a letter from Princess Rebecca." He handed me the letter.

"Thank you, Joseph. When will we be meeting up with Edward?"

"In two days' time. He carries with him more supplies and more men."

I smiled. Our little caravan was getting bigger. I was sure that Samuel had not expected this to come about.

"I thought it best that we do not go directly to the cottage. We shall take a longer way, so we can be sure that we are not followed."

"Thank you, Joseph." He rode back into position at the front.

My dearest Sabine,

My Edward is in your hands. Please take care of him. I am nervous about this journey you are on and so fearful of your safety, but I have faith that Edward will do his best to keep you safe. I will play my part in this charade until we can meet again.

All my love,

Rebecca

I tucked the letter into my bodice next to my locket and the note from Jared. This was going to be a bigger adventure than I anticipated. Our ride that day went just until the light of the day was nearing the end. We made camp, and Joseph sent a small scouting party out to revisit our trail, looking for more who could follow. Westin made it clear that he was sleeping next to me to keep me safe. We sat there with Camille, watching the guards' mill about and set up our camp. Camille was not her usual chattering self. I think she was rethinking her decision to join us. There was nothing I could do but reassure her that we were safe and that these men would give their lives to protect us. She seemed confident with that. The light of day had left the sky and was replaced with the dark of the night. I remembered that night we spent in the forest on our way to Wellington. The sounds of the forest were loud and deceitful. Every little noise had me up, looking around. This feeling of fear was one I would have to get used to. Charles was next to us on one side, and Blake on the other. I felt very safe and secure. There were roaming guards keeping watch over our camp, and they seemed to switch every few hours. When Charles rose to take his turn, I asked to join him. While we sat at our post, I needed to tell him of the jewels I left at Whispering Wind.

"Charles, I am not foolish enough to think that more men will not come to end my life, but I need to confide in you a little secret I have, and I want you to decide if it is worth anything."

"Well, Sabine, you have done nothing but astound me with your wit, so I am sure that whatever it is you have to say to me, it will be worth it."

I smiled. "Well, what I had said to that man today was only a half truth. I did give the jewels to Samuel. I just did not give them all to him. You see, the trunk that I discovered with the jewels, the ones that I gave to Samuel, was Ardes and Jenna's. Theirs was the second one that I had found. There was another, my mother's, and her trunk held the same if not more. Those jewels, I hid at Whispering Wind. Do you think it would be wise for us to retrieve them for the future?"

He sat there, looking at me. "See, I am astounded yet again. Sabine, considering what lies ahead for all of us, perhaps retrieving them would be helpful in procuring the army we are going to need to accomplish the task you have set before us."

"Yes, I thought so too, but I am not sure who to trust to retrieve them. What lies buried in the earth is a king's ransom. Anyone not trustworthy would take them and run."

"Well, if that is the case, then there would be just one I would truly trust besides myself."

At the same time, we both said the same name, "Blake"

We sat in silence for a bit, just enjoying the night. It was the vibration of the earth that startled us both. "Get back to the camp, Sabine. Get your brother and hide in the dark of the night."

I was on my feet in a full on dead run to Westin and Camille. Blake had already woken them, and they stood ready. I reached out and grabbed Westin by the arm, and off the three of us went into the dark of the night. I felt silly hiding in the trees, but Westin would fight beside me, and he was not good enough to fight off trained swordsmen. So we hid.

CHAPTER FOURTEEN

In the dark of the night, fear became our friend. We could not see anything through the trees. We could hear the guards running around and getting into position to fight to the death if need be. We were silent, and even the noises of the forest seemed to disappear. The thunder of the hooves as they pounded the earth grew louder and louder. One word echoed through the dark. It was Charles, yelling, "HALT!" The thunder ended, there were voices, and then Blake appeared in my view.

"Sabine, Westin, it is safe. You can come out now."

We made our way back to the camp to see more guards. With them, lying across the saddles of five horses, were five dead men. Samuel was not going to let me go easily. He really wanted me dead. I could not imagine why he would hate me so much that he would have to send so many after us.

"We were in the barracks when we heard voices out in the court-yard," the lead rider was saying to Charles. "I looked out the window, and King Samuel was talking to these men. He had instructed them to follow you and to kill the princess."

We were walking up when Charles turned to look at me. "Sabine, this is Gerald Apparently..."

"I heard what he said, Charles. Thank you. Please, Gerald, go on. I would like to hear what my friend, King Samuel, had to say to these men." Charles chuckled and turned to Gerald.

"He instructed them, as I said, to follow you and to kill you. He had said that you were traveling west toward Blackmore and beyond. I woke these men, and we secretly followed them. A fight ensued when we stopped them to talk about what their mission was. We won." He smiled.

"Charles, may we talk?"

"Of course."

We walked a bit away from the guards. "How would Samuel know which direction we have come?"

"Well, there has to be more than just this lot of men following us. It must be a chain of them. Some follow and some run back to tell the rest which direction to go. I trust these men, Sabine. I trust them with my life."

"Well, Charles, I hope you are not wrong with that trust because I need you. I trust you, and if you say they are all faithful, then I will believe you. As for our errand Blake is going to go on for us, I think we need to postpone that. Joseph said that Edward had many supplies with him, so perhaps when Joseph returns for Jared and Rebecca, Blake can make his way to Whispering Wind."

"I believe you might be right about that. We do not want whoever these people are to get their hands on that. It is nearly the beginning of the new day, so perhaps we should break camp and move on."

We walked back to the camp, and Charles instructed the new men to dispose of the bodies where they would not be found, then told the rest of the men to pack up and that we were moving forward. There were three groups that Charles sent to scour the countryside to see who else had decided to join us, and I thought it might be nice to have a chat with our barbarian friends. Charles escorted me.

"Well, gentleman, as you can see, it is going to take a great deal to end my life. The more that you come at me, the more men seem to appear to defend me. You do know why Samuel wants me dead, and you have just over three days' time to decide to tell me what it is that

Samuel has up his sleeve before your life is to end." There were no
words spoken.

We had moved east for a bit, then West, then North, back to the
South, and then West again. Joseph thought it would be best this way,
so that we might confuse anyone who could be following us. By the
end of the day, we would be close to Edward, and more people would
join our caravan. I could not help but think of Samuel and the mood
he must be in, with no word coming back from his newfound friends.
I could only hope that Jared was not in his line of fire. I could not
think about that. I had to keep my wits about me. The road had
proven to be a treacherous one.

When we made camp, I did the only thing my body would let it do,
and that was to sleep. The noises of the forest that came with the dark
of the night were silent in my head. I had visions of Mother and
Father, and it was comforting to see them in my mind. When I woke, I
seemed to be in an uplifted mood. Charles had filled me in on the
evening, and thankfully, it was uneventful. All the scouts returned
with no news, and he had sent out five new groups to do the scouting
for the day. Today, we would meet up with Edward and begin a
different approach to our final destination. We packed up camp and
moved forward. Although Westin, Camille, and I had begun to relax a
bit, the guards were just as jumpy as ever. I understood why; Charles
had made it perfectly clear that, no matter what the cost of life, I was
to be protected. I felt bad for them all, being ordered to protect me,
even if it could cost their lives. Somehow, it seemed very wrong. Our
morning went by quickly and it was midday when Joseph came to talk
to me.

"Sabine, would you come and talk to me in private please?"

"Of course, Joseph. Is everything all right?"

"Oh yes, I just need to speak to you." We moved away from the
group and traveled alongside of them. "We should be close to where
Edward is waiting for us. Sabine, I was informed by Princess Rebecca
that you had met Edward once on the plain."

"Yes. He arrived with a few of his friends. He was very kind."

"Well, those men were not his friends. They were his guards. He is a prince as well, Prince Edward of Collingwood. He is the oldest son of King Marcus. I am aware that you know not of these lands that I speak of, and I would not expect you to know of these things, but Collingwood is not in the grace of Blackmore."

"What you are saying to me, Joseph, is that Edward's father and Rebecca's father are on the brink of a war?"

"I would not say a war, but they just are not on good terms. It is a very intense relationship, and the fact that Rebecca and Edward are in love has made the situation even worse between the two lands."

"This quest of mine to be free of Samuel and to find who slaughtered my family has turned out to possibly cause a war between two otherwise peaceful kingdoms. When Edward, Rebecca, and Jared all turn up missing, I feel that it will not be just the barbarians who we will be fighting to stay alive."

"I know not of the details of the Collingwood's or those of the Blackmore's. I only know that the tension is as great as it is with you and Wellington. We will make it to the cottage, and we will deal with it all when Jared and Rebecca arrive. I am going myself to meet them. With it just being a few of us, we can ride hard and should make it back in good time. Have no fear, Sabine. I will deliver Jared to you, or I will die trying. We need to get you to safety first."

"Thank you, Joseph. You have given me much to think about, and now I must return the favor. We cannot risk our company escaping and getting word back to Samuel. I believe it is time to relieve them of their struggle."

"I agree. I shall take care of it myself."

While Joseph went off to entertain our guests, I went back to Westin and Camille.

"Sabine, how long are we going to be riding?"

"Well, Westin, I am not sure. I think four more days."

"Four more days? That is a long time, Sabine. I do not like sleeping on the ground. I would like to sleep in my big bed."

I giggled. "Oh, I would love nothing more, Westin, but right now, we need to be strong, and we need to do what Charles requires us to do. I promise that when we get to our destination, there will be a great big bed waiting just for you."

The light of the day moved through the sky, and the pink and orange glow streamed through the trees. Soon, it would be gone, and the dark of the night would be upon us. Joseph rode up fast alongside of me.

"The task is done, my lady. I have news to share when we make camp. We are near to Edward, so I am riding ahead to let him know we are arriving."

"Thank you, Joseph."

He bowed his head and rode off. When we arrived in Edward's camp, I knew I should not have been surprised after the news that Joseph revealed to me about Edward's lineage, but I was. There were at least thirty, possibly more, guards with him. Our little caravan had grown into a small army. All of this was to protect me and Westin. I was certain I did not have the whole story.

Edward approached me once we all settled in for the night. "Your Highness, will you walk with me?"

I was taken aback by his words, but I complied, and we walked around the camp.

"Why did you call me Your Highness, Edward?"

"Are you not Princess Sabine of Whispering Wind?"

"Why would you say that?"

He chuckled. "The sword you carry; you had said that day on the plain that it was your father's. It is one of a kind, as is every sword of every king in every land."

"But what makes you think my father was a king?"

"Because, Sabine, as Jared and Rebecca were promised in marriage by their fathers, you and I were promised in marriage by ours."

I began to laugh. I could not control it. The guards were all looking at me like I had lost my mind. I could not catch my breath. I thought I had offended Edward, for the look on his face was one of shock. I managed to compose myself enough to say, "You know nothing of me, Edward. Until that day on the plain, you and I knew nothing of one another. I was not promised to you in marriage by my father. My father was not a king. He was just a villager who was slaughtered with the rest of a kingdom. I just happened to be gone from home that day and survived." I walked away from him. I did not know Edward, and although he might have been a prince, I was not going to contribute any information to him.

He ran after me and grabbed my arm. "You are who I say you are."

"You, sire, will unhand me."

He smiled. "Not until you admit that you are Princess Sabine of Whispering Wind."

"I will admit nothing to you, and you will unhand me. I will not ask you again, sire."

"And I will not release you until you tell me the truth of your bloodline."

I could not hold back my irritation, and before he or anyone else realized, Prince Edward was lying on the ground with my sword pressed against his throat. "Now, sire, please do not touch me again without my permission, or I will not be held responsible for my reaction to your invasion of my body." I got up and walked away. I looked around as I walked back to Westin. Some guards were sword ready, others were laughing, and a few even applauded.

I passed Charles, and he just smiled at me. Westin was amazed that I did that to Edward. "Sabine, who taught you to do that?" he asked, his eyes wide.

I laughed. "Jared did," I whispered to him.

Joseph came up to me. "Well done." I smiled. "Can we talk, Sabine?"

"Of course."

We walked for a bit. "I had an interesting talk with our guests before they departed. It seems that Samuel is willing to part with a great deal to see your demise. There are no more coming for you. The eight were all that there were. I will make sure and continue to send out our scouts."

"Thank you, Joseph. I cannot figure out why Samuel wants me dead." We walked back to camp.

Edward did not come around again for the rest of the night. When the light of the day came, the groups of scouts had returned. It was becoming clearer that the barbarians may have been telling the truth before they died. It seemed as if they had ceased in their pursuit of us. Our next few days of travel went along slowly. Edward kept his distance from me, and Charles and Blake made sure that we were not followed. At the dusk of the day on our sixth day, Joseph came along in a most cheerful mood.

"My lady, I am glad to inform you that this will be the last night we sleep in the wilds. Your new home awaits you in this land."

Westin was so excited to hear the news, as was Camille. I did not want to ruin it for him, but there was still the threat of barbarian intruders arriving. We were not safe. We needed to wait now for Jared and Rebecca. When they made it to us safe and unnoticed, then I would relax.

"Thank you, Joseph. The light of the day cannot come fast enough."

I was right, too. The dark of night was long, and sleep would not come for me. I went in search of Charles, as he had become a friend to me, and I felt it comforting to speak with him. "May I sit with you?"

"Of course. Anytime." We sat there in silence for a little while.

"Charles, do you think we succeeded in avoiding those who are seeking us?"

"Yes, Sabine. I believe we are safe now. After a day or two, I shall send Joseph, Blake, and a few others to return and retrieve Rebecca and Jared, and I will have Blake attend to that matter in which we spoke."

"Thank you, Charles."

"May I make an observation?"

"Yes, Charles, any time you wish."

"That day Edward found himself on the ground at the end of your sword, I must say that you impressed me with your quickness and your precision in placing him there. Lord Jared has taught you well. He would have been proud of you."

I could not help but laugh. "He called me Princess Sabine of Whispering Wind, and he said that my father and his father had promised us in marriage. I laughed at him, and he did not like that. I laughed, I think, Charles, because I was scared. Scared that he knew who I was."

"Sabine, everyone knows who you are. We have known all along. Even though King Samuel told us you were his orphaned niece, we knew the truth. In time, you will know who you are and why it is important that we keep you alive."

"What does that mean exactly, Charles? Joseph had said something similar to me a few days ago. Why am I so important?"

"In time, Sabine, you shall know the truth of your birth and the truth of your destiny. The time is not right. Will you trust me enough not to inquire anymore?"

"I trust you, Charles, but you will tell me what this intrigue is?"

"I shall, my lady, in time." We sat there for a while longer. The light of the day began to show in the sky. "We should be going now. It is time for you to see your new home." Charles smiled.

I sighed as I said, "And give up this glorious life on the run?" He chuckled and helped me up. The ride was simple, and by midday we had approached what looked to be big hills.

"Just on the other side," Charles said.

It took us sometime to climb the hills, and just as I thought we had reached the top, there was another. Finally, at the top of the last hill, we stopped. Looking out over the valley left us all speechless. It was something out of a dream; the grass was so green, and there was what looked to be water falling off the hills in the distance. The trees were in abundance, as were wildflowers. I could see some animals, fencing, and then I saw the roof of the cottage peeking through the trees. It was bigger than I had imagined. With the hills that surrounded the valley, it was our very own little fortress.

"Joseph," I heard myself whisper.

"I searched a long time to find the perfect valley fit for a queen. Your kingdom awaits you, my lady."

We rode down into the valley. Westin was so excited. "Oh, Sabine, it is wonderful. Just think of the adventures we are going to have."

"Yes, my love, I am."

We moved closer and closer, and Westin's excitement only grew. "Look, Sabine, cows. Look, Sabine, pigs. Look, Sabine, sheep. Look,

Sabine, an orchard. Look, Sabine, vegetables. Look, Sabine, horses. Look, Sabine, stables."

Each time, I said, "Yes, I see that, Westin."

He was so happy to just be at a place he could relax. When he saw the cottage, he cried. He said it was so pretty. Camille had been virtually invisible throughout our journey. I was very aware of her quietness. It was so out of her nature to be quiet that it had me on edge, but I did not let her know that I had been watching her. I was not sure if she was to be trusted or not. I wanted to believe that it was the journey and not something more that had silenced her. I could not forget that she came with us so willingly and had been in Samuel's employ for a long period of time.

The cottage was more than I could have imagined. It was stocked with food, and there was a staff in place. Joseph had thought of everything. I could not help but wonder how or why, but when I entered the kitchen, I was greeted with smiles and bows and curtsies. The cook was the one who spoke to me.

"Your Highness, I shall have the evening meal ready for you and Lord Westin in a matter of moments."

I was taken aback by her greeting. "My lady, please call me Sabine."

She smiled, curtsied, and then went about her duties. I went to find Joseph and Charles. I wandered around the outside of the cottage, and when I spotted a roof in the tree line, I headed toward it. I had no idea what it was. As I drew closer to the building, I realized that it was a barracks of some sort. The building was bigger than the cottage. It had multiple floors and was hidden rather well in the trees. The men were moving around doing this and doing that. I spied a face that looked familiar, and I spoke, "Excuse me, sir. Would you please find Charles and Joseph for me?"

The man looked shocked that I spoke to him. He immediately bowed his head. "Of course, Your Highness, right away."

I was really going to have to put a stop to this Highness business. It was getting a bit overwhelming. Even at Whispering Wind I was not addressed as 'Your Highness'. I was walking back and forth, thinking, when Charles and Joseph appeared.

"My lady, is everything acceptable with the cottage?"

"Yes, Joseph, as far as I could tell. I need to speak to you both. Come and let us walk for a bit." I started walking. I did not look back to see if they were behind me. I somehow knew that they were. "I have a few questions I need answered. First of all, I am finding it difficult to understand what this place is, and better yet, why this place? Please explain to me what is going on here. I was just in the kitchen, and the lovely lady who is to cook for us." I turned to give Joseph an odd look. "When I entered the room, she addressed me as Your Highness. That needs to end please. I would like for you to inform everyone that they are to address me as Sabine. I have no kingdom, and I have no king. I am not a Highness, but merely Sabine." They both nodded. "I am a bit confused, Joseph. Why is there housing for so many men? There are fields here, an orchard, animals, and stables. You could not have known that we would even come here."

"Sabine, when you came to Wellington, we knew who you were. We were all sworn to secrecy by the king. When I was sent to find you a place to live far enough away, I imagined that you would need these things. I was informed that there would be a troop of guards to accompany you, so logically, they would need a place to live. When I found this cottage, I employed people to build all the out buildings and to tend the fields and orchards, and I employed a staff to care for the cottage."

"Where did you get all this money?"

"That is the funny part of this. Samuel gave me a king's ransom to do it, and he has no idea as to where we are. Sabine, we will depart in the morning to return to Wellington and Blackmore and retrieve Jared and Rebecca. I am taking with me twenty guards. We should return in eight days' time, barring no interruptions, and when we return, there will be much to tell you."

"Thank you, Joseph, for all that you have done and all that you do."

"It is my honor, Sabine. Now, if you will excuse me, I need to go prepare for our departure."

"Of course. Charles, will you walk with me?" I headed away from the cottage and into the field away from those who could hear. "I am to believe that Blake will be completing our task?"

"Yes, he is prepared and is waiting for his instructions."

"I have not seen him since we arrived."

"He has been tending to Edward. Apparently, Edward is not happy with his accommodation of having to sleep in the barracks with the guards. He thinks it preposterous that he not be allowed to sleep in the cottage."

"I suppose Edward is used to having his own way, and I am sure that the damage I did to his self-esteem is what fuels his flames."

Charles chuckled. "Oh, I am sure it was more than just his self-esteem that you bruised that day. To be bested when you believe you are the best is one thing, but to be bested by a woman is totally different."

"Yes, well, I am sure that Prince Edward of Collingwood will think before he presumes he can touch me again."

A whistle echoed through the valley. Charles and I both turned toward the cottage and saw Blake. Charles waved him over. We needed to discuss his approach to Whispering Wind. As he arrived, Charles spoke first, "Did you get the matter with Edward sorted out?"

Blake was smiling. "Oh, he will stay in the barracks. He will not like it, but he will stay."

"Thank you, Blake. That man is lucky my friend loves him. Listen, I need for you to retrieve a few things from Whispering Wind for me when you go back to retrieve Jared. You need to be cunning and very careful, for you will be carrying a king's ransom. It has proven to be the reason my family was slaughtered." Blake gave Charles an odd look of concern at that statement. "If you can find an alternate route into Whispering Wind, into the back courtyard of the castle, it would best. There is a hedge that runs along the grass, just past the court-yard. If you follow it to the end, you will be able to go behind the hedge and follow the rocks to an opening. It is a cave. You will not see it, for it is covered and over grown. When you happen upon it, push through the underbrush. Once inside, you will find many things that I have hidden there, but they are not to worry you. What you will be doing is digging in the ground. Buried just beneath the surface, you will find fourteen different containers, and hidden within those containers are jewels. Jewels as you have never seen, as you will never see. Bring them all back to us here. Say nothing of your mission. No one other than the three of us is to know of this. Do not stop for the others on your return."

"Again, I say to you, I am astounded." Charles smiled at me.

"It would be my honor, and I will not fail you," Blake said.

"Blake, you must give me your word that if there is danger of any kind, you will abandon this mission, for your life means more to me than what lies in the ground."

"Thank you, my lady. I give you my word. I will leave after I have had a meal."

"I do not know about the two of you, but I think I would like a bath and some sleep. So I will excuse myself, so you two can finish whatever it is that you do." I moved away from them toward the cottage.

Inside, I found my way through the cottage, which was bigger than any cottage I had ever known. Camille was standing in the hall outside of a door. "This would be your room, my lady."

"Thank you, Camille. I just wish to bathe and sleep."

"Your bath is waiting for you, my lady, and I will retrieve a meal for you."

"Thank you, Camille." I went into my room, undressed, and climbed into the bath. It was wonderful to wash the journey off. When I finished, I put on my sleeping gown and climbed into the huge bed. There was a knock on the door, and I know Camille would not knock. Opening the door, I found myself a bit without words. Standing there was Edward.

"Excuse me for disturbing you, Sabine, but I was wondering if we could have a talk?"

"Edward, I do not think it is appropriate for you to be here alone. I am going to sleep. Tomorrow we will talk. Please, excuse me now." I went to close the door, and he put his foot in it.

"Excuse me, Princess." He was angry.

"Excuse me, Edward," I yelled. I heard a tray drop in the hall; Camille with my dinner.

"No, Princess, you will allow me to enter your room, you will hear what I have to say, and you will answer my questions." He shoved the door, and with the door, he shoved me back. I lost my footing and slammed to the floor. Before I could gain my composure, he was standing over me. "Not so sure of yourself when the positions are reversed, are you, Princess?"

"Edward, it would be in your best interest to leave now."

"Do not think you are able to best me again, Princess, for I am the chosen one, and you are nothing but a mere woman." He reached for me, grabbing me by the arm and pulling me off the floor. Before I knew what was happening, he shoved me backwards into the chair. The chair lifted off the floor and flipped backwards. I was in shock that this man was the man that Rebecca chose as her mate. He was going to hurt me, and I knew I had no other choice but to stop him. I looked around for something to use as a weapon, but there was nothing within my reach. Edward grabbed me again, only this time, when he pulled me up, I swung my fist, connecting with his neck. He let go of me and bent over in pain. I took my foot and planted it right on his shoulder, shoving as hard I could. He slammed into my bed, moving it. I ran to the door, to unbolt it, but he was quick to recover, grabbing my hair and pulling me back landing me flat on the floor. His foot connected with my side, and the pain was so intense that my breath left me. In my ear, I could hear him say, "You will listen to me, even if I have to beat you to death."

My anger had emerged, and I whipped my arm around, connecting it with his face. He let out a yelp that would have matched my own. "No, sire, I believe you have that wrong. It is I who will do the talking." I was on my feet, and I hit him again in the face. I heard my hand snap. I swung the other, connecting it with his jaw, it felt like it broke under my blow. He fell to the floor in agony, and that is when my door flew open, and Charles came running in. He grabbed me and carried me out of the room to the arms of Blake, who in turn, removed me from the cottage. As we were moving down the halls, guards were everywhere, and cowering in the corner was Camille and Westin. My heart went out to them both. How frightened they must be. I motioned for them to follow Blake. When we were outside, I told Blake that I was fine and that he could put me down.

"Are you all right, Sabine?" he asked, looking me over. He reached up to touch my eye where I had hit it on the chair when Edward threw me into it.

"I am fine, Blake, but I think that Edward is in need of some assistance. I heard some bones break when I reciprocated his force-fulness."

Blake's laughter was loud in the dark of the night as it echoed off the hills. Soon, we were all laughing. Charles came out of the house with Edward in tow and handed him off to a few guards. I heard him say, "Restrain this man, and do not under any circumstances allow him his freedom until I return."

We started walking toward one another. "Sabine, are you hurt?"

"I think I might have hurt my hand," I said, holding it up for inspection.

"What in the world took place? Camille came running into the barracks, screaming that you were being beaten. I thought the girl had lost her mind."

I turned to look at Camille. "Thank you, my dear."

"I am sorry about your meal, my lady. I will retrieve another for you."

"Thank you, Camille."

"Sabine, why would Edward want to hurt you like that?" Westin asked.

"Well, Westin, I think that he was a bit angry that I bested him that day in the forest. I believe that Edward is full of drink, and I am sure that he will be sorry for what he did in the morning. I am fine. Really, I am. There is no need to be frightened. I promise." Westin smiled, hugged me, and then followed Camille into the cottage.

"Charles, Edward's anger was not because I bested him. He said something about the chosen one being him and not me. Do you know what he was talking about?"

"The ramblings of a man who has had too much to drink is my guess." He looked at Blake. "You must return to Whispering Wind and retrieve the items Sabine asked you to. We are fine here."

"I will leave now."

"Please be safe, Blake."

"Sabine, let us get you in the cottage, so I can look at your hand." I knew there was something more going on, but I trusted Charles, and I knew he would tell me in time. We had just arrived here, and Edward had already proven to be a huge mistake. He could not be allowed to leave, for he would know the way back. I would be stuck with him until Rebecca arrived. Joseph and the others were leaving at the break of the light of the day, and then all we could do was wait.

In my room, Charles examined my hand and assured me that it was not broken, but it would be sore. "Jared has taught you well, Sabine. I do not know of another woman who could have fought Edward off the way that you had."

"I just did what I needed to do. Charles, I am hungry, angry, and tired. Can we please deal with this later?"

"Yes, of course. I will be just outside the door if you need anything." Camille came in with a tray full of food. I smiled at her, thanked her, ate, and then went to sleep.

The light of the day came and left. My body was in need of sleep, and my mind shut down. The past weeks had taken their toll on me. Charles made sure that no one bothered me and that there was absolutely no noise. When the light of the day came on the second day, my body was refreshed and ready to arise. I woke feeling peaceful, but as I moved, I could feel the aches of the fight I had with Edward. Poor Edward; I could not help but think of how distraught he was. His anger was intense. I was sure that he felt quite terrible for what he had done. Rebecca would not be happy at his decision, and Jared would want his head. That thought made me smile. I reached to my neck to hold my locket, and panic engulfed me when I could not feel it. It was gone. Out of the bed and across the room my feet took me. I was searching the floor on my knees, moving things around, when there was a knock on the door. "Sabine, is everything all right?"

"Yes and no," I shouted back.

The door flew open, and Charles was by my side. "What is it?"

"I have lost my locket from Jared. Will you please help me find it?"

How silly we must have looked on our hands and knees, scurrying around on the floor. Charles had discovered it under the bed. The chain was intact, so it must have managed to get off my neck in the struggle.

"Thank you, Charles. I feel a bit silly now. It is just a locket."

"Not at all. To you, it must be important. I am just glad that it is intact and that we found it. Camille has been worried about you, but I would not let her disturb you. I opened the door a few times just to make sure you were all right."

"Thank you, Charles. You have been a good friend to me, and I will not forget that. Jared chose wisely when he chose you to protect me."

"Sabine, Jared did not choose me. I requested the honor of protecting you, as we all have."

I found his words a bit disturbing, but I was not going to push him, for I knew in time he would tell me what the intrigue was all about.

"I will tell Camille that you are awake."

"Thank you, Charles."

He left, and before I finished dressing, Camille was at the door with food. "You must be starving, my lady."

"Thank you, Camille. It is good to see you coming back to your old self. I was a bit worried about you."

"You were worried about me? Well, that is just silly... a princess worried about her servants."

"Camille, I do not think of you as my servant. I think of you as my friend."

She brushed my hair for me and then plaited it. When I finished the morning meal, she disappeared with my tray. I thought it was time Westin and I did some exploring. He would like that. He was probably so scared, since nothing had been explained to him. He had been ignored, and I would not do that to my brother. I took Simon's sword, and out the door I went. I found Westin in the kitchen, and he was so happy to see me.

170

"Sabine," he yelled when I walked in.

"Hello, my love," I replied, and we hugged. "Westin, do you want to come exploring with me today?" The look on his face was all I needed for an answer. "Why not bring your sword? We can duel on the plain if you want."

He was gone before I could finish my thought. It was going to be a good day. We walked hand and hand to the stables with Charles a few steps behind us. Raiden was so excited to see me; he was snorting and stomping his feet. I swear the horse thought himself a dog. I saddled him up, and off we went. The valley was beautiful. We climbed trees and hills, found a few caves to explore, practiced our swords in the field, and picked flowers. We lay in the grass and just spent the entire day together. We needed to feel free again.

"So, Westin, what do you think of Joseph's choice for our new home?"

"I love it, Sabine, but the journey here was not nice. Who were all those men trying to hurt us? Why would anyone want to kill you? Why would Edward be so mean to you? You know, Sabine, I went to the barracks where he is tied up, and I hit him in the mouth and told him he was not nice and if he ever hurt you again that I would kill him."

I did not know if I should be terrified or impressed with my brother.

"Thank you, Westin. That was very brave and very sweet of you to protect me."

"You are my sister, Sabine. You know I listen to the guards talk. They do not know that I am there because I hide," he said with a giggle. "They say you are special. I know you are special. You are my sister, but they say that you are a prophecy. I do not like when they say that. What is a prophecy, Sabine?"

I could not help but giggle. "Westin, you should not be hiding and listening to others talk. That is not nice. A prophecy is like a story that someone tells someone else about something that will happen in the future, and it goes on and on through time. Do you understand?"

"I am not sure, but I think I do. So you are a story that someone told a very long time ago?"

I laughed. "No Westin, I am not a story, but we cannot fault others for what they think. I know not of this story, and trust me, I am not special. Only to you and to Jared."

We lay there in the grass for a long time, just looking at the clouds. It was good to just be with Westin. Camille had sent one of the guards with food to find us.

"Camille is funny, Sabine. I like her a great deal. She plays tricks with me and she makes me laugh." My heart was full of love for my brother. He had found a friend. I really did not want to think that it might be more than a friend. I was just happy for my brother.

The light of the day was leaving the sky, and I could not believe that we had stayed out here all day. "I think it is time to get back to the cottage for the evening meal. Westin, do we have a room to eat in at the cottage?"

His laughter filled the air. "Yes, Sabine, we have lots of rooms. We even have a library full of books and a study like Samuel's."

"Well, that Joseph thinks of everything, does he not?"

"Yes, he does."

We raced back to the stables, and I let Westin win. Well, Raiden let Westin win. It was the perfect ending to a perfect day. We had the evening meal together in a room with a table, and then we went to our rooms. It was a good day, and it was another day gone until Jared was to arrive.

When the light of day came through my windows the next morning, I dressed in my boy clothes and requested to speak to Edward.

"I am not sure that is a wise decision, Sabine."

"I have dressed for the occasion, Charles, so he will not best me again."

We walked to the barracks, and Charles asked everyone to please leave us alone. Edward was lying on a bed, so I sat on the one next to him. When he sat up, I realized that he was chained to the floor.

"I did not deserve your aggressive behavior toward me, Edward. I have done you no wrong."

"Sabine, I cannot apologize enough for my behavior the other night. I have never, nor would I ever, strike a woman. I have no excuse. I will expect Lord Jared to have my head when he arrives, and I suspect that my love Rebecca will not want a part in my life."

"I cannot pretend to assume what Jared or Rebecca will choose to do, and I will not keep this from them. If you house such anger, Rebecca should be made aware of that. You would have taken my life, Edward. I am sure of it. Your anger and rage were immense. What would bring such vile behavior toward me? You do not know me."

"It is not you, Sabine. It is the idea that you are the one."

I laughed. "Edward, I am not anyone but an orphan from a kingdom that no longer exists."

"Clearly you have not been told why you are so important, or why I am chained to the floor of a barracks."

"Well, Edward, you are chained to the floor of a barracks simply because you tried to kill me, and well, I am not ready to die just yet. I can see that your mind has not come back to its normal state of being, so I am going to leave. Sleep well, Edward, for Rebecca shall arrive soon." I could not get out of there fast enough. Poor Edward; I started to think his mind was broken.

The days and nights passed without word from Joseph. We lived each day as if it were our last. I felt bad for not telling Westin the true danger we were in. I could not let him live whatever days were left for us in fear. We fell into a routine as we did in Wellington, except that our table was not filled with the chattering of others. It was just Westin and I, and our conversations were mostly about what trick he played on whom, and about his adventures of exploration of the land. Some of his stories included Camille, although I believed Camille was present more than Westin had shared. I thought it was lovely that he had someone who was becoming very special in his life. I only wanted happiness for him after all that was taken from him. It brought tears to my eyes thinking of all we had lost.

While we sat eating our evening meal, we heard shouts coming from the direction of the barracks. Westin was on his feet with his sword in hand.

"I will protect you, Sabine." I knew instantly that he was afraid Edward had escaped.

"Westin, it is fine. Charles is outside, and he will not let anything happen to me. You can put your sword down. Thank you for protecting me."

His sword went reluctantly back into its sheath. When there was a knock on the door, we went together to open it. Charles stood there with a smile on his face.

"Blake has returned. He just reached the top of the hill and should be here soon. With him, he should have news of Jared and Rebecca."

We all went outside to wait for Blake. It took him some time to reach the cottage. Upon his arrival, he wore a smile from ear to ear. "Sabine, I come bearing good news. Lord Jared and Lady Rebecca are but two days' ride from here, and all went well with their escape. Wellington and Blackmore are both in an uproar over the disappearances of the prince and princess. I have achieved the task you set forth for me. I carry with me the items you requested. Shall we go inside and take care of matters?"

I looked at Charles. We had already decided that one of the caves that Westin and I discovered would be the best place to put them, so we went to the stables and off we went. It was difficult to see with the dark of night fast approaching, but we managed to secure the jewels. On our way back to the cottage, I found it to be the perfect opportunity to ask Blake about Wellington. "Blake, what is it that you heard while in Wellington?"

"Well, the king is beside himself. I had a very difficult time moving through the lands without detection. He has patrols of guards and more of our barbarian friends everywhere, looking for Jared and looking for a trail. Joseph did a fantastic job of confusing them. When I got to Whispering Wind, now that was the biggest challenge. Your barbarian friends have moved into the castle. There are camps everywhere, but I managed to get past them and retrieve the jewels without being detected."

"Perhaps because Samuel could not give them the jewels he

promised. He removed me so he could give them my father's kingdom."

"Yes, I agree. Along my route on my return, I passed through several villages as a nomad and heard talk among the people of the uprising of evil that is over taking Whispering Wind. The talk is one of fear. All the people in all the lands are fearful of what is to come now that your father is dead. In Blackmore and the surrounding kingdoms, there is talk that Samuel blames Blackmore for the disappearance of Jared, and he has threatened to destroy King Gerald. In Collingwood, the talk is that Blackmore had Edward killed so he could not interfere with Rebecca's marriage to Jared. Blackmore in turn has said that Collingwood has kidnapped Rebecca to prevent the marriage. The world as we know it, Sabine, no longer exists. Charles, do you believe it is time to tell her?"

"When Jared arrives, we will sit, and we will share the truth with Sabine. Is that acceptable, Sabine?"

I busted out laughing. "You men and all your secret chatter, you make it sound like I am some kind of messenger from God himself. I will listen to all that you have to say, but that does not mean I will believe you."

They both looked at one another with shock on their faces. I laughed again, kicked Raiden in the sides, and we bolted across the field.

I went to my room with a light heart and a happy disposition, all the while shaking my head at the thought that they believed me to be something more than just ordinary. Camille was in the chair next to the fireplace.

"My lady, may I talk to you about something?"

"Of course, my dear. What has you looking so low?"

"My lady, I am not sure what is happening to me. I am confused."

I tried not to laugh. "What do you mean, Camille? What has you confused?"

"Westin. When I spend time with him now, I feel different than I did before. I do not understand why."

I knew exactly what she was talking about. Rebecca and I had so many conversations about this very subject. Camille was falling in love, or was already in love, with Westin. I knew that Westin was feeling the same way.

"Camille, I believe that your feelings for Westin are changing. You are learning to care more for him than you have in the past. Perhaps you want to protect him, or you want to spend all your time with him, or you cannot wait to be with him."

"Yes, yes, my lady. That is it exactly, but why do I feel this way?"

"Oh, Camille, you are falling in love."

She did not respond. She just sat there with a blank look on her face. When she did speak, it was a whisper. "Do you think he feels the same way?"

"Yes, Camille, I do. Is that all right with you?"

"My lady, is it all right with you?"

I laughed. "Oh, Camille, I could want for nothing less. Westin is a wonderful man, and he deserves to be loved by no less than a wonderful woman as you. Yes, it is all right with me that you love my brother."

She jumped up and threw her arms around my neck. Whatever worries I had concerning Camille's loyalty were just thrown out the window. I wished her all the luck, and she was gone.

CHAPTER FIFTEEN

I slept well that night. When the light of day came, it marked the beginning of the changing of seasons. The workers were busy harvesting the crops, while Westin, Camille, and I went to the orchards to help harvest the trees. We had a day full of laughter and good company. The guards even helped. We sat in the fields and ate some of the fruits and some of the vegetables. We laughed and talked until there was the sound of a trumpet in the distance that caught our attention. "Jared?" I said, looking at Charles.

"I would not think so. Blake said they were at least two days' ride from here. We must get you back to the cottage, Sabine."

We all made our way back to the cottage. Blake and a few other guards mounted their horses and took off toward the hills. Charles planted himself right next to me. It was some time before we heard the thunder of the horses that were arriving. Every guard was at his ready. Westin had retrieved my sword for me and had taken Camille and the house staff to the cave where we told them to hide. I was ready to fight, ready to die to save him. The thunder was approaching fast, and Charles and I stood in front of the cottage waiting. Our first sight was Blake, and he was waving to signal that all was safe. Then I saw them, Jared and Rebecca, riding next to one another. I dropped my sword and took off running toward him. He jumped off his horse, and we met somewhere in the middle. Our embrace knocked us both to the ground, where we lay in one another's arms laughing and kissing.

"My love, oh how I have missed you." His kisses suffocated my response.

Rebecca sat on her horse laughing. "Well, if someone would direct me to the location of my beloved Edward, I would like to commence with my welcoming."

We all laughed. Jared helped me up, and I embraced my friend. "Oh, Rebecca, it is so good to see you safe. I am afraid that I have some distressing news of Edward." I felt her stiffen in my embrace.

"What has happened to Edward," she asked, her voice panicked.

"Rebecca, I am fearful he is not the man you believe him to be. While on our journey here, he became forceful with me, and I needed to put him in his place." Jared went to speak, and Charles put his hand on his shoulder. "When we arrived here, on our first night, Edward came to my room. It was clear that he had partaken in drink, and he proceeded to attempt to kill me. Again, I needed to put him in his place."

"Oh, Sabine, are you all right? He did not hurt you, did he?"

"I am fine, but your concern should not be for me. It should be for Edward. I am fearful that his mind has left him. He continues to spout ramblings that I should not be allowed to live."

"Where is he? Will you take me to him please?"

"Yes, of course. He is in the barracks under guard."

We all walked together, Jared and me hand in hand. Charles had sent someone to get Westin, giving him orders to bring him to the barracks. We all arrived at the same time, and together we went to see Edward. The reunion was uncomfortable between Rebecca and Edward, and Jared was shooting looks of death at him. Westin stayed by the door out of fear. It was all an uncomfortable situation. "Rebecca, you must listen to me. She is not the chosen one. I am. She is not to be allowed to live. She will ruin everything."

"Edward, what are you talking about? What has happened to you?"

Charles cleared his throat. "I believe I can bring this all into the light. Perhaps we should all get comfortable. Sabine, the ramblings of Edward are not ramblings at all. They hold more truth than you know."

"Charles, you are going to have to enlighten us," Jared said in a joking manner.

"I suppose you are right, Jared. There is a legend, a prophecy so to speak. It comes from the time of Merlin, the great sorcerer."

"Charles, you cannot possibly believe that Merlin was an actual person, can you? Those stories were childhood stories, such that they were told as bedtime stories to us all," Jared cut in.

"I only know what I have been told, Jared, what I have seen, and what I have been privileged to experience."

"Then, by all means, tell us this fable of yours."

"Well, the story," he smiled, "begins with a tale of a very powerful man, one who swung a sword that was nearly his equal in height. He was not a large man in body, as the story would have you believe. He was invincible, and everyone feared him, but he was a peaceful man. Many would come to take his life, but no one could touch his abilities. He hated to fight. He hated to kill, but it was either kill or be killed. He requested that men leave him in peace and leave him to be happy and to grow old. It was the fear of his power that convinced the people in the lands to abide by his request. It was believed that it was indeed his sword that made him so powerful. He married, had children, and died, just like all men. It was said that Merlin put a spell on him and his sword, and only those worthy could wield it. Sabine, may I ask you, have you ever had the acquaintance of someone other than yourself who has the golden red hair you do?"

I thought it a funny question, and it caused me to take notice of Edward. "Well, Edward does, but other than him, no. My father's hair was similar, but not as red as mine, and my mother's was golden, as is Rebecca's, so it was thought that my strange color was a mixture of theirs."

"The man of this story had hair the color of yours, Sabine, a color no man had ever seen before, nor has seen since. It is said that when

Merlin cast his spell that the man's hair changed color, and only a man whose hair was the color of this great warrior, would and could wield the sword. When he died, his sword was naturally passed on to his son, who became the new king, as tradition would call for. Not every new king chose to keep his father's sword, and would have one forged for himself, and then pass both on through the family bloodline. It is believed that none of the succeeding kings could wield that famed sword. There has been no one who has been born in hundreds of years with that golden red hair. The sword was passed on and on through time. It is said that the one who wields the sword will unite the lands, and peace will be forged."

"I am he," shouted Edward. "I am the one to wield the sword. I am the bringer of peace."

"Edward, do not make me gag you again," Charles said in a soft tone.

"Now, we have come through hundreds of years of one particular bloodline, and we come to your father, Sabine. As he grew into a young man and became of age to receive the training to be king, he was passed on the sword, the sword you now carry. Your father has been the only man who could wield it, and he did. He brought peace to the lands, but he did not fit the legend. He was feared because of the sword, but those who believed in the legend, or prophecy if you would like, knew he was not the chosen one. It is not you, Edward. You have not been born into the bloodline, and although your hair is similar in color to Sabine's, it is not the same. When you were born, Sabine, men such as Samuel and Rebecca's father, along with Edward's father, knew that the legend was true. We believe your father knew this as well, and that is why you were allowed to train with a sword. That is why your brothers taught you all that you know. You are the bringer of peace. We believe that is why Samuel and the others destroyed Whispering Wind and killed your family. They could not be involved, so the barbarians were hired. When Samuel discovered you had not been killed, he was outraged." He paused looking at Jared.

"I know this because I was in his study when Westin left after he had told him what had happened. The plan was then set into motion, to possess you, to control you, and when Samuel watched your progress with Jared, he knew that the only thing he could do to control all the land was to kill you. We have been watching over you from day one. Your every move has been seen by at least one of us. When I first saw you pick up your father's sword and swing it at Jared, I knew that the story, the legend, the prophecy, was true. Sabine, no woman would be able to pick that sword up, let alone swing it with the force that you do. That day on the plain when Edward handed you that sword, I saw the look on his face. I knew then that he knew it to be truth. He has been the only man with that red hair that has been born in hundreds of years."

"I am not this person, Charles. Perhaps it is Edward."

"Sabine, you must understand that a king's sword can only be handed down to the next king. Edward is not that king."

"Well, Charles, in case you have not noticed, I am not that king either."

Jared wrapped his arms around me and said, "I would certainly hope not, for I should look a fool for being in love with a man." We all laughed, all of us except for Charles.

"Sabine, you do not even realize what it is you have already done. In this room are three kingdoms all ready to fight together for you and with you. Even Edward's faithful guards have chained him to the floor because the belief is so deep."

"Charles, what if I do not want to be this person in this story? What if Edward is this person? I think we should unchain him and let him wield my sword. Let him have the power he so richly wants. I have no use for it. My only desire is to live here and be happy with Jared."

"I say Sabine is correct. Let us unchain Edward. Let us go out and see what he can do with her sword. I will fight with him, and if he can best me using this mighty sword, then he can be the hero of the story." Jared just wanted an excuse to fight with Edward.

Charles agreed. He unchained Edward, keeping careful watch on him, and we all went out into the dark of night. I took my sword and handed it to Edward. It was obvious that he was going to have difficulty; it hit the ground hard. He picked it up, but with great effort. Jared raised his sword and hit mine with it. The fight ensued, and swing for swing, Edward matched Jared's. It was the grimaced look on Edward's face when Jared struck my sword that made everyone aware that Edward was in pain. After a few minutes, Charles signaled for them to stop.

"Edward, it is time for Sabine to try."

Edward handed me the sword. I turned to face Jared with a wide grin on my face. "Are you ready, my dear?" I taunted him.

"As ready as I will ever be, my love."

I swung first. My blow was powerful, and sparks flew from our swords. I stopped and stared in amazement. "Well, that has never happened before." I swung again, and again, and each time, sparks flew through the air. Jared and I sparred for some time, each time with sparks flying. It was amazing. Westin kept yelling, "Again, again!" Jared was the one that conceded.

"My love, you have been practicing."

"That is the strange thing, Jared. I have not. Charles, will you wield this sword with Jared?" I handed it to Charles.

They went around and around, but there were no sparks. Next was Blake, then Joseph. When I went again, there they were. Sparks flew. These men were all stronger than me, all taller and more capable of hitting hard, but I was the only one who caused sparks to emerge.

"What is going on, Charles? This has never happened before this day." Each time I swung my sword and connected with Jared's, sparks flew. It was amazing to see. We stayed there in front of the barracks, swinging our swords. It looked as if Jared and Charles were just as amazed as I was. Charles cleared his throat, and we stopped.

"Sabine, how old are you?"

"Eighteen years. Why?"

"Have you swung your swords since you became eighteen?

"What are you thinking, old friend?" Jared said as he wrapped his arm around my waist. His touch sent shivers through me, and I could not help but smile.

"Edward, how old are you?" Edward was miserable. I felt bad for him. Although I did not want to believe what Charles was saying, it was obvious that Edward did.

"I am eighteen as well," he said in a huff.

"Sabine, have you practiced swords with anyone since you became of age?" I had to admit that I could not remember.

"That day on the plain with Rebecca, had you come of age then?" Charles asked.

"I believe that I had. Why, Charles? What are you not saying to us?"

"Rebecca, would you please be so kind as to fight with Sabine?"

Rebecca laughed. "I would love to wield a sword at the chosen one." She eyed me up in her playful manner.

We took our places and began swinging, and to all of our surprise there were no more sparks. We stopped swinging because Charles was laughing.

"My lord, it is truth. All of it is truth." Between his gasps for air, he managed to say, "Jared, would you be so kind as to fight with Rebecca please?"

We all just stood there, watching Charles laugh. He composed himself after a few minutes. "If the legend is true, when the two of you fight, sparks will fly."

Jared bowed toward Rebecca and raised his sword. Rebecca laughed at him, swung her sword just one time, and Jared's sword went straight to the ground in a stream of sparks. Not one word was spoken for a very long time. Rebecca and I stood there, just looking at one another. Could all that Charles had been saying be truth?

Edward was the first to speak, although it was more of a guttural groan. "Impossible… What magic is this?"

Charles said but one word, "Truth."

"How is it possible, Charles? How did I just put Jared's sword on the ground?"

"Rebecca, what is your age?"

"I just began my eighteenth year, just as Sabine and Edward. Please, Charles, tell us what you know."

Charles suggested that we all go back into the barracks, and then with all of us comfortable, he began again. "Now, the story does have a twist, but no one ever believed it to be truth, so it was lost to history. I believe now that Samuel and Gerald had this knowledge as well, but it was not until the day that Rebecca came to Wellington for the burial of Juliana. After the evening meal, I was called to Samuel's study. In attendance was myself, Samuel, Gerald, and Steven over there." He bowed toward the door with his head.

We all turned back to look in the direction, and leaning against the door was a midsized man. I had seen him with Charles on numerous occasions, but honestly, I had never spoken to him.

"And what was said in this meeting, Charles?" Jared's voice was hard and firm. He was deeply angry at his father for conspiring to have me killed.

"Samuel and Gerald were well into conversation when we arrived, so I have no real knowledge as to what was spoken before, but I have an idea. Samuel asked me in detail the extent of your relationship, Sabine, with Rebecca. I told him what I had observed and that I had no knowledge of the conversations the two of you have had. Then I asked him why he would inquire this of me. It was Gerald who answered. When the two of you embraced in the dining hall earlier that day, apparently something became even clearer to them, something about the power the two of you hold. It made sense to me in that moment why Samuel wanted you dead, Sabine, and Rebecca and Jared to marry."

"Enlighten us, would you please, Charles?" Jared's voice was more agitated.

"Well, the part of the story that was lost in history because it was so hard to believe was this. The bringer of peace had a soul mate, another which held the same power as the first, one that would complement and strengthen the first. Together they would be invincible. Samuel and Gerald, along with countless other kings, knew this and held it close to their breasts. It was a legend that holds great power and the promise of great wealth. Those kings whose hearts were not true, and whose greed embraced their black hearts, wanted nothing more than to possess this power. Sabine, remember when I told you that Samuel wanted to control you?" I nodded my head.

"Well, when your family was murdered, it left the door open for Jared's match to Rebecca to move forward. Samuel and Gerald thought they knew who Rebecca was from her unbelievable abilities with a sword. Forging that union was the hope of creating another chosen one. I believe that is why Jenna was married to Ardes, but when she produced a girl instead of a boy, she became irrelevant. A woman was not to hold this position. Samuel knew he had a better chance in grooming a male child to take the position, a male child that belonged to him. Your brother, Simon, was the one who was promised in marriage to Rebecca, but Samuel knew the truth of Rebecca and yourself, another reason for murdering your family. Which brings Jared into the picture. Jared, you are indeed the best swordsman in all the lands, well, now that Sabine's father is no longer living. It was not by chance that you became this way. It was with great detail and secrecy that you were trained from infancy, and it is the same with Rebecca. The legend says that the golden red haired man and the golden haired man would unite and become the bringers of peace. No one ever imagined it to be two women, two very capable women, I want to add. So Sabine, when I rode into Whispering Wind on that day, and you came running out of the castle to greet Westin, I knew in that instant who you were. We had all heard the stories growing up, but not once was it said or did we believe that this person would be a woman. As Samuel's guards, we had heard things that made us believe that it was indeed Samuel who carried out the slaughter and murder of your family. We did not have proof until the day Westin showed up at Wellington. We knew then that the legend we were all told as children was indeed truth."

"Well, that is some story, Charles, but how do you expect us to believe this as truth?" Jared was in shock, just as the rest of us were.

"I am not finished yet, Jared. Rebecca, may I inquire as to where you got your sword."

Rebecca sat there looking at me as if I knew the answer. "My father had it made for me, but it was not in our kingdom. It was in fact made in Whispering Wind, or at least that is what he said."

"May I see your sword?"

Rebecca rose from her spot next to Edward and handed her sword to Charles. He looked it over, turning it this way and that way, and then he asked me for mine. After giving my sword the same scrutiny, he then pointed the tips of each sword to the ground. It was obvious that my sword was larger than Rebecca's.

Charles continued, "These two swords are identical in markings. If you look here on the hilts, you can see that they both have a sun and a moon on them. The way they are arranged means becoming more powerful with age. These markings here, the way the sun sits over the moon, means that when two come together something is born that is more than the sum of its parts. When these symbols are brought together, they cancel one another out and the power becomes the whole, which is unstoppable. The sun is greater than the moon so that represents you Sabine, and the moon would represent Rebecca. Sabine, I am positive that your father knew this tale as well. Together, the kings forged Rebecca's sword, and she was trained as you were. Only Samuel and Gerald thought it preposterous that two women would rule, so the plan was devised. Fortunately, you survived, and then when you met Rebecca by accident, things changed drastically. You needed to be eliminated, hence the summons to Samuel's study. I was told, along with Steven, to make sure you never survived the journey. We were promised great wealth and promotion in the guard to carry out Samuel and Gerald's orders. I am sorry to say, Edward that you were part of that plan as well. You were to be killed alongside Sabine and Westin."

"Well, that is some story, Charles, but forgive me for not believing it. There is no way that either King Samuel or King Gerald would ever go against my father or his army. With Sabine's father dead, my father is the most powerful."

"Edward, my apologies, as I do not mean to demean you or your father, but the most powerful is in this room with us. Together, they will lead us into peace, and our army will become invincible. The legend is true, and in your heart you know it is not you. In your heart, Edward, you know that, together, it is Sabine and your beloved Rebecca. When you come to peace with that, then and only then will you be released from your restraints." Charles paused and looked to me and Rebecca then. "Our time now is to train the two of you and to ready you for the coming battles. We must fight to retrieve Juliana and the children, to bring peace to all the land, and to deal with Samuel and Gerald. I am sorry, Jared, but in the end, I know Samuel will not give up without a fight, and he will fight to the death. Greed is a powerful motivator, and I am sure that your father would not hesitate to kill you himself, especially since he murdered his daughter for less. He knows now that you have betrayed him and disobeyed him for Sabine. His fury is more than any of us can comprehend. Our presence in this valley is hidden for a short time, but they will come, and we will need to be ready."

I do not think that any of us could speak, let alone move. The silence was only broken by the sound of Raiden's neighing and kicking of the stables, and then a guard ran into the room out of breath. "There are horses arriving, a great deal of horses."

We were on our feet quickly. I grabbed my sword from Charles and took off running toward the stables. When I reached Raiden, he had nearly knocked his gate off the hinges. He was nudging me with his nose, being very persistent, so I climbed on his back, and he took off into the dark of the night. I could not see where it was that he was taking me, but his legs were moving so fast that what I could see was a blur. I heard Jared's yells as we bolted across the grass in front of the cottage, but they became silent with the wind whipping through my ears. I leaned into Raiden's neck and asked him, "What is wrong, boy?" He just ran faster. I wrapped my arms around the great horse's neck and held on. He slowed as we came to the foot of the massive hills that surrounded the valley, only to climb them. I had no idea what direction he had taken me in, but I trusted him. Up and up we climbed, until we reached the top. Then and only then did he stop and turn to face the valley. The only sounds were his breathing and mine. I looked into the darkness, seeing just little flickers of light from torches and the buildings in the valley below, and then I heard it. Thunder.

In my heart, I knew that sound, and I feared it. My beloved Jared, Westin, and my friends were all left in the valley. I had abandoned them. I should be down there with them, ready to fight. I kicked Raiden in the sides, but he did not budge. "What is it, boy? Why have you brought me here?" He just bobbed his head up and down. The fear in my chest was more than I could bear, so I climbed off Raiden and started to climb down. I did not get very far, however, because Raiden managed to continuously block my way. "Why will you not let me help them?" I asked him. I was not sure if I actually expected an answer, but I wanted one.

The thunder stopped as I stared into the darkness of the valley. I could hear the screams of the horses, and I could see sparks from the swords colliding. Some were brighter than others; those would have been Rebecca's. My friends, the people I loved, were fighting, and I was forced away by a horse. The fight seemed to go on forever, but it did end. My fear was that they were all dead, and I was going to be left alone. Raiden nudged me with his nose, nearly knocking me off the rock I had perched myself upon. I climbed back on him, and he led me down the hills to the plain, and off we went. When we arrived at the cottage, Charles, Blake, and Jared were on their horses coming to find me.

I climbed off of Raiden, yelling, "What in the world happened?"

"I am sorry to say, Sabine, that the barbarians have discovered us. We have no way of knowing if we got them all or not, but we managed to capture a few of them, and we killed the rest."

"Where are Westin and Camille? Where is Rebecca?"

"I am here," I heard Rebecca say. As she approached, I could see her gown was covered in blood. "This sword is unbelievable. Not one of those barbarians could touch me." She was smiling ear to ear. "Where did you go?"

"I went to check on Raiden, and he...well, I got on his back, and he took me away and would not bring me back until now."

Jared laughed. "I always said that horse was strange."

"No, that horse is her guardian," Charles said.

We all looked at Charles, and I asked, "What do you mean, my guardian?"

He just smiled. "There is much you do not know, Sabine, but you will in time."

"Charles, I am finding you to be a good friend, so please excuse me if I offend you, but all this secrecy is becoming a hindrance. I wish to know all that you know. If you say to me, 'In due time,' I swear it, I might not be able to control my anger. You have given us very little. I would like to know the rest, and I would like to know it right now!"

"The day has been long. I give you my word that in the light of the day, I will reveal all that I know."

"Agreed. I wish to speak to Blake, and then, will you take me to these barbarians? I wish to speak to them."

"Yes, Sabine," Charles replied, and Blake walked out of the dark of night.

I walked with him away from the others. "Will you go to the cave and retrieve for me one of each of those jewels we buried, please? Meet us wherever it is they have taken the barbarians, once you have them."

"Yes, of course. I will return shortly." He was gone quickly.

I turned to face Jared and Charles. "Please take me to these barbarians."

We walked toward the barracks, and Raiden followed me. I swear, that horse thought he was a dog. All around were the dead bodies of those that were killed. We did not go into the barracks, but around to the back of the building. Sitting tied up were five men. The stench was a scent I was all too familiar with. As I walked toward them, I could see the murderous glow in their eyes. One of them growled at me, "You will die."

Jared moved to strike him, but I stopped him. "You, Lord Jared, are as your father said, taken by a woman who is not worthy, a woman who should not be allowed to draw another breath."

I laughed. "Well, it seems that you are the one tied up."

"You will die," he said again.

"It seems to be the plan, but it will not become a reality."

"We will not stop until all the descendants of Whispering Wind are dead."

I knelt down in front of him and said, "Well then, I suppose we shall have to stop you. I am not going anywhere. You can continue to come, and you will continue to die. I will avenge my family, and you must know by now that the legend is truth, and that myself and Rebecca will bring peace, and you will surely die."

"The legend speaks of no woman. Women are insignificant. You are not who you think you are."

"Then why is it that you are trying to kill me? Why did you slaughter my family?"

Just then, I heard Blake say, "You certainly did not do it for these."

I stood and walked to Blake to retrieve the jewels. I turned and laid them on the ground in front of the barbarians. "This is what you fight for. These are what you are promised by King Samuel, but these are just a few, for King Samuel holds the bulk of these stones. I know because I gave them to him."

The men stared at the jewels. Never before had I seen any so big. One man looked up at me and said, "These jewels are not part of the legend. They are part of our history. How is it that you possess them? You are but a mere woman. A king owns these. Who did you steal these from?"

"I did not thieve them from anyone. I found them hidden in Whispering Wind when I returned to find my family slaughtered by you and your friends." My voice was louder than usual. These men were making me angry.

"Liar," he yelled. "You are not the bringer of peace. That is a story. YOU WILL DIE!!"

I was shocked at my reaction. I stood and drew my sword, and before anyone could stop me, I swung it. The brilliance of light that flashed as I struck the man in the neck knocked us all back a step. His head went rolling along the ground. No one moved. No one dared to breathe. It was Charles who spoke, and it was a whisper. "Truth is before you."

I looked at Jared, then past him to Rebecca, who smiled her brilliant smile as she said, "See what I mean?" I did indeed see what she meant. Jared just stood there, staring at me. I was worried he did not care for what he had just seen. His eyes were not the same as he gazed upon me.

"It is truth. Oh, Sabine." Before I knew what was happening, he pulled me into his arms. My sword fell to the ground as we embraced.

"The day and night have been long. Let us all retire, for tomorrow will bring more truth," Charles said as he picked up my sword. Then speaking to Blake, he said, "Make sure the bodies are buried far from here, and make sure that these four are never left unattended. Send more men to stand at the ready, and send someone to retrieve Westin and Camille. Joseph, gather all who remain and meet me in front of the cottage. Sabine, Rebecca, and Jared, please come with me as we need to talk." He bent to pick up the jewels.

Before we walked away, I turned to face the barbarians. "I will return in the light of the day, and we shall chat again." None of them spoke. Jared put his arm around me, and we made our way back to the cottage.

The majority of the guards were assembled in front of the cottage when we arrived. Charles started putting everyone to work and giving them their orders for the night. "Rest assured that more will come. It was indeed a great army that destroyed Whispering Wind, so we can expect that they will come here. We are going to need reinforcements, so I am going to have you, Joseph, direct Steven to take with him a few select guards and go back to Blackmore, Collingwood, and to Wellington. Find more troops or men who will be willing to train and fight with us. Tell him to try not to give too much information. We do not want Wellington to hear of this. Blake, in the light of the day, I will need you to go to the neighboring villages and employ workers to build more barracks to house those who will come and join us. Joseph will tell you where to go, for he did the same to employ those who built what is here. Now, get some sleep, for the light of the day shall be upon us soon." Everyone dispersed, and Charles turned to face us. "Sabine, Rebecca, there is much Jared and I must teach you both. I know you have plenty of questions, and I will do my best to answer all of them, but for now, you must eat and rest. Westin and my sister are safe in the cottage, and there should be a meal waiting for you."

"Your sister? Camille is your sister?"

"Yes, she is, Sabine, and I am grateful that you decided to bring her along. I was fearful of leaving her behind, for I am sure that Samuel would have surely put her to death once he realized we were not returning."

"Funny, she never said anything to me."

"It is not her station to speak of these things, but nevertheless, I am in your debt. Now, go get some food and some rest. I will be here keeping watch."

We bid everyone goodnight and went into the cottage. Not much was said while we ate. I think we were all just so very tired. Camille took Jared to his room, which was next to Westin's, and that made him very happy to have Jared there with him. Rebecca stayed in a room across from mine. We said our good nights and retired. Camille had drawn us both baths, and it felt wonderful to climb into the hot water and scrub the dirt off. I put on my sleeping gown and climbed into the huge oversized bed. Just as I was getting ready to blow out the candle, there was a knock on my door. "Come in," I called, but the door did not open. I climbed out and went to the door. I should have known it would be Jared.

"I wish not to add to the chatter about, so I will not enter your chamber, but I could not sleep without doing this first." He reached in and pulled me into the hall, then thoroughly kissed me. I could not have been happier that he escaped from Wellington and that he had made it safely to me. By the time we finished our embrace, I was short of breath. He smiled at me, touching my face, and said, "I love only you, Sabine."

"I love only you, Jared."

He walked away with that brilliant smile of his. I watched him until he turned to go down to his room. Closing my door, I knew sleep would come quick, and I could not wait. I was tired.

CHAPTER SIXTEEN

Before I knew it, the light of the day was warming my face. There was a fire burning in the fireplace, so it must have gotten cold overnight. A knock came at the door. "Sabine, are you awake?" It was Rebecca.

"Yes, of course. Come in."

When she came into the room, she did it twirling around in circles. "How do you like my man clothes?" She began to giggle.

"I like them indeed. Where did you acquire those?"

"Edward. I went to see him this morning. He is so angry about all of this. I am still so confused. Sabine, do you believe any of this? I mean, it is not all that hard to believe after the events of last night. Did you see that brilliant flash of light come out of your sword when you cut that barbarian's head off? I thought mine was bright, but yours was ten times more than mine."

"To be honest with you, Rebecca, I do not understand any of this. Two years ago, I was just a girl whose father was a king. None of what Charles has said was ever heard by me. I mean, some of it makes a bit of sense. How many princesses do you know of, or have you ever known of, who were allowed to train with a sword? None. Women are just that. Women. My father would never have let me go to the training grounds, let alone fight a real fight with a sword. I was only allowed to fight with my brothers."

"I know that my father was very hesitant in allowing me to practice. He wanted sons, but he got me and my sister instead. Mother could not bear any more children."

"I am afraid of what lies ahead for us, Rebecca."

"Oh, Sabine, I agree with you. I mean, fighting is fun, but the barbarians are fierce. I am just as fearful as you."

We sat there looking at one another, fearing for our very existence. If Samuel and Gerald succeeded, we would perish, and they would win. That man would not outwit me. Ardes and Simon made sure of that.

"I will put on my boy clothes, and then we can go find Charles and get some answers."

"I will meet you in the dining hall," she said, giggling, knowing well we had no dining hall.

I smiled at her as she left my room, and I got out my boy clothes. I neatly folded the gown that Camille had laid out for me and placed it in the wardrobe for another day. Today, I would dress as a boy. I made my way down to the room with the table, finding Jared, Westin, and Rebecca waiting for me.

"Am I to wait for you every morning?" Jared said, smiling as he stood to greet me.

"You shall, sire," I snapped back at him playfully. I was always the last to arrive. We ate a feast for our morning meal. It was fun to watch Camille fawning over Westin. They would smile at one another and giggle every now and again. With all that was going on, I was glad that they had one another. I was grateful that Camille was making it bearable for him. Westin looked up at me admiring him and smiled. The dents in his cheeks reminded me of Mother. I missed her so.

"Sabine?"

"Yes, my love?"

"Are you all right?"

"Of course I am, Westin. Why would you ask?"

"You are crying."

I reached up to touch my cheek and wiped the tears I had not felt, "Well, I do not know why I am crying. I was just thinking about Mother and how much your smile reminds me of hers."

"I think of Mother and Father all the time. I miss them, Sabine."

"Yes, I know, my love. I miss them as well."

"Camille and I are going to ride to the caves today. Do you want to come with us?"

"I wish that I could say yes, Westin, but there are a few things I need to discuss with Charles. Perhaps tomorrow we can all go for a fun ride. Maybe we could take a basket of food along with us, make an afternoon of it. Would that be nice?"

"I would love it, Sabine. I cannot wait." He stood to leave and turned to me. "I love you, Sabine."

"I love you too, Westin."

He left the room. I looked after him with a smile. "You really love him deeply." Jared touched my hand.

"I do. He is all that is left of my family."

"Until you marry me, and then I will be your family as well." He picked up my hand and kissed it. "Let us go find Charles and get to the bottom of this tale he has spun."

We walked out into the light of day to find Charles and Joseph waiting for us with our horses. "Good morning, ladies. Would you be so kind as to bring your swords along for the ride?"

"I will get them for you." Jared turned and was gone. Rebecca and I mounted our horses.

"Where would we be going this morning, Charles?"

"Well, Sabine, I thought it best to distance ourselves from the others." He raised his eyebrows at me. I could not stop myself from smiling.

"I wanted to speak to the barbarians this morning to see if they decided to give up a bit of their plan. Do you think we could stop and speak with them before we head off?"

"I can assure you, my lady that the barbarians have nothing to say."

"Charles, although I appreciate all that you have done for me and all that you do in protecting me, I would really rather you not decide what is important and what is not. I want to deal with these barbarians, and I would appreciate it if you would not stop me from doing so."

"As you wish, Sabine." He turned his horse to face the barracks just as Jared came out of the cottage.

We went to the back of the barracks where the barbarians were tied up. Raiden walked up and stopped right in front of them, giving a snort, and it seemed as if he was trying to stomp on them. I climbed off and said to him, "You can stop trying to frighten them. I do not think that you scared them." He snorted at me and took a step back.

"Good Morning. I trust that your night was comfortable." I smiled at them. "I just stopped by to see if you had any thoughts you would like to share with us today. Your time left here is minimal, and I hear that confession is good for the soul." Not one word was spoken.

"Have it your way. I will return at midday to see if you would like to chat then. Have a good morning." I climbed back on Raiden, and he gave a little jump after I mounted him. I think he was trying to scare them. I had to laugh; silly horse.

We came out in front of the cottage. "Sabine, shall we?" Rebecca held her hand out toward the open plain in front of us.

"With every part of my being," I replied and kicked Raiden in the sides, and off we went. It felt so good to just fly with my friend. We had not a care in the world when we were riding like this. It was just us, our horses, and the wind. Raiden did his arch, and before I knew it, we were riding back toward Jared, Charles, and Joseph. We came to a stop just short of Charles. He bowed his head and started out onto the plain, and we all followed him. No one said a word. The sun felt good on my face, and I tilted my head so it warmed me. Jared just watched me in silence as he did a great deal of the time.

"Why do you watch me so?"

"Because I cannot believe that I could ever love someone as I love you."

I could not help but smile. Raiden came to a halt without me having to tell him, and I opened my eyes. Charles and Joseph had dismounted their horses and were walking, so we did the same. We finally stopped and sat in a circle; Charles, Joseph, Rebecca, Jared and myself. We waited for Charles to collect his thoughts. He cleared his throat and began.

"You know the legend of the swords and of the power that Sabine and Rebecca hold when they unite. I must confess, Sabine that your meeting Rebecca was not by chance. It was in fact my doing." He waited for one of us to say something, but as always, we learned to just let Charles talk. "As I said before, when I saw you that day at Whispering Wind, I knew who you were, and I knew that the legend was true. Rebecca was known to us through her guard, and we all watched over her. The legend is of the fire haired warrior and his companion with the hair like the golden sun.

"When Rebecca's father asked the guard to allow her to play out her desire to learn to fight with a sword, we saw it as an opportunity to train her. We had no knowledge of who you were, Sabine. We had only heard of the child that was sired with the golden red hair, but you were a girl. Edward had been born first, so we really did not pay close enough attention. We all assumed it was Edward. Apparently, so did Edward, as it turns out. Rebecca, we believe that is why he paired himself with you. He believed you to be the companion in the legend, but he did not have the sword. Sabine, your father knew who you were, and your brothers were allowed to teach you all that they knew. With Ardes being the best swordsman in all the known land, we were not concerned with you or your training. It was not until your family was brutally murdered and you survived that we knew. There are more who know of this legend, and there will be many more that will join us here. Joseph did not just happen upon this valley. It is part of the legend as well. When Joseph was ordered by Samuel to acquire a residence for you and Westin, we knew he needed to find this valley."

"It was not an easy feat to accomplish," Joseph added. "We only had bits of knowledge concerning this part of the legend. It was said to be in the East surrounded by black hills, and contained within the hills was a lush green valley. The legend speaks of an energy not known by mere man, but only by Merlin. He foretold this legend to the first king, who in turn passed it to his son, and then his son passed it on to his son. Through the generations, this story was shared with few, and a great deal of the detail was lost." Joseph did not look up as he spoke. It was almost as if he was afraid of the power of his words.

Charles continued on, "This valley is where the two of you will finish your training. This valley is where your army will grow. This valley's ground will produce the food needed to sustain us all. This valley will protect you both. It has a very defendable perimeter, and we will have enough time to defend you. This valley is where you will realize and learn the truth of the power the two of you hold."

Rebecca and I looked at one another. This seemed all a bit hard to swallow. We smiled in unison as Charles continued.

"I told you I would tell you, of Raiden's part in all of this. Raiden was your father's horse; am I correct?"

"Yes, he is…or was my father's, but I do not understand how he escaped the slaughter, when all the other animals and horses were murdered right along with everyone else."

"Well, if I am not mistaken, Raiden was indeed your father's, father's horse as well, and his father's before him, and his before him." Raiden snorted and stomped his foot.

Jared laughed deeply and loudly. "That is the most preposterous story I have ever heard. Charles, you cannot assume we could ever entertain that to have any truth to it. A horse that old would be impossible. What you are saying is that this horse is over a hundred years."

"I believe, Jared, that Raiden is closer to three hundred years." I sat there looking at my horse. Could he really be three hundred years? Raiden stood there looking back at me as if he knew what I was thinking. I heard myself say as I stared into Raiden's eyes,

"How is this possible, Charles?"

"It is not possible, Sabine. You cannot tell me that you honestly believe him, do you?"

"Jared, you said it yourself. He follows me around like a dog. When I talk to him, he acts and responds as if he knows what it is I am saying. When the barbarians came into the valley, he went crazy. When I went to him, he forced me to go with him, and he took me to the top of the hills, away from the danger. While I was there, I tried to come back to fight, and he stopped me. Only when it was over did he bring me back."

"I believe he took you away because he knows you are not ready to fight," Charles said, and Raiden snorted.

"So I guess now, Charles, you are going to explain to us how you believe this horse to be three hundred years or more in age?"

"Well, Jared, if you keep an open mind, I will gladly share the knowledge I do have."

"By all means, my friend." Jared waved his hand in a motion to suggest Charles walk through a door.

Charles bowed his head and smiled, saying, "To be truthful, I know very little of Raiden, but it is said that he has not left the sword since the time of Merlin."

Jared interrupted Charles, "Are you wanting us to believe that Merlin was indeed a real person, and not just a story of make believe told to us as children, and told to our fathers and to their fathers?"

"I am telling you that the stories told to me through generations of my family, and to this day, all that I know, has been truth."

"Jared," I said as I reached over and touched his hand. "All Charles has revealed so far has been truth. You have seen and felt," I smiled, "the power of my sword, have you not?"

"Yes, indeed I have."

"Well, do you not at least owe it to Charles to listen with an open mind, just as he has requested of you?"

"Forgive me, Charles. You may continue."

"Thank you, Jared. What I know of Raiden is when the first king was given the sword from Merlin, he was also given a horse. We believe it to have been Raiden. This horse was said to have speed not known to any man. I have seen him run with Sabine on his back, and he never falters. He is said to have power beyond that of any man or horse. His size is unique and greater than any other horse. He holds special abilities that allow him to maneuver in a manner in which men move. It is said that he can ride for days without ever stopping, and that he needs no food or drink. Some say that he is Merlin himself, while others think he has been conjured from the spirits of a thousand horses who lived before him. It has been said that the spirit of the owner is embodied within him when he passes. No one knows the true origin of Raiden, but the truth has been set before us, and it has not yet faltered. He will stand by your side, Sabine, he will never leave you unprotected, and he has proven himself worthy of such an honor already."

I sat there in disbelief, looking at the great horse who had become my friend. I could not help but wonder if he would ever die. Had he really waited all these years for me? I had a great deal to think about. I was not ready for any of this; to lead an army, to unite the land in peace. I just wanted to find who murdered my family and save Juliana.

"This is very difficult to accept, Charles. I am not sure that I am worthy or up to the tasks you have set before me. I am but a girl without a kingdom or a family. I will follow your direction, for you have kept me alive this long." I smiled.

"Sabine, I know that you are ready for what lies ahead, and you will see that in time. I wanted you to bring your sword out here so you and Rebecca can fight. It is important that you two practice, and you must practice with one another now. For your swords alone will cause great harm to those whom fight with you. Remember, against one another, you cancel the other out, and that should allow you to fight one another equally. Joseph, we are done here. I would appreciate it if you would take care of that business we spoke of at the beginning of the day. Would you also please stop by the cottage and ask Westin and Camille to come and join us and bring food with them? We shall be here for a while."

Joseph rose from the grass, as we all did. He walked by me and paused. I almost did not hear him when he whispered. "It is an honor to be in your service, Your Highness."

I reached out to touch his arm and smiled at him. Rebecca was the first to draw her sword. She loved to fight, so we did just that. We went at it for some time before Westin and Camille came with the food. We had a lovely meal sitting in the grass, laughing and talking. Charles finally relaxed enough to enjoy himself. It was nice to see him and Camille together. I would have never placed them as brother and sister. Camille is a tiny girl, like me, and Charles is a giant in comparison. The day moved quickly, and we headed back to the cottage.

"Charles, I would like to speak to the barbarians before I retire for the night."

"As you wish, Sabine." He smiled and bowed his head.

We all rode to the barracks, but I did not bother getting off of Raiden. "Well, it seems that your time here is coming to an end. There is much to do before we ride to Whispering Wind and beyond to destroy you all. Is there anything you wish to say to me before I retire for the night?"

"It is our wish that you do not see the light of the day. It is our wish that you take your last breath and die."

"Well then, I suppose that my offer to spare your lives is something that would not interest you." I looked at Charles. "Would you please see to it that our visitors have a swift and painless evening?"

"Yes, my lady. Consider it done."

"Well, I will say this to you, gentlemen. Your friends will not have such a peaceful end." With that, I rode Raiden to the stables and got him prepared for the night. I could not help myself from staring at him. Looking into his eyes, as he did mine, I swore he smiled at me. I could not help but wonder if, in his eyes, I saw my father. I giggled, patted him on the head, and bid him good night.

CHAPTER SEVENTEEN

As I left the stables and walked past the barracks, one of the guards motioned for me to come toward him. As I approached, he whispered, "My lady, Lady Rebecca has gone in to talk to Prince Edward alone. I have a guard standing outside the door, just in case. I thought you might like to know."

"Thank you," I told him, and I made way into the barracks. I could see the guard leaning into the door as if to listen in on the conversation. I whispered to him, "Is there anything going on?" He seemed a bit embarrassed at me catching him and shook his head no. He straightened up, and I moved in to take his place listening. The door was cracked, and I could see Rebecca sitting on the bed, and Edward's back was facing me.

Rebecca just sat there looking at Edward. She looked as if she was struggling to find the words to begin. Charles had delivered a blow to her today on the plain. I could see the pain in her eyes, but she did not show it any other way.

"Edward, I was informed today that your feelings for me are not true." I could see that she was struggling with her anger.

"Who told you that, your imposter friend, Sabine?"

"No, Edward. It was not Sabine, and please do not blame Sabine for this. Is what I say true?"

"Rebecca, it is supposed to be you and I who are the chosen ones, not that red haired replica. She is not who she claims to be. My father told me that it was me. I was born first, and he told me that a man could only be the chosen one. Sabine's existence was not known for many years. Her father kept her birth a secret, and then he kept her hidden within the walls of Whispering Wind."

I could not believe what he was saying. I flashed on a few memories as a child. I was never allowed out of the back garden as a young child. It was not until I was in my thirteenth year that father allowed me to go anywhere, and Ardes or Simon would always have to accompany me. When Mother and Father had their great fancy balls, I was always in my room with Westin. We were never allowed to come down and join in. Even when I was older, it was never allowed. Had Father really kept me hidden?

Rebecca continued, "Edward, you are avoiding my query. Are your feelings for me true?"

"Rebecca, you have been told untruths concerning this legend. You are not to be a swordsman. You are to compliment me, not fight side by side. That is preposterous to think that a woman could best a man. You are to produce an heir to carry on my reign as the keeper of peace. That is all. Why do you think Samuel wanted the binding of you and that worthless Jared? He thought that because Jenna did him no good by producing a girl that perhaps his son could do a better job, and who else would he pair him with, but you, the supposed compliment? How does it feel, Rebecca, to know that you are nothing without me? That alone, you are just a woman, and everyone knows that a woman is good for one thing, and that is to bare an heir. Without that ability, you are worthless, just as Jenna was. She got just what she deserved. And to think that Samuel placed so much hope on her. What a disappointment she turned out to be. I am sure that Samuel found great joy in knowing she is now dead."

"Edward, I suggest you mind your words. I do not think you are in the position to speak this way."

"What, do you think these chains will stop the inevitable, Rebecca? Do you think that you and that Sabine will rise to the occasion?" He laughed a deep and evil laugh. "You are mad if you think the two of you, two WOMEN," he screamed the word at her, "can stop an army of barbarians, or Samuel's army, or my father's army, or your father's for that matter. What do you think, Rebecca? That your father would stop just to save you? He was the one that sold you into marriage with Jared. He wants the power just as my father, Samuel, and even Sabine's father wanted. This will not end well for you, Rebecca. You will die, and I will laugh when they all come back to me for help. I will crush them all."

I did not see her move, but I heard the slapping sound as she slapped Edward across the face.

"How dare you speak to me this way! So then, it is truth? You never cared for me? You never loved me?"

He laughed again. "Who in their right mind would ever love someone like you? You are a weak minded girl who lives in a fantasy. You will die, Rebecca, along with your friend, Sabine, and then they will come to me. I will show them how to rule."

I was standing in the doorway now. I wanted nothing more than to remove Rebecca from his violent ranting's. She was my friend, and he was hurting her with his words. The look on her face was a mixture of pain and anger, but more so anger, for she stood up and looked me right in the face. I saw her eyes. I saw what he had done to her with his words, and before I could move, before I could scream, Rebecca drew her sword and swung it. The flash of light was brilliant. The whole room was white from it. Edward's head rolled across the room and stopped just in front of me.

"Well, I guess you will not be ruling anyone." Was all she said. I stood there, unable to move. I could hear footsteps running up behind me. I felt a hand on my shoulder, someone saying my name, but my eyes never left hers. She turned and stepped over his body and walked up to me. We stood there looking at one another, and then I saw them, her eyes filled with tears. My arms instinctively reached out to hold her. We stood there, not hearing all the voices around us, just me and my friend embracing, silently crying.

She whispered in my ear, "I need to ride. Will you come with me?" I nodded, and we turned and left Edward's body and everyone else in the room. We walked arm in arm to the stables. I was not even sure how we managed to put the saddles on the horses, but we did. Then we slowly walked them out into the night. I climbed on Raiden and she on Spirit. It was instinct for them both, I think. We did not even have to kick them, and they were off. Raiden steadied his pace to stay with Spirit. I could hear shouts behind us, but in the end, I knew Charles would stop them from coming after us.

We rode and rode, always in an arch, never really getting too far from the lights of the cottage and barracks. I knew Raiden would keep a suitable distance. I do not know how long we rode. Rebecca finally slowed to a trot and then to a walk. I did not say a word to her, as I knew she needed to come to terms with the fact that she just beheaded Edward. I needed to come to terms with it.

Her words were soft. "What did I do, Sabine?"

I was not sure how to respond to her, so I said nothing. I looked at my friend, and I could see her tears.

"Sabine?"

"Yes, Rebecca?"

"I killed Edward."

"I know. I saw."

"Why did I do that? I mean, he made me so angry."

"I know. I heard the things he said to you, and I am so sorry." I did not expect her to laugh, but she did.

"Why do you have to be sorry, Sabine? You did not say those things. This thing we are together makes men lose their minds. I have never known Edward to be so cruel. Do you believe it to be truth, the things that Charles has told us?"

"I do not know, Rebecca. I just know that the things Charles has said are truth. It is so beyond real that there has to be some truth to it. Why would they tell a tale such as this?"

"I murdered the man I love, Sabine."

"I know, Rebecca. I know." She climbed off Spirit, and I followed. We sat in the grass in silence. I spoke first, reaching out to touch her hand. "Rebecca, I heard everything Edward said to you. It was cruel. He was obviously not in his right mind. He has been this way since I met him on the road here. Whatever happened to him, I do not think he would have recovered from it. Perhaps you did him a favor by ending his pain."

She giggled. "I ended it all right."

"You sure did."

And then we laughed together. "Did you see the light from my sword when I struck him?"

"The light was so bright I could see nothing but you in the center of it."

"The only thing I could see was you as well."

We sat there for a while, not saying anything until we heard the horses. Neither of us moved, but I could not help but wonder how they found us. The dark of the night was black. I had a difficult time seeing Rebecca, but Jared and Charles rode up and stopped just in front of us.

"Rebecca, are you all right?" Charles said in a soft voice.

"I am fine, Charles, but I am fearful that Edward has lost his head," she replied with a giggle.

In a laughing manner, Charles said, "Yes, I am afraid he did."

We all laughed then. Jared came to sit next to me, and Charles sat next to Rebecca. "Rebecca," Charles began, "Edward would not have recovered from his thoughts. He truly believed that he was the one the legend speaks of. His father trained him and convinced him that he was worthy to carry the sword of Sabine's father. As I told you earlier, your training began at a very young age as well, only you were not told of your place in all this. Edward, however, knew of you, and he was promised to you in marriage by both of your fathers. It was Samuel who changed the plan when Jenna did not produce a male heir. It was Samuel who organized the death of Sabine's family and the arrangement of you and Jared to marry. Edward showed signs of madness long before he met you. We have kept a close watch over him. At first, we thought it was Edward and his father who sent the barbarians."

"Why did no one stop me from falling in love with Edward?"

"I am sorry, Rebecca. We could not risk telling you the truth when we were not sure of what knowledge was true."

"Well, I am not surprised that Edward lost his mind with this knowledge. It is very far from the truth of what we know. I am having a hard time believing it myself." She smiled.

"As am I." It was more of a whisper to myself. "But so far, all that Charles has told us, Rebecca, has been the truth."

Raiden snorted and stomped his foot, and we all kind of laughed. "We have taken care of Edward. I will send word to his father in the morning. I will simply tell him that the barbarians were too much for us to handle and Edward was taken from us. That should hurt him enough to question Samuel's intent."

"Thank you, Charles. I am tired, and I wish to return to the cottage. Sabine, will you ride with me?"

"Of course I will, Rebecca." We mounted our horses and rode off into the dark of the night. Jared and Charles rode with us, but let us have our privacy. Once back at the cottage, we ate in silence, and then we retired to our rooms. I was lying in bed when there was a slight knock on the door. I went to open it, and it was Rebecca.

"Would you mind if I slept here with you tonight?"

"Not at all. Please come on in."

We did not say a word to one another. She just climbed in my bed and under the covers. When the light of the day came, she was gone.

CHAPTER EIGHTEEN

I sat there in my bed thinking of how my friend must have felt. She beheaded the man she loved last night, and no one said a word about it. I would not know what I would do if I beheaded Jared. I got up and dressed in my girl clothes. I did not feel like looking like a boy. I did not want to practice, and I did not want to fight. I just wanted to find my friend and make sure she was all right. I made my way downstairs and out the door. I heard Jared and Westin calling my name, but I kept on moving. I made it to the stables when Jared caught up to me.

"Sabine, what are you doing? Did you not hear Westin and me calling you?"

I kept on walking, almost running into the stables. My head turned toward Spirit's stall. I saw that he was gone. I kept on walking to Raiden. He stood there ready for me, as if he knew I was coming. I started to put his saddle on, and Jared grabbed my arm. "Sabine!"

"I do not have time for this, Jared. Please let me go!"

With that, Raiden nudged Jared and knocked him back. I continued to saddle him.

"Jared, I am sorry. We will talk when I return. Rebecca needs me, and I have to go." I climbed on Raiden, and he trotted out of the stable. I leaned into him and said, "Take me to Rebecca, boy." I did not even have to kick him, and he was gone. We were flying. The cottage was a blur as he rode out onto the plain. I leaned in and wrapped my arms around his neck as he ran. He continued to the hills, where he took me the night the barbarians came into the valley. He slowed only to climb to the top, and down the other side. When he hit flat ground, he was off again. Where did she go? I cannot say how long I was on Raiden, but it was not long before I met up with Rebecca. Spirit was in a full run when Raiden galloped up next to him.

"Rebecca, where are you going?" The look on her face was that of shock. She pulled on Spirit's reigns and came to a stop. Raiden did the same.

"How in the world did you find me?"

"I asked Raiden to bring me to you. Where are you going?"

"I do not know. I just know I cannot stay there, not after last night. Everyone is looking at me, talking about me. I think I need to tell Edward's father that it was me who took his son's life. I snuck away. How did you find me?"

"I told you. I asked Raiden to bring me to you. Rebecca, you must not feel guilty for what happened to Edward. He was not himself. His mind had been tainted by his father years ago, and it had nothing to do with you. Eventually, his life would have ended. You just relieved him of his insanity sooner rather than later."

"I murdered him, you mean."

"No, Rebecca. He would have tried to kill me and possibly even you. You saved my life by taking his."

I was not expecting her reaction. She started to cry, so I reached out to hold her. We sat there on our horses for some time; I could imagine how silly we looked. I just held her until she was cried out. She pulled away from me.

"I am sorry, Sabine. I must look like a child."

"There is nothing to be sorry for. You are my friend, you needed me and I came."

"Does anyone know where you are?"

"Well, I am sure that by now, there are guards all over the place looking for us." I could not help but giggle. "Jared followed me into the stables, and when I would not talk to him, he grabbed my arm, and Raiden knocked him to the ground. So I am sure that he alerted the guards, and I think we might even be in trouble with Charles."

"Thank you for coming after me. I still do not know how you found me. I left before dawn, and Spirit has not stopped running."

"To be honest, I just discovered you gone a little bit ago. Raiden is faster than I think any of us suspected, for I have not been gone long. We really should get back. I am sure that they will be looking for us in the valley."

She smiled at me and turned her horse around, kicked Spirit in the sides, and off they went. I sat there for a minute, just watching her golden hair fly in the air as they rode off. Raiden snorted, and his ears started twitching. "What is it, boy?" He turned so we were facing the opposite direction of Rebecca. I looked and looked and saw nothing, but Raiden's ears would not stop twitching. "I do not see anything, boy. What is it?" Just after I said it, I saw them. "Barbarians!" I could not see how many of them there were, but they were coming. "Go, boy! Can we make it back to the valley?" Raiden reared up on his hind legs. I nearly fell off, but he hit the ground with a thump, spun around, and then took off. We were next to Rebecca before I knew what was happening. "Barbarians!" I screamed at her. She kicked Spirit in the sides, and he took off. I was not sure if Raiden was keeping pace with him, or he with Raiden, but we were flying again. The hills came fast.

Raiden and Spirit climbed them at a very fast pace. When we reached the top, Raiden stopped and turned. I could see them more clearly at this height; there were at least fifty of them if not more. Rebecca and Spirit had already made it to the bottom of the hills and had started across the plain. I could see the guards riding toward us. Raiden was moving again. He made it down in what seemed no time at all, and was passing Spirit in moments. We rode up to Charles, and I told him, "You can yell at me later, but barbarians are coming. They are right behind us. We need to sound the alarm and get ready!"

Not a word was said. Raiden took off and stopped in front of the cottage, so I jumped off of him, ran up to my room to change my clothes, and got my sword. Jared met me in the hall on my way out.

"What were you thinking?"

"If I had not gone to get Rebecca, she would be dead right now. Help me fight and yell at me later." I kissed him and pushed passed him and down the stairs. Westin was in the kitchen hall, so I yelled at him, "Get Camille and go to the caves now!" He nodded and was gone.

I ran out the door and climbed on Raiden, and Jared was right behind me. Charles was riding up with Rebecca. "I will be right back," she said. "Wait for me." She was gone quickly.

When she returned, we rode to the center of the plain. Beside me on my left was Charles, who said, "We will be successful, Sabine."

"I have no fear, Charles. These men murdered my family. They will not best me."

On my right was Rebecca, and on her right was Jared. She looked at me and smiled. I saw in her eyes that same gleam the first night they came, the night Raiden whisked me away. I looked down the line and could not remember having so many guards. Where did they all come from? I would ask that of Charles when this was over. Raiden's ears started twitching again. "They are coming," I whispered. Charles looked at me, and I motioned to Raiden's ears. He followed my gaze and smiled.

Not a moment later, the first one cleared the hills, then the next and the next. They made a trail down the hills. I knew they had to have seen us. Soon, the last was on the plain. Their line was greater than ours. I could not help but smile as I leaned into Charles and said, "This is not a fair fight, Charles. They should have brought more."

He laughed so loud that I jumped. Soon, we were both laughing. I could just imagine what the barbarians were thinking, but before we could catch our breath, they were on us and coming fast and hard. Raiden did not move. I had no idea what to do. I had never been in a fight before, not one like this. *Should we not be riding toward them?* Raiden stomped his hoof on the ground, and it was like a signal that all the other horses sensed. I felt his body under me tighten. My instinct was to hang on, so my hand gripped his reigns tighter, and with my other hand on my sword I raised it in the air. Rebecca did the same, and then it happened. Nothing could have ever prepared any of us for what took place. No one moved. The lightning was so fierce and so bright. Raiden and Spirit both reared up on their hind legs, perhaps to protect us from the brightness of the light. When they landed on their feet, the light was gone, and lying on the ground in front of us were dead men and horses. There was a black burn mark that ran across the land. I had never seen anything like it in all my life.

We all just sat there on our horses, no one moving, no one speaking. I was not sure if any of us were breathing. It was Rebecca who broke the silence. "Did that just happen?"

I looked at her and said, "Apart, we are nothing, but together, we will level armies." Then I turned to Charles.

"Do you believe me now?" he asked.

"I think I must be dreaming because there is no way that just happened. How is this possible?"

"I told you, Sabine that together, the two of you will bring peace and unite the lands. I know nothing of this magic. I only know the legend that was told to me. This was not in the legend. This is something no one knew about. I thought that you were unstoppable with the sword, not untouchable. We may not need more men. Our little army here may be enough, but you still need to train. You need more hand to hand combat. We know nothing of this power you two just demonstrated, and we do not know if it will work again."

Raiden stomped his hoof on the ground and snorted. "Apparently, Raiden thinks it will. Rebecca, we should try this again to see if it works."

"I think you are right, Sabine. You ready?"

We raised our swords in the air, and nothing happened. We both laughed and looked at Charles.

"Why are you looking at me? I had nothing to do with this. Perhaps it was Raiden who ignited the swords." Raiden gave a little jump and neighed.

"Well, if that is the case, boy, then let us do it again and see if you are as magical, as Charles thinks you are."

He turned his head and looked at me, and I swear he was smiling. I felt his body tense up underneath me. I could not help but think he was the magic.

"Come on, Rebecca." I raised my sword, and she did the same. The light was so brilliant, more so than the first time. Raiden and Spirit both reared up on their hind legs, and when they slammed them to the ground, the light ended. The bodies and horses that were lying on the ground were in flames. We looked at one another with shock and disbelief on our faces.

"What is this magic?" Jared's voice was low.

I just looked at him. He was in shock, as we all were. "My love, I know not what this is, only that it is. Come. Let us go back to the cottage and talk." I reached out to him. His horse moved into mine, and we moved toward the cottage. Charles sent some men to get Westin and Camille.

I had not eaten, so when we entered the cottage, I asked one of the kitchen girls to bring us food to my room. She gave me a look. I knew the look; it was unheard of for a man to accompany a young woman to her room, but she saw Rebecca and Charles walk in behind us, and she bowed her head and went off to the kitchen.

"Come on," I said as I motioned to everyone to follow.

It was Charles who broke in, "Would it be more appropriate for us to talk in here?" He motioned to the sitting room.

"Charles, I think we are beyond traditional arrangements. I prefer my room, where I know that our words will be semi private. It is fine, and I am not worried about what people will think. We just literally burned to death a small army of men, and there is nothing traditional about that."

He nodded his head, and we made our way upstairs and into my room. Jared sat in one chair, and Charles in the other. Rebecca and I sat on the bed. Camille brought in more food than any of us could eat, and then she excused herself. We ate in silence. It was Jared who spoke first. "Sabine, before I knew any of these legends concerning you, I just knew you as the girl who captured my heart."

His tone frightened me. "And now?" I did not want to hear what he had to say, but I needed to hear it. I needed to know if his feelings for me had changed.

"And now you have become this woman of a legend, possibly more than three hundred years in the making. You possess a power that no one has ever known. I am just wondering if I am worthy of having these feelings of love for you that I have. I think that there is much more ahead of you, and perhaps I will hinder the course your life is on."

I could feel the tears welling in my eyes. My heart felt as if it would leap from my chest. Charles was watching me and broke in. "Jared, I believe that your love for her, and your presence in her life, are a part of this as well. Without it, she would not know compassion, love, or sympathy. Your father removed that part of her life with the slaughter of her family. She knew only hate and revenge until she gave in to her feelings for you. It is important, I believe, that she has you, a man who is true at heart."

"But how do you know that I am true at heart, Charles? I could end up like Edward."

"Well, Jared, if you were not true at heart with your feelings toward Sabine, you would not have just offered to bow out of her life and allow her to fulfill her destiny. But her destiny lies with you and with Rebecca."

"And with you, Charles. If you had not stepped in and intervened with Samuel, I would not be here."

"I know not what my purpose in all this is, Sabine. I only know that I am to protect you, even if it means giving my life."

Jared stood and crossed my room to the bed, he sat next to me. "You are the most incredible woman I have ever known. From that first day in the courtyard at Whispering Wind, when you tackled me, I knew that I was going to love you until the day I left this world. If you will have me, Sabine, would you do me the honor of becoming my wife someday?"

I sat there looking at him. I knew I was going to say yes, but I just could not get the words to come out of my mouth. "Jared, I have never known anyone like you. When I am not with you, I cannot stop thinking about you, and when I am with you, I cannot believe you love me the way you do. If someday means when this is over, then my answer is yes. If someday means you are not sure of this, then my answer is no. Jared, I love you, and I would give all that I have to spend the rest of my life, however long that is, with you."

"To me, Sabine, tomorrow is someday."

I threw myself into his arms and kissed him. "I love you, and yes, I will marry you," I managed to say between kisses.

Charles cleared his throat, and we parted laughing. As he walked back to his chair, I glanced over at Rebecca. She was crying. I reached out and took her hand. "I love you."

"I know, and I am grateful you came after me this morning. I just realized that, without you, I would not be here."

"I am not so sure about that, Rebecca. May I ask where you got Spirit from?" Charles asked her.

She looked at him. "I do not know, Charles. As far back as I can remember, he has always been in my father's stables. When I was little, he would follow me around. Everyone would laugh and call him a dog. My mother thought it was sweet. I learned to ride him when I was in my fourth year. Now that you mention it, Charles, he is older than I am. I do not think he has aged at all. What are you thinking?"

"I do not know, Rebecca. I know nothing of your part in this legend, except that you are the compliment to Sabine. I just find it amazing."

We all just sat there, not saying a word and looking at one another. I could not help but think that we were just people who happened to walk into a world of made up bedtime stories that just happened to be real. I thought we were all thinking the same thing because it was the knock on the door that jolted us all back to reality.

"Come in," we all said at once, then chuckled.

It was Westin. "Sabine, did you see the fire out on the plain?"

"I did indeed. I am glad you are here. I was going to find you later so we could talk. Would you come and sit with me?"

His smile grew huge. "You were coming to find me? I thought you were going to be too busy for me, Sabine."

"Oh, Westin, I am so sorry for not having time to ride and spend time with you, but you do understand that we are trying to make sure that no one will hurt us anymore. We are also working on going to find Juliana."

"But, Sabine, Juliana is dead. Remember, we buried her at Samuel's."

"There is so much we need to talk about. How about you go down to the kitchen and ask Camille to put some food in a sack for us, and me, you, and Jared will go for a ride and have a nice chat under a tree somewhere."

His face lit up, and he turned to face Jared. "You are going to come with us?" He was so excited.

"I would not miss it, Westin. We have not spent any time together in a long while. It will be good to just be the three of us."

"This is going to be fun, just the three of us. I will be ready and waiting for you in front. I will get the horses ready after I talk to Camille." He was soon out the door.

"Rebecca, will you be all right?"

"I am fine, Sabine. Please go. You and Westin have much to talk about. I will be all right. Charles is here. He can keep me from running away again." She giggled.

I threw my arms around her and kissed her on the cheek. "I love you."

"I love you too. Now go on and spend the afternoon with Westin, because tomorrow I think everything is going to change."

"Charles, you take care of her." I smiled at him.

"I have never let you down before, Sabine, and I shall not let you down now."

With that, Jared and I went down and met Westin in front of the cottage. He was more than excited to have time with us. I loved my brother so much, and he and Juliana were all I had left, besides Jared. We rode for a while, playing and racing. Raiden always let Westin win. We found a nice place far from the fires to rest and eat. "Sabine, what did you mean when you said that we had to find Juliana?"

"Westin, that baby we buried at Wellington was not Juliana.

Samuel had that baby killed so we would believe that it was her, so we would believe that there was nothing left for us to hang onto. I knew it was not her when I held her in my arms. That poor child that we buried, Westin, was not Juliana. She is out there somewhere with all the rest of the children of Whispering Wind, and I know we are going to find them and bring them home."

"I do not understand, Sabine. Why would Samuel be so cruel like that? To kill an innocent little girl just makes no sense."

It was Jared who spoke next, "Westin, I did not want to believe anything that was said about my father, but what Sabine says is the truth. Things have come to light that make my father out to be a monster, along with Rebecca's father and Edward's father. They are bad men, Westin, and we are going to do everything in our power to stop them so we can go home."

"Which is why I wanted to talk to you. When we go home, Jared has asked me to marry him, and I said yes. Is that all right with you?"

I did not expect his response. He screamed, "Yes, yes, yes! Oh, Sabine, yes! I knew that Jared loved you, and I was hoping that you loved him back. I am going to have a brother again!" He was so happy he hugged us both in his big arms. We laughed and hugged.

"Sabine, can I marry Camille too?"

I cannot say that I was shocked. I think I was more shocked that my older brother asked me for permission to marry a girl. "Well, it is all right with me, but I think that you need to ask Charles."

"Charles? Why would I ask Charles? He is not my brother."

"No, he is not, but he is Camille's brother."

"He is? She never told me that. I think I love her, Sabine. She makes me feel funny inside. I think she feels the same way, but, Sabine." His face went sad.

"What is it, Westin?"

"I do not want to wait until we go home. Do I have to wait like you and Jared?"

I could not stop from laughing. "No, you do not have to wait. Jared and I are waiting because we have so much to do before we can be safe, but you are safe here. If Charles says yes, then you can marry Camille when you want."

He kissed me and jumped up. "I am going to find Charles and ask him so I can ask Camille." He climbed on his horse and was gone.

"You know that boy loves you."

"As I do him, and what about this boy?" I touched his chest.

"Oh, this boy has more love for you than the dark of night has stars," he said, and he kissed me. "Why must we wait, Sabine? I understand your thoughts on the matter, but why?"

"Jared, I want to be able to love you without fear of dying. I would not want our children to grow up without a mother."

"Children? You want to have children with me?" He could not contain his smile.

"Many children, Jared. Many, many children." I fell into his arms, and we lay in the grass and kissed for most of the afternoon, stopping only when it became too much for us.

CHAPTER NINETEEN

Westin could not contain himself. He raced to the barracks, but Charles was not there. He ran to the cottage and back up to my room, hoping he was still there with Rebecca, but he was not. He ran to the stables, but Charles' horse was gone and so was Rebecca's. He went back out into the courtyard and asked every guard he could find if they had seen Charles or knew where he had gone. No one seemed to know. He climbed back on his horse and headed out onto the plain. He ran his horse from one end to the other; no Charles and no Rebecca.

On his way back to the cottage, completely depleted from his efforts, he spotted Charles and Rebecca riding toward him. He kicked his horse, and off he went. Riding up to Charles with a panicked look on his face, he could not stop himself as he said, "Charles, I have been looking for you."

"Is everything all right, Westin? Is Sabine all right?"

"Oh, yes. Sabine is fine. I left her on the plain with Jared, and they were kissing. I need to talk to you about something. Rebecca, could I please talk to Charles alone? It is man stuff."

Rebecca smiled at him. "Why of course, Westin. I would not want to hear man stuff."

"Thank you, Rebecca," Westin said as she rode off.

"What can I do to help you, Westin?"

"I do not need help, Charles. Sabine said yes, but she said I needed to ask you first."

"Well then, what is it, Westin? Please feel free to speak."

"I did not know that you were Camille's brother, but I think I love her. I am supposed to ask you if it is all right if I marry Camille."

Charles smiled. "Westin, does Camille feel the same way about you?"

"I think she does. She said she feels funny like I do when we are together, and Sabine said that is how she feels when she is with Jared, and she loves Jared, and Jared loves her. So I think, yes. Camille loves me too."

"I am beginning to understand that funny feeling, Westin. To be honest, I feel that way when I am around Rebecca as well, so I will tell you this. If Camille wants to marry you, then you have my blessing."

"Thank you, Charles, for your blessing, but can I marry her?"

Charles laughed hardily. "Yes, Westin, you can marry Camille."

"Thank you, Charles. Now I have to go and ask Camille if she wants to marry me." Before he left, Westin asked one more question. "Charles, what does it mean to be married?"

Charles could not contain himself. His laughter came out in gasps. "That is the question all men ask, Westin, but I think the best answer is that it means that the person you want to marry is the only person you want to spend all your time with, every day for the rest of your life."

"That is what I thought. I spend every day with Camille now, so this would mean that I can do it for the rest of my life, and she does not ever have to go away. Yes, that is what I want. Thank you, Charles."

Before he could say anything, Westin was gone, racing back to the cottage to find Camille. Charles just smiled. He knew that Camille would say yes, as she had spoken to him days before about the same thing. Camille was unsure if it was acceptable for her to love or want to marry a prince because she was just a servant, but Charles had reassured her that the line drawn by society was not one that mattered any longer.

Westin jumped off his horse before it had a chance to stop and ran into the house screaming Camille's name. She came running down the stairs. Her foot slipped, and she fell, bouncing to the floor. Westin ran to her side. "Camille, are you all right?"

"I am, Westin. Are you all right?" She sat up on the stairs, rubbing her arm.

"I just spoke to Sabine and Charles, so now I can ask you. Camille, will you marry me? I like it a great deal when we spend time with one another. You know you make me feel funny inside when we are together, and when I told Sabine about it, she said that is how she feels about Jared, and she loves Jared. I think that I love you, Camille, and I want to know if you will marry me so we can be together forever."

Camille threw her arms around Westin's neck and hugged him. "Yes, Westin, I will marry you, and yes, I love you as well." She pulled back and kissed him on the mouth. Westin did not know what to do, so he pushed Camille away.

"What are you doing, Camille?"

"I am kissing you, Westin."

"I do not think we should do that, Camille. We are not married. Only married people do that."

"Sabine and Jared kiss."

"Sabine and Jared are getting married." He thought about that. They were getting married, and he and Camille were getting married, so he smiled. "Do that again, Camille." She kissed him, and he kissed her back. "Camille, I feel strange," he said to her when they separated. "Why do I feel like this?"

"I do not know, Westin. I am not a boy. Maybe Jared can tell you."

"I will go find him and ask him. Camille, can we get married tomorrow?"

"I will ask Charles, and we can talk when you get back from talking to Jared."

"Okay, I will be back later." Out the door he went to find Jared. Westin did not need to go far. Jared and I were on our way back to the cottage. We had spent too much time on the plain alone. It was not a good idea to do it too often.

"Jared, can we have a man talk?"

I could not help but smile. "You two go ahead. I am going to get cleaned up for the evening meal." Jared kissed me, and I went on to the stables to put Raiden up for the night. They continued on a casual walk onto the plain.

"So what can I do for you, Westin?"

"I asked Camille to marry me, and she said yes, then she kissed me. You know like you and Sabine kiss, and I felt funny. My body was doing things that I could not explain."

Jared felt himself go red. "What kinds of things, Westin?"

"Well, my mind got unclear, my heart was beating fast, and I was shaking, and a part of me started to…well, you know, right?"

Jared did his best to keep himself composed. "I do indeed know what you mean, Westin. Trust me when I tell you that it is normal. My suggestion is not to do those things with Camille until you are married. After that, I think we can continue this conversation, all right?"

"Ok, and you are sure that it is normal? I know that I am not as smart as you, Jared, but you are as close to a brother as I have right now, and I just do not think that Sabine can help me."

"I will do my best as your future brother to not let you down."

"Thank you, Jared. I asked Camille to marry me tomorrow. Do you think we can get married tomorrow?"

"Well, I do not know, Westin. I think we need to go have a chat with Charles. Do you know where he is?"

"No, I do not, but when I found him, he was with Rebecca, so maybe he is with her again. We can go look for him."

"Then let us do just that."

They found Charles in the barracks. "Charles, Camille said she would marry me, so I want to know if I can marry her tomorrow."

"Well, I do not see why you could not marry her tomorrow, Westin. Would it be all right if I married you?"

Westin laughed so hard. "Charles, you are a boy. You cannot marry me! I love Camille, and I want to marry her."

Charles smiled at him. "No, I do not mean you and I get married, Westin. I meant would you like for me to marry you and Camille?"

"You can do that?"

"Yes, I can. Would you like that?"

"Yes! That would be wonderful, Charles. Can we do it after the morning meal?"

"Of course we can." Before Charles could finish, Westin was running back to the cottage to find Camille and give her the news. "So you are clergy? This is good to know. I might need your services soon."

Charles laughed. "I am here to serve."

Westin ran into the cottage, yelling for Camille, he found her in the kitchen. "Charles said yes. We can get married tomorrow after the morning meal. Is that all right with you, Camille?"

"That is all right with me, Westin. Are you sure you want to do this?"

"Oh, I am sure. Jared said that the weird way I was feeling when we were kissing was okay, and that tomorrow he will explain it all to me after we are married. So when we are done, I am going to have to go and talk to him. Okay?"

She smiled and kissed him. "That is fine, Westin."

"I am going to find Sabine and tell her."

"Westin, Sabine is sleeping right now, so perhaps you can wait for a bit?"

"Okay, I will go wait by her door for her to wake up." He brought the chair from the end of the hall and sat right outside my door. I am not sure how long Westin sat there. I fell asleep almost instantly. It had been a very busy morning, and I really did not have a great deal of food to eat. When he heard me moving about, he knocked on my door.

"Come in," I said.

"Sabine, can I talk to you?"

"Of course, my love. What is it?"

"Camille and I are going to marry tomorrow after the morning meal. Charles said he could marry us. Is that all right? And then I have to go talk to Jared right after because he is going to explain to me why my body feels weird when Camille kisses me."

I would have to say that Westin caught me by surprise. I had no knowledge as to the male body or its functions, so for that, I would be forever grateful to Jared.

"I am glad that you feel close enough to Jared to trust him with such an important task."

"I do, Sabine. He is going to be my brother."

"He is indeed, Westin."

When Westin came into my room, he did not shut the door. I looked up, and Rebecca was in the doorway. "I understand there is going to be a marriage here tomorrow."

Westin could not contain himself. "Yes, Rebecca, there is, and it is mine and Camille's. We are going to be married." Turning to me, he asked, "Sabine, what does one wear to a marriage?"

"Well, I would imagine his best clothing."

"I am going to go to my room to look for something to wear. To look for my best clothing. I love you, Sabine."

"I love you too, Westin, with all my heart."

"Sabine, what is Camille going wear? I have a gown that I brought with me, and well, I was going to wear it when I married Edward. Do you think Camille would want to wear it? I am not going to need it now, and there is no reason why it should go to waste."

"I am sure she would love the gesture. We can go and find out." I stood, and we went to find Camille.

We found her in the kitchen and swept her upstairs to Rebecca's room. She was completely amazed at the beauty of the gown. "Oh, my lady, this is too expensive for me to wear. I have a lovely gown that I only wear for special occasions. I am fine with wearing that."

"Do not be silly, Camille. This gown is just going to sit in this trunk until it rots. So rather than do that, I want you to have it. Wear it to marry the man you love, since that is what it was made for."

"Really?" Her eyes were wide, and her smile matched them. She

put the dress on, and it was a bit big, but we managed, with the help of the ladies in the kitchen, to fit it to Camille. It was nice to just be with women, because in this valley and in this cottage, we were all the same. There were no princes or princesses, and there were no servants. We were just us; strong women.

The dark of night fell upon the valley, and we ate the evening meal with great anticipation for the coming day. My brother was about to be married; something I think my parents would have been proud of. I could not be happier for Westin. Camille was a wonderful girl, and she seemed genuine in her feelings for him. Charles had reassured me that she was. He had said that they had a talk a few days before about whether or not it was acceptable for her to love a prince. I was pleased that he reassured her that it was indeed.

After the meal, I excused myself and went to my room. When I left Whispering Wind, I had managed to hide a few of Father's trinkets that I had found in my satchel. I went to my trunk and reached in; there they were tucked in the bottom just where I put them. I climbed onto my bed, opened the satchel, and poured them out onto the white top covering. I pushed my finger through them, spreading them out. Father's collar was among these items, and that is what I wanted Westin to have. He was still the King of Whispering Wind, and he should at least, for his marriage day, look like a king. I picked up one end of it and pulled it up in the air. Other trinkets fell to the covering; a few rings, a locket, Mother's locket. I pulled it away from the collar, and I did not realize I was crying until a tear hit my hand. I remembered the day Father gave it to her. It was the day we celebrated her birth, and Father always insisted that it was the best day. His voice was as clear in my head today as it was then as he said, "If she had not been born on this day; then you would not exist, and I would not be the happiest man alive. So we need to celebrate the birth of your mother and my wife, Julia." He had given her this locket on that day many years ago.

Westin said she had it on the day he found her. It was tucked into her bodice, just as the one Jared had given me was. I reached up and took out the tiny locket and turned it over in my hand. I had not noticed the letters on it. One side had an S, and the other had a J. *Is our love the same as my parents? Is it a love that we can build a life with and a family with?* Time would tell. There was so much that we would do together, and taking down his father was one of them. *Would Jared love me when I brought his father to his knees for giving the order to slaughter my family?* I could not marry him until this is over. I had to make sure he would stand by my side for the rest of our lives, however short that may be. I tucked the locket back into my bodice, gathered up the trinkets, and put them back in the trunk. With my father's collar in hand, I made my way to Westin's room. I knocked lightly, just in case he was sleeping, but I knew better. When Westin was excited, it was very rare for him to sleep.

He opened the door with a giant smile on his face. "Sabine, what are you doing at my room? You have never come to my room. What would bring you here now?"

"I am sorry for that, Westin. May I come in? I would like to talk to you."

"Of course, Sabine. You are always welcome in my room."

I walked in and noticed that it was a nice room, very manly. I went to sit on the bed, which seemed much larger than mine. Joseph certainly did a good job preparing this cottage for us. "Come sit by me, Westin."

"Sabine, is everything all right? Are you going to tell me I cannot marry Camille?"

"Oh, no, sweetie, not at all. I just want to talk to you for minute. I have something for you."

He came over and sat next to me. "What is it, Sabine? I like when you give me things because you always give the best things."

I laughed. "Thank you, Westin, but I think you give the best gifts. Remember the sheath for my sword? That was the greatest gift."

"I worked really hard on that sheath. It took a very long time."

"I can tell, Westin. I love it, and I take it with me everywhere I go. Westin, tomorrow is an important day for you and Camille. You are, by all rights, the King of Whispering Wind now."

"Sabine, I do not want to be king. You be the king. I give the throne to you. King Sabine."

We laughed. "Westin, I am a girl. I cannot be the king."

"Well then, you can be the queen. I give the Kingdom of Whispering Wind to you, Sabine. I just want to be me and marry Camille."

"Thank you, Westin, but I still want to give you this." I pulled the collar out of the cloth I wrapped it in. "I found it after you left to go to Samuel's. It is Father's collar. I think it would look wonderful on you, and it would be nice to have something of his with you on your special day."

He put his head down, and I saw his shoulders shake. "Westin, are you all right?" I reached up to take his chin in my hand to lift his face, but instead, he threw his arms around me and gave me a huge hug. He squeezed me so hard I could not breathe. I tried to wiggle free, and he lessened his grip on me, but before I realized what was happening, he was sobbing. "Oh, Westin, what is the matter? Are you all right?"

"Oh, Sabine," he sobbed. "I miss Mother and Father so much. I wish they were not dead."

"I know, my love. I miss them as well, but I do know that they would be so happy for you and so very proud of you, especially Father. He would be proud that his son has chosen a fine woman such as Camille to marry."

"I remember the last time I saw Father wear this collar, Sabine. That is why I am crying. It was when Ardes married Jenna, and that was such a happy day. Now it is just me and you Sabine. No one else is here from our family."

"I know, Westin, but you are going to marry Camille, and she will become a part of our family, just as Charles will become part of our family because he is Camille's brother. When this mess is all over and we go home to Whispering Wind, then Jared will become a part of our family, and we will have Juliana back with us, and she is our family. So you see, Westin, we will grow a new family, and we will make Mother and Father proud of us. That is why I want you to have Father's collar. He would want you to have it."

"Thank you, Sabine. I will wear it, but I want you to keep it. You will need to wear it when we get home to Whispering Wind. You will need it, Sabine, because you will be the queen, and you will rule."

"All right, I will keep it for you. You never know. You might just change your mind and want to be the king."

"No, Sabine. I like being just me." He smiled and hugged me again.

"Are you all right then about tomorrow? Is there anything you want to ask me before you become Camille's husband?"

"I get to kiss her whenever I want, right?"

I could not help but laugh. "Yes, Westin, but only if she wants to kiss you back."

"She wants to," he said, and then in a very hushed tone he went on to say, "We kiss now all the time, but do not tell Charles. I do not want him mad at me or at Camille."

"I promise I will not tell anyone," I whispered back to him. "I love you, Westin, and I am so happy that you found love in your life."

"I love you too, Sabine, and I am happy you found Jared."

I got up and went to the door. I turned to say good night to him, and he was holding Father's collar up to the light with his very interested face on. I quietly closed the door behind me and headed to my room. Sleep was easy. When I felt the light of the day on my face, I could not help the smile that filled my face. Today was the day my big brother, the rightful King of Whispering Wind, was to wed a woman who loved him unconditionally. Even Mother and Father could not have asked for anything more. I climbed out of bed and searched for my best gown. Camille, of course, was not here to help me, but I remembered her packing it. "You might need it", she had said. I opened the trunk and started ruffling through it when there was a knock on the door.

"Come in," I said as I dug deeper. I think I must have looked pretty silly. Half of my body was inside the trunk when Camille walked in.

"My lady, what are you doing?"

"I am looking for that gown you packed when we left Wellington. Camille, where did you put it?"

"Would this be the gown, my lady?" She giggled.

I half climbed out of the trunk. "There it is. Thank you, Camille, but you do not have to do things like this for me any longer, especially today. You are going to be my sister. Today you are going to marry my brother. Why would you be taking care of me?"

"It is my station, my lady, to care for you. I would still like to continue after Westin and I are married. I like that I earn my way. I was not born of privilege. I cannot even think of doing nothing all day, so if it is all right with you, my lady, I would like to continue taking care of you."

"We will talk about it later, Camille." I smiled. "But we need to get you ready. You are getting married soon."

"Oh, I am ready, my lady."

"Camille, after today, I insist that you call me Sabine. That is my name, and you will be my sister, so if you want to continue doing what you do, then I am going to have to insist that you call me Sabine."

"Thank you my...I mean, Sabine. I do not have a sister, only brothers, so I am a bit excited about gaining a sister as well."

"I know when Jenna came to live with us, I could not have been happier. It was so nice to have a sister, another female in the house. I have three brothers, as you know. How many brothers do you have, Camille? I thought that it was just you and Charles?"

Camille giggled. "Sabine, I have seven brothers, and you know three of them."

"I know three of them? What do you mean?"

"Well, you know Charles, Joseph, and Blake. Then there is Steven, Aidan, Edward, and James. I am the youngest."

I was amazed. The look on my face must have been terribly funny because Camille started laughing.

"Joseph and Blake are your brothers?"

"Yes, Sabine, they are, and I believe that in time, you will know my other brothers as well."

"Your whole family is going to fight with us? Somehow, that does not seem fair to your parents. To risk the loss of all their sons is unacceptable. I will not allow it."

"Sabine," she said, and she looked at me as if I was a child, and her years were greater than my own. "You have met my brother, Charles, have you not?" I could only nod. I found myself mesmerized by her tone. "You know that they believe the legend. We all do. Even Jared knows that one day you will have no other choice but to end his father's life. It seems, in this instance, that you and Rebecca are the only ones who remain in the darkness of disbelief. We will all stand beside you, and if necessary we will all die for you. You will see in time, when they start to come to train. As your army grows, so does your power. You are the bringer of peace."

Her words hung in the air as a thick smoke. Everything that Charles had tried to make me believe had always been believed. This girl standing before me had more conviction in her words than anything I had ever done in my life. I felt humble and small in comparison. I raised my eyes to meet hers, and the eyes that met mine were smiling.

"I am going to marry the man I love today, so let us get you dressed."

I was shocked at her casualness concerning all of what she had just said. I smiled back at her.

"You are right, Camille, but I think Rebecca and I should be helping you today, not the other way around."

Just then, a winded Rebecca burst through the door. "There you are, Camille. I thought you might have run off."

We all laughed. "I am not going anywhere, except down to the field to marry Westin."

"Well then, let us get you ready, shall we?"

We went back to Camille's room, and by the time Rebecca and I were finished with her, she had been transformed into a Lady of the Manor, which in truth, she should have looked like a queen. I wondered if Camille realized that after today, she would actually be the Queen of Whispering Wind. It felt good to know that those things were not important to her, that she was marrying Westin because she loved him and not because it was her station in life to do so.

It was the look on Westin's face that made everything bad in our life disappear. He cried when he saw how beautiful Camille was. The ceremony was simple and lovely. Charles was marrying his little sister to the King of Whispering Wind. He beamed with joy at his sister and her chosen mate, just as we all did. They kissed one another when it was over, and Westin turned to me and Jared and said, "Sabine, you and Jared can get married too, as long as we are all here."

I did not know what to say to him. Jared was the one who spoke for us. "Westin, I would love nothing more than to marry Sabine, but we have a great task set before us, and we both think it would be best to deal with that before we commit ourselves to wed."

"Thank you, Jared," I said to him and walked up to Westin. "My sweet Westin, thank you for wanting to share this day with me and Jared, but this is your day, yours and Camille's. This is the day we celebrate your love for one another. Jared and I will have our day. I love you, and I am so happy to have Camille as my sister." I kissed him on the cheek, turned, and said to everyone present, "I present to you Westin and Camille of Whispering Wind."

All in attendance cheered. We made our way back to the cottage where there was a feast waiting for us. It was a good day; we laughed, we sang, we danced, and most of all, we shared love. There were no boundaries of stations. We were all one.

CHAPTER TWENTY

The light of the day came quick. Today was the beginning of our training. Rebecca did not have a great deal of combat training. She knew how to wield her sword, but not in a real fight. Today Charles, Jared, and a few other guards would offer us some real fighting experience. I got up and put on my boy clothes and made my way down to have my morning meal. As usual, everyone was there waiting on me. Jared smiled as he rose to pull out my chair. "On time as usual, my lady," he said as he pushed my chair in for me.

"I am on time. You are just early."

We all laughed, and then the topic of discussion was our training for the day. Charles had six guards plus him and Jared. Rebecca's eyes were huge with anticipation and excitement. She was going to have a good time, I could tell. It seemed that all of her disdain about killing Edward had left her, and her focus now was to end this and get back home. I could not help but notice the glances between her and Charles. I made a mental note to inquire about that later when we had some time to ourselves.

Neither Westin nor Camille were present this morning. I was sure they were still in bed, discovering things about one another. I really envied them. One day, Jared and I would know the love and the passion they shared.

The days that passed were full of training. None of us had any time to do much more. Joseph had returned with many more troops, as did Blake. I met the rest of Camille's brothers and many more. There were workers all over, building new barracks and adding onto the stables. There were more workers in the fields, and more help in the kitchen. It seemed as if we were building a village right here in our valley, and the cottage just, like a castle, became the center. Day after day, time flew by. The days turned into months, and the cold season was upon us. We moved our training into the stables for warmth. Rebecca and I could just about best all the guards in both swords and hand to hand combat.

It was Jared and Charles we could not take down. It was determined that when we could best them in both swords and hand to hand combat, we would then make our plans to move our little army across the lands to look for the barbarians that slaughtered my family.

By the time the cold months had passed and the season of the blossoms was upon us, a wonderful announcement came along with the newness of the ground. A new baby was coming to Westin and Camille, which was the best news anyone could have. My heart was so full. There was just one thing that tugged at me, and that was Juliana. She would be coming to the beginning of her third year. She needed to be found. I needed to have her with me, for Jenna and Ardes. She needed to be safe at home.

It was a beautiful day. The sun was high in the sky, the flowers were beginning to bloom, and the wind was warm on our faces when I did what I thought was the impossible. I bested Charles in both swords and hand to hand combat. It was a few days later that Rebecca did the same. There was only Jared left for us to beat. It took a few weeks to best him, but in the end, we did. Rebecca and I were now an unstoppable force.

Our little army had grown immensely. There were close to four hundred of us, and it was amazing to see our little valley now from the top of the hills that surrounded it. Everyone was training and waiting for Charles to say it was time to go. I think secretly that he wanted to wait for the birth of Camille's baby, but that would not be until the cold season returned, and we could not march in the cold season.

At our evening meal, Charles asked us all to meet in the main barracks the next morning. It was time to make our plans.

I wandered out into the dark of night when we finished our meal to look at the stars in our serene little valley. It was such a peaceful place, and I was concerned that I would have to leave there one day soon, probably not to ever return. I wanted with all my heart to rebuild Whispering Wind and live out my days with Jared and Juliana. Deep down inside, I feared that it would not happen as such. There was a very real possibility that I would not return at all. Jared walked up behind me and wrapped his arms around my waist. He could feel the tension in my body.

"Do not worry, my love. All will work itself out. We will return, and we will bring Juliana home."

"It is what is in my heart, Jared, but I have to think of the worst. I have to think that I am not going to return here or to Whispering Wind, that I may never see my brother again. I am just so happy for him that he has Camille and now a baby on the way. His life will be rich. He will miss me, but I trust that he will be safe here in our valley, and I know that he will live his life out as my parents would want him to."

"We will survive this, Sabine, and we will marry, and we will raise Juliana alongside our own children. I love you, and I do not believe that we will be separated in this life." I turned in his arms and kissed him. Tomorrow would determine the course of our lives.

The light of the day came quick; I do not think I slept. There was so much going on in my head. My future was blank. Nothing was in it but blood and death. It seemed that since my family had been murdered and our kingdom slaughtered, that was all my life had known. I had kings looking for me to put me to death, barbarians looking for me to put me to death, and I was about to go to a meeting that would ultimately send me out into their midst to put them to death, or to at least try.

I took my time getting dressed and making my way down to the dining table. There was a strange energy in the room. It felt as if everyone was sitting on pins. I could not bring myself to feel excitement at the possibility of dying. Rebecca was beside herself with excitement. She was such a sphere of energy anyway, so this had her sitting on the edge of her seat. Jared just sat next to me and held my hand, looking at me. Westin and Camille, as always, just stared at one another smiling. It was all so surreal. Our meal ended, and Charles was the first to rise from his chair.

"I will see you all in the barracks?"

We all agreed, and once he had left, Rebecca turned to me. "Sabine, I am worried about you."

"Why would you worry about me?"

"Well, you seem a bit distracted, and we need to be in the right frame of mind. We need to be ready for this. If you are not ready, then we must delay our departure. If you are not ready, Sabine, we shall fail."

I smiled at my friend and said, "I am ready. I guess I have just become comfortable here, and the thought that we may not come home has me a bit thwarted. But I assure you, I am ready. This mood will pass. I have no choice but to be ready. I want...no, I need to avenge my family, and I will find Juliana, and I will take back Whispering Wind."

"That is the girl I know and love. Come on. Let us go hear what plans Charles has for our departure." She reached out and took my hand.

As I left the room, I looked back at my brother. He looked at me with love and sadness in his eyes, but beyond that, I saw nothing but happiness. That is what I would drive myself with; giving Westin the opportunity to have happiness for the rest of his life.

We made our way to the barracks. There were so many men. We made our way into the building as men moved to make a path. The windows were all open, and I could see nothing but eager faces; faces of sons, fathers and brothers of those who would be left behind. Charles had waited for us to arrive before he began to speak.

"Well, it seems as if the time has come for us to make our plans, to make our move on those who destroyed Whispering Wind and who seek to destroy and put to death Sabine and Rebecca. We all know the legend, and we all know our part in it. Although our army is small, we have the power within these two ladies to take on armies much greater than our own. I think that in six days' time, we should be ready to begin our journey to find the barbarians and bring back the children of Whispering Wind that were stolen. Yesterday, I put most of you into groups of ten men each. I have your tasks for the upcoming departure. We have plenty to do in the next six days, and on the seventh day, we will leave at the break of the light of the day."

"Charles, may I say something please?"

"Of course, Sabine."

I stood and walked to the front of the room. "I am Sabine, for those of you whom I have not met. I just want to say thank you all for giving up your lives, for leaving your families, and for willingly marching into battle with me. I know that you are all aware of what happened to my family, and I have no right to expect any of you to die for me in the days to come."

A man stood and interrupted me, "My lady, if I may speak? We are doing what we are doing not only for you, but for ourselves. We cannot live in kingdoms run by tyrants who do not care about us, and we will not be ruled by kings who would plot to destroy others for power. It has been told to us by our fathers the peace you will bring, and that is what we are willing to die for. Peace."

"Thank you for that. I just wanted to say thank you to all of you, and I will never be able to repay any of you for all you have done and all you are about to give to me."

It was like no sound I ever heard before, but every single man shouted at the same time, "Long live the bringers of Peace!" It was very overwhelming.

Charles led the way to the stables where Raiden and the other horses were ready and waiting. It was good to see him, and it would be even better to ride him. He had not gotten much exercise over the previous months with all our training, so it would be good to ride again. I climbed up on top of him, leaned in, and said, "Good to you see you, old boy." He reared his head up and down and stomped on the ground. "Are you ready for some training?" He stomped again. He walked us out into the sunshine where Rebecca and Spirit were waiting.

"You up for a run. Sabine?"

"You are on!" I kicked Raiden in the sides. Like a gust of wind, we were flying out of the grounds that surrounded the stable and barracks, past the cottage, and out onto the plain. It felt so good to just hang on and let him carry me away from everything. Spirit held his own against Raiden, but Raiden would not let him get even a nose ahead of him. We were free, and we were together. The horses made their arch across the plain and headed back to the cottage. Charles, Jared, and about a hundred men were riding hard toward us, so Raiden and Spirit slowed when we got closer to them.

"All right, ladies, feel like some lightning?" Charles said with a huge smile on his face.

We could not help but smile. Although we had been trained in swords and hand to hand combat, we had not tried the reign of lightning that our swords and horses produced. It was a onetime thing months ago when the barbarians came into the valley. Neither Rebecca nor I knew how to harness the power. We turned our horses so we were in front of the men. I looked over at her and smiled, saying, "You ready for this?"

Her eyes were wild, and her smile was bigger than all the times before. Rebecca said, "Oh, you know I am!"

We drew our swords and raised them high above our heads, while Raiden and Spirit reared up on their hind legs. Lightning flew across the land, burning everything in its path. When the horses landed on the ground, we looked at one another and smiled.

"Well, I guess that is how it works then," Charles chuckled.

We turned to face them. Besides Charles and Jared, the rest of the men were literally stunned. The laughter could not be contained within us. Rebecca and I laughed hard. I could not resist saying, "Now, who wants to fight?" All of them shook their heads with obvious fear in their eyes. It was time, and I knew then that I was ready to fulfill this legend or die trying. As long as Rebecca was at my side, we were indeed unstoppable.

On the morning of the sixth day, I made it a point to seek out Westin, and of course, I found him with Camille. "Westin, would you come for a ride with me today? I would like to spend some time with you before we leave in the morning."

"I would love to go riding with you, Sabine. Camille, is it all right if I leave you for the day?"

"Of course, Westin. I was going to ask you if you would mind if I spent some time with my brothers before they left."

He kissed her good bye, and we went out to the stables to get our horses. We did not ride hard, but just walked through the plain until we got to the caves where Blake had buried the jewels.

"Westin, I wanted you to come here with me today because I wanted to say goodbye to you, just in case..."

He interrupted me, "Sabine, do not be silly. You are coming home, and you are bringing Juliana with you. I am not worried, just scared that you will not be here when my baby comes into the world."

"Westin, there is a real chance that we will not make it back here, I like your positive attitude, but there is something else. Remember when I sent you to Samuel to get help when we went back to Whispering Wind?" He nodded. "Well, while you were gone, I was going through the house and taking things that were of value. I hid them in the caves behind the hedge at the back of the castle. Do you remember, we use to play there as children?" A smile crossed his face, and he nodded. "Well, while I was putting Mother's things back in her trunk, I discovered a false bottom in the trunk. Inside it were jewels, hundreds and hundreds of jewels."

"Like the ones you gave Samuel?"

"Exactly like the ones I gave Samuel, only in Mother's trunk, there were many, many more than what I found in Jenna's trunk. I did not tell Samuel about those, but I hid them in the cave. When we came here, I asked Blake to go and get them. Do you remember bringing me to these caves when we got here?"

"I do. This is one of my favorite places, Sabine, and no one knows they are here."

"Yes, I know, Westin. That is why I brought you here. I need to tell you something, and I need for you to give me your word that you will listen to me and follow my instructions."

I knew Westin, and I knew he could not pass up a good intrigue. He smiled again and nodded in compliance.

"I am leaving in the morning, and I do not know when I shall return. Charles is leaving some men here to look after you and Camille and to protect you. No one knows of these caves except me, you, and Blake. Westin, if anyone comes here, if the barbarians come here, you are to bring Camille here to hide. If the baby comes and you are ever in danger, you are to come here with them. You stay here until it is safe to leave. You are a smart man, Westin. You saved me from being murdered along with our family, and I know you can and will do the same for Camille and your baby. When it is safe to come out of the caves, you must leave here and never come back."

"But, Sabine, what if when you come back, we are not here? How will you find me?"

"Westin, I need to tell you something." I leaned in and whispered to him, "I think Raiden is magic." Raiden snorted and stomped his hoof into the ground. "I really believe, Westin, that Raiden would be able to find you."

"Wow, Sabine! Father's horse is magic? That is unbelievable!"

"I know it is, but there is so much more I need for you to know. Now, inside this cave are all the jewels I found in Mother's trunk. They are buried in the ground, so you will need to dig them up. I had Blake bring some supplies here that you would need if you had to run from here. There are tools and blankets, all the things you would need. You are to dig up the jewels so that you can trade them for things when you find a new place to live. You must never tell anyone that you have more than you do. There are some not nice people out in the world, Westin, and I do not want someone to hurt you just to take the jewels from you. Do not go back toward Whispering Wind or Wellington. You and Camille must go in the other direction. You will go East and follow the rising sun. Do you understand?"

I looked up at him, and he was crying. "Westin, what is wrong?"

He threw his arms around me, crying, "Oh, Sabine, I cannot think about you not coming home."

"Westin, this is not only about me not ever coming back. While we are away, there is a good chance that Samuel or Rebecca's father will try to find you and take you prisoner so they could stop me. They know that I would never put you in danger, so they will know that I left you behind. Do you understand?" He nodded. "Now, promise me, Westin. Promise me that you will not stay here if danger comes."

"I promise, Sabine, but you must promise me that if we have to leave this valley, and you do not die and you return home, you will come with your magic horse, Raiden, and find us."

"With all that I am, Westin, I promise. I love you so much it hurts me to leave you, but I trust Charles, and he assured me that you will be safe here."

"I love you too, Sabine, for you are my only sister and Queen of Whispering Wind. You need to come home, so we can go back home to Whispering Wind. I want my baby to grow up where we did, to play in the forests and run through the village like we used to when we were little."

My whole body was full of love for this man before me, my older brother, whose mind was that of an older child. He was so innocent and beautiful. My only hope was that he survived this, intact with his wife and child.

We took our time making our way back to the cottage as we talked about our parents and our brothers. We remembered all that we could about our life before Samuel. We spent the majority of the day together remembering. I wanted Westin to have all the fresh memories of our life together in his mind before I, his last surviving family, left him alone in a valley six days ride from his home. When we got back to the cottage, it was time for our last evening meal together. When it came time to say goodnight, I could not stop hugging him and Camille. The tears flowed from my eyes uncontrollably. I would miss them both. We all walked upstairs together, and I walked them to their room.

"Goodnight, Westin. I love you. Goodnight, Camille. I love you."

"I love you too, Sabine," they said together and then laughed. I walked to my room alone and sad. This would be the last night that I slept in this beautiful cottage. This would be the last time I would be with my family. So much had happened in the two years since my family had been slaughtered, so much that it was hard to believe. How did one's life turn out this way? I walked into my room, shut the door, and leaned my head against it while I cried. The arms that wrapped around me were familiar. I spun in them, and they embraced me. Jared held me while I cried, never saying a word. When my tears stopped, only then did he speak. "I think that you need me tonight. I know I need you. We are about to embark on a journey that both excites me and terrifies me. If it is with your permission, I wish to stay with you tonight."

"Thank you," is all I could say.

Jared waited for me to change into my sleeping gown and to crawl into the bed. He walked over and blew out the candle as he trailed his fingers down my cheek. He slowly moved around the bed to the other side where he removed his clothing, leaving him in his undergarments. Pulling back the covers, he slid into the huge bed next to me, wrapping his arms around me, and settled in for the night. I do not think in my whole life that I ever slept more soundly. We never moved; we just held one another. It was what we both needed, to feel the love we shared and to just feel safe and at peace. When the light of the day was just breaking through the dark of the night, he whispered in my ear, "My beautiful Sabine, it is time to arise."

I could not help but smile. That was the voice I wanted to hear every morning for the rest of my life. "I do not want to rise and go off to war today, Jared. Can we just stay in bed and go another day?"

His laughter was soft, and his breath warm on my face. My eyes fluttered open to see his beautiful face so close to my own. His mouth covered mine, and his embrace was not one I had ever felt before. I could sense my body stirring in an emotion I did not know. Our breathing became deep as did the kiss. When he finished with me, he pulled away and whispered, "I love only you until the day I die."

"I love only you," was all I could get out.

He trailed his fingertips along my face to my lips, and then he kissed me again. I would have done anything to have it never stop, but it did. This was the day. It was the end of this beautiful life I had in this magical valley.

We got out of bed and dressed. As Jared quietly left my room, he turned and said, "No matter what lies ahead of us, Sabine, I love only you," and he closed the door quietly.

I sat on my bed, thinking about the last two years; about how I felt when I walked into the village at Whispering Wind, how it felt to see my family's blood on the floors of my childhood home, the fear I felt when I saw Juliana's cot covered in blood, Jenna's blood, and the holes in the great gate that had held my father's dying body. Samuel would pay for all he had done to me, and I knew it would be at Jared's expense. I believed he knew what would come in the end. I could only hope that he would forgive me for ending his father's life.

The voices outside brought me back to the reality of what was about to take place. Horses, wagons, guards... everything was coming together. It was time to get moving. I grabbed my things, my sword, and turned to look at my room. "Goodbye room," I said and left.

Downstairs, everyone was waiting for me at the table as usual. We had a good morning meal, went over some early plans, said our good-byes, and went out to the front of the cottage. I was taken aback by the amount of men that spanned out onto the plain; hundreds of men and wagons, more than I had imagined. Raiden was there looking at me. I think he sensed my nervousness. He made his way up to me and put his head down so he could look me in the eyes. "Hey, boy," I said as I reached up to rub his nose. "You ready for this?"

He stomped his hoof on the ground and snorted. I swear he was smiling as he nodded his head up and down. I heard Jared laugh, and looked up at him.

"I swear it, that horse is human," he chuckled.

We all had a giggle. I turned to find Westin and Camille standing behind me. I reached out and grabbed him, and hugging him tightly, I said. "I love you so much, Westin. You take care of Camille, and I promise you that I will do my best to come back. Remember what I told you yesterday?"

"Yes, Sabine, I remember. I love you too, and do not fret, sister. You will return to us, and you will be here in time for the baby to come. I can feel it. Now, go so you can hurry home."

I kissed him on the cheek, hugged Camille, and told them I loved them a few more times. I climbed up on Raiden, and before I knew what was happening, I turned to look at the cottage and Westin behind me. They seemed so far away.

Charles had sent guards ahead of us; five teams of twenty-five in five different directions. Every few hours, men would come to check in and give reports. So far, there were no sightings of the barbarians. It seemed that, as we gained closer ground to villages, others would join us. Days and days passed with no word of barbarians. We had traveled past Edward's father's kingdom, Collingwood. We had passed Rebecca's kingdom, Blackmore, and we had passed Wellington. We were less than a half of a day's ride from Whispering Wind, when Charles thought it best we stop for the day so we could be fresh for the morning. We made camp close to where Westin had brought me on that day.

The dark of night was upon us when I went in search of Charles. I found him standing guard. "May I sit with you a while?"

"Of course, Sabine. Is everything all right?"

"I am not sure. I am scared, Charles. I do not know what to expect tomorrow."

We heard horses coming. "Well, I will tell you shortly, Sabine, what we are to expect." Just then, three men rode up on horses; Blake, Joseph, and Steven. Of course Charles would trust none but his own brothers.

"There are at least two, maybe three hundred barbarians in Whispering Wind, Charles," Joseph started, "And there are numerous bands scattered throughout the land. All the scouts have not returned yet, so we do not know exactly how many."

"I was hoping there would not be anyone at Whispering Wind," I heard myself say.

Charles turned to look at me. "I was expecting this. Samuel knows what he is doing, Sabine, and he knows you are coming for him. If we attack Whispering Wind, there is no doubt that the other bands of barbarians are strategically placed to reinforce."

"Has anyone reported any children? We need to be careful how we attack, Charles. We cannot harm any children. Those children are the children of the villagers that were slaughtered with my family, and then there is Juliana."

"So far, from the information we have, there has been no sign of the children, Sabine," Blake said concerned.

"They could have them at Whispering Wind someplace. I had not realized how big and complex the grounds were. They could be anywhere. I will have a few men work their way into the castle tonight and see if they can find them or hear something concerning them. Charles, should we wait until we find the children?" Joseph was looking at me as he spoke.

"My concern with that plan, Joseph, is that we will be found here, and that would eliminate our element of surprise. We take Whispering Wind in the morning. I think we would stand a better chance defending it against the bands of barbarians scattered throughout the country side. My guess would be that the castle is their stronghold, and that is where the children are most likely to be. We will have to make sure we stop any scouts from leaving the castle. Steven, you, Aidan, and Edward will go to Whispering Wind now and get as much information as you can. Report back here as soon as you hear something or just before dawn. Sabine, you need to get some sleep. We have a big day tomorrow."

He smiled at me. I had been dismissed, yet I did not argue with him. I felt comfortable with him telling me what to do. I smiled back and did as I was told. I wandered back to my sleeping tent that I shared with Rebecca. She was lying on her back, looking up at me.

"Sabine, I have been thinking. Do you think we could not kill my father?"

"Rebecca, I have no intention on killing your father or Jared's. My fear is that they will not leave us a choice. They plotted together along with Edwards's father to slaughter me and my family. How could I not want revenge? Samuel has not stopped trying to murder me. I cannot live like this, always looking over my shoulder, and neither can you. You are as much of this legend as I am, Rebecca. Without you, there is nothing. I will understand if you do not want to do this with us. I will fight on my own. I must avenge my family, however. Please understand that, if it comes to your father or me, I must apologize now for killing him."

"I understand how you feel, and no, I do not want to leave you. I have never had a friend such as you, and I fear that I will never have one again. We are in this together. Those barbarians on that plain wanted me dead just as much as they wanted you dead. I am just finding it hard to believe that my father had ordered my death. I do not think I can be the one to end his life, nor do I believe I can watch as you do. I am, however, going to have to ask him why before he dies, so perhaps I should just close my eyes when you strike him down."

I could not help but giggle. "Rebecca, I am not going to kill your father intentionally. If he fights, which I think he will, he will die with honor."

"Well, I could live with that."

"Good. So can I. Now we need to sleep. The light of the day will be upon us soon." I reached over and squeezed her hand.

Sleep was not something that came easily for me that night. Thoughts of the new day were flooding my mind. It could all go wrong. We were going for the element of surprise. *What if we were the ones that were going to be surprised? And Jared... Could I live if he did not? Could I live if anyone did not?* I was thinking too much. I knew I must sleep. I tried to focus on the last night at the cottage, the night I slept in Jared's arms for the first time. It was with hope that I would live to sleep in his arms again. I must have fallen asleep because Charles woke me.

"I am sorry to wake you, Sabine, but I have news from our scouts."

"It is fine, Charles. Please tell me what you know."

"Well, the children are nowhere to be seen. There has been no talk of them at the castle, and we still have scouts that have not returned."

"They have to be someplace. We need to find them. The children are out there somewhere. Charles, are we great enough in our numbers to do this?" I was terrified of his answer but I was willing to lose my life in this vendetta.

"Sabine, you have seen the power you and Rebecca hold. My fear is that we will have nothing to do but clean up all the dead." He smiled. "It is time to prepare. We should wake the others."

I woke Rebecca, and we dressed and headed out for a meal. I could see Jared across the way, and his warm smile warmed my heart. The look in his eyes sent fear coursing through my body. I rushed passed the others and right into his arms. As we embraced, I whispered in his ear, "What is wrong?"

"Nothing is wrong my love," he whispered back. "I am just fearful that this may be our last day together."

"I know. I did not sleep myself. I love only you."

"I love only you," he whispered, and then kissed me. It was the first time he had ever kissed me in front of people before, but I did not care what anyone thought. This day could have been the last day for all of us. It was Charles who cleared his throat, which was followed with laughter and cheers by the men who could see us. I was a bit flush in the face. We parted and joined the group around the food. We ate and went over the plan. Everything was to stay here, and we would go in groups. Rebecca and I walked away from the others while they finalized the plan.

"You all right?" Rebecca asked. "I think I am. How about you?" It was the look in her eyes that told the truth. "You know I am. Are you not excited?"

"I think I am more terrified than I am anything."

Her laughter was sort of evil. "You do know what we can do together, right? You were there on that plain in the valley, were you not? Sabine, they cannot touch us, and even if they get close, Raiden and Spirit will out run them all."

"Yes, but Rebecca, we cannot out run them forever."

"Sabine, you worry too much. Come on. Let us go get your family home back, and after that, we shall go and find Juliana. When we finish with all those barbarians, we will go put a stop to Wellington and Blackmore together. I was thinking last night, and you are right. My father needs to answer for his actions, and I know him. He will fight for his honor, so let us go fight for the honor that was taken from your family." She reached out and took my hand. "Together, we are invincible. Together we are the bringers of peace, so let us go and bring the peace."

I looked at her, and I could not help but smile. "Let us go then." We walked over to Raiden and Spirit, and I reached up to run my hand along Raiden's neck. "You ready for this, boy?" He nodded his head. "I am glad you are. To be honest, I am terrified." If I did not know better, I would swear he smiled at me. I just shook my head and chuckled. I put his saddle on and climbed up. We walked over to where the rest of the men were mounting their horses.

Charles came up to us. "Are you ready?"

"As ready as I will ever be," I said as I smiled.

We moved out, taking our time. The light of the day was breaking, and the sky was the color of the soft pink flowers in Katherine's garden. The dark of night still clung to the sky behind us. The closer we came to the hill, in which Westin and I had ridden up, the deeper the color pink became in the sky. It was almost blood red by the time we reached the top, and I thought it fitting considering what was about to take place. It was with hope that it was not our blood that ran that day.

CHAPTER TWENTY ONE

I could imagine how we looked, Rebecca and I in the middle, with Jared to my left, then Joseph, Steven, and James. To Rebecca's right were Charles, Blake, Edward, and Aidan, and the rest of our troops were behind us and out of sight. We probably looked like we were just waiting for them to come and kill us.

Looking down at Whispering Wind, we could see the smoke from the fires in the village and in the courtyard of the castle. I wondered how many were down there and how many of them we could kill before they killed us.

My eyes swept the expanse that lay before me; the expanse that once was a thriving village, a happy childhood I had there. Now, it was tainted with the blood of its people, the blood of my family. I think Jared sensed my apprehension, and he reached over and took my hand in his.

"I am going to marry you when this is over."

"And I you," I said.

"I love only you, Sabine. You own my heart."

Just then, a horn blared through the silent dead air. I did not think I had ever heard a more eerie sound. I think it was the realization that those could very well be my last moments of life. I looked across to

Charles, and he had a small smile on his face. I did not know why he would be smiling.

"Are you ready, ladies? We are about to see if this legend is truth or not."

"You are about to be dazzled, my friend," Rebecca said.

We just sat there on the hill, no one moving, and no one advancing forward. "Are we just going to sit here?"

"Sabine, we need to let them come to us. I am not sure if your power works while you are in full gallop. I think it has something to do with the way Raiden and Spirit rear up."

Thinking about it, I realized he was probably right. It was hard to rear a horse in full gallop. I was feeling a bit foolish, sitting there on a hill, waiting for death to come to me. Raiden felt my tension and neighed at me. I swear, he could read my thoughts.

It was obvious that the movement, in what used to be the village of our kingdom, was the barbarians preparing to come and kill us. You could not see into the castle grounds, but I was sure that there was plenty of excitement there as well. I let out a little nervous chuckle. When I looked up, everyone was staring at me.

"I was just thinking about what was running through their heads."

"Yes, I can imagine that myself, Sabine." Charles said, "But I would not think of it as funny."

"Well, Charles, that is the difference between you and me. I can see the humor in the very possible reality that we are all going to die here on this hill today."

"Sabine," Rebecca laughed, "we are not going to die today." She slapped me on the shoulder. "We are invincible, remember? Bringers of peace and all."

"I can also imagine what they are saying to one another, wondering how stupid we are to come without an army to fight with us. I suppose they will be surprised when they get closer, now, won't they!" I said.

"More than you know, sister. More than you know," she replied, and we laughed.

Jared and Charles just sat there looking at us. If I had not known better myself, I would have thought we had lost our minds and were on the brink of going mad. I looked out over the village. The horses were coming, and there were a lot of them. You could see the dust stirring in the air as they moved.

"Here we go," Jared whispered as his hand tightened around mine.

We sat there watching and waiting. They were coming ten in the front line. As we stood there, we could see that these ten were farther ahead of the rest. They rode half way up the hill while the others waited. We slowly edged toward them. As we drew closer, I saw that the leader of this group was in fact a woman. She spoke in a hard, nasty voice.

"Who are you, and what do you want? You are on the lands of The Pantheons. You will not live to see the dark of the night."

I could not help it. The laughter came out of nowhere. I had no intention on speaking, as I had planned to let Charles be the speaker, but when she said these were her lands, I could not stop it. The sound of my laugh shocked everyone who was within earshot. The woman scowled at me, as did Charles and Jared. Rebecca, however, had a huge smile on her face. She loved this stuff.

I finally managed to get control and the words flew out of my mouth just like the laughter, "You are wrong. These are not your lands. They belong to me, and I am here to take them back!"

The woman laughed, but it was not a real laugh. Her laugh had a trace of fear in it. She said, "I believe these lands were abandoned. No one was here when we arrived, so they now belong to Pantheon."

"See, that is where you are mistaken," I said. "You and your band of barbarian fiends slaughtered those who lived and worked in this land, along with its king, my father, so this land rightfully belongs to me. I can tell by the looks on your faces that you know I speak the truth."

Laughter came from all of them this time. "You will die here today, you and your little merry band of horseman," the woman said.

Rebecca and I drew our swords. "The only ones that will be dying today, my lady, are you and your little alliance of murdering thieves." Rebecca's eyes were wide, and her smile was even wider. The band of ten started to back up as the woman turned completely around and was moving faster than the others. No one on our line, other than Rebecca and me, moved or drew their swords. We just sat there. When they were far enough away so that I was sure they could not hear me, I whispered to Charles, "How far do you think this power we have, reaches?"

"I do not know, Sabine," he replied as he laughed. "Perhaps you should give it a try."

I looked at Rebecca, and I knew she was ready. "I love only you Jared," I said, never looking away from Rebecca. We raised our arms high above our heads, and then Raiden and Spirit neighed at one another, and up they went. The light was intense, and it seemed to last as long as they were reared up. When they landed, the light ended, and the ground was in flames just along the front line of barbarians. Their horses were jumping to get away from them.

"Well, I guess that answers your question, Sabine." Charles stated.

Rebecca and I nodded together, as if we were one mind, one entity. We started walking forward. I turned to face Charles and said, "Stay here." He nodded. The closer we got to the flames, the less they became. The woman on her horse was standing on our side of the flames.

"You have a choice. Either leave and give me back what rightfully belongs to me, along with all the children you stole from my kingdom, or die. The choice is yours, but you will not win. You will not beat us, and I can see it in your eyes that you know this to be the truth. You know who I am, and you know the legend is truth. I will give you until the light of the day comes again to decide, but you will not defeat me. You will not defeat us."

"I do not need until the light of the day comes again. I give you my decision now. We will not back down, and what you say is a lie. We know not of any legend, and you have no claim on this land. It was given to us by Wellington. You forfeited this land when you stole the heir to Wellington." She nodded toward Jared. "In exchange, we are to annihilate you and your mere merry band of fighters."

I could feel the thunder of our troops coming up the hill, and then

I saw their faces. "I suppose our merry little band of soldiers is more than you anticipated."

"You will die here, Princess, and so will the heir to Wellington. It is with his father's blessing that we end this now."

Rebecca raised her sword in the air. "If you insist," she said. I followed, Raiden and Spirit did their thing, and the light that ensued engulfed the barbarians behind this mysterious woman. When it was done, all that stood behind her were dead. The woman turned on her horse, looking at the death behind her.

Jared and the rest had come up behind us. "Wellington has made a deal with you knowing you will die, and with hopes that at least you kill me before you do. I am sorry to tell you, my lady that Wellington will pay." Jared smiled at her.

"You would defy your own king, and then you would kill your own father? I can understand why Wellington wants you both dead!" she hissed.

"You are wrong. You will be the only one dying today. I want my kingdom back, and you will give it to me along with the children." I was losing my patience.

As we shared words with this mysterious woman, more barbarians had ridden up, and from the plums of dust in the horizon and the faint sound of thunder, I knew more were coming. I was scared and excited. Perhaps the end would be here. I would finally get Juliana back, and I could send for Westin. As the first group of barbarians arrived, they were both shocked and outraged at the deaths that lay before them. I could see the murderous thoughts in their eyes. They believed they would win. I believed they would win, but the fact that Rebecca and I just killed a hundred or more barbarians was right in front of my face.

"Do you choose to stand and fight this day, or do you choose to yield and retreat?" I asked.

"I will not be delivered ultimatums, for you are but a mere child. You can do me no harm."

Rebecca was the one that spoke, well, she laughed first. "Listen to me, you, old woman. You have nothing but this rabble to stand with you, for we have truth and honor on our side. Our youth has more of an advantage than you have on your side. You are nothing but a bunch of ruthless murderers, and you will die today!"

Charles, Jared, Blake, Joseph, Steven, James, Aidan, and Edward moved into position in front of us. Raiden and Spirit complied with the movement and proceeded to back us up into the troops behind us.

"What's the matter, little girls? You afraid you are going to get hurt?"

Charles laughed. "With all strategic moves, protecting your assets are the best laid plans. Our little girls will be protected with our lives, and you will not harm them today or any other day. This is your last chance to leave this place alive, to live to tell the story of truth concerning the legend of the bringers of peace. Before you they stand, and they will stand after you. Today is the day of the stories our father's and their father's before them have told us as children. You know the stories. You lived throughout the reign of Sabine's father. Now, show your kindness, return our children, and leave Whispering Wind never to return."

The mysterious woman sat on her horse while the hundreds and hundreds of barbarians rode in behind her; all looking, trying to get a glance at the dead. "You are a foolish man, Charles, if you believe this rubbish of legends, you and you brothers." She nodded at them. "It will be a shame to kill such great warriors, but a pleasure all the same. Your kind has been nothing but a pain in my side, with killing my men and threatening me."

Rebecca and I were five soldiers back. "You ready to do this?" she whispered to me.

"I am as ready as I will ever be. Let us take the back row first. Raiden, can you get the back line of barbarians?"

He neighed, we raised our arms, and Raiden and Spirit reared up. The light came again. Men were screaming in terror, and the flash was brilliant. We came down, and it stopped. I could hear Charles saying, "As you can see, my lady, there will be only your death today. You cannot win."

A man rode up to her. "We cannot fight this trickery. She is a witch. They both are. The legend of Merlin is truth, and we cannot win against this."

She slapped him. "We can win, and we will win! All of you fools just need to find your courage. Kill them!"

"We will not fight against this magic. We will all die."

"You are right. You will die," she said as she drew her sword and struck him down. "Anyone else want to turn and run?" No one moved. "Now, raise your swords and fight!" She spun around on her horse, raised her sword, and swung it at Jared. He was faster than her, and the fight began. I heard Charles yell, "Protect them with your lives!" Men were everywhere around us, moving us further back into the troops.

"Now, Rebecca!" I yelled.

With our arms in the air, Raiden and Spirit reared up. The light was brighter than I had ever seen it, and the screams were loud. Our men fought, and her men died where they stood. Our horses stood high on their hind legs, and the light only intensified. The smell of burning flesh reminded me of the days when Jared and I burned the bodies of the villagers. Raiden dropped first, then Spirit, and then I noticed the silence. We pushed our way through the troops. A few of them tried to stop us, but we pushed on anyway. After we made it up to Charles, the sight before him was pure devastation. Hundreds of men and horses lay dead. The only one left standing was the mysterious woman.

"I am Sabine of Whispering Wind, this is my kingdom, and you will yield." I could not help myself. I felt braver than I had that day in the courtyard when I jumped Jared. I was scared to death, but I knew nothing was going to happen to us; not now, not ever.

The woman was angry, and that anger came out in her words, "I will never yield to the likes of you, little girl, for I am Devious the great barbarian, daughter of Kelvin, and granddaughter of Kracken. You will not destroy me or my army. We are great. The dead that lay before you are just mere hundreds of the thousands that await you. You will die, Sabine of Whispering Wind, and you will beg me for your life, just as your father did."

I reached out and grabbed her by her wild hair and threw her to the ground. I jumped off of Raiden and threw myself on top of her. I could not control the anger, nor could I get the image of my father hanging on the great gates out of my head. She fought well in return. I was sure she was concerned with my abilities in hand to hand combat, but she did not show fear. She just fought harder. We rolled around on the ground, hitting one another. It was not until Jared pulled me off of her that I stopped trying to kill her with my bare hands.

She scuffled away from me and gained her footing. "I will kill you!" I screamed at her.

She laughed and said, "It was wise of Wellington to pull you away."

"Be careful, woman, or I will release her."

"Oh, please do, young Jared, for it will be my pleasure to slice the throat of this wild beast. You should come and join me, Sabine. You have the killer instinct I admire in my warriors."

I do not know if it was Jared who let me go, or if I managed to get free of his iron grip on me, but I lunged at her, knocking her to the ground. She had a blade in her hand, and she swiped it at me. I heard Charles gasp, and before I knew it, I was flying in the air with a firm grip on me. Charles stood over the woman with his foot on her wrist and the blade lying on the ground next to it.

"You will not harm her, not now, not tomorrow, not ever! You know who I am, old woman, and you know that I will protect her with my life. We are the guardians of the bringers of peace, and you also know you cannot kill me. Now, Aidan, bring some rope and tie this woman up. She is coming with us."

Aidan and Steven tied her and put her up on her horse. She started shouting things at me and Rebecca. Charles rode up and tied a piece of cloth around her mouth, and we all laughed.

"Sabine, Rebecca, would you mind?" Charles looked back at the bodies.

We raised our swords, and our horses did their thing. The fire burned all the horses and bodies that were lying on the ground to ash, the ground charred black from the fire and the light. I sat there on

Raiden for a long time, looking at the place where hundreds of men had died in only a few moments of time.

None of this can be real. *How can this be real? What mysteries lie within me?* My father knew that one day I would discover this power. I wondered what he would have told me. I wondered why he would have chosen Edward for me to marry, or if he might not have chosen anyone at all. "Father," I whispered. I bowed my head and felt the warmth of the tears on my cheeks. How I missed him. How I wished he was here to explain this to me.

Jared pulled me from Raiden's back onto his horse and into his arms. Again, I cried while he held me, not saying a word. It felt good to be in his embrace. When I finally gained control of myself, I pulled away from him, only to see in his eyes the love he felt for me, which brought on another round of tears. *How could he love me like this?* I am a murderer, just like that mysterious woman. *Have I not just slaughtered hundreds of men? Have I not just tumbled on the ground with a crazy barbarian woman?* But he did. He loved me no matter what. I gained my composure and kissed his neck.

He chuckled. "You might be careful, my lady. I was quite taken by your lack of self-control. It was quite appealing to watch you rolling around in the dirt like a banshee."

We laughed, kissed, and then laughed some more. "We should get you back to camp. I am sure that Charles has a plan we will need to discuss."

I pouted my lip out. He kissed it, and I climbed back on to Raiden. "I love only you, Jared."

"I love only you, Sabine."

As we moved closer to camp, it seemed to have gotten smaller. There were troops surrounding it. Charles was not leaving anything to chance. The soldiers nodded as we passed through them into the camp. "You go find Charles, and I will put the horses up," Jared said as he dismounted his horse. I slid off of Raiden, patting his neck.

"Stay close," I whispered to him.

He neighed at me and nodded his head. I smiled at Jared. He just chuckled as he took his reigns and walked away.

I wandered through the camp toward Charles' tent, but he was not there. Aidan was walking up and said, "There you are. Charles was wondering where you were. He is over by your tent, talking to Rebecca and waiting for you."

"Thank you, Aidan, and thank you for today. Can I ask you a question?"

"You can ask me anything you like."

"Today, Charles said something to that barbarian woman about her knowing who he was and that she could not kill him. What was he talking about?"

"You do not know who we are, Your Highness?"

"Please call me Sabine, and no, I do not know who you are. Who are you?"

"We are your guardians. Our lineage is said to go back to Merlin. In fact, we are supposedly direct descendants of Merlin. I am not sure I believe it all, but Charles, Blake, and Joseph believe."

I stood there, just staring at him. *Did he just say that they were direct descendants of Merlin?* This truly was turning out to be a fantastic story. *How could any of it be real?* I think Aidan sensed my confusion. "Sabine, go and find Charles. I am sure he will tell you the story if you ask him. If I know anything of my brother, it is that he does not give out information unless he is asked."

I nodded, still stunned at what he had just said to me. It did not take me long to find Charles sitting with Rebecca. I guess the stunned look on my face caused alarm because Charles stood and rushed to my side. "Sabine, are you all right? What has happened?"

I just looked at him. "Well, Charles, it seems that you have happened. Is it true that you are direct descendants of Merlin?"

"I do not know that to be truth, Sabine. I only know what we were told our whole lives, but seeing all that I have seen with you and Rebecca, I am inclined to believe." We started walking toward Rebecca. "I believe in the legend. I had to, with the things that had been taking place, and then the murder of your family. I was guided to the belief that all I had been told by my father was the truth. We are your guardians, Sabine, and as I was told, we cannot be killed while we are protecting you. We will all die, but it will not be in your service."

"What else are you not telling us, Charles?" We had reached Rebecca and were sitting.

"Yes, Charles, what else have you left out of the story?"

"I do not know anything. There were many vague stories passed down through the generations of my family."

"Well, I think you should fill us in, old friend," Jared said as he came walking up.

"Most of what I know, you already know."

"That is a very vague statement, Charles, even for you."

"Jared, I am not trying to be evasive. I am just not sure what would be relevant to our journey."

"Charles," I interrupted Jared. "Would you be so kind as to tell us all you know, and let us decide what is relevant?"

"All right, I can do that."

"Would you please start with how that woman knows who you are?"

"Devious knows me from Samuel. She was there at Wellington just before your family was murdered. When she saw me, she singled me out and told me that my purpose for existing was about to be removed, and she said that I would perish soon after. I had known the story of our role in the legend, but I never believed that part of it. It was not until I saw you, Sabine, at Whispering Wind, that I knew it was all truth. It is difficult to understand, or even grasp the truth of this legend. I struggle with it each day, but the way I see it is, if you and Rebecca are the truth, then all the rest must be the same." he cleared his throat, and his voice fell to a whisper before he continued, "I will marry Rebecca."

We looked at Rebecca, who was sitting there with a look of disbelief on her face. "You are a bit forward with your thinking, are you not, Charles?" she sputtered out.

"I am just telling you what the legend has foretold. Rebecca, it is said that you will marry a guardian. I already feel the closeness we have shared, and my feelings for you are very real to me. It is with hope that you share those feelings, or that you will in time."

Rebecca's face was flush, and if I had reached over to touch it I was sure it would be fire hot as well. I was not sure if she was angry at his assumption, or if she shared his sentiment. Her mouth opened, but nothing came out. She stood abruptly and stormed off, not looking back. Charles stood, excused himself, and went after her. Jared and I just looked at one another.

CHAPTER TWENTY TWO

Charles caught up with Rebecca by the horses. "Rebecca, may I speak with you?"

"Charles, I am not sure there is any more that you can say to me. You seem to have my future mapped out for me already. It is exactly what my father would have done. Well, it is exactly what he did do, when he tried to sell me off to Jared."

"You must give me the opportunity to explain."

"Must I, Charles? I think the liberties you already instilled upon me were quite enough."

"I understand your anger toward me, but you do not have all the information that goes along with my assumption that you and I will be together."

"Then I will give you the opportunity to explain yourself, for I fear that you have damaged the friendship we have."

"If we remain as we are, as friends, then I could not be happier in my life. Rebecca, it is an honor to know you and to share this part of your life with you. I will be with you and Sabine for the rest of my days. It is required of me by my father and his father before him. We were born, raised, and trained to fulfill our destiny. It is all that we know. My younger brothers are skeptical of this life we were born into, but Joseph and Blake know that this is the path we must follow."

"I can understand that, Charles, but what I do not understand is why you would think that you and I will marry."

"There are parts of the legend that seemed so insignificant that they had all been forgotten. The main parts were the red hair, the blonde hair, the swords, and the horses. We had no knowledge of the power of your swords when brought together. It was not until things started to happen that I went back to my family and searched the writings for clues as to what we were supposed to do. When I overheard Samuel order the slaughter of Sabine's family, I thought he wanted King Stephan's land. I later heard him talking to Devious about you and Jared and Edward. Devious knows this legend. Her family was slaughtered by Sabine's father. She was just a child, but he left them alive. We think it was to bring it all to this moment. Rebecca, when I rode into Whispering Wind that day with Samuel, and Sabine came running out of the castle to greet her brother, I thought I was imagining her hair as it flew out behind her."

"It is quite red."

"A color no one had ever seen before. The legend had to be truth, but she was a woman. Nowhere in the legend does it speak of it being a woman. We knew of the golden haired woman who would accompany the bringer of peace, so you were not a surprise." He reached up and ran his finger down her hair. "But for it to be a woman, and she was not even a woman. She is so tiny, and she was so very childlike that first day, but her hair was as real as all of this is. Samuel knew the minute he saw her. You see, Sabine had been kept very close to Whispering Wind. She was not traveled as a young woman her age would have been, and she was never left unattended, for fear someone would discover her. Her father knew who she was, as did Samuel, and I am sorry to also say your father. Stephan, Samuel, and Gerald were friends growing up. The friendship lasted most of their lives, until Stephan went out and slaughtered the barbarians and brought back all the jewels that were stolen from his father. Samuel and Gerald were not happy that Stephan denied finding the jewels, but they knew he had them. The stories were floating around the kingdoms of his brutal assault on the barbarians and what he took back from them. Samuel and Gerald parted ways with Stephan, and unrest settled into the lands. It was not until Jenna and Ardes fell in love that Samuel found his way into the legend. Keep in mind that Sabine was not known to them, not until Samuel and Katherine went to Whispering Wind to marry their oldest daughter off to a family Samuel despised. He knew that Stephan's lineage was that of the legend, so I think he thought that if Jenna was to produce an heir with the red hair, then he would finally get his hands on those jewels, and he would rule all the lands as he saw fit.

"But when they arrived at Whispering Wind, and he met Sabine, everything changed for Samuel. He left immediately after the wedding and started researching the legend. He had my father brought to Wellington to tell him all that he knew. My father only told him enough to keep his life. That was when the plan was set into motion to destroy Whispering Wind. Keep in mind also, that I only knew bits and pieces. When I got word from my mother that my father had been brought to Wellington, I went home for a few days. My father told me the parts of the legend that included you, the more detailed ones. He also told me that you would be the one I was to marry. I had no knowledge of this until that day, but you were already in love with Edward, and it is not proper to want someone who wants another."

"Why did you wait so long, Charles, to tell me this?"

"I was told by my father to reveal as little as possible, and to only do so when it needed to be revealed. There is more to the legend, but my father told me that if I shared it all, it would make some jealous, and they would seek to destroy you and Sabine. When I realized that I loved you, I could not, and I will not risk your life."

"But you are to protect Sabine. I am just second."

"Without Sabine, your power does not exist, and without you, Sabine cannot bring peace. It is a double edged sword, so to speak. I am bound by blood to be her guardian, and I am bound by legend to wed you, but my heart is bound to you because I am in love with you. I have been since that second visit to the plain, when I brought Sabine to meet with you. I knew when I saw that look in your eyes, that look you get when your mind is whirling with adventure. That morning, after you took Edward's life, I heard you in the stables. I came out to see what you were doing, and then you rode right past me."

"I did not see you, but I was not looking either. Why did you not come after me?"

"I could not. I am not supposed to interfere with the natural order of things. I cannot stop you from doing what you need to do. I think it is because it would interfere with the progress of what is to come. If I change anything, if I cause you or Sabine to think in any way except for the way you think, it could change things. Does that make sense to you?"

"So, Sabine needed to come for me. We needed to experience our horses, or rather, I needed to learn that Spirit is just as fast as Raiden, and we needed to see those barbarians in order to bring them into the valley, and then our power was unleashed."

"Exactly. If I had stopped you, none of those things would have happened, and we would not be here right now. Would you please accept my apology for putting my feelings out there when you were not ready for them? I had no right to mess with your mind."

Giggling, Rebecca said, "You really did not tell me anything, that I already did not know."

"Am I that obvious?"

"No, I think I know because I think I might have feelings for you as well. I think that is why I seemed so angry. I think I was more upset that it may have been that obvious to everyone else that I felt that way about you."

"Well, if it is not too much to ask, could you please be a bit more careful of yourself for me? I cannot interfere with what you choose to do, but I would appreciate it if you could choose wisely."

"I would appreciate the same from you. We have a great deal to do, and a great many battles to fight, before this is over."

"Yes, Rebecca, we do."

They started walking back to where Jared and I were sitting, only they were not alone. They were being followed. Acting suspiciously, Raiden and Spirit were following behind. Neither Charles nor Rebecca had noticed them.

CHAPTER TWENTY THREE

The scream was more guttural and unnatural, not like a scream of terror or pain, more like a calling. It echoed off the trees, the hills, and it felt like the ground even shook. It lasted longer than I could hold my breath, and just as it began, fast and unexpected, it ended.

When Charles and Rebecca arrived, we were standing. Everyone was standing and looking around. "What was that, Charles?"

"I do not know, Sabine, but you stay here. I am going to find out." He turned to walk away, and Raiden blocked his path. "What are you doing here?"

It was as if Charles was waiting for him to answer. Raiden nudged him back with his nose, and Spirit walked up to Rebecca, as if he was standing guard over her. Joseph, Blake, Aidan, Steven, Edward, and James came running over to join us. There was confusion everywhere. Men were running here and there, unable to make up their minds where they were going, or where they were supposed to be. Raiden moved from Charles and came to stand by me. He nudged me with his nose. It was more like he was directing me, tucking me into his shoulder. I remembered he had done the same thing the night the barbarians came; the night he ran with me. I looked over at Rebecca, and Spirit was doing the same thing.

"Your sword, Rebecca. Get your sword."

I reached for mine and climbed on Raiden, and Rebecca did the same. "There is something terribly wrong, Charles. Something bad is happening or going to happen."

Just then, Raiden was up on his hind legs, and Spirit followed. Instinctively, Rebecca and I raised our swords. In the dark of the night, the light that radiated from our swords was brilliant. It was directed outward, far beyond our perimeter of guards. I had no idea what was out there, or what was happening. Raiden and Spirit were turning as they were up, and the brilliant light was moving in a circle around our camp. Then, we could hear them; the screams of terror, the screams of men about to die. We were surrounded, but not for long. Raiden made a complete circle before he dropped to the ground. Charles was yelling orders to his brothers, and the men started to become calmer. Blake and Joseph went to get the mysterious woman, and when they dragged her back, she was laughing. "You will die! You will die! You will die!" She was chanting these words and laughing.

I climbed off of Raiden and walked up to her. She was on her knees, so I knelt down in front of her. "When are you going to realize that you cannot harm me? I have given you a choice, to give me back the children, leave this place, and live, or to die."

She just laughed. I had not really looked at her up close. Even when I was rolling on the ground with her, I had not looked at her. Her eyes were wide and so brown they almost looked black. Her skin was dark and rough, like the hide of a cow. Her teeth were black, and her breath smelt like eggs that had been left out to rot. Her hair was a dark brown color, knotted and dirty. Her clothing was ragged and worn, and her scent was horrific, like the covering that Westin had covered me with. I got up and went into our tent, looking for my sack. I returned with the covering, and it matched the one she wore around her shoulders.

"This belongs to one of your men." It was more a question than it was a statement. She just smiled and sucked in her breath. The sound only had a chance to begin again before Charles kicked her in the face and ended it. She fell to the ground and laid there like a heap of hay.

"It was her who made that noise. Is it like a call or something?"

"I think it was more than that," Jared said. He smiled and wrapped his arm around me.

"She seems to have some kind of powers. It was that sound that caused the confusion in the men. It also was a call, I think, that brought the barbarians here."

Just then, a few men came running up. "Charles, there are hundreds of dead just outside the perimeter, an entire circle."

Charles stood over the mysterious woman with a smile on his face. "This is just the beginning. Ladies, would you mind destroying the bodies? Raiden, Spirit, we are forever in your debt."

I climbed back on Raiden, and we lit up the dark of the night once again. The fires burned for a long time, leaving a glow around our camp well into the night.

I had a restless sleep. I could not help but wonder who this mysterious woman was. She had to be some sort of sorceress to have done what she did with her voice. I could not sleep, so I quietly left the tent. I had not noticed that Rebecca was not in the tent either. I could not remember if I had heard her leave. Perhaps I did fall asleep. I wandered around, looking for Charles, and I found him sitting with Rebecca and Jared in front of a small fire, engrossed in conversation. I almost did not want to interrupt them, but Jared heard me and turned with a smile on his face.

"You should be sleeping, my love."

"So should all of you. I suppose after tonight, none of us are going to sleep for a while. Charles, do you have any idea what this woman is? I was thinking that if the legend is true, therefore, Merlin must have been a real person. So, if Merlin was real, then it would not be absurd to assume that this woman is some sort of sorceress."

"I was thinking exactly that, Sabine. I am not sure that she can be killed. If she is a sorceress, we are going to have to find a way to destroy her. I am sure that she is only here so she can bring her men to us. If she wanted to leave, I am positive she could go," Charles said.

"Well, if she is bringing them to us, then we should make sure she is comfortable." We all kind of chuckled.

"The light of the day is upon us, so I think we need to pack up our camp and move onward. Sitting here is not going to get Whispering Wind back, or the children. I will go and get things started. Sabine and Rebecca, you both need to eat. I have noticed that you have not eaten since the midday meal yesterday, so that is a direct order." He raised his eyebrows at us. I saluted him, and Rebecca stuck her tongue out at him.

"I will make sure they eat, my friend," Jared said.

Charles laughed as he walked away. Jared went to get us some food, which left me and Rebecca sitting alone. "You did not get a chance to tell me what happened last night between you and Charles."

She leaned closer to me. "He told me he was in love with me."

I gasped. "I thought I was imagining the way he looked at you, and the way you looked back at him. You love him as well?"

"I think I do, but we cannot act on it. Just as you and Jared, we have bigger things to concern ourselves with. Perhaps when this is all done, we might have a chance, that is, if we live through this." She smiled.

"Oh, Rebecca, I am so happy for you. I know Charles is a wonderful man, and you could find no other who would be true to you."

"I know, Sabine, but it is not something I can let distract me. Just knowing he will be there when this is over will have to be enough."

"You are right. We need to keep our focus on what lies ahead. This woman, this Devious, I think she is the key. Did you happen to notice last night, that you, Jared, Charles, his brothers, and I were the only ones who were not affected by her scream?"

"I did. I wonder if we are immune."

"It is worth mentioning to Charles."

Just then, Jared returned with food; a great deal of food. "Do you think we are going to be able to eat all that?"

We all laughed and proceeded to eat until we could not eat anymore. "Looks like we have some company," Jared said as he nodded in Rebecca's direction. I looked up to see Raiden and Spirit walking up to us. "I swear that horse thinks he is a dog." Jared was laughing.

"You should not make fun of him. He is going to save us all, are you not Raiden?" He nodded his head and snorted. I fed him some leftovers and then went to find Charles, and as with any good dog, Raiden followed. As I walked, I could see that the majority of the tents were gone, the wagons were filled, and the men were standing in a large circle around Charles, probably getting their orders. As I approached them, the mysterious woman was still out, lying on the ground. I stopped to look at her, but she seemed helpless in this state of being. I, however, knew just how dangerous she was. Charles was right. Killing her would not stop this woman. We were going to have to find a way to destroy her.

"Sabine, are you all right?"

"Oh, yes, Charles. I was just thinking. That is all. Are we ready to move onward? We have a baby coming, and we need to finish this, although I am fearful we are not going to make it back to the valley in time. I can remember the cloud and the amount of barbarians that were here that day. There were thousands, tens of thousands. Raiden and Spirit may not be able to handle them all. I am afraid that we may lose some of our men, and I am just having a hard time with any of you dying for me, or because of me."

"Sabine, every man here knows the risk of being here. They are here of their own accord, all fighting for the same freedom. If Samuel and Gerald have their way, the lands will fall to treachery, and I am fearful that all will plummet into nothingness. Samuel wants the power, and he wants the wealth that goes with it. Gerald, I believe, is in too far to get out, even if he wanted to. He knows now that by joining Samuel, he has ordered his eldest daughter to death. I am sure he is a regretful man these days."

I could not help but chuckle. "Somehow, Charles, I want to believe you, but I just do not. Rebecca's father knew exactly what he was doing. It has always been a mystery to me why people would want more than what they have. Is it not just enough to have found love and happiness?"

"I think women think differently than men, Sabine. For a woman, those things are just what she needs and wants. For men, I think it is more about being the best, having the most, and being the most powerful."

"Perhaps that is why I am a woman and not a man, as everyone anticipated. Perhaps this power Rebecca and I hold is not to be trusted with a man. The wrong man, such as Edward, would use it to destroy and conquer, whereas, we as women do not wish for that. We wish for peace and harmony."

He stood there looking at me. "You know, Sabine, what you just said makes very good sense. Perhaps we all misinterpreted the legend. I will have a good think about this, and perhaps more will make sense to us. I believe we are ready to move out."

"You will fill me in when you figure it all out, will you not?"

"Of course I will."

I climbed on Raiden and rode off to find Jared and Rebecca. Together, the ten of us rode in the front of our small army of men toward Whispering Wind, toward what would ultimately be the beginning of the end.

CHAPTER TWENTY FOUR

For weeks, we moved forward, throughout the lands, killing all that stood in our way. Every barbarian that came up against us died. There were times when Raiden and Spirit could not get them all, especially when they came at us wave after wave. This Devious woman seemed to be able to control them all, either that or they were her followers and would do anything she asked them to do.

We lost a few of our troops, maybe a hundred or more, but as we passed through each land, we gained more. It seemed as if this legend was something everyone, except for me, was aware of. In the weeks we progressed, I constantly searched my mind for any hint of this legend in the stories my father had told us, in stories my brothers had told me, but there was nothing. Father had kept this secret to himself.

I wondered sometimes how he must have felt when I was born. Was he afraid? Did he know that this was the way my life would end up? My memories of my family life were fading. The voices of my brothers, my mother, and my father were fading from my memory. I needed this to be finished.

Weeks turned into months, and we were so far from home, driving the barbarians further West. Soon, the land came to an end, and we were faced with a giant body of water, an ocean Charles had called it.

I had never seen anything like it before, but where were we to go from there?

"I believe, Sabine, that this is where we make our stand. I believe this is the end of our journey."

"What exactly does that mean, Charles? Is this where we shall all die?"

"No, this is where it will end. The legend says that at the water's edge, the end will come."

"Well, my old friend, those are not encouraging words. With our back against the water, where are we to go?" Jared asked.

"We are to go nowhere, Jared. We are to stand and fight. They will come to us. They want her back, and when the last of them come to die for her, then she shall die as well."

"We need to find the children, Charles. I need to find Juliana. We have not come across her as of yet."

"They will bring her, Sabine. I guarantee it. They will use her and the children as a tool to get Devious back. That is when we will trade her, and she will die with her men."

"Well, Charles, through all of this, you have been my guide, so I shall not mistrust you now, but I am tired. I must sleep. Jared, would you accompany me? I wish to talk to you alone."

"It would be my pleasure, my lady." He bowed his head and smiled.

The men had finished putting up our tent, and Rebecca was practicing swords with Aidan. I could not be bothered, as I had not slept in weeks. I had not felt safe in months, and I remembered that last night in the cottage when Jared snuck into my room and held me while I slept. "Would you hold me tonight? I am scared, tired, and unsettled. I fear the only place I will find peace is in your arms. I know it is not proper, but I need you tonight, Jared. I just need you to hold me tight."

"Sabine, there is nothing wrong with needing me, and I will set anyone who says a word against you on their back sides. It would be my pleasure to hold you, my love, while you sleep." He bowed and moved his arm in a gesturing manner toward the opening of the tent.

Inside, I removed as much of my clothing that was allowed. Jared lay on the cot watching me, waiting for me. I climbed in next to him, and he wrapped his arms around me. I felt safe with him. I settled in, kissed his neck, and closed my eyes. I do not remember much else. I thought a few times I heard voices, but I could not be sure whose they were, or what they were saying. It felt so good to feel safe and to rest. It was the soft moist lips on my forehead, my cheeks, and then my lips that woke me. I responded to the kiss on my lips, pretending to still be sleeping. My lips parted just a bit then, and I felt his smile.

"You are awake, my love." His breath was hot on my mouth.

"Shhhh… No, I am sleeping, and this is the most wonderful vision ever."

He covered my mouth with his, and we did not part until we heard someone clear their throat. We separated, breathless and smiling. "Can I help you, my friend?" Jared asked Charles, who was standing at the opening of the tent with a red face.

"Um, well, the light of the day is upon us, and there has been word from our scouts."

I wanted to die of embarrassment, as I am sure that was what Charles was already doing. I just kept my head buried in Jared's chest. "Thank you, Charles. We will be right there."

Charles left, and we started laughing and kissing again. Jared was the one who stopped. I wanted to keep on kissing him. "We really should get up and go talk to Charles. You have been asleep for a long time, my love."

"Mmmm, I do not want to go anywhere. I want to go home and marry you and spend all my days in bed with you."

"I would love that more than anything, but we cannot go home until it is safe and we finish this."

I agreed, and we got up. Jared stepped out of the tent while I put on fresh clothing. I was a little apprehensive about walking out. I knew that Charles and his brothers would be out there but I did not do anything wrong, so I did not care. I walked out of the tent into the bright light of the day. "How long have I been asleep?"

"Well, you went to sleep before the evening meal, and it is now midday, so I would say a very long time, which is fine. You needed to sleep. I only wish Rebecca would follow your lead and sleep herself." Charles smiled at me.

"Well, if I had strong arms to hold me while I slept, perhaps I would," pouted Rebecca

Charles looked at her adoringly. "You just need to ask, my lady, and I will be happy to comply."

We all giggled. "Now, our scouts have returned, and there are a couple thousand barbarians headed this way from the North and the East. Our scouts from the South have not checked in yet, which makes me think they have been captured or killed. They are coming, just like we anticipated. We will be ready. Blake figures they should be here just before the dark of the night is upon us, so our visibility will be minimal. Rebecca, Sabine, you two will stay behind the front line, and you will follow that order. You must be protected at all costs. Jared, Blake, Joseph, and I will stay with you. If I tell you to run, you run, no questions asked. There are thousands coming, and we are but hundreds. I know we can do this, but I need to make sure the two of you are safe. With our lives, we vowed to protect you, and we will. This is about to get as real as it gets, so let us not make any mistakes."

"Charles," I interrupted him. "Is this the end? We have killed thousands of them. How many more could there be? We have been gone for months, and the killing never ends."

"Sabine, I cannot imagine the amount of barbarians you saw at Whispering Wind the day your family was murdered, but I can only assume that there cannot be many more of them left."

"When we are done with this here, the woman must die in order for this to be ended, and we need to find the children, Charles. I need to find Juliana. She is nearly in her third year of life. I can only imagine what they have done to her."

"I know, Sabine. You and Rebecca and Jared need to eat and then prepare, for the time we have left until they arrive is limited."

There was a commotion in the camp by the horses. Some men came running up to us. "Charles, one of the scouts is back from the South. He brings terrifying news with him."

"Bring him here quickly."

A few minutes later, some men were running up, and in their arms was one of our scouts. He looked as if he had been beaten. He was bloody and tattered. His voice was week. "Charles, there are many coming from the South. They have the children. They plan on using them as a shield, so you cannot harm them. They want the woman and said they will kill one child each time you refuse to turn her over to them." He looked at me. "Starting with Juliana." The rage that flowed through my body was greater than the rage I felt at seeing Whispering Wind in ruins, greater than I felt knowing my family had been murdered.

"Thank you, Mathew. Your service to us will be well rewarded. Please take him and tend to him."

The men left, and Charles turned to me. "Sabine, this is what we have been waiting for. The fact that they are willing to use the children tells us that their numbers are nearly finished. This is the end. We need to be very careful."

"Charles, we cannot risk the children."

"I have faith in the two of you, Sabine. You and Rebecca can do this. I know you can. When it is finished, we shall set our path for home, we will deal with Samuel and Gerald, and then peace will reign throughout the lands."

Rebecca was at my side with her arms around me. "We will end this, and we will be victorious. You know it in your heart, Sabine, but you cannot let your rage dictate you. We must be confident, and we must stand united. You cannot see the children as the reason for our failure. Raiden and Spirit will keep them safe. You must believe that, Sabine. You must."

"I know, Rebecca, and I will. Right now, will you come with me? I want to talk to that woman."

She nodded, and we started walking toward the mysterious woman named Devious. The guards were looking at us. I was sure that Charles had instructed them to not allow us near her. Rebecca smiled at one, and they let us pass. The woman was sitting on the ground, bound and gagged. Rebecca and I sat in front of her. "They are coming here to get you, or at least they think they are," I said to her. I could tell that she was smiling. "They will not succeed. You do know that you have sentenced them all to their deaths, the same fate you will receive."

She mumbled something, but I could not understand her. I reached up to remove her gag. Her laughter was loud and hoarse, "There are tens of thousands coming for you, Sabine, all with one goal in their minds, to put you to death. You cannot escape this. Your leader, Charles, has backed you into a corner. There is no way out for you now. It will be a great pleasure when I watch you draw your last breath."

"You have seen the power we hold. You cannot touch us."

"Yes, but I have the one thing you seek, your brother's child, little sweet Juliana. I have been training her to be just like me, for the child has powers that you are unaware of. She has a gift like me. She will grow to be my daughter, and you will die knowing this."

I do not know what happened to me, but I snapped. I lunged forward and wrapped my hands around her neck, squeezing. Her black teeth and her acid breath laughed in my face. It was Rebecca who pulled me off of her, saying, "We need her alive, Sabine!"

When she pulled me back, my fingers latched onto something that hung on the woman's neck. It tugged and tore free in my grip. She let out a gasp, as if she was frightened. I looked down at it as it lay in my hand. She started screaming at me, "Give it back! Give it back! You do not know the power it holds. Give it back!"

Rebecca reached up and put the gag back on her, while I sat there looking into her eyes. They were filled with a variety of emotions. "Is this important to you?" I asked her. The woman just shook her head, violently trying to get the gag off.

I looked down at the object in my hand. It was a glass ball of sorts, almost in a teardrop shape. It was green in color, but as I looked closely, I could see that there was some sort of mist swirling around inside a chamber. It was beautiful and terrifying at the same time. I looked up at the woman with amazement in my eyes. She was becoming violent, so Rebecca put her hand on my arm to pull me up. The guards had come around to see what all the commotion was. We turned to walk away, and the woman was growling like a rabid dog. With one blow from a guard's foot, she fell silent. As we walked toward the camp, Charles and Blake came running up.

"Are you all right? What were you thinking?"

"I was thinking, Charles, that I wanted to hear what she had to say about the children. She told us that tens of thousands of barbarians were coming, and that we were all going to die. She told me that Juliana has some kind of special powers, and that she was going to raise her as her own. I got a little angry."

Rebecca cut me off, saying, "You got more than a little angry. You tried to kill her."

"Yes, I did, but when Rebecca pulled me off of her, my fingers got tangled in this, and it pulled off her neck." I held the strange bauble in the air.

"It is again truth," Charles said as he reached up and took the bauble.

"What are you talking about, Charles?"

"The legend talks of a magic sphere that gives the person who wears it the ability to become invisible."

I could not contain the laughter. "Invisible? That is preposterous." Charles put the glowing teardrop of mist around his neck. "Is it?" He reached up and wrapped his hand around the sphere, closed his eyes, and then he disappeared. He could see us, but we could not see him. He laughed. "Is it, Sabine? I can tell by the look on your face that it is truth."

"No wonder the old woman wanted to kill you Sabine," Rebecca said with a laugh.

Charles removed his hand and reappeared. "Amazing," he said. "Sabine, you wear it and see if it works for you." He took the bauble off and placed it around my neck. I closed my eyes and wrapped my hand around it. I did not feel different, but Rebecca started laughing again. I could see them.

"Can you see me?"

"No, we cannot. This is perfect," Rebecca said laughing. "Hey, Jared, come here. I want to show you something," she yelled after

Jared. "Keep your hand on it, Sabine. Let us see if we can confuse him."

Jared came running up. "Have you seen Sabine? The guards said that you and she went to see that woman." I released the bauble and scared him. "What in the world? How is this possible?"

"Well, Rebecca and I did go see Devious. She said some things to me, and I tried to choke her. When Rebecca pulled me off, this came with my hands." I held out the bauble. "It makes the wearer invisible."

"How is this possible, Charles?"

"There are parts of the legend that are not known to many, forgotten in time, I suppose, but there is a story in there about a mysterious bauble that allows the wearer to become invisible. No one ever really believed in such a story, but it is truth, as with all the stories associated with the legend. "Sabine, touch Rebecca, and then hold the bauble. Let us see if it works that way as well."

"You ready?" I asked her as I took her hand in mine.

"Oh, I am more than ready! This could be even better for us if it works. We will not have to hide then."

I wrapped my hand around the bauble, and both of us disappeared. "Did it work?"

"It did indeed. Rebecca, take Jared's hand."

She did, and he too disappeared. The laughter that escaped Charles was booming. He reached over and touched Jared's arm, and then he disappeared as well.

"So this is how they move without being noticed. This is an incredible find, Sabine."

"This is terrifying. I can only imagine," I paused as I let go of the bauble, and we all reappeared, "how many times this was used to gain access to my family, to me. When this is over, this bauble must be destroyed."

"I agree, but for now, we can use it to our advantage. We no longer have to hide you or use guards to protect you. You both can be in plain sight but yet hidden. We need to prepare now. The light of the day is leaving, and we shall soon be surrounded by barbarians. Please, Sabine, do not allow yourself to get angry at what you will see concerning the children. Trust in your bond with Raiden. He will protect her from the light. You concentrate on what needs to be done, both of you. If we falter just once, we could all end up dead. Now, go prepare. Get your swords and your horses and meet us at the woman."

No one moved. We all just stood there, looking at one another in amazement. I could not ever have imagined that things like this could be real. I was just a girl whose family was slaughtered by vicious people. Two years ago, I was lying on a hill just outside my father's kingdom, day dreaming of the wonderful life I had, and today, I was preparing for battle with the very people who murdered my family. I held in my hand a mysterious bauble filled with a green mist that made the wearer invisible. I had a horse with mystical powers, and I could force a burning light from my father's sword. I had the knowledge that my brother's child may possess magical powers of the mind. It was all so very unbelievable. How was I supposed to move from this spot?

"You all right, love?" Jared was looking at me with a slight smile on his face.

"No, Jared, I am not all right. I do not think I can do this. We have come so far from home to find Juliana, and now she is mere moments away from me, and there is a great possibility that she is going to die in front of me. I cannot do this. I cannot risk her."

"Sabine, you are right. We have come a very long way to find her. If you look back at the months we have moved across the land, and all that we have accomplished, you cannot possibly doubt what is to come. The legend is true. You and Rebecca are accomplishing things that no one should ever be able to do. The size of the barbarian camps that we have annihilated with our small army is unheard of. Thousands of men we have taken down, and thousands more will fall. You need to do what Charles said. You need to trust Raiden, trust yourself, and most of all, you need to believe that you can do this. Believe that you can save her. You can save them all and take them home."

"Take them home to what, Jared? Their parents are all dead. The village is destroyed. Who is going to raise them?"

"You are worrying about things you should not be. Please, my love, just believe in yourself. They are coming, and they are coming fast. We need to prepare. How about this? I will stand by your side, and I will not leave you. If we fail at this task, we are all dead anyway, and if I am going to leave this place, I am leaving it with you, dead or alive." He bent down and kissed my head.

I threw myself into his arms. "Oh, Jared, I am so scared."

"I know, love. I am scared as well."

CHAPTER TWENTY FIVE

Our line of defense was small compared to what approached us. The cloud that spread across the horizon was the same cloud that I remembered seeing that day on the hill. My heart was pounding, more so than from Jared's kisses.

"Rebecca, we do not know if this bauble will work if you hold onto me. I have to have one hand on my sword and one on the bauble, so put your free hand on my leg." She reached out and touched me as I wrapped my hand around the bauble. "Jared, can you see us?"

"No."

"All right then, maybe this will work. Do not let me go, Rebecca, no matter what, and please make sure I stay put."

She giggled. "Like I have any control over you, Sabine. You know what is at stake here, so I think you will behave yourself." Raiden snorted.

"See, even he has faith in you."

The cloud gained ground quickly, and the sound of the thunder was immense. They were close, very close. I shifted in my saddle and stretched my neck to see above the heads of the troops in front of me. I could see them coming now. Closer and closer they came, and then the thunder stopped. When the dust settled, there were thousands of men before us.

I heard laughter, and then a voice, coming from the front of the barbarians. "You call this an army? You could not be the same army that has destroyed my men."

"We are one and the same," Charles called out.

"Well, this is going to be easy. Are you prepared to die?"

Charles laughed then. "We will not be doing any dying this day."

Just then I heard it. I was not sure if anyone else heard it, but I could hear the soft cries of children. I could not help but wonder if Juliana would know me. Would she be afraid of me? I strained my neck and my body to look through the men, nearly falling off of Raiden, and there they were. Some barbarians were dragging them and pushing them. One of the men struck one of the older children. I could not stop myself. "Leave them alone," I shouted. Jared reached out to settle me, and the barbarian in front started laughing.

"Well, well, well… What do we have here? You brought a woman. There are a few of us who have not had the company of a woman in a long time." He turned and said to his men, "Keep the woman alive," and laughed.

Raiden did not like what he heard. He reared up, and Spirit followed. Rebecca and I raised our swords, and it began. The light was brilliant, the screams were loud, and the smell of burning flesh was strong. Raiden dropped to the ground, putting an end to it.

"So the legend is true," the voice said. "I am impressed, but we are many, Princess, and we have what you seek." He held up a small child, filthy and screaming. I could not tell if it was a boy or a girl. The child's hair was matted to its head, and its face was so dirty you could not tell if it was white. I studied what little of the face I could see, when my eyes connected with the eyes of the child. My breath froze in my chest as my voice disappeared.

"Juliana," I whispered, but only Jared and Rebecca heard me. I felt Rebecca's hand tighten on my leg. Raiden twitched under me.

"Oh, yes, Princess, you know who this child is. She is the daughter of your brother. I found her asleep in her cot just after I slit the throat of her mother. If you pull that again, I will slit her throat as well."

It was Jared who moved first. "No," I said, and I reached out to him. "It is what he wants. Remember what you told me earlier, that you will not leave me?"

"I will keep my word." That was all he said, but I could see the murder in his eyes and the anger on his face.

"I would not anger her. You will not like the outcome of this meeting," Charles said, trying to be diplomatic.

I leaned into Raiden, whispering, "Can you do this? Can you get them all and not hurt the children?"

He leaned his head into me, almost like he was going to talk, but he wanted to look into my eyes. When he did, I saw the answer in them that he would, and he could. I sat up and looked at Rebecca. "We do this or we die."

"I am prepared for either. I will not live like this, Sabine, in fear for my life. Let us end it now."

"Charles," I said softly.

"Sabine," it was a whisper.

"We are prepared," I whispered back.

"So let it begin. I love you, Rebecca," he said. "I love you, Charles."

"I love only you, Jared."

"I love only you, Sabine."

Rebecca let go of me, and I let go of the bauble, so that I could look the man in the eye. The look he returned was that of shock. Raiden rose, and Spirit followed. My eyes never left the man's as I raised my father's sword. I was amazed at how long Raiden stood on his hind legs. The screams were loud, and our troops were fighting, but we stood in our spot, and we burned them. When Raiden dropped, and the light had ended, the barbarians that were holding onto the children were the only ones left in the front, and there were not many left behind them.

"I will kill her!" he yelled.

"You will not. You know who I am, and you know the truth of what will become of you. I will give you a choice, the same choice I gave your leader, this Devious. Give me what belongs to me and disappear, and I will allow you to live, or you can stand and die." I never turned my eyes from his.

"Devious is not my leader. I lead myself. I choose to fight with her. I make my own decisions. You will not soon forget my name. I am Guffster, and I will not yield."

I leaned into Raiden. "Can you kill him without hurting Juliana?" I do not know what I expected. Perhaps I hoped that with all the magic around me, he would answer. He stomped his hoof on the ground. I could not tell if that was a yes or a no, but I was not about to take that chance. I kicked him in the side, and we moved to face this Guffster.

"I will fight you one on one for the child," I said as I approached him. "If I win, the rest of you will yield and release the children."

"You are a foolish child, Princess, but what do I get if I win?"

"Is it not obvious?"

"Why not humor me and tell me."

"If you win, then you win. My promise is that no one here will avenge my death."

"Sabine, NO!!!" It was Jared. He rode up next to me. "This barbarian is twice your size. You cannot win against him."

"What do we have here? Wellington? Well, this would be an interesting fact to pass on to your father. I have orders to end your life as well, traitor."

"The only life that will end here, sire, is yours," I said.

"You spout big words for such a little person, Princess. We shall see. You have my word, if you beat me, they will yield, and the children are yours. If I win, then Whispering Wind belongs to me, and the rest of you had better ride for your lives." He scanned the troops behind me, and I saw his eyes stop and focus on one person. Rebecca. "Is that the Princess of Blackmore? Well, well, this is turning out to be a very profitable day for me, Princess. There is a price on your head as well. I do not know what the three of you have done to warrant such extreme measures, but when I end your lives I will be a very rich man."

I climbed off of Raiden. He did not like that I was going to fight hand to hand. No one did.

"Sabine, please do not do this," Jared was pleading.

"It is fine, Jared. I want our niece, and if I have to fight this Guffster, then I will. I love only you."

He grabbed my arm turned me to face him. I could see the fear in his eyes. "I love only you," he said and kissed me.

"Well, is this not fun? Shall we, Princess, or are you going to ravage her right in front of me, Wellington?"

I spun around with sword in hand. "You will not live through this, Guffster."

He laughed, dropped Juliana on the ground, and it took all that I had not to run up to her. She was crying. Another barbarian grabbed her by the hair and dragged her back. I stepped forward, wanting to run to her, but Raiden's neigh stopped me. Guffster drew his sword and swung it at me, thinking I was not paying attention. My sword met his in mid swing.

"Well, the littlest Princess is quick, but not as quick as me." He swung again and again. I could only defend. He pushed me back, and I fought him the best I could, but I tripped and fell flat on my back. I heard Jared scream out, and Charles grabbed him. Guffster lunged at me. It was instinct to put my feet up to block him, and they landed in his gut, flipping him over my head. I did not look to see where he landed, but it was my opportunity to gain my footing. I jumped up and spun around, wielding my sword. It came down hard on his, and the sparks flew. He was taken aback by the power of my sword. I hit him again and again. He fell a few times, but got up quickly. He was fast, but as long as I was just a second faster, I was still in control. I swung at him time and time again, each time with a bit more power than the last. I could see and feel that he was weakening. I did not stop my ascent on him. Strike after strike, flash after flash, his power was depleting. I swung hard the next time, and his sword went flying out of his hand. He knelt there, looking at me in amazement. "Yield or die."

"I will never yield to you." Those were the last words he spoke. I swung my sword, and with a brilliant flash of light, his head rolled away, and his body fell to a slump on the ground. There was silence behind me. I could hear the heartbeats of those around me.

"Juliana," I whispered. I spun around with my sword in the air to find her, ready to kill any who got in my way. I saw no one but her, the tear streaked little face looking at me with fear in her eyes. I moved slowly toward her. "RELEASE THE CHILD!" I screamed to the barbarian holding her by the hair. He stood there with rotten teeth smiling at me, as if he was going to kill her before I could get to her. I heard the arrow fly through the air beside me, and I watched it as it entered the barbarian's eye. He released her and fell to the ground. She ran toward me, and I toward her. Before I knew what was happening, the troops had surrounded us, keeping her safe as we drew closer together. I dropped to my knees as she neared, but she stopped short and stood there looking at me. This beautiful child looked like a banshee. It was obvious that she was terrified and unsure of who I was. "It is me, Sabine. You remember me, do you not?"

Her eyes never left mine. I started to hum the lullaby I would hum to her when she slept, the same one my mother would hum to me. She tilted her head, as if she was pulling a memory from the back of her little mind. I heard nothing around me except her heartbeat. I saw only her as I hummed. I saw it in her eyes the moment she remembered the song. There was no stopping her; she hit me so hard that it knocked us both to the ground. My arms wrapped around her. Yes, this was Juliana. The years could never remove how she felt in my arms. They may have changed her appearance, but not her eyes or her heart. "I found you, my love. I found you."

Our reunion was short lived, however. I felt arms all around us as we were lifted to our feet. Someone was pulling her away from me. "NO," I shouted.

"Sabine, this is not over." It was Charles.

The reality of where I was, and what had happened, came swirling back to me. I let her go. I knew whoever had her would die to protect her.

"Go, Juliana. I will be right back." I spun around, ready to face whatever was left. They were fighting around us, barbarians and our troops. There were dead men everywhere. I searched for Rebecca, but I could not see her. "REBECCA!" I screamed.

"I am here!" I spun to follow the voice. I moved my way through the fighting, killing anyone in my way. I found her fighting with a huge smile on her face. She killed one, then another. "We need our horses," she said as she swung again.

"RAIDEN!" I yelled. He made his way to us with Spirit at his side. We climbed up, and Raiden rose on his hind legs. The light was so intense, but a short time later, it was silent. The only thing I could hear were the sobs of the children. Raiden landed, the light subsided, and death surrounded us. The only men standing were ours. The scene that lay out before me was one from a nightmare. Something was different, however. Something was out of place. Something was wrong. I searched the faces; Charles, Blake, Joseph, but I could not see Jared. My heart stopped beating in my chest. I could not breathe. It felt like that day in Samuel's study, the day I thought Jared had been killed. Jared could not be dead. "NOOOOOO!" I screamed. Raiden moved quickly, jumping over the bodies, and he stopped right next to him. "NOOOOOO!" I screamed again. I do not know how I moved so quickly, but I was on the ground with Jared in my arms. He was bleeding from his gut. The tears I could not control. "NOOOOOO!" I screamed again. "Jared." I touched his face. "Jared, do not leave me."

His eyes fluttered. "I love only you," he managed to say before he closed his eyes and went limp in my arms.

"NOOOOO!" I screamed again. Charles, Rebecca, and Blake were at my side. I could not take my eyes off of him. "No, no, no," was all I could say. Rebecca put her arms around me. Charles leaned down to listen to his chest. "No, no, no, Jared. Please do not leave me." Then I heard her, the mysterious woman named Devious, and she was laughing.

"Sabine, I am sorry, but he is gone," Charles said with tears streaming down his face.

"No, he cannot be gone. We are supposed to be together forever, Charles."

"I am so sorry." His voice was a whisper.

The laughter was louder now, and then she spoke, "I will trade you."

"SHUT UP, OLD WOMAN!" I screamed at her.

"All right, but I know how you can save him."

I looked at Charles and then Rebecca. Charles had that look in his eyes, that one he has every time something unnatural is about to occur. I laid Jared on the ground as gently as I could. Charles helped me up, and we went to the mysterious woman.

"What is this babble you spew?" I asked her.

"I will trade my life for his." She was staring at the bauble on my neck.

"Your life is not worth his."

"But is my life worth his to you, Princess? Would you do anything to save your love, like letting me keep mine?"

"What are you saying, that you can bring him back from the dead? What do I look like, a fool?"

"I cannot bring him back, but I know how you can." Her eyes never left the bauble.

I looked down at it and laid it in my hand. "I suppose you will trade the information for this bauble of yours?"

She smiled, her black teeth showing. "You agree to release me, and I will tell you how to save him from the dark underworld, but you are running out of time, Princess. You only have a few moments left to decide before he is lost forever."

I looked at Charles. His eyes said agree, but his body said kill her where she sat.

"Agreed, but you will not get your bauble back."

"It is the bauble that will save him. The mist inside will give him back his life. Break the glass on him, and he will live again."

"If you are lying, I will cut your head off myself."

"Oh, I am not lying, Princess, but you better hurry. Death waits for no man." She laughed.

I ran back to Jared, tore the bauble from my neck, and slammed it against Jared's chest. It shattered, cutting my hand and his chest. The mist seeped out and covered his body and the parts of me that were holding him. We were all very still, staring at him, waiting for something, anything, to happen. Minutes went by, and nothing. "You lied to me, old woman!" I yelled at her.

"Patience, Princess," she said with a chuckle.

"Charles, how did this happen?"

"When you beat Guffster, and the child ran to you, the barbarians moved with her."

"But why did I not see that?"

"I do not know, but we surrounded you to protect you while you got Juliana. When she ran to you, and you fell on the ground, a barbarian got through us somehow. He had his sword raised above his head to strike you both down. Jared put himself in front of the sword. That was all I could see. It was Blake and Joseph who removed you and the child."

"I remember hands on me. Who took Juliana?"

"It was Blake. Jared must not have been fast enough to strike back. He must have felt the full force of that sword."

I looked down at him. "He gave his life to protect me."

"That is why you can get him back," the mysterious woman said.

I turned to look at her. "What are you babbling about old woman?"

"When someone dies for love or out of love is the only time the mist will work. If he had died in battle, it would be useless."

I looked at Charles. "This cannot be true, can it?"

"Sabine, everything you have accomplished, everything you have been through, and the things we have seen together, why would I not believe this as well?"

Just then, I felt Jared's chest move, or did I? I looked down at him, but he was not moving, not that I could see. I moved my hand to where his heart was. "Uh…" I did not want to imagine what I was feeling. His chest rose once, twice. I ripped open his shirt to see the wound, and my eyes could not be deceiving me. He was healing. We all were silent as we watched what none of us could believe.

"Mmm, grrrr," he was making sounds.

"Jared," I whispered, terrified I was imagining this. "Jared, can you hear me?"

There was nothing, no movement, no sound. I moved my hand back to his heart. I could still feel it beating. He was alive, but at what cost?

The old woman laughed again. "Time, Princess... You should pray to whatever God you pray to that you got to him in time."

"What are you rumbling about, old woman?" Rebecca snapped at her.

"We shall wait and see. We shall wait and see," she said.

Jared's eye fluttered. "Jared, can you hear me?"

"Mmm, yes my love," he whispered.

I could not contain the tears any longer. He was alive. My love was alive. I could not explain how this made me feel, but I was still hearing the words of the old woman in my head. His hands started to move toward his wound, and mine covered his. "Do not fear, my love. All is well."

"But how is this possible?"

"The mist in the bauble. It had magical healing powers, or so the old woman said it did. I was willing to try just about anything. With all the magic that surrounds us, I had to at least try. You were gone from me, and we had just started our life together. I could not bear to think of having to continue on without you." I bent over him to wrap my arms around him. It felt glorious when he returned the gesture. "I love only you."

He gave a choked laugh. "I love only you."

Our embrace was interrupted by the mysterious woman. "A deal has been made. Release me."

"I will release you only when I see fit to do so, old woman."

"Taking this power of yours, Princess, to a new level, are we?"

Charles interjected, "It would be wise to mind your tongue, woman."

"Now, Charles, I can see that you are truly a man of your word..."

He interrupted her, "I did not give you my word on anything, woman."

"Yes, but what I was going to say is that you are a man of your word, so I would imagine you would do your best to make sure those you surround yourself with are in the same manner as yourself. Although, I am not sure why you would be in the position you are in, when you know that this is not the end but the beginning."

It was Rebecca who rose in anger. Walking up to the woman she said, "This babble you spew from your treacherous mouth is your problem. Do not infect us with your sayings, or Sabine's word will mean nothing. I will cut off your head, just as your friends have lost theirs. You cannot play your trickery on me."

She laughed at Rebecca. "Oh, Blackmore, you know not what you speak. There is no treachery in my words, only truth. Your Charles here knows that what I say is just that. None of you know what lies ahead of you."

"And I suppose you do, old woman?"

"I know as much as your Charles here knows. I see he has not told you all of the truth, Princess. I would imagine he wants to spare you the ugliness that awaits you. Tell me, Princess. How will you feel when your Sabine brings to your father the same fate you just threatened me with? Will you love her then? Will you follow her then? I think not, for the rage will eat at you for the rest of your days. Your spite and jealously will be just as your father's was toward the great King Stephan of Whispering Wind, and we all know what happened to him."

I looked over at Rebecca. She was furious at the words. I could see it in her eyes. "Charles," I said with great alarm in my voice.

"Rebecca, calm down. What she says is the truth. I know more than I have told, but you know why I have not told you. I am bound not to interfere in the future outcome. What will come has to take place in order to fulfill the prophecy. Come. Let us leave this place and go home."

Rebecca heard his words and walked away from the old woman. I could see the anger in her eyes. She was not going to forget this any time soon. It was time to begin our long journey home. We needed to deal with Samuel and with Gerald. I did not want to kill either of them, but I knew the pride these men had, and they would force my hand. They would not yield to me or to Rebecca. The key would be to allow Rebecca to choose her father's fate, and I would have to do the same for Jared. I could not take the lives of their fathers. I knew what it had done to me to lose mine in such a fashion, and I did not want that for either of them. I loved them both too much to inflict that pain on them.

"Charles, can we speak please?"

"Of course, Sabine."

"Rebecca, would you please sit here with Jared for me?"

"Yes," she replied shortly. Her anger still had a hold of her.

I walked away with Charles, far enough so no one could hear us. "What are you not telling us, Charles? Are the ramblings of that old woman truth?"

"They are truth, Sabine, but I cannot say the outcome of what lies ahead. The decisions must be made by you and Rebecca. It is not my place to interfere, but I have faith in you that you will choose wisely. The two of you have been through a great deal, but I think for now, we just need to move forward and work our way home."

"I agree, Charles, but I wanted to know if you would have any insight as to how Jared will fair in all of this."

"Well, I believe, for now, he is going to make a full recovery, but when we return home, there is much I need to research. I will have more information for you then. I know not of the mystical powers of the green mist, just that it makes the wearer invisible. The old woman is the clue. I know you agreed to release her, and I know that when you give your word, you stay true to it, but you did not tell her when you would release her. I think perhaps we should bring her back with us. She knows more than she is saying, and I think it would be beneficial for us to hang onto her."

"I think you are right, Charles, and as soon as Jared is strong enough to travel, we should leave."

"I believe, my lady that he is indeed well enough now." He nodded toward Rebecca.

I turned to see Jared trying to stand with Rebecca's help. My heart was elated; my love was alive.

The mysterious woman, this Devious, was not happy with my decision not to release her just yet, but I did keep my word not to cut her head off. I had to do what Charles suggested. This woman knew more than she was saying, and until Charles had the opportunity to discover any information concerning this magic green mist that brought Jared back to life, we needed to keep her close. Our journey home was weeks, if not months, away, or so I thought. The children had all been fed. Rebecca and I cleaned them the best we could as we moved across the land. When we would stop at villages along the way, we were presented with food, clothing, and in some instances, shelter. The children all had clean clothing to wear, and they finally began to feel safe.

Jared seemed to be himself, although sometimes I would find him sitting alone and staring at nothing at all. He was still his loving self, and his touch still felt the same. His kisses became more passionate, and I could not be sure if it was from the relief that we survived all of this or if there was something more behind it. I thought that I might be reading more into the mysterious green mist and the words of Devious than I should allow myself. However, the things that had taken place over the last few months alone were unrealistic and surpassed any fantasy story anyone could have imagined.

Juliana had not left my side since we began the trek home. She rode on my horse with me, she slept with me, and she would bathe with me. I was never going to let her out of my sight again. One night, as we lay on my cot together, she reached up to move the hair from my face while I slept.

"What is the matter, sweetheart?" I asked her.

"Are you my mother?" she whispered.

My heart broke in two. I was not sure how much information she had, or how much I should tell her. I supposed if she wanted to know, then I needed to tell her.

"That old ugly woman told me she was my mother, but she was

mean to me. When I would not do what she would tell me to do, she would hit me and kick me."

I could not stop the tears. I wrapped my arms around her and pulled her closer to my chest. "No, Juliana, that woman is not your mother. Your mother's name was Jenna, she was Jared's sister. Your father was my brother. His name was Ardes. The ugly old woman and her mean old men killed everyone in our family and stole you and all the other children. I am your father's sister. My name is Sabine, and I have loved you your whole life. I have been looking for you for a very long time. You are safe now. We are safe, and we are going home."

"I do not have a mother or a father, so what does that make me?"

"It makes you loved." It was all I could think of to say to this child who was nearing her fourth year. "It is time for sleep, my love. As you grow, I will tell you more, and I will never let you forget your mother and father." She snuggled up to my chest, placed her little hand on my cheek, and fell asleep.

I could not remember falling asleep, but the crash outside my tent woke me in a panic. I moved from Juliana without disturbing her, shook Rebecca, and then grabbed my sword. I pulled back the flap of our tent slowly and carefully. There were two men standing outside, whispering. "I think this is the one with the women in it," the first man said.

"Are you sure? I thought it was that one over there," said the second.

"Well, there is only one way to find out," the first said.

Rebecca came up beside me. She nearly made me scream because she was so quiet. I pointed to the other side of the opening of our tent. She moved silently to position herself. I was not sure if we should go out and greet them or let them wander in. Wandering in seemed the best choice. I was not sure if there were others in the camp as well. The first man stepped forward toward the opening and reached out to pull back the flap. The second man followed and pulled the other flap. I looked at Rebecca, noticing the grin from ear to ear on her face. She seemed to like this cloak and dagger stuff way too much. When their arms came into view, I grabbed one, and Rebecca grabbed the other.

Together in harmony, as we always were, we ripped the two men into our tent, knocking them to the ground. I stepped over one and placed the tip of my blade on his throat, and Rebecca, who loved the dramatics of it all, jumped on top of hers and laid the blade along his throat.

"Do you not have manners? Did you not know that it was rude to enter a lady's quarters without asking her permission first?" Rebecca glared at the man.

"I do not see any ladies here," the man shot back. Rebecca applied pressure to her sword.

"I suggest you speak with manners, sir, or she is liable to cut your head off. She has been known to do that a time or two." I could not help myself. I leaned down a bit and whispered, "She beheaded the man she loved because he angered her, so I would be careful." I looked at the man at the tip of my sword. "Me, on the other hand, well, I do not need a reason to cut someone's head off, so what brings you to my tent?"

The man lying on his back under my feet spoke first, "We were sent by Wellington and Blackmore to seek you out and to bring you back with us."

"Well, it appears you were misinformed, because it will take a great deal more than the two of you to take us anywhere."

The man under Rebecca's sword laughed. "What makes you think we are alone?"

Not a moment passed after he said those words, and the world went black.

CHAPTER TWENTY SIX

It was Juliana's screams that woke everyone in our camp. Jared and Charles were the first to reach our tent and Blake and Joseph were not far behind. They found Juliana alone, and on the floor just inside, were our swords.

Jared rushed to Juliana. "Shhh, little one. What happened?" He scooped her up in his arms and cradled her.

"Two men came in. Rebecca and Sabine threw them on the ground," she said through tears.

Jared could not help but smile, along with Charles. "Then what happened, sweetheart."

"Then more men came and hit them on the head. They fell down and they took them away."

Panic set in. "Charles, search the camp now. Send out scouts to find them." Charles was already on his way out of the tent. "Do you remember anything else, sweetheart?"

She shook her head. "They were whispering."

"Did they say any names?"

"I think so."

"It is all right, sweetheart. We will find them. If you can remember anything that they said, you tell me, all right?"

She nodded at him. Jared went to find Charles.

"I sent some men out, and one of our trackers. We will find them. Juliana, do you remember anything else?"

"I think they were names, but I do not know."

"Names, like people's names?"

She nodded. "They were big names."

Jared stood there, looking at Charles, and at the same time, they said, "Was one of those names Wellington?" Juliana smiled and nodded.

Jared could feel the fear well up in him. The anger rose at a rapid pace along with it. "Juliana, sweetheart, was the other name Blackmore?"

In a small voice she said, "Yes."

Charles and Jared both stood there frozen, unable to move. Blake interrupted the stare of fear. "Then we must be close, and we need to move now to get them back. Their horses are still here."

Charles spoke, but his eyes never left Jared's. "Prepare the old woman. Gather fifty or so men and prepare to ride. Find some men to take the children to Wellington, Blackmore and Collingwood. This is not over, and we have a war on our hands."

Jared looked to Juliana and said, "Sweetheart, I am going to have to go get Sabine back, but we are going to make sure that you and the other children are safe. We are close to home now, so I am going to send you to your father's brother, Westin. He will look after you until I can get Sabine back, all right?"

She started to cry. "But Sabine said she would never leave me."

"She did not leave you on her own accord, sweetheart. Someone took her, just like they took you, and just like she came to find you, I need to go find her. Do you understand?"

"Yes," she said and threw her arms around Jared's neck. "Please do not make me leave you," she sobbed into his neck. Jared held her while she sobbed and shook in his arms. He knew how terrified she was.

It was Blake that spoke, "Excuse me, sire, but if Sabine promised her, and the child wishes to stay, then I believe she should stay. I can keep her close."

"Yes, Jared," agreed Charles. "We must keep the child with us. We know not the danger that lies ahead for her."

Jared could not resist Juliana and smiled. "Well, my little love, it looks like you are going to stay with us."

There were smiles everywhere. Even Charles smiled, only no one knew his was forced. No one knew the truth of what lay ahead for all of us, except him.

Charles had arranged for a hundred men to escort the children, and the rest came to find us.

CHAPTER TWENTY SEVEN

My eyes fluttered open, and my head was pounding. I tried to focus, but I could not, so I closed my eyes again. My hands and feet were bound, and I could hear breathing, so chances were Rebecca was near. I did not want to move, just in case we were not alone, and I did not want our captors to know I was awake. I listened, but there were no other sounds, so I thought it best to just stay still. I was not sure how much time had passed before I heard footsteps. It was more than one set. Then I heard voices, deep male voices. There was the sound of keys, and then I heard the door being unlocked with a voice saying, "Is this really necessary? They are just girls."

Laughter came, and the other voice said, "Just girls? Now that is funny. Just girls collectively wiped out an entire army. Tens of thousands of men are dead. I think this is mild. You do not know the power these two girls hold. You have always been blind to the reality of your daughter's abilities, Gerald."

Gerald was Rebecca's father, so the other man must be Samuel. We were at Wellington. I should have known Samuel would attempt to end this his way. The door swung open, and I heard Gerald gasp and move across the room.

"What have you done, Samuel? Rebecca, my dear Rebecca. Is she dead? Would you go so far as to kill my daughter, Samuel?"

"Relax, Gerald. She is merely unconscious. Here, throws some water on her face. I am sure she will snap out of it."

I heard the water splash on the floor, and then I felt it as Samuel poured it over me as well. Rebecca woke up fierce, but I took my time. She was screaming at her father, "How dare you think it acceptable to bind me like a common thief. Everyone was right about you, Father. Everyone told me you did this, and I did not want to listen to them. Does Mother know you are such a treacherous man? Will you have me burned at the stake, as you did Sabine's village and family? Or shall it be a hanging for treason in the courtyard of Blackmore, so your subjects will heed and be warned? Come on, Father, and tell me what my fate is. You send goons after me in the dark of the night to kidnap me and my friend in our sleep, and then you bind us and throw us in this place. What is this place? Are we in a dungeon, Father? We are in a dungeon. I thought we did not have a dun..." She stopped talking when she realized that Samuel was in the room. "Oh, this just keeps getting better, Samuel of Wellington. Father, do you really lie with snakes and murderers? You are no father of mine. I want nothing to do with you. Be gone and leave me to rot in this place with my friend." She tried to get away from him.

"Rebecca, none of what you say is truth."

She laughed as she spoke, "Are you kidding me, Father? I have seen what you have done. I have been a part of what you have done. I have had tens of thousands of men trying to do what you and Samuel hired them to do. KILL ME!"

"No, Rebecca, they did what I hired them to do. They brought you back to me."

My eyes had focused, and I could see Rebecca's face, and those were the wrong words to say.

"What? Are you serious, Father? I know the truth. I know everything, so stop pretending that you are my father. Be a man. Better yet, be the man who had his friend murdered along with his entire family."

"Now, Rebecca, you are being a bit hard on your father," Samuel said in his condescending voice. "We needed to protect the lands from Stephan's evil plan. He would have annihilated us and taken what we owned for himself to grow stronger than all of us, so we just beat him at his own game. Would you want to live under a man who treated his people in such a despicable way? Unfortunately for me, a few of them were missed. Now, we only have this one to take care of, and then Whispering Wind will be gone." He nodded toward me.

I knew how Samuel liked to play his mind games. There was no way he could have gotten to Westin. I had to trust Charles in protecting him. After all, Camille was his sister, and he would have died for her. I chose not to say a word to Samuel. I lay there not moving, only breathing, waiting, and letting Rebecca do what she must do.

"Oh, Samuel, you lie just as easily as you breathe, but rest assured that will not be for much longer. Do you really think they will not come for us? Do you really think that Jared will allow you to kill his beloved?"

"Jared is nothing to me now. He is as insignificant as his mother and his sisters. He serves no purpose. Once he chose this orphan over his duty to me, he became nothing to me. Those who will come for you will not discover you until it is too late. They will be dealt with and suffer the same fate as Whispering Wind."

She laughed, and it was never a good thing when Rebecca laughed like that. "Oh Samuel, a fool you are if you believe you can end this here in this dungeon. If you thought it was that easy, then why are we here? Why not just slit our throats when your thugs came for us? I know why. It is because you know the truth, or what you perceive to be the truth." She laughed again. "And you, Father, you gave me only one thing that I am grateful for, and that is my life. Nothing else means a thing to me. You sentenced me to death, and I am no longer your child. I was dead to you the moment you made the decision to side with Wellington."

"No, Rebecca that is not how it happened. You just do not understand what Stephan was going to do."

"Are you kidding me, Father? You are going to stand there, looking down on your oldest daughter, bound in a dungeon, and spew lies to me. I think, considering the fact that your friend here plans on ending our lives, you could at least tell me the truth. It was the thought of all those jewels, was it not, Father?"

The look on Gerald's face was enough to see that he was shocked that we knew about the jewels. I stifled a giggle, but Rebecca was furious. She needed to get this out of her.

"Rebecca, please. Do not be ridiculous. There are no such jewels. We did this for the safety of the entire land."

"Oh, Father." Her voice had changed. She became calm, and she never took her eyes off of him, but I knew my friend. I knew that these were going to be the last moments for her and her father to be father and daughter. "You sadden me with your pathetic and condescending ways. I know the truth. I have seen the jewels with my own eyes." I felt Samuel shift at this realization. "I know this is what it is all about. I know that you and Samuel knew of their existence, and I know that long before Sabine and her brothers were born, that her father went and took them back from the barbarians. I also know that my arranged marriage to Wellington was to bond your kingdoms, to unite against the rest of the land, and to produce the heir to the legend. Father, did you not know that this was the reason behind Jenna and Ardes, and that when Jenna had a daughter, she became irrelevant just as her mother and sisters? You sicken me with your lies and your condescending words. I disown you as my father. Please leave and allow Samuel to do what he is going to do. I want nothing more from you."

She turned her eyes from him and focused on me. I knew it was time, and we needed to fight our way out of here.

We can do this, Sabine,

I heard her in my head. I was stunned. *How was that possible? How was any of this possible?* I gave up trying to figure it all out a long time ago. I concentrated and tried to project my thoughts to her.

Say when.

Her look let me know she had heard me.

"Rebecca, please. You are my daughter, and I love you."

Samuel interjected with his poisonous thoughts, "Gerald, it is obvious that your daughter is lost to you, just as Jared is lost to me. These lies that have been spread about us have obviously been drilled into their heads, and they are not going to listen to us. I say we just let them stay here for a bit and come to their senses." He then directed his words toward me as he continued, "And you, Sabine, you have been very quiet through all this. Do you not want to ask me how I found your brother, or what has happened to the simple Westin?"

He was baiting me, but I would not answer him. I would not give him the satisfaction. He would not beat me.

"Humph, perhaps my guard hit her a bit too hard on the head."

It was in that instant that I heard Rebecca scream in my head.

NOW!

I swung my feet around, as did Rebecca, knocking Samuel and Gerald to the floor. I managed, with great pain, to flip myself on top of Samuel, placing my knee on his throat. Rebecca did the same to her father. While I lay there on the floor, I had managed to loosen the straps around my hands, but not enough to free them. I fumbled around for Samuel's sword. Finding it, I pulled it out a bit so I could cut my hands free. I replaced my knee with my hands. It was difficult at best not to choke the life out of him, but I managed to squeeze just hard enough to cause him to go into the dark. I turned to face Rebecca, and saw that she had not had much success. I untied my feet and then untied her. She had a harder time stopping herself from killing her father, but she managed to stop once he was out.

"I need to leave him alive, so that I can show my mother what kind of man she married."

"I know. Katherine needs to know as well. I wonder why there are no guards here."

"I am sure that they want no one to know our location. We need to tie them up and get out of here, wherever here is. Sabine, do you have any clue as to where we are?"

"I can only imagine where we are. It is going to be interesting finding out. I wonder if they got our swords or if they left them behind."

"I do not think they are that smart. So should we leave them here, or should we take them with us for hostages?"

"I say we gag them and leave them for now. Here are the keys. Make sure the knots are tight." I took the keys from Samuel. "You ready for this?"

She chuckled. "As ready as I will ever be. Oh, one more thing, Sabine, I do not think I will have a problem with you killing my father. I thought I might, but after this, he is not my father."

I sort of smiled. "Okay then, let us go before someone comes looking for them."

As we made our way through the labyrinth of halls, there was no sign of anyone. It was strange. I could not imagine where we would be that there would be no guards.

"Sabine," Rebecca whispered. I turned to see that she was nodding toward some stairs to the right. I nodded back, and we slithered our way up the stairs, not knowing what to expect. Curiously, there was no one in sight. We were nowhere that looked familiar, just another level of the labyrinth; more hallways, more corners, and then another staircase. As we ascended, I heard some voices, so we stopped to listen.

"This place gives me the creeps. I wonder how long they are going to be down there?" one voice said.

"Who knows? It is all a big secret. Did you know that all the guards who went out on that mission were put to their death?"

"How did you find that out? You do not know anyone in Wellington, do you?"

I looked at Rebecca. She had that look in her eyes again.

"It has been the talk around the village. No one could believe that Wellington would be so brutal. The king had said they had committed treason and gone against him. It was his way of showing his people that he would not tolerate disobedience."

"Well, I am glad that we live in Blackmore then."

"Yeah, but our guys were put to death as well."

"What are you talking about? The king said they had not returned yet."

"Oh, I am sure they will not be returning any time soon. The king will probably say they were defeated in battle against the barbarians that took Princess Rebecca."

When Rebecca heard that, I could not stop her, not that I would have tried, but she flew past me, nearly knocking me down the steps.

"So that is what you were told, was it?"

The men nearly fell over when she spoke. I came up behind her. Their faces were distorted. "Princess, what are you doing here? Your father said you were kidnapped by barbarians."

She laughed. "Blackmore was lying, as is Wellington. You know this to be truth, for my father and Wellington are locked in the very dungeon they put us in. Now, the choice is yours. Tell us where we are and give us some horses, or you can meet the same fate as those you serve."

"Well, Princess, we are at Whispering Wind, and you are welcome to our horses."

I could not believe what the man had said. Whispering Wind did not have dungeons. I looked around, but I did not recognize where we were. "Where are we?" I said miffed.

"Princess Sabine." He bowed. "We are in the barracks to the south of the castle."

My father had dungeons? Who did he keep in them? Perhaps they were built before my father was born. If that was so, then how did Wellington know of them? Could this be what the barbarians were looking for, secret passages?

"Tell us what you know. How many times have you come here?" Rebecca demanded.

"This would be our first trip."

She looked at me. "It is a two-day ride from Wellington. We have been gone for at least three days, Sabine."

"Jared and Charles must be looking for us. The first place they would go would be Wellington. Jared would know his father would try something. We need to get to Wellington, Rebecca. You two breathe none of this to anyone, or I will cut your head off myself."

"Yes, my lady."

We ran to the horses, making our way through the castle grounds, and then into the village, or what was left of the village. We were just about to the fields when I heard the thunder again.

"Rebecca, do you hear that?"

"Horses, and lots of them."

"Come on." I turned my horse and headed through the fields to the hill. I stopped before I started my ascent. "It could be Charles and Jared."

"It could also be Wellington."

"We cannot be seen from here. We shall wait and see."

The thunder grew louder, and then it stopped short. There was not a sound in the dark of the night. I listened carefully for a voice, but heard nothing.

I looked at Rebecca, but she was just as stumped as I was. Then I saw him, a shadow in the dark night. He was walking slowly. *Could it be him?* The closer he got, the better I could hear him, but he was not alone. I could not stop the scream when I saw him, "Raiden!!" I was off my horse before I finished screaming. I ran up to him and threw my arms around his neck. He neighed and neighed. I heard the other horses coming, and then I felt Jared's arms around my waist, pulling me into him. "Oh, thank God you are alive," he said as he suffocated me with his kisses. "Do not ever do that to me again. Do you hear me?"

I laughed at him. "Well, it was not by my own choice." We laughed together then, and he kissed me some more.

I heard Charles yell Rebecca's name, and I felt her run past me. When Jared finally let me go, I turned to see them kissing and laughed. I was glad that they had finally given in to their feelings. Life would be good again.

"So, why are you both here?" Charles asked when he was finished kissing Rebecca.

"Well, it seems that Samuel and Gerald had us kidnapped with the intention of ending our lives."

Charles looked at Rebecca, and she smiled. "What they did not expect was for us to reverse the role and take them captive." We both laughed.

"My father kidnapped you?" Jared asked.

"Not only did he kidnap us, he also admitted to having my family slaughtered, and he said that he took care of Westin as well. We locked them in the dungeon. Did you know my father had dungeons?"

"No, I did not know that. Shall we go see my father and see what he has to say for himself?"

"Jared, where is Juliana?"

Charles answered, "We sent the children to the surrounding kingdoms with about a hundred men. They should be arriving there in a few days. Joseph, would you have some men go to the valley and let Westin and Camille know we are returning soon?" He looked at me and read the concern in my eyes. "Juliana is with Blake."

I nodded. "Thank you, Charles."

Joseph nodded his head, and we started walking. Raiden followed me. I did not think he was going to let me out of his sight for a long time. We made our way through the village, through the courtyard, and then back toward the barracks.

"Where are these dungeons? I would have imagined that they were in the castle."

"One would imagine that to be so, but in this case, they are beneath the barracks."

Only me, Jared, Rebecca, Charles, and the rest of our guardians went into the dungeons. We made our way through the labyrinths and down into the deep dungeon. While we walked, Jared looked around. "Impressive place you have here, my dear."

I laughed. "Why, thank you, my love."

We arrived at the door where Gerald and Samuel were. I took the keys from my bodice and unlocked it. We all made our way into the room. They were both still unconscious, but Jared saw the bucket of water and poured it on them both. Samuel woke, spitting and coughing, and Jared rolled him over with his foot.

"Hello, Father."

"Jared, untie me, my boy. This banshee has taken me prisoner, and she must be dealt with."

Jared laughed. "Oh, Father, you will have to do better than that."

"Jared, you have been lied to and misled, son."

"Do not call me son. I have seen things you could only dream of seeing. Would you like to see something else?" He lifted his shirt. "You see this, Father? This is where a sword plunged into my flesh and ended my life, a sword you hired to murder me."

"That is preposterous! I would never do such a thing. LIES! It's all lies. You cannot believe what that girl says."

He pulled out my sword from its sheath and showed Samuel. "You see this sword, Father? This sword is what you seek, is it not? The sword that you believe holds so much power, that you have wanted for years, is nothing but just a sword. It is but a piece of metal that was forged a long time ago. It holds no power for you, Father. You see this girl?" He turned and pointed to me. "She is just a girl, the girl I love and intend to wed, but just a girl. You see that horse?" Raiden had followed us into the dungeon. "That is just a horse, a horse who belonged to the girl's father, whom you had murdered. So, you see, this is just a sword made of metal, a girl I love, and a horse, and the other girl, sword, and horse are just that... a girl, a sword, and a horse. But, Father, what you do not know is that when you combine them," he paused as he handed me my sword, just as Charles handed Rebecca her sword, "they become something you really need to see. Ladies, would you do me the honor of enlightening my father?"

I turned to climb on Raiden, noticing that Spirit was right behind him, and Rebecca climbed up as well. The ceiling was low, so we had to go out into the hall. I leaned into Raiden, saying, "I know you want them dead, but try not to kill them, for they have knowledge we need." He neighed at me. "I know, but do it for me," I said to him. I looked into his eye, and he looked like he was smirking at me. I raised my sword, as did Rebecca. The horses jumped up on their hind legs, and the brilliant light flooded the room. I could hear Samuel and Gerald's screams of fear. I could not help but smile. Raiden dropped to the floor, and I climbed off and went back into the room. Rebecca laughed loudly as she followed me.

"Now, Father, there is something more you need to know. When these girls hold these swords and fight with them, this is what happens. Ladies," he said as he turned with his sword in hand. I swung first, and the light was intense in the darkness, and then Rebecca did the same. "Would you please fight one another?" We complied, and as usual, nothing happened. Jared turned to face his Father. "One more demonstration... Sabine, could I have your sword please?" I handed it to him. "Charles, would you be so kind?"

"But of course." He drew his sword and swung it at Jared. The swords clanked as they struck one another, but without the brilliant light. "Thank you, Charles, Sabine." He handed me my sword back.

He turned to face his father again, only this time, he squatted down in front of him. "So you see, Father, this power you seek does not belong to you. It belongs to Sabine of Whispering Wind and to Rebecca of Blackmore. You killed an entire family, an entire kingdom, so you and Gerald could obtain this power. You tried to force me and Rebecca into a marriage neither of us wanted. You murdered my sister when she did not birth a male child. You hunted us, as if we were thieves," his voice cracked. "You stole my sister's child, your grandchild. You murdered another child to make us believe Juliana was dead, but you could not kill her. You knew what would have happened to you if she died, did you not Father?" Samuel stared at Jared, but he did not speak. I could not help but wonder if it was fear that Jared would strike him, or fear that we knew the truth. We knew most of the truth, but Charles had not told us everything.

"So, Father, the way I see it is that you are the monster. You are the one who needs to be stopped, and I am glad to tell you that this girl is the one who has done you in. If she does not end your life, then your life will end here. You will remain in this dungeon until the end of your days. Wellington will be told you died in battle, as will Blackmore. My mother will take your place in Wellington. She will become the queen, and she will pass the kingdom onto Francine. Sabine will take her place as Queen of Whispering Wind, and Rebecca will take her place in Blackmore. You see, Father, peace will reign true. You know your crimes, and you will pay for them. When I leave this place, you will never see my face again. You will know that I am happy, and you will know that our children will grow and laugh and play in the halls of Whispering Wind. Charles will make sure that the light of the day will never cross your face again."

Samuel and Gerald did not move, nor did they speak. The fear was still in their eyes.

Gerald finally spoke through his tears, "Rebecca, I cannot say how sorry I am for all of this. It was not my intention to cause you harm. The only thing you had to do was marry Jared, and none of this would have happened."

"Excuse me," Charles interrupted him. "This you would have been able to stop. Your first mistake was to mistrust your friend, Stephan. Your second was to believe that Wellington would have let you live with the knowledge you have."

"A fool's bet made by a fool, right Father?" Rebecca did not wait for an answer. "Can we get out of here? I need a bath."

Charles laughed. "After you, my lady."

Samuel was saying something, some sort of threat, as we walked out. Jared shut the big door behind us and locked it. "Charles, we are going to need some men posted here, men we trust."

"Already done, Jared. Now let us get these ladies what they need."

Jared came up and wrapped his arm around my waist. "My love, will you do me the honor of becoming my bride?" He said it loud enough for his father to hear, so I did the same.

I kissed him. "Yes, my lord, I will, just as soon as Westin and Camille get home."

We climbed out of the labyrinth to find all our men waiting for some kind of news. Charles addressed them, "Men, we are home. Let us make camp for the night, get some well needed rest, and we will all decide what to do in the morning."

That seemed to be enough for everyone. Charles was talking to a few men and then came back to us. "Sabine, your kingdom awaits you."

I could not help but laugh. "Some kingdom, but, Charles, this is not over, is it? What about Devious?"

"Well, I think Devious will enjoy her accommodations below with Samuel and Gerald," he said with a smile. "Come with me, ladies. Real beds await you."

"Beds that barbarians slept in. I think I will sleep in my tent, if you do not mind. Jared, would you please stay with me? I think I have had enough of getting hit on the head and being thrown in dungeons."

He laughed. "Whatever the lady wishes, but there is someone who awaits you, my lady."

I looked past him to see Blake holding a sleeping Juliana in his arms. She was so tiny set against his great frame. He leaned his head down and said something to Juliana. Her head lifted off his shoulder, her eyes widened, and her mother's smile flashed across her face. Blake set her down, and she was in my arms before I knew what happened.

We walked to where the soldiers were setting up the tents. I started to help set ours up. I was tired, and I just wanted to lie in Jared's arms and let the exhaustion over run me. I always slept best in his arms, and that is exactly what I did.

CHAPTER TWENTY EIGHT

I was not aware of the movements outside the tent. I was only aware of the arms that were around me and the slight snore of the man who held me. I did not want to move, but there was much that needed to be done. I wanted to see, and I needed to be with, Westin. *Had their baby been born yet? Were they even still alive?* Charles must know something, anything. I knew the cottage was a six-day ride, but it was a six-day ride when you were just traveling slowly. I was not sure how fast it actually took to get there if you were riding hard. I tried to remember how long it took Blake when he came here, to Whispering Wind, to get the jewels. So much had happened. I could not bring the memories up in my mind. I shook my head, as if to shake off the fog. Jared stirred next me, and his breathing changed, so I knew he was awake.

"Mmm, good morning, my love."

"Good morning." His arms tightened around me, and his mouth found mine. We kissed until our breathing became irregular. "I never want this to end," he whispered.

"Me neither, but we have things to do. You need to see your mother and tell her the lie, and you need to make the transition for her as easy as possible," I whispered back as not to awaken Juliana.

He chuckled. "If you think I am leaving you for one moment in time, you are mistaken," he kissed me again.

I pulled away from him. "Do not be silly. We have been gone for a long time, Jared, and you have been away from home for a year. Your mother has got to be crazed."

"How about we go together? I am sure my mother will be glad to receive you, and I know she will want to meet Juliana." His hand left my waist to stroke my cheek.

"Let us go talk to Charles, and then we will decide."

"Deal," he said as he released me.

I ran my fingers through my hair and made a loose plait, tied it with a leather strap, and straightened my clothes. "There. I am ready."

Juliana was still sleeping, so we left her. Outside the tent, I saw Blake and motioned for him to come over. "Would you please stay with her until she awakens and then come find us? She knows you."

"Of course, Sabine," Blake said.

We went looking for Charles. He was with Rebecca down by the stream. I could hear her laughing as we walked up. "Good day, you two. Did you sleep well?"

"I sleep best when I am in his arms, so yes, I slept well. Charles, I need to talk to you about Westin and Camille."

"It is already done, Sabine. I sent Aidan and a few men to bring them home. Rebecca and I were just talking about this story we are going to tell Wellington and Blackmore."

"I think we should just tell them the truth, Charles. Enough lies have already been told. I am sure that Katherine, as well as Rebecca's mother, may know more than we give them credit for. Only if the truth seems too much for them to handle as we tell it, then we can fabricate the lie and tell them of their deaths."

"I second that, Sabine. I have always been honest with my mother, and I really would not want to lie to her now. Also, I just want to clarify one thing. I am not going to be taking over the rule of Blackmore. I will leave that to my mother and to my sister. I am going to stay here with Charles. He is your guardian, and as it turns out, he is going to be my husband." She smiled her wicked smile at him.

I hugged my friend tightly, and I whispered in her ear, "Legends do come true." We both rolled with laughter.

We made our plans, the four of us, to depart as soon as we had our morning meal. We needed to get to Wellington, and then to Blackmore and back, before Westin and Camille got to Whispering Wind. I could only hope that all was well with my brother, for I missed him dearly.

As we walked to the camp in the courtyard talking, I happened to notice a lovely little girl in a beautiful white gown, standing in the midst of all the otherwise dirty men, looking sad and lost. I could not look away, and then her eyes looked up into mine as I approached her. I gasped when I realized that it was Juliana. She was beautiful, so beautiful. I could see Ardes in her eyes looking at me, and I could see Jenna in her face. She was a perfect blend of them both. I let go of Jared's hand and ran up to her, scooping her into my arms. Her little hands wrapped around my neck, and she hung on as we twirled in the courtyard.

"My beautiful Juliana, you look so lovely. I missed you so much. Have these men been good to you?"

"Yes, Sabine, but I missed you, and they said you were leaving me again."

She melted my heart. "They said that, did they?" She nodded her head as the tears began to roll down her frightfully thin cheeks. "Oh, my love, do not cry. I told you I would not leave you again. I was going to ask you if you would like to go on an adventure with us to meet your grandmother. Would you like that?" She squeezed my neck tighter and nodded her little head in my hair. "Well, good. Right after we have had some food, we are going to leave, so you must go help Blake get everything ready. When you are done, you come right back here to get me, and we will go, all right?"

"All right," she said, and I sat her on her feet. I looked up to see Blake waiting for her with his hand held out. As she ran to him, she turned and looked at me. I reassured her, "I promise. I will be right here waiting for you," and she continued on.

"Charles, could you send someone to the cottage to have them bring Westin and Camille to Wellington. I think Camille needs to see her mother, your mother, and I would like to marry Jared there with Katherine and the girls."

"I will send someone now," he said and walked away. There was not much said while we ate. I could not believe how hungry I was. I think I ate more than Jared did. He sat there watching me with huge eyes, and I could not help but laugh to myself.

Charles came walking up with Juliana in his arms, and they were laughing about something. She had changed out of her pretty white gown into some make shift boy clothes. She looked like a totally different child.

"Look, Sabine. Charles made me boy clothes, just like yours!"

"I see that, and you look just as lovely in them as you did your pretty white gown."

"Blake said we had to pack it up, so that when I meet Grandmother, I can look like the little princess that I am and not some boy. Am I a princess like you, Sabine?"

"You are, my love, as was your mother, Jenna." I reached for her. "Now, are we all ready for our adventure?" She nodded her head, and I hugged her.

"All right, my two beautiful ladies, shall we get going?" Jared said as he kissed her on the cheek. We all walked to where the horses were. "Hi Raiden." Juliana said. He stomped his hoof and snorted at her, which sent her into a fit of giggles.

I climbed up on him, and Jared handed Juliana up to me. "Now, you hang onto Raiden and Sabine, all right?"

"I will, Jared." She smiled at him.

He looked deep into my eyes and said, "I love only you."

"I love only you," I replied as I bent to kiss him. Juliana giggled. As we rode out of Whispering Wind, I noticed the men beginning to rebuild. Somehow, I knew that when we returned, it would be nearly as it was that day I lay up on the hill; except that when I returned, it would still be void of my family.

CHAPTER TWENTY NINE

We rode gently for a while, just enjoying the forest and each other. We stopped by the brook, so the horses could have a drink. Jared and I sat on the grass, while Juliana chatted with her new friend, Raiden.

"I was watching you as we left Whispering Wind," Jared said in almost a whisper. "We will rebuild it, and we will fill it with the love that still grows there." He reached up and wiped the tear from my cheek.

I could not say anything. I just looked into his eyes, and I knew what he was saying to me was true. There were just no words to tell him how I felt, to tell him that I missed my family. I missed my brothers and my mother and father. I could only hope that they would be proud of me, and that they were at peace.

Charles cleared his throat. "I think we should be going. We have a long ride ahead of us."

"Yes, we do." Jared smiled at me, and then he kissed me.

We began our journey once more. I could tell that Juliana was getting a bit fidgety, so I leaned down and asked her, "Do you want to go faster?" She nodded her head. "Raiden," I whispered, "Would you like to show Juliana how fast you can run? But be careful."

He neighed at me, and I wrapped my arm around her so she would not fall off. Raiden did not hold back. Before I knew it, we were flying through the forest. I could hear the others behind us, and then I heard Spirit and Rebecca closing in. When the two of them ran, there was nothing like it. The ride was easy and gentle; our hair flying out behind us, and the wind on our faces. I could hear Juliana giggling, yelling, "Faster! Faster!" Raiden obeyed her. I could not tell you how long we rode like this, but just as the sun was about to set on the horizon, Wellington came into view. I pulled back on Raiden's reigns for him to slow.

"We must wait for Jared and Charles," I said as Raiden pulled to a stop.

"We need to change out of our boy clothes and into our beautiful gowns to meet your Grandmother."

Rebecca came over to take Juliana, so I could get off of Raiden. We quickly changed from our boy clothes, climbed back up on our horses, and waited for them to catch up. It took a little while for them to reach us, and when they did, their laughter bellowed through the trees.

"I believe you lovely ladies are in need of some water to wash your faces of the days' ride," Charles said as he handed me a skin of water and a cloth, and then one to Rebecca as well. I poured some water onto the cloth and washed Juliana's face and then my own.

"There." I smiled at her. "Pretty as ever. Your Grandmother is going to be very surprised to see you."

In the softest of whispers, Juliana said, "Do you think she will like me?"

It was Jared who spoke in the softest of voices, "Of course, sweetheart. She is going to be so happy to meet you." He reached out and ran his finger along her cheek. Juliana smiled at him. He saw the same thing I saw. When she smiled, he saw Jenna.

"Shall we go, my ladies?"

I looked at Juliana, and she nodded. We took our time riding into Wellington. As we rode through the village, we could hear the whispers. The people were shocked to see Jared. It was a guard who rode up that explained the faces of the villagers.

"Lord Jared? Is it really you?"

"Well, yes it is me, and Princess Sabine of Whispering Wind, as well as Princess Rebecca of Blackmore."

"Charles, my friend," he said in shock. "We were told you had perished."

Charles laughed. "You have been misled, my friend, but please tell me what you have heard."

The guard nodded toward me and Rebecca. "His Majesty told us that while on your way to take Sabine to her new home, you were all met with death by the barbarians. He said that Jared and Rebecca had run off to find the barbarians, and they too were taken. Your family has grieved for years at the loss of you and your brothers."

Charles looked at me as he spoke, "Well, the story was not truth. We are all alive and well. Sabine, I am going to see my mother and father, if that is all right?"

"Of course, Charles. We will be at the castle."

He kissed Rebecca and was gone in an instant. We rode the rest of the way to the castle without speaking. As we came through the gates into the courtyard, I heard Kaitlin scream for her mother. Jared was off his horse, and he had her in his arms, twirling her around. Then Katherine and Francine came out. Katherine was crying so hard she could hardly stand. Jared put Kaitlin down and ran to his mother. It was such a beautiful sight to behold. They stood there for a long time without speaking and without moving. A mother and her son; the son she was made to believe was dead. At that moment, I could not have hated Samuel more.

Francine was the one who broke the silence, "Sabine?"

I smiled at her as Katherine opened her eyes. "Oh, Jared, you found her." Then she saw Juliana peer around my arm, and she gasped. In a whispered voice she asked, "Jared, is that your child?"

Jared laughed. "No, Mother." He started walking over to me. He reached to take Juliana, but she buried her head in my chest. I leaned into him, and he held me as I swung my leg to slide down into his arms. Before I could move, Katherine's arms were around us.

"Oh, child, it is so good to see you. I was so torn when Samuel told us that you had been killed."

I could not help it. The tears just streamed down my cheeks. I could not imagine what this poor woman had been told. Her grief had to have been spectacular in size.

"Mother," Jared said as he pulled us apart. "I would like to introduce you to your Granddaughter."

"But, you said the child was not yours."

"She is not," he said softly as he waited for her to figure it out. It was not until Katherine saw Juliana's face that she knew. "Mother, I would like you to meet Juliana. Juliana, this is your grandmother." Katherine touched her face. "How could this be, Jared? She was killed along with your sister." Her eyes shot up, and she searched the courtyard looking for Jenna.

"Mother, Jenna is not here. She died that day at Whispering Wind, but Juliana did not. She was taken, along with all the other children. We have been searching the known lands for her for a very long time. Sabine knew the child Father had presented to us was not Juliana. Our departure was planned, Mother. The stories you have been told by Father have been nothing but untruths. Come inside, and we will tell you the truth of our time apart." He guided us into the castle, with Katherine hugging us all the way. We made our way into the grand room, none of us wanting to part, and we all sat.

It was Katherine who spoke first, "Rebecca, my dear, your mother will be so happy to know that her first born daughter has not perished. We mourned together for so long. Should we send word?"

"No, Mother, we are going there in the morning to tell Rebecca's mother what we will tell you tonight. It is a tale of murder and lies, a tale that has been in play for hundreds of years, an intrigue beyond belief."

"Jared." I smiled at him. "Juliana must eat. We all must eat, and she really should be in bed."

"No, I do not want to leave you, Sabine," her tiny voice came out as nearly a whisper.

"I know, my love, but will you at least eat?" She nodded her head.

319

"I will be right back," Jared said as he excused himself. He went out into the courtyard and found a guard. "Raymond, would you and a few others go to Blackmore and bring Rebecca's mother and sister here please? Tell them nothing, just that Wellington requests their presence right away. Do not bring the carriage. I know Blackmore knows how to ride a horse. Do this as fast as you can. You should return quickly, and please, send someone to find Charles and his brothers. Tell them their presence is required directly."

"Of course, sire," Raymond said and bowed.

"Please, do not bow to me. I am not Lord of this manner, and you may call me Jared. Please, call me Jared."

"Yes, Jared. We will return as fast as we can."

Jared came back into the house and sat next to Juliana. "Sweetheart, how about you and I go and see what we can find to eat in the kitchen?"

Juliana loved an adventure, and to go to the kitchen would be just that. She had never seen a kitchen, so it would be fun for her. "May I come along as well?"

Jared leaned over and kissed me. "Of course, my love. Mother, Rebecca, would you care to join us on our little adventure? We shall hunt and seek out some food," he said and smiled at Juliana. I could see the love he had for her, how sweet and gentle he was with her. He would not scare her any more than she already was. He was going to be a wonderful father.

As we all played the game of seeking out the kitchen, Jared had said to Rebecca, "I have sent some guards to Blackmore to retrieve your mother and sister, and to send for Charles. I think the telling of this journey we have all been on for more than a year's time now should only be told once."

"Thank you, Jared." Rebecca reached out to embrace him.

Juliana found the kitchen on her own. It was the smell of the cooking food that gave her direction, and it was the shock of the cook who screamed when she pounced into the kitchen unannounced that scared her into Jared's arms. We had a good laugh at the bit of excitement our presence made as we all piled into the kitchen. I was sure that Katherine had never been in this room, and that the cooks and servants were just as shocked as she was to be having us in here. At the cottage, it was an everyday occurrence. We did not consider ourselves any better than those who cared for us.

"Ladies, we have hunted the scents of your exploits and ask your permission to indulge our hunger on such treasures as those in which you have prepared." Jared bowed, and Juliana giggled wildly and bowed with him.

The cook did not know what to say. She just stood there, staring at Jared, and before we could say anything more, her arms were wrapped around him. "Oh, Lord Jared, you are alive!" She picked him up and swung him around in a circle. Juliana saw this as funny and giggled louder. The spinning stopped, the cook let him go, and then she turned to face Juliana. She was a rather large woman, and this terrified her. She moved behind me and buried her face in my skirt. "Do not be frightened, little one. I will not hurt you." Juliana peered out from behind me, and the cook gasped. "Could it be?" she whispered as her eyes searched my face and then Jared's. "This is Juliana, Jenna's daughter," Jared said to her. "Juliana, this is Ruth. She used to sneak me and your mother cookies."

The cook Ruth gasped and stuttered, "But... she... how could this be?"

"I am sorry, Ruth, but the stories of our demise have been greatly exaggerated. The story will be told when everyone is present, but for now, we would love to indulge in your fine cooking." He smiled at her, and that was all it took.

"Please, my lord, go to the dining hall and let us serve you."

"That will not be necessary, Ruth. We would feel more comfortable here with you all. I am afraid that we have lost any desire to be anything other than who we are. We do not consider ourselves above your station. We are just Jared, Sabine, Rebecca, and Juliana, so if you would not mind, we would like to stay."

Ruth smiled an awkward smile and nodded. We made our way to the table in the center of the great room. Rebecca and I set the table with plates and cups we found on shelves over the work station. Jared held out the chair for his shocked mother and his sisters. We chatted as we ate, waiting for Rebecca's mother and sister. Charles had come and sat next to Rebecca, and we ate and laughed and talked for a long time. It was important that Juliana get to know her grandmother, and that we all got familiar with one another again. When Rebecca's mother arrived, we moved back into the great hall to greet her. When she came through the doors and saw her daughter, she fell to the floor. Charles was closest and caught her before her head hit the stone floor. He carried her to the big sofa in the great room and laid her gently down. Rebecca was at her side when she started to wake. "Mother, Mother," she whispered.

Her mother's eyes fluttered as she woke to see her daughter sitting next to her, holding her hand. "How could this be?" her mother whispered. "You are dead! Am I dreaming?"

Rebecca giggled. "No, Mother, you are not dreaming. I am not dead. You were told an untruth."

Her mother regained herself and sat up. "But how could this be? We have mourned you all for so long. Your father said you were killed by the barbarians. Why would he tell me such a thing if it were not the truth?"

It was Jared who answered her question. "You have all been led to believe things that just are not true. We brought you all here to tell you at the same time what Wellington and Blackmore have done to Whispering Wind, and to all of us." Jared proceeded to tell the story, as Juliana snuggled into my lap and fell asleep. Jared and Rebecca's families sat and listened in horror, as Jared gave them all the details of the last year and a half. Charles interjected where his part and his knowledge were needed. As he neared the end, it was obvious that we needed to tell the truth, and not the untruth we agreed upon, concerning Samuel and Gerald.

"Now, this is the part that we were hesitant to tell the truth about, but it is obvious that enough untruths have been told for more than one lifetime. Samuel and Gerald did not parish. We will leave it up to the both of you," he continued as he gestured to his mother and to Rebecca's, "As to what their future holds. They are locked away in the dungeons of Whispering Wind, along with the leader of the barbarians. I have sworn to them that they will never see the light of day again."

Katherine spoke first, "Jared, you are the king now, and it is your decision."

"You see, that is the thing, Mother. I do not wish to be king. You and Margret are now the queens that rule our kingdoms."

Margret looked at Rebecca. "But, that honor is bestowed upon you, our first born."

"No, Mother. My place is with Sabine. I know that now, and with Charles." She looked at him and smiled. "We are to be married. He is Sabine's guardian, and I will be with him. Mother, we will all live at Whispering Wind. Blackmore is yours, and then you shall pass it on to Kate, and she will pass it on to her daughter, just as Katherine will pass Wellington on to Francine, and she will pass it on to her daughter, just as Sabine will pass Whispering Wind on to her daughter."

We all sat there for some time, not saying a word. Katherine and Margret needed to absorb all that we had told them. Jared came to take Juliana from my arms, and in a whisper, he said, "Mother, is Sabine's room still Sabine's room? This child needs a proper place to sleep."

"Of course, Jared."

"Oh, and I do not want you to be shocked or surprised, but I will be sleeping with Sabine and Juliana. I will not ever let them out of my sight again, but do not worry Mother, for we shall be wed just as soon as Westin arrives." He smiled at her, and we left the room.

I heard Charles say to Rebecca as we were leaving, "We shall sleep in Jared's room. It is just down the hall from Sabine's."

Margret looked at Rebecca with shock. "This is not proper for you to bed together. None of this is proper. I will not have it."

I reached out and touched Jared's arm. "Hold on. We need to explain this." I turned and went back to where Margret and Katherine were. "May I speak?" They nodded.

"These men have watched over us for a long time now. They have stood guard while we slept, fought to keep us alive, and have sacrificed everything they have to protect us. They deserve your respect and your trust as men of honor. I trust them both with my life, so why would I not trust them with my virtue as well?"

It was silent. I could feel Jared's smile at my back. He knew what I was saying was truth. Although he would have it his way if he could, he did protect my virtue.

"My lady, I would never compromise Rebecca's virtue or her honor in any way. I am a proper man, but I do not trust Wellington or Blackmore, and I am sorry, but I will not leave her alone. If it suits you, we will move Jared's bed to Sabine's room, and we will all sleep there. Jared, will you help me?" Charles spoke with a gentle but firm voice. He did not wait for a response from Margret. Jared handed me Juliana and followed Charles out of the room. I could not help but smile at the look on Margret's face.

"Goodnight, Mother. I will see you at the morning meal." Rebecca kissed her mother on the cheek, and we left the room.

We waited until we were upstairs before we started to giggle. "I have been gone for a year and a half, and she is worried about my virtue."

"You are her daughter. It is expected." I smiled at her.

When we reached my old room, Jared and Charles were just finishing up. I laid Juliana on the bed and climbed in next to her. Jared fixed a small fire, and Charles and Rebecca climbed into Jared's bed. I cannot remember anything after that. I just knew that when I woke in his arms as the light of the day beamed into the windows and across my face. I felt safe.

CHAPTER THIRTY

The light of the day brought with it a whole new line of inquiries. When we arrived in the dining hall, everyone was seated, and the chatter was in full swing. Katherine and Margret were discussing the marriages of Rebecca and myself. Margaret was not sure it was a good idea for Rebecca to marry a guard, and Katherine wanted Jared to rule Wellington. It seemed that they were planning our futures for us and becoming stern with their decisions for us. To the four of us, it did not matter what they thought, or what they wanted, for we knew what was going to take place. Time and tradition had changed for us, and we were not going to live by the barbaric rules that our forefathers had set into place.

"Mother," Jared addressed Katherine. "It is not your decision to choose for me my future. I will love only Sabine, and we will marry and live in Whispering Wind. It is my choice, and you will not make it for me."

I reached over to touch his arm. "Jared, please be kind to your mother. She is only thinking of your best interest."

He smiled at me. "I am aware, my love, what my mother wants for me, but she must understand that I never wanted Wellington."

"May I say something?" Charles interrupted. "We are all aware of tradition, but if I may be so bold as to say, a new dawn is upon us. These two women, no matter how out of reach the intrigue is, are the bringers of peace. They are the legend we have all known our whole lives, and our fathers' lives, and their fathers before them. We have all passed the stories off as just that, stories, but the things we have seen, the things we have done, have proved them to be truth and not stories. If I may suggest we all go out into the courtyard when we finish the meal, and we will prove to you just what it is we are saying. My lady," he said, gesturing toward Margret. "I love Rebecca, and our union has been foretold in the legend. I have not presumed that she will love me in return. I am only grateful that it has happened. I will love her until the day I leave this world, and I will protect her with my life. If she chooses not to return my affection, it would not stop me from protecting her. I am just honored that she does."

"Thank you, Charles, and I understand how you feel, but you must understand that we were given in our marriages to men we did not love. It is my place now to choose her husband for her."

"Excuse me, Mother, but I will do my own choosing. I have already accepted Charles' proposal, and I do return his affection with all that I am. Tradition is not something that will stand in my way."

"May I suggest something?" I was so hungry and just wanted to eat. "We have plenty of time to discuss this. I know that I am hungry, as is Juliana. I would like to eat, and then, Rebecca, we can show them all that we are together, and we can explain in more detail how the four of us are bound together."

Rebecca agreed, and we ate our meal in silence. Difficult glances were shared between Charles and Margret, as well as between Jared and Katherine. It was Juliana who became the center of attention, which I was grateful for. Her skills with the eating implements seem to be lacking. I tried to show her, but she was dropping more off than she was getting into her mouth. I smiled at her and let her use her hands. Teaching her to use utensils was not the task for this day, and I knew that in time, she would learn.

When we finished our meal, Charles led us out into the courtyard, saying, "I believe the best place to do this is in the training grounds."

"I agree," Jared responded. "Mother, do you care to walk, or should I get your carriage?"

"I am fine with the walk."

We started walking toward the stables. Juliana was running ahead of us. She stopped and turned around to make sure it was safe because she was still unsure of how far she was willing to be away from us. I smiled at her and nodded that it was indeed fine. As we reached the stables, two guards were walking out with Raiden and Spirit, and Juliana squealed with delight as she saw him.

"Hi, Raiden," she squealed. He complied with a snort and a stomp.

She ran up to him and wrapped her arms around his leg. Katherine let out a gasp. "Jared, get her before that horse stomps her to the ground!"

"It is all right, Katherine. He will not hurt her. They are old friends."

"Sabine, he is but an animal."

"On the contrary, Katherine. He is more than just an animal. Are you not, boy?" I said as I walked up to him, and he brushed his head against mine. I lifted Juliana up to ride him by herself to the training ground.

I really thought Katherine was going to faint when I let go of Raiden's reigns. "Sabine!" she said, panicked. "She will get hurt most assuredly, maybe even killed. She is much too young to ride alone."

"I assure you, Mother, that Raiden will not harm her," Jared said with a smile on his face as he reached over and took my hand in his. We continued out to the training grounds. Raiden stopped when we got there, so Jared could take Juliana off. She hugged his neck and thanked him for the ride.

Charles began, "Now, we know the legend speaks of a force so powerful that it could stop an army in its tracks. I would like to present to you that force." He gestured to me and Rebecca. "These swords," he continued as he took Rebecca's from his sheath, and Jared took mine. "Jared, would you mind?" Jared swung the sword at Charles with all that he had, and as usual, nothing happened. He handed Rebecca her sword, and Jared gave me mine. "Ladies," he said.

"What are you doing, Charles? These girls could not possibly lift those swords. They are going to get hurt." Katherine was panicked.

I could see that look in Rebecca's eyes, and then the smile came. Before another word was spoken, she swung her sword at me with all that she had. Her mother screamed, as I blocked her advance. Again and again, she swung at me, and nothing happened.

"Please, Jared, before one of them gets hurt."

"It is fine, Mother. These two have been doing this for years now, even when Sabine lived here with us at Wellington. Her and Rebecca used to meet on the plain to practice. They know what they are doing. Trust me."

"Now, as you can see, when Jared and I use these swords, they are just that, swords. The same when Rebecca and Sabine fight with one another. But what happens when they fight someone else with those swords?" Charles said.

He raised his sword to me, as Jared did to Rebecca. This time, both Margret and Katherine screamed out, "NO!" But it was too late. I responded, as did Rebecca. When Charles' sword hit mine, nothing happened. It was not until I swung at him that the force and the flash of light brought him to his knees. The same with Jared, and when the light vanished, Rebecca and I stood over them in victory.

"What was that?" Katherine was stunned.

"That, my lady, was the power these two women have, the power of the bringers of peace. When someone else uses their swords, the power stays hidden, and when they fight one another they cancel one another out. When they strike an opponent, the force and the power come to life. These women, these fragile tiny women, can bring a man to his knees."

"Are you telling me that they fought hundreds, if not thousands, of men alone?" Margret was visibly upset at the thought that her daughter may have fought in hand to hand combat.

Rebecca laughed. "Mother, I can best any man and drop him to his knees without even straining myself."

A crowd had gathered, and she searched the men for the biggest.

"You, sir, would you be so kind as to assist me?" She nodded to the biggest guy in the crowd.

"It would be my pleasure, my lady."

The man was huge, bigger than Charles. He walked up and bowed gently toward Rebecca, saying, "Are you sure, my lady?"

She smiled that wicked smile of hers, and I almost felt sorry for the man. "My name is Rebecca, and I am sure."

The man raised his sword in full swing at Rebecca, and it was quick. When it struck her, she did not move her body, only her arms. She swung his sword around, and with a powerful blow, slammed her blade into his. The light was brilliant, and the man fell to the ground on his knees. Her laughter was all that was heard after the blow. She apologized to the man, and then turned to face her mother. "You see, Mother, I can take care of myself."

"Now, my ladies, would you mind?" Charles gestured toward Raiden and Spirit, and then turned to face Katherine and Margret. "That is not all that they can do together. The legend tells of the one with the fire red hair, who everyone thought was Edward of Collingwood, and the compliment of the golden haired one. The two of them would be invincible. Samuel and Gerald had this knowledge, and it was not until Jenna and Ardes married that Sabine was discovered. Samuel knew from the moment he saw her who she was, hence your immediate departure from Whispering Wind after the marriage ceremony." He was speaking to Katherine.

"That is when Blackmore and Wellington devised their plan to murder all at Whispering Wind. Samuel wanted to wait for Jenna to have a child to see if it was a boy, as perhaps then he would have the upper hand, but when she produced a girl instead, he knew what needed to be done. They wiped out Whispering Wind, only Sabine and Westin were not there that day. When Samuel discovered this, and Sabine gave him the jewels, he knew it all to be truth. Every story we were told as children was truth. He panicked and did the only thing his ego would allow. He would not submit himself to a woman, not the way he despised them, so he decided that two more deaths would not mean a thing. The two things he did not factor into his plan were me and the love Jared has for her. He did not know who her guardian was. That was never told in the legend, just that there was one. And he certainly did not expect this." He turned to us. "Ladies, if you would be so kind."

Rebecca was wild with excitement. "It would be our pleasure, my love."

I leaned into Raiden and said, "Be careful. As far from them as you can go." He neighed at me. We raised our arms with swords in hand, and Raiden and Spirit jumped on their hind legs. The light was brilliant as it shot out onto the plain. When they landed on the ground, I saw Jared kneeling next to his mother. I jumped off Raiden and ran to him. Katherine had fallen to the ground and lay there unresponsive. I looked back at Raiden, but the look in his eyes assured me that she was untouched.

"Mother? Mother, can you hear me? Mother?" Jared looked at me, and I saw the fear in his eyes. I put my hand on his arm as she flinched. "Mother," his voice cracked. "Mother, are you all right?"

"What was that?" she mumbled.

Jared smiled. "That was what Father wanted. He wanted the power to destroy everyone."

"Sabine, are you all right?"

I could not help but giggle. "Yes, Katherine, we are fine. I know it is a great deal to take in all at once, but we are fine."

Jared helped her up. There was not much said as we made our way back up the path to the courtyard. In fact, there was not much said for the better part of the day. Katherine and Margret disappeared into Samuel's study. Jared and I played with Juliana, and Rebecca went to meet Charles' family. Soon, it was time for the afternoon meal. Sitting around the huge table, it felt like everyone was on edge.

"Katherine," I started, and my voice sounded loud in the otherwise quiet room. "I know that this is all unimaginable but..."

She raised her hand to silence me. A new look came across her face, and a sternness I had never heard came from her voice as she spoke, "I wish for you to take me to Samuel. Margret and I wish to speak to our husbands. This abomination of trickery is beyond us.

You and Rebecca have had some sort of witchery cast upon you. No one can do the things you have showed me. I also wish for you to leave Wellington. I am requesting you leave Juliana here with us, for she is my granddaughter, and I will not allow her to be put in harm's way again. You must leave immediately after the meal."

"Mother, you cannot be serious!" Jared spoke with great anger.

"Jared, you will not be leaving with Sabine and Rebecca. They have Charles to defend them. You will remain here with me, and you will retain your title as king while your father is indisposed. I want him released. I want you to take me to him and to release him. I believe he had the right intention when he sent those to Whispering Wind to remove this witch and her family."

Jared was angry. I had not seen him like this before. As he stood, he directed it outward toward his mother. "You will not speak to me in such a manner, Mother. Sabine is to be my wife, and there is nothing you can say or do about it. I will not take you to Father, and he will not be released EVER! We will leave Wellington, and you will not see me again for the rest of your days. You know not of what you are speaking about. My father, your husband, the King of Wellington, murdered an entire village of people, an entire family, because he thought he deserved to be the ruler of all the lands. He put into play a plan to murder me, as well as Rebecca, and if you find that noble, then you and I are not seeing the same things." He turned to face me, and in a softer, gentler tone, he said, "Sabine, would you please gather your things as well as Juliana's."

Katherine stood up. "Juliana will not be leaving with you. She is my daughter's child, and she will remain in Wellington."

Before I could speak or react, Jared spun on his heels to face her. "She will be coming with us, and the only way you will stop that from happening, Mother, is to strike me dead where I stand. You and I are finished!" He turned to me, and I was already on my feet. He picked up Juliana, and we walked out.

Rebecca stood and said to her mother. "I suppose you feel the same, Mother?"

Margret was fierce. "I do indeed, Rebecca. You will not marry a man who is beneath you. You are the Princess of Blackmore, and you will marry a prince, not a servant of the land."

I paused at the doorway. I knew that tone in her voice. Margret was about to witness a side of her daughter she did not know. Rebecca began to laugh, and it was never a good thing when she laughed in anger. "You really do not get it, Mother, do you? This has nothing to do with my station in this life. This has been foretold for hundreds of years..."

Margret interrupted her, "You cannot honestly stand there and tell me you believe this babble? This witch," she said, pointing to me, "has invaded your mind with her trickery. You will listen to me, and you will obey me, or..."

"Or what, Mother? You will send an army to murder me, like Father did? Well, I say this to you, Mother. Good luck finding one who will do as you ask. This has greater reach than Blackmore or Wellington. You cannot touch us. I am sad to say that we should have all let you believe the lie of our deaths." She turned to Charles. "Please take me away from this place. Please take me home. I wish to begin our life together."

The five of us walked out the front doors of Wellington to face the guards who had been ordered by Katherine to stop us. Charles reached for his sword, saying, "Shall you take your chances with us, or will you let us pass?"

They separated and let us pass. They had saddled our horses, and there were many who had requested to join us. As I climbed on Raiden, I noticed that Katherine and Margret rushed out into the courtyard. Katherine yelled in a desperate shriek, "Stop them! I order you to stop them. That woman is a witch, and she has cast a spell upon your king!"

One of the guards that was not going with us spoke, "I am sorry, my lady, but we do not agree with you. Change is coming, and we believe it to be truth."

"Anyone who does not agree with me is dismissed. You remove yourselves from Wellington immediately."

One by one, the guards walked away. Only a few stayed behind.

We rode out of Wellington, feeling saddened by the outcome of our efforts. Jared had parted company with his family on bad terms, and now Juliana would not know her grandmother. Rebecca and her mother had placed a wedge in their relationship that would not mend easily. This was not the way it was supposed to be. We were all so happy the day before. I looked at Jared, and he at me. "What now?" I mouthed to him. Juliana was so upset by all the anger in the dining hall. She was so small and had suffered so much. Jared just smiled and shrugged his shoulders.

As we rode through the village, we were met with no opposition. It was just the opposite. People were walking along with us. Some were pulling carts filled with their belongings. Wellington was coming with us. I rode up to where Charles and Rebecca were.

"Charles, what is happening?"

"I believe, Sabine, that we have a following, rather, I should say you have a following."

"This is not right, Charles. These people have lived here their whole lives. They are Wellington."

"Sabine, I do not want to sound harsh, so forgive me if I do, but you have lived a life of privilege, just as Rebecca and Jared have, so you have not been subjected to the stories handed down through generations. You have all been sheltered from the truth. These people have heard the stories. They have seen the things that Samuel has done, and they know that the legend is truth. I told you this was bigger than all of us. I am but one person in all of this, as we all are, but collectively, we have set into motion a tale that has been told for hundreds of years, a tale that the most repressed villagers clung to for their salvation. We have not all lived like those in Whispering Wind lived, with fairness and courtesy. Samuel, as well as Gerald, along with Collingwood, are tyrants who believe that the burden lies with the common people. These people have all been worked to the bone, taxed to the point of starvation, and dealt with violently if they could not provide the king with what he wanted. You see, Sabine, your father and mother knew the very second you were born who you were, and that is why you were never allowed to leave your kingdom.

I believe that if Ardes had not loved Jenna, that their union would have never taken place. Your father went to great lengths to keep you hidden from everyone. The villagers could only speculate about you. The talk was filtered through the kingdoms, but you were a girl, and nowhere in the legend or the stories was it ever inferred that a woman would be the one. As I told you before, the moment I saw you, I knew that it was true, and so did Samuel that day he came for Jenna and Ardes' marriage. Why do you think he left immediately after? I am sure that your father had tried to prevent all that happened to them. I think after Juliana was born, that he felt a bit more secure, and that is probably what ended Whispering Wind."

"This is too much to believe, Charles. Three years ago, I was just a girl lying on a hilltop, day dreaming, and now I am some mythical legend who is to save the land. Will I ever be just that girl again?"

"In my eyes, and in my heart, my love, you will always be that girl," Jared said as he smiled at me.

"We need to stop Westin and Camille from coming here."

"It is already done, Sabine. They will be to Whispering Wind in a day or two, and Camille has not yet had her baby."

We rode out of Wellington with our heads held high and with more than half of the villagers and guards. I supposed we were a sight to see. I could not help but wonder how Katherine felt. She so desperately wanted her son back, and for one short day, she had him. Samuel must have told her horrible things about me for her to turn on her own son. I could only hope that now that everyone knew the legend was true, that she and Wellington would be safe.

"We need to keep the location of Samuel and Gerald secret. No one must ever know where they are. Charles, can the men who guard them be trusted?"

He chuckled. "Sabine, those who will follow you will be true at heart. There will be no one who is with us that will ever be against you."

We climbed the hill at the end of Samuel's land, and we turned to look at the kingdom below us. It was sad to know that it would be a very long time until we would be welcomed there again, if ever. I looked over at Jared, and I could see the distress in his eyes. My hand found his. "I love only you, and I am sorry for what has happened."

"My love, this is not your doing. My father did this. His greed for power did this. My mother will forgive me one day."

Our ride to Whispering Wind seemed to take forever. We needed to camp for the night. The villagers walked or pulled carts, so our pace was slow.

When the light of the day broke through the sky, I woke. I was not sure if I had even slept. It bothered me to think of the things that Katherine said to me, and the way Jared had spoken to her was not in his character. He was a very kind man with a beautiful heart, but that man in that room was not Jared. I could not help but wonder how much of Samuel was in him. I quietly left Jared and Juliana sleeping, and I made my way over to Raiden. The camp was quiet since everyone was still asleep with the exception of the guards.

Raiden sensed me coming and made his way to greet me. "Hey, boy. Ready to go home?" He stomped his foot on the ground. I could not help but giggle. I swear he thought he was human. Well, according to Charles, he very well could be. "I could not sleep. I am worried about what lies ahead. I know that sounds silly, considering what we have been through." Raiden put his head next to mine, and I reached up to hug him. I turned to look at our camp. "Look at all these people, Raiden. They are following me. Why would someone leave all that they had to follow a girl, a fatherless girl, an orphan? I have no idea what I am doing, and everyone seems to think I am this legend. I do not believe that, but then I look at you and what happens when you do what you do. I think you are the one made of legends. Maybe we should all follow you." I giggled, and Raiden snorted.

I stood there with him for a moment, wondering what my future was to be. How was I going to rebuild Whispering Wind? Would I be able to live there with the ghosts of my family? Would these people finally figure out that I was just a girl and turn against me? I think that the revenge I pledged to my Father, standing at the gate that day, had taken on a life of its own and manifested into an uprising I could not control. "I need to ride," I whispered to myself, but Raiden heard me and nudged me, as if he was saying, 'Me too'.

I looked around and found his saddle. I put it on him, which is something I was not sure where I learned. When it was secure, I climbed up, and he quietly made his way out of camp and onto the plain. I leaned into him and whispered, "Do not hold back. I think we both need this." Before I sat back up, he was off. I closed my eyes and flew with him. Riding him this way was like flying, soaring through the sky, like a bird in flight. I could hardly feel him move underneath me. I could not tell how long we rode like this. Raiden never seemed to tire. I felt him arc, and my body slightly moved to the left, and then he was on his return to the camp. When I opened my eyes, I could not contain the giggle. Standing on the edge of the plain were at least fifteen men. Apparently, someone woke and discovered I was gone. As we got closer, I saw Charles and Jared in the middle. Raiden slowed as we approached them, and I could see that I was going to get reprimanded for leaving without telling anyone, but as we got even closer, I could see the grin on Charles' face. Jared was a bit more serious, but all was well.

"I just needed to ride," I said.

"I understand, Sabine, but next time, would you please let me know, so I do not send out an army to search for you?"

"Jared, I am not afraid of what lies in wait for me, and I am not a child. I am, after all, the legend, so what harm could come to me?" I was half joking. "Besides, Raiden can out run even the fastest horses. He would not let anything happen to me."

"I know, Sabine, but you must not forget that he is but a horse and not a guard with a sword."

"Perhaps to you and everyone else he is but a horse. You were not there when he killed the wolf now, were you? I would take my chances with Raiden protecting me more than I would a man with a sword any day."

Not another word was spoken. I thought that maybe I was a bit hard on Jared, but he had no right to treat me as if I were a child, especially in front of all those men. By the time we got back to camp, it was packed and ready to go. Juliana was eating with Rebecca when I walked up. "Good morning, beautiful girl. Are you ready to go home?"

She smiled and nodded her head. I scooped her up, and we went and climbed on Raiden. Jared lifted her up to me, saying, "I am sorry, Sabine, for being so firm with you…"

"It is fine, Jared. I hold no ill will toward you. I understand that you were worried, and the next time, I promise to leave word with someone. Now, let us go home. I am tired of roaming the lands."

He smiled. "Agreed."

When we were half a day's ride away from Whispering Wind, I turned to Charles and Rebecca. "I think we are going ahead of you all. Rebecca, would you and Spirit care to ride with us?" Her wicked smile was all I needed to see.

"Charles, Jared, we shall see you at home." Charles nodded, and Jared winked at me. I leaned down and whispered to Juliana, "You want to fly, my love?"

"Yes," she whispered and leaned into Raiden. "Go fast please." He did not disappoint her.

CHAPTER THIRTY ONE

After all, that we had been through, after all that we had done, going home sounded like a dream. I was going back to Whispering Wind, to my home. My family was with me now; I had Jared and Juliana, Charles and Rebecca, and Westin and Camille would be arriving in the days to come. We would make it a home again, and it would be filled with love, laughter, and joy. Those thoughts were all that I would allow to fill my mind, for I had seen enough death and despair to last three lifetimes. Samuel and Gerald would remain hidden from Katherine and Margret. The old crone, Devious, would never see the light of day. If Charles had not felt she would be of use, she would have died with her men. I took back my life, and I would live it as my father had wished, in peace.

Riding this way with Raiden was beyond words. I held Juliana tightly against me. She was still so small, and falling off this horse would definitely have ended her life. We flew through the forest, the trees almost a blur at his speed. It was when we broke free of the trees and onto the plain, onto the lands of Whispering Wind that Raiden slowed. I pulled him to a stop in amazement at what lay before me. It was as if I had walked out of a horrible dream, as if nothing had happened. Whispering Wind looked just as it had that day I had laid on the hilltop and looked down upon it. It was full of life again, as if the past three years had not happened. I knew I could not be dreaming. I heard myself say, "Where did they come from?" It was the answer that shocked me.

"It is not where they come from that you should ask, Your Highness. It is why they came."

I turned in my saddle to see Aidan sitting on his horse just a few feet away from me. I could not help but smile. If Aidan was here, that meant that Westin and Camille were here as well.

"Aidan, I am so happy to see you."

"It is good to see you, Your Highness."

"I told you, my name is Sabine." I sort of giggled and shook my head.

"It was Sabine when you had no kingdom to rule, but as you can see, Your Highness, you are now the Queen of Whispering Wind, and I am but a humble servant in your employ."

We all laughed. "Where did they all come from, Aidan? Who are all these people?"

"Well, they have come from the North and the West. Some came from Collingwood, some from Blackmore, and some from Wellington. They came for you, Sabine. They came to stand with you, to live in your kingdom, to live the dream they have all dreamed of for hundreds of years. They came to live in peace and to be free."

"We have been gone for just a few days. How is this even possible?"

"You forget that word does travel through the lands. When I left for the cottage, I came across many people on the roads, many people on their way here. They asked if it was true that peace was to come, and that the bringer of peace was in Whispering Wind. You forget the tragedy of your family sent fear throughout the lands. The legend spoke of the bringer of peace coming from the South, so it was believed that all was lost. When we started our journey home, every village we stopped in, every kingdom, word started to spread throughout the lands, and the people started to come."

"I am just a girl, Aidan."

"You are far from just a girl," Jared said from behind me. I turned to face him as he approached. "Good to see you, Aidan."

"Good to see you, my lord."

"Jared, would you look at all these people who have come here. We have been gone but a few days, and they have already built so many cottages. The fields are tilled. It is amazing how much they have accomplished."

"Sabine, my love, when people are happy, they are productive."

I heard my name from across the plain, but it was faint. I whirled my head and body. Riding full force was a horse, and on this horse was my brother. "Westin," I whispered. Before I knew it, I was off of Raiden handing Juliana to Jared, and I was running toward him. He slowed his horse as he gained on me, and he jumped off, running right into my arms. When our bodies collided, we slammed onto the ground in laughter.

"Oh, Sabine, I missed you so much. I was so afraid you were dead. I cried so much the longer you were gone, and when Aiden came and said we could come home, I cried even more."

"Oh, Westin, I have missed you so much. There is much to tell you, much you need to know."

We lay there in the grass, laughing and talking. It was not until we felt the pounding ground underneath us that we sat up. I turned to face the direction in which I came from to see everyone approaching, and right in front sat Juliana on Raiden.

"Who is that little boy on your horse, Sabine?"

My heart was pounding in my chest, and my smile was from ear to ear. I had asked Adian not to say anything about Juliana to Westin. I wanted it to be a surprise. "Come on, Westin. I want you to meet someone."

"Sabine, did you have a child?"

I could not contain my laughter. "Westin, I still have my virtue," was all I could manage to get out between my guff's of laughter.

We walked to meet Raiden. I reached up and took Juliana off

Raiden, and then stood her in front of me and waited. Westin stood there with a funny look on his face. He knelt down in front of her and just stared at her, but no one said a word. Juliana reached out to touch his face, and Westin returned the gesture. When Juliana smiled, Westin let out a gasp and fell backwards to get away from her. Juliana turned to face me, burying her face in my legs.

"It cannot be," Westin said with tears streaming down his cheeks. "Is this."

"Yes, Westin. I found her."

He reached out and grabbed her and drew her into his arms. "Juliana," he whispered through his sobs of happiness. "Beautiful Juliana… You found her, Sabine. You really found her!"

I stooped down and embraced them both. "Yes, my love, I did. We are home now, and nothing will separate us again."

I could not say how long we stayed there, holding one another, but it was Charles who spoke gently to me, "Sabine, the light of the day is leaving us we should get back to the castle."

"Can she ride with me, Sabine?"

I looked at Juliana, and she smiled, nodding that she wanted to ride with him. She pulled on my pant leg, and I bent down so I could hear what she wanted to say. "Sabine, is he my father?"

"No, my love. Your father and mother are gone. He is your Uncle, your father's brother. His name is Westin, and he loves you very much."

With that, she turned and ran up to Westin, who in turn scooped her into his arms. We made our way to the village, and as we rode through it, people clapped and cheered. It was all so strange; I did not know who any of them were, but they seemed to know me. As we approached the gates to the castle, I could not help but notice that they had been replaced. I turned to look at Blake.

"They have been preserved, Your Highness."

I nodded to him as we passed through the gates and into the court-yard. It did not look the same as when I left here two years ago. The ground was not stained with blood and bodies, the doors on the castle were put back in place, there were people milling about, and gardeners were finishing for the day. We climbed off our horses and made our way to the great hall. The place was filled with the scents of food, and sitting on the stairs was Camille; big, fat, plump Camille, full with Westin's child. She looked so beautiful and in a bit of pain. I ran right past Westin to hug her.

"I am so glad you are safe, my lady."

"I am your sister, Camille. My name is Sabine."

"Yes, that may be true, my lady, but you are also my queen, and I was taught to respect my queen."

"I insist, Camille, please."

"As you wish."

The others came over to see their sister, and then it was time for the real reunion. Camille's parents had made the journey with us. They had not seen their daughter in over a years' time, so it was quite the reunion. We made our way into the dining hall, and for the first time I think in my whole life, the entire room was filled with people. Every chair was taken, and some were standing. We told of our adventures while we ate the food that was prepared for our return. We laughed, we cried, and we knew we were home. I had insisted that Charles' parents live with us in the castle, along with Charles and his brothers, for there was more than enough room. We had all been living together for over a year, and it would just feel strange not to have them with me, or near me.

As we all made our way up the stairs, it was not mentioned, but it was a silent understanding; Ardes and Jenna's room and my mother and father's rooms were not to be chosen by anyone. There were strange looks when Jared, Charles, and Blake moved a bed from one of the rooms into my room for Charles and Rebecca to sleep in. I think everyone thought we were all crazy.

Charles' father was the only one that said anything. "Excuse me, son. I know you are a grown man, and a fine man indeed, but you are not married to Princess Rebecca, yet you share a bed with her. Would this be the wisest choice, son?"

"Father, it is true that I am not married to Rebecca, but I am going to wed her in the future, and you can rest assured, Father, that Rebecca's virtue is intact. We have been through some horrible dealings with the barbarians, and it seems that every time Jared and I are apart from Rebecca and Sabine, trouble seems to find them. I promise you, this is the reason for the bed in Sabine's quarters. We are aware of how it looks to others, so the solution we came up with was this one. Surely, you cannot think that I would dishonor a princess?"

His father smiled and laughed a very uncomfortable laugh. "No, son, I do not believe that you would do such a thing. Though you may not be of noble blood, you are of strong character, and I believe you will do the right thing."

"Thank you for your understanding, Father."

His father leaned in and whispered to him, "This is all so odd, us sleeping in a castle. We are just common folk. It just feels wrong."

I could not stop myself from saying, "Excuse me, my lord, but you are anything but common. You are the father of my guardian. You should never have to feel common. If it were not for Charles, I am sure I would be dead. He has saved my life more times than I could ever thank him for. If taking care of his family is a way to repay him for all that he has done for me and all that he has sacrificed for me, then I shall do it with nothing but the greatest joy. Whispering Wind is your home. Please do not feel like a guest here. The room you choose shall remain your room until you leave this life."

"That is very kind of you, Princess. This will take some getting used to." He smiled and patted my hand. I stood there in the hall with Charles, as his father slowly walked down the long hall.

"Thank you, Sabine," he whispered

"It is not even the slightest inconvenience, Charles. You would die for me. The least I can do for you is make sure your mother and father have the best life for as long as they live."

He put his arm on my shoulder and squeezed me close to him. We turned to walk in the room, and Jared was standing in the middle of the room with Rebecca. "Am I to worry about the two of you?" I laughed out loud and ran into his arms.

"I love only you, my love."

"As I love only you," he replied, and then he kissed me.

Juliana was already asleep. It was amazing how crowded my room was with these two giant beds in it, but somehow, it felt right. I closed my eyes with Jared's arm securely around me, and the dark of the night took control. Sleep came, but it was not peaceful.

CHAPTER THIRTY TWO

My sleep was restless, and the light of day came all too quickly. I did not feel the need to say anything to anyone. It was probably my body trying to absorb a sense of normalcy. We carried on our days, filling them with joy and laughter. Westin and I took walks with Juliana, telling her everything about Ardes and Jenna. I was sure it was more than a little girl of just four years could understand, but she already had her favorite stories, and she especially liked the ones that Westin told her about her father. She adjusted well to being with us. I woke a few times to her having nightmares, but they were becoming less and less, and mine were becoming more and more. I could not be sure what mine were of, but nevertheless, as long as Jared was next to me, I felt safe.

Days had passed with no discussion of the witch or of Gerald and Samuel. After the morning meal, I asked Rebecca to join me on a walk. We strolled through Mother's gardens, and I asked her, "Have you been to see your father?"

Her reply was not what I expected, she laughed. "I have not, and I have no intentions of ever seeing him again. Why do you ask?"

"I am just wondering, and I wanted to let you know that if you wanted to go, that I would gladly accompany you."

"Thank you. I did think about going to tell him that I was to wed Charles, just to torture him, but then I thought better of it. I do not care to see him, Sabine. He ordered my death. My own father ordered barbarians to murder me, to murder us. To me, that is an unforgivable act."

"I am sorry. Please just know that I am here if you change your mind. So, have you and Charles decided when you might be married?"

"We have actually. I was waiting to say something until you and Jared decided. I wanted you to be first. After all, you have waited longer than us."

"That is sweet of you, Rebecca, but Jared and I wanted to wait until we were all in a comfortable place. I suppose it will be soon, since we all have a routine now. It feels normal, does it not?"

"It feels pretty normal to me."

"I will talk to Jared after the evening meal and see what he thinks about it. Do you have a day in mind?"

"Well, we wanted to do it sooner rather than later, so you let me know."

I could not help but laugh. "Rebecca, if you and Charles want to marry, then please do not worry about Jared and I. Your happiness means the world to me."

"As yours does to me, Sabine. The problem I am having with it all is I am not sure that I am ready to be a mother. I am just now learning how to live a normal life. I think we are hoping that you and Jared take your time, but we have already decided that you are first," she said, half smiling.

"To be honest with you, Rebecca, I am not so sure I want to be a mother at all. What if something happens? What if the witch gets away? What if we have to fight again? We are supposed to be the bringers of peace and all, but somewhere deep inside of me, I do not think this is over."

"Yeah, me neither. It is a strange feeling indeed. You know my sleep has been off these past days. I have been having flickers of things flash in my mind while I sleep. Something is not right."

"My sleep has been the same. Are we so off of normal that our minds are making up stuff to worry about? I mean, for so long, we lived on the edge, not knowing what was coming or who was coming. Now, no one is coming, and we have what we fought so hard to have, and neither one of us can calm down."

We both laughed. "Yeah, that is us, the crazy girls from Whispering Wind," she said

I laughed, but deep down inside, I was terrified that she could be right. "Would you mind if I borrowed Charles for a little while? I need to talk to him."

"Sabine, he is your guardian. You can borrow him whenever you need."

I kissed her on the cheek. "Thank you. We will chat later," I told her and then took off running. I needed to have some of his knowledge, the kind he was not allowed to tell me. Something was not right here at Whispering Wind, and it had not been since our return from Wellington.

I found Charles coming out of the barracks as I ran into the courtyard. "Sabine, is everything all right?"

"Yes, Charles. All is fine. Are you busy? I need to talk. Can you go for a ride with me?"

"Of course. You do know that I am at your service anytime?" We went to the stables to get our horses, and he asked me again, "Sabine is everything all right?"

"I just need to talk to you," I said as I finished putting Raiden's saddle on.

"You do know that you do not have to do that. I can have him saddled for you if you would like."

"It is all right. I think he prefers if I do it." Raiden stomped his hoof on the ground. "See!" We both laughed.

"To the hilltop, my lady?"

"The hilltop, my lord."

When we arrived, I climbed off of Raiden and waited for Charles. "You do know that you are not staying here? I need for you to take Charles' horse back to the stables with you and wait for him to whistle. I know you do not like it when I make you go, but I need to be alone with him. You understand, right?" He just nodded his head. Charles arrived, and Raiden and his horse left.

"You know it is amazing how that horse listens to you."

I chuckled. "He is magic, remember?" We sat down and waited until they were back at the castle before I began. "I need for you to tell me the things you are not."

"I know it must be frustrating for you, Sabine, but I cannot interfere with the future."

"So, what you are saying to me, Charles, is that this is not over? I cannot marry Jared, nor you Rebecca, until this is done. Neither of us can bring a child into this mess, so I need to know."

"As much as I would like to tell you all will be well, I cannot."

"You are being very mysterious, Charles, and it is setting me on edge."

"Sabine, if I tell you what has been foretold, then you and Rebecca will not learn. To fulfill the prophecy, it must come from the two of you. Neither I nor anyone else can tell you what will come or what will be. A chain of events must occur before the prophecy can be fulfilled."

"Are there others who know this chain of events?"

"Yes, there are, Sabine. With being the keepers of this knowledge, the guardians, we have sworn not to interfere. The only thing I can tell you for sure is that I will protect you with my life, as well as my brothers."

"You keep saying that. You are not going to die, are you, Charles? I mean, Rebecca would never forgive me if you died saving me."

He laughed. "It is not my intention to die anytime soon, Sabine. My intention is to marry Rebecca, have lots of fat babies, and live a long life."

"Yes, that may be your intention, Charles, but is that what is going to happen?"

"I cannot tell what the future holds for any of us. I just feel that you and Rebecca will figure out what to do when the time comes."

"Charles, I have not told Jared this, but I am sure he can sense it. I have been having strange flashes of things while I sleep."

"What sorts of things?"

"Fire, screams, death… It is always the same. Sometimes there is more, and they seem to be coming more frequent as well."

"I could not imagine what it would be about. I have noticed that Rebecca is not sleeping well either."

"I know. She told me that she is having disturbing thoughts as well. She cannot remember hers when she wakes. She just knows they were bad. Have you spoken to Jared about this not being over? He was so intent on marrying me, and he has not said a word about it since we have been back."

"We have discussed the possibility that this is not over, but remember, Sabine, it very well may be over. I only know what I have been told and what is written down, but Jared has never given me the inclination that he did not want to marry you."

"I know, Charles. I am just fearful that I am going to have to decline if he does ask again, at least until this feeling of dread leaves me."

"There should be no reason you cannot have your life. Remember, we have been through a great deal. Not many people can say that they have done all that we have done and come out of it…well, normal. Your mind needs to rest. You need to just be you. What are the things you did before all of this started?"

I laughed. "Charles, I was just a child when all this began. To me, it feels like a lifetime ago. I had no plans. I had nothing to do but be me, but then one day, I was forced to grow up. I was faced with things I did not have the skills for. I suppose you are right in a sense, but I know you, just as you know me, and I know this is not over. Thank you, Charles."

"You are most welcome, and please consider Jared's offer to marry when he gives it again. You cannot allow yourself not to be happy. I mean, how silly would it be for the bringer of peace to live without happiness?" He bumped my shoulder, and we sort of laughed.

"Will you promise me one thing?"

"I will do my best."

"If you see that Rebecca and I are missing something, will you gently guide us to figure it out?"

"I always do. Remember, Sabine, I am your guardian."

I smiled at him. I knew he was not going to reveal anything to me. If I was this person that they say I was, this bringer of peace, whatever that meant, then I should trust my instincts. I should know that the feelings I had were feelings I should be aware of. I should not just continue to pretend it is nothing.

Charles whistled for Raiden, and it really was almost like he was a dog. I could not help but smile as he trotted up the hillside. "Charles, I think I am going to ride for a while. Would you please let Jared know if he comes looking for me?"

"May I inquire as to where you will be riding to, so I can send Blake and Joseph to keep an eye out?"

"Charles, Raiden will not let anything happen to me. You know that he senses everything and that he can outrun any horse."

"You are right, Sabine. Enjoy your ride. Will you please let me know when you return, so I do not worry?"

I nodded. "Of course, Charles, and thank you. I will try not to be long." I climbed on Raiden and said, "Take me for a ride, boy." We reached the plain just on the other side of the village, and Raiden let loose. I just closed my eyes and let the wind take control of me. It was amazing how he moved so fast, and how I barely feel him move beneath me. This feeling of freedom was how I wished I felt when I was not riding him. I had so much to think about, so much we needed to figure out. I could feel Raiden turn slightly; he was making his arch. I felt him tense up under me, and I opened my eyes to see many guards riding toward Whispering Wind.

He slowed to a trot. "Should we worry?"

He stopped. It was almost like he was smelling the air to get a handle on who was coming. His ears were twitching, and out of nowhere, he started moving. Before I knew what was happening, we were at the village. A dead run to the castle gates, and to the barracks, and then he stopped and reared up, neighing and stomping his feet. Jared and Charles came running out of the barracks.

"Horses are coming, a lot of them."

Men were running everywhere, horses were being saddled, and in a matter of minutes, about two hundred guards were mounted and ready to go.

Rebecca came running up with our swords, threw mine to me, and then she climbed on Spirit. We rode out to the end of the village to meet them. Rebecca leaned over and whispered, "I have to admit, Sabine that this is what I live for. Can you feel the energy?"

"I know what you mean."

The horses rode up, and we could see that the guards were a mixture of Wellington, Blackmore, and Collingwood.

"What brings you here?" Charles spoke.

"Charles," one man said with a nod, "Wellington is mounting an attack. The story is that the princess is a witch and has taken Lord Jared prisoner with some sort of mind control, and Wellington wants him returned."

"Well, that is an untruth, but why are Blackmore and Collingwood here as well?"

"Blackmore says the same of Princess Rebecca, and Collingwood wants revenge for the death of Prince Edward."

Rebecca laughed, and it was never a good thing when she laughed. "Edward was insane, and I did Collingwood a great service when I removed his head for him."

"Yes, we were told that, but we were also told that Princess Sabine has control of your mind as well, and that she made you do it."

It is never a good idea to anger Rebecca, especially when she is in her fighting frame of mind. "NO ONE CONTROLS ME!!! You go back and tell my mother that if she wants a fight, we will gladly give her one. I am here of my own free will, as is Jared. If anyone is out of control, it is my mother, Wellington, and Collingwood. You do not want this fight, unless of course you wish to die."

"We are not here to fight, Princess. We are here to join you and to deliver to you a message from the kingdoms."

"What is your message?"

"Blackmore and Wellington say that this will never end. As long as you, Princess, and His Highness Prince Jared, are under the spell of Princess Sabine, they will not stop coming."

Laughter was all Rebecca could respond with. "Would you like to see what awaits Blackmore? Sabine, shall we show them?"

"My pleasure." I drew my sword.

When Raiden and Spirit hit the ground, Rebecca said, "Now you send some men back to Blackmore and to Wellington, and you tell them all, that this is the fate that awaits them. You cannot stop us, and Jared and I are not going anywhere." With that, she turned on her horse to face me. "Will you ride with me?"

"To the hill top?"

"To the hill top!"

She looked at Charles. "My love, I will be back in a bit. Sabine and I have some things we need to discuss."

He just nodded at her. Jared leaned over to me and whispered, "I love only you." I kissed him, and we were off.

We climbed off our horses and sent Raiden and Spirit back to the castle. Rebecca was pacing. I could not tell if she was angry or lost in thought, so I said nothing to her.

"You know something is not right here. I cannot put my finger on it, but something is not right." She said.

"I just said those same words to Charles. Since we came back from Wellington, things have been strange. You and I are not different, but everyone else is."

"After we talked today, I was thinking about what that witch said concerning Juliana. Do you remember?"

"Yes, that she had gifts, and that she was like her."

"Right, so with all this talk of mind control, that you have control over mine and Jared's minds, where in the world would my mother get such a crazy idea from? Wellington has been poisoned. That is obvious, but my mother has not been privy to my father's doings. I could tell by the look of confusion on her face, but Katherine did not blink. She did not shed one tear. It felt so false to me. I did not want to say anything. I thought that it was just in my mind, but after today, after talking to you about Juliana's sleep becoming less and less disturbed, and mine and yours more disturbed, I am wondering if that witch has more control over this situation, as we believe her to have."

"You know she was in Wellington. She could have cast a spell there. She was here while we were there. She could have done the same here. We need to keep this to ourselves, Rebecca, or we will look like the ones who are crazy."

"You are right, Sabine. We need to think about this and observe the people around us. Charles has said, time and time again, that we need to figure this out, that we need to do it together. Let us say that she cannot control us, but she can plant seeds in our heads through Juliana. She can cause us to question what is happening around us. I wonder what she is up to. We should have killed her at the water's edge."

"I think there is something more to this. Charles told me today that we needed to learn things on our own to fulfill the prophecy, so I took it that it is not over yet. I agree, however. We need to keep our eyes open and keep this out of our thoughts. If she is controlling things, we need to be careful."

"Agreed. Now, how do we get the horses back?"

I stood up and yelled for Raiden, and it only took a moment before he and Spirit were running from the village. We rode back to the castle and went on about our day. The new guards were getting settled. It was funny how they avoided me and Rebecca at every turn. I supposed I would avoid me as well, had I seen what we could do. It made me smile.

Jared was waiting for me in the back courtyard. "How was your ride, my love?"

"It was fine. What are you doing out here?"

"I was waiting for you. Will you come with me?" He put out his hand, and I placed mine in it. He led me to our room and closed the door behind us. "I know that you have not been sleeping well, and I thought it would be nice if we could have a rest together."

Finding this odd, I smiled at him. "That sounds wonderful," I said, and I climbed into the bed. He lay next to me and wrapped his arms around me. It was the safest place for me. I really did not expect to fall asleep, but I did. It was a very peaceful sleep, so much so that we slept right through the midday meal and the evening meal, and straight through to the light of day. There were no flickers of anything in my mind while I slept. When we woke, we both looked at one another and smiled.

"How long have we been sleeping?"

"All day and all night, and now it is day again," I heard Westin say. "I came in here to watch over you. I was not sure if that witch did something bad to you to make you sleep."

"Well, thank you, Westin. That was very kind of you to look after us." Jared got up to shake his hand.

"You are my brother now. That witch took my other brothers, and I will not let her take you." Jared hugged him. "Juliana slept with me and Camille last night. She moves a lot and cries out a lot, Sabine. No wonder you and Jared slept so long."

I smiled at him. "I suppose she does, but she has been through a lot, Westin. She will get better."

Just then, Juliana came running into the room. "Sabine," she squealed as she flung herself in my arms. "I missed you. Are you ill?"

"Why, no, sweetheart. Jared and I were just tired, I suppose." I looked at him and smiled.

We all went down to the morning meal, and it was good to see the table full and to hear the chatter. I sat there, looking around at everyone I loved, and I wondered what, if anything, was wrong with them. This was how I spent my day, wondering around watching everyone, engaging when it was necessary, but mostly I watched.

The dark of the night was upon us faster than I expected. We had our evening meal, and then we all parted company and retired to our rooms. I changed into my sleeping gown, got Juliana ready, and then we curled up in bed. Sleep came, but again, it was not pleasant.

CHAPTER THIRTY THREE

The pounding in my head was horrific. It felt as if someone was bashing it with a rock. I tried to scream, but my body would not work. I opened my eyes to find myself standing and not lying on the ground as I thought I was. I could make out the shapes of bodies lying on the ground in front of me, and it was silent. My sight was blurred from the pounding in my head. I tried to focus. My face was wet, so I reached up to wipe away the moisture, and as I took my hand away to look at it, I could see that it was not the right color. *What was wrong with me? Where was everyone?* Jared, Rebecca, Charles, Juliana, where was she? I turned slowly, looking through the fog in my eyes, searching the ground for her. Blinking my eyes, trying to clear whatever was in them, the fog in my brain finally lifted, and my mind became my own again. I realized that my eyes were not foggy at all, but blocked by something, a shade of color. As I turned, my mind started to put together the scene in front of me. Bodies were laying everywhere I turned, horses, and fires that did not burn red. I began to search the faces of those dead on the ground; Blake, Steven, James, guards I did not know, and then I saw Charles. I tried to move, but I could feel nothing but pain. I focused on his face, and just under him, I saw her hair; Rebecca. I could feel the scream within me, but I could not get it out. A few bodies away from them were Westin and Camille. I tried to force my body to move, but my mind was not cooperating. Tears filled my eyes as I slowly turned, searching for Jared, searching for Juliana, searching for Raiden, for anyone.

The tears washed away some of what blurred my sight, so I could see clearer now. The fires were turning red. My hands were sticky, and I looked down at them. They were covered in blood. And then I saw them, lying on the ground right in front of me; Raiden and Juliana. I could feel the low rumble of the guttural growl that was forming in my chest. My hand searched my side for my sword, but it was the banshee scream that froze my heart and forced my head up. My eyes focused, and I saw her off in the distance. I saw that witch, Devious, and standing next to her was my beloved Jared with a smile pressed across his lips.

My heart pounded louder than the thunder in my head. He was covered in blood. His lips were pulled back to show his teeth, and they were red from blood. I looked down at Juliana and Raiden, and that is when I saw it. That is when I realized that their hearts were ripped from their bodies. I felt sick, and I could feel my evening meal coming up from inside my body. As I leaned over to wretch, I heard a sound, like a branch on the forest floor cracking as someone stepped on it. I look up in time to see Jared running toward me. My hand found my sword, and I drew it. I found my voice in that instant, screaming at him, "NOOOOOO!" But he would not stop. I raised my sword, ready to strike, still screaming, "NOOOOOO!" I pulled back. I was shaking so hard that I was not sure I could kill him. I love him so, but he did this. Did he do this? He was running harder and faster, and I knew I had to time this right or I would be dead just like everyone else. I swung my sword, screaming, "NOOOOOO!" There was a brilliant light. I could feel my body shaking. I could hear voices. I could feel the light in my eyes, warmth on my face. I could hear myself screaming above the voices. I heard crying and pleading, and I felt pressure all over my body. I would not let her win. I would not let her have me. I tried to get away, hitting and clawing at what was holding me down. One grip was gone, then another and another, until finally I was free. I could not see. She must have blinded me, I thought. I scrambled away from whatever was there. I fell a fair distance to the ground, hurting my leg, but I managed to feel my way along the ground. I ran into something flat, so I followed it, hitting my head. It felt as if I was in a corner, so I stopped moving. Then I heard my name, "Sabine." It was softly spoken, almost a whisper. I tilted my head to hear it again.

"Sabine, my love."

"NOOOOOO!" I screamed at him. I thrashed my arms outward, trying to strike at the voice. It could not be Jared. I had killed him. My hands waved around, and then I felt him grab my arms.

"Sabine, my love," his voice panicked.

"NOOOOOO!" I screamed.

"SABINE, WAKE UP!" he screamed back at me. What was he saying? "SABINE!" He shook me, his hand warm on my face. I stopped trying to hit him. My mind was coming out of the fog. Wake up? What? I could feel my body slump, and then I felt him lift me into his arms. The sounds around me were sobs and whispers. I could hear Jared saying, "Shhhh, Sabine. Come on, my love. Wake up."

My eyes fluttered open, and the light of the day was bright. I felt Jared climb on the bed with me in his arms, never letting me go, being so careful not to jostle me around. He felt so warm. His heart was slamming in his chest. It was over now. I opened my eyes to see his staring back at me.

"What happened?" I whispered.

"I was hoping you could tell me. I have never seen anyone act that way while they were asleep."

"It was so real."

"It must have been. You were screaming and crying. You were shaking. What was going on in your head, my love?"

I looked away from him to see that my room was filled. Westin was sitting on the edge of the bed holding Juliana, and both of them were crying. She tried to wiggle away from him, but he just held her tighter.

"It is all right, Westin," I said, trying to reassure him that I had not gone mad.

He let her go, and she scrambled up into my arms. "I was so scared, Sabine. Where did you go?"

"I do not know, my love, where I was, and I was so scared as well." I held her close.

Charles looked like he had seen a ghost, and I could see that Rebecca had been crying. Camille was in the corner, being held by her mother and father, while Joseph and Blake remained by the door.

"I am so sorry to have worried you all. I am all right. I promise," I said to them.

It took a little while before anyone believed me. I think they just needed to make sure. I made Juliana go with Westin and Camille. I promised her I would meet her in the dining hall in a little while. When Rebecca and Charles went to leave, I asked them to stay. Charles closed the door behind Westin and Juliana and turned to face me.

I sat up in the middle of the bed. "Please come and sit with me." I motioned to Rebecca and Charles. "In all my days, I have never experienced anything such as this. It was so real. Charles, do you have any idea what happened to me?"

"Sabine, I have no clues as to what was in your head. Perhaps you had a vision. Can you tell us what you have seen?"

"Well, that is just it, Charles. I could not really see anything until the end. My head hurt like someone was beating me in the head with a rock. My vision was blurred. How long was I screaming?"

"It was quite a while. Enough time had passed for everyone to appear at your door." I thought about that for a minute before I could continue. "It was not until I saw Jared that my vision became clear." I looked at him and said, "You were with that barbarian witch, Devious, and you were going to kill me."

No one said a word. No one moved. I am not so sure a breath passed through anyone's lips. I whispered, "I killed you."

Jared reached for me the instant the words came out of my mouth. He pulled me into his arms holding me. "Shhhh, my love. Shhhh, I will never try to kill you, and you shall never have cause to kill me. Whatever it was that has happened to you, it is over now."

I could see the exchange of looks between Rebecca, Charles, and Jared. They were frightened, as they should be.

"I will be fine," I said as I pulled away from Jared. "Would you two please excuse us? We need to change. I promised Juliana that I would meet her in the dining hall, and I think I scared everyone enough that I should reassure them that I am all right."

Jared and Charles left, and I changed along with Rebecca. "You know you scared me half to death."

"I am sorry. My head is still cloudy with thoughts. Later, would you ride with me, so we can talk without ears?" I pointed to the door.

She smiled at me. "I would love nothing more. It is good to be home, Sabine, and back to normal again."

I smiled and nodded, but I knew that there was nothing normal about what just happened to me, and I could feel it deep inside that nothing would ever be the same again. Something was changing, or had changed, and I feared that this was just the beginning and not the end.

We made our way down to the dining hall. Along the way, I could not help but notice that the blood in the halls and on the stairs was gone. Most of the furnishings had been replaced. Of course, it was not my mother's things, but it was furnished. When we walked into the dining hall, all the chairs around our huge table were full, except for two where Rebecca and I sat down. We did not talk about what happened to me. Instead there was chatter about how well the village was coming along, when Camille was expected to have her baby, and how we would all get along living together in the castle. We talked of how I was to be named queen by Westin, who was the rightful King of Whispering Wind. "Are you sure, my love, that you do not want to be king?"

"I am sure, Sabine. Camille and I are happy just being us, and we are having a baby." He smiled ear to ear when he said that. "I want to be able to play with it. I am sure, Sabine. I do not want to rule a kingdom. I just want to be me."

Jared interrupted us, "Well then, now that, that is settled, there is one more thing I would like to bring to your attention, my lady." He was looking at me.

"Yes, my love." I smiled back at him.

"Well, I would like to address this feeling I have within me for the future Queen of Whispering Wind, this feeling of longing and love to spend the rest of my days with you. Your Highness, would you do me the great honor of becoming my wife?"

I stood up and ran to him, kissing him in front of everyone in the room. "I would love nothing more, sire." Everyone clapped and cheered.

"Would tomorrow be too soon, my lady?"

"Tomorrow would be fine, my lord."

"Tomorrow," Charles' mother gasped. "There is no way we can manage a wedding for a queen in less than a day. You must wait, so that we can do it the right way."

I could not help but giggle. "My lady, we do not require anything fancy. We just want our family with us, nothing more, just something simple please."

People were getting up from their chairs, and Charles' mother was telling everyone what needed to be done. Camille and Juliana went to the kitchen, and I excused myself to go see Raiden. "Jared, Rebecca and I are going for a ride. We will be fine, so please do not worry." I looked at Rebecca, she nodded, and we left the dining hall.

We walked to the stables without a word. We said nothing as we saddled Raiden and Spirit. When we left the stables, we left through the back gates. I did not want to go through the village. When we hit the meadow, Raiden and Spirit took control. "To the top of the hill, Raiden." He took the long way to the hill. I think he wanted to run for a bit. I did not mind. I had to figure out how I was going to tell Rebecca what happened in my mind last night. *How would I tell her that I saw her dead body in the forest?* Riding Raiden like this always felt wonderful. To just feel the wind on my face and the air pulsing through my chest, there was nothing like it for me. As we reached the top of the hill, I looked down at Whispering Wind. It felt strange to see it full of people. The last time I was on this hill, all I saw was death. Now, I saw nothing but life. I sighed.

"Are you all right, Sabine?"

"I am not sure," I said as I climbed off of Raiden. "Rebecca, I need to talk to you, but I need for you to swear to me that what I am going to say to you will remain between us. I wish for you to not even tell Charles."

"Sabine, after all that we have been through, I see you as my sister. You never have to ask me that. I will keep this between us."

"I know that I can trust you, but when I tell you what I am going to tell you, I fear you will feel the need to include Charles and Jared, but they must not know this, not yet."

"I love Charles, but he does not own my thoughts, just my heart." she smiled. "Now, please tell me what is going on."

I proceeded to tell her all that I saw in my mind the night before. She gasped and held my hand. Raiden and Spirit were uneasy as I spoke. It played out in my head as if it was a real memory. I could feel the fear with each word I spoke. When I finished, Rebecca sat there, not saying a word, with a look of horror on her face.

"What do you think it all means?" she asked.

"I do not know, Rebecca, but Charles had mentioned a vision. Why would I have a vision such as this? Do you think we should end Devious' life, so there is no chance of this becoming true?"

"Sabine, I am not so sure she can be killed. Remember what she said about Juliana? That she had magical powers or something like that? What if she somehow connected herself to Juliana? You sleep with her at your side, and perhaps this barbarian witch is playing mind games with you. What if she is trying to make you go mad? We need to go talk to her."

"She will not tell us the truth, Rebecca. She will just laugh and try to make us angry at her. Maybe what you are saying is the truth. What if she did tie herself to Juliana? If I kill her, then will Juliana die as well?"

"I think we can manage to keep one another from killing her. Come on. Let us go see her."

Raiden snorted, so I looked up at him. "You can come too." I giggled. "Crazy horse, I swear he thinks he is human."

We both laughed then. As we stood, I turned to face Whispering Wind, only this time when I looked at it, I felt different, like there was mystery that surrounded it.

"You coming?" I heard from behind me.

I turned and climbed onto Raiden. "We should get our swords before we go down there."

"Agreed. I will race you back to the castle."

"You are on," I said, knowing very well that Raiden could, and probably would, beat Spirit.

We were down the hill in a shot, through the fields and to the edge of the village. I held Raiden back, so Rebecca could gain some ground. When we started through the village, the people cleared the road. We flew like birds toward the gates. When we hit the gates and bound into the courtyard, guards came running. Jared and Charles came running out of the castle to meet us.

"What is it, Sabine?"

I laughed as we came to a stop just in front of them. "Nothing, we were just having a little race."

His smile was forced, but I could tell that he was not happy with my response. "Charles, you need to lighten up. We are home, and we are safe."

The look on his face somehow told me just how wrong I was, but it did not matter. He may have known things I did not, but Rebecca and I were figuring things out, just like he said we would. He could not hold that against me.

We hurried past them and into the castle, up the staircase, and to our room. It made me think that after tomorrow, this would not be our room any longer. It would be mine and Jared's room. I stood there, looking at the bed where we all slept, the three of us. *How would Juliana take this? Would she be frightened to not be sleeping with me? Should we wait until she was comfortable with her surroundings?*

"What is wrong, Sabine?"

I looked at her and smiled. "Nothing really. I was just thinking that this would be the last night we all sleep in the same room. And Juliana, where will she sleep? Will she be all right? Should we wait until she is comfortable before we separate us all?"

"No. you should not wait, Sabine. You and Jared have waited long enough to be man and wife, and she will be fine. This is her life now, and she needs to know that you are just down the hall. If you want, she can stay with me and Charles tomorrow night, and the nights that follow. Charles and I are not planning to marry any time in the near future," she said, that last part coming out a bit sarcastically.

"Thank you, Rebecca, but we will figure this out later. Right now, we need to go have a chat with our guest." The smile on her face was one I knew well. She was ready for battle. "We cannot go killing her now."

She laughed. "Oh, I know that, but you never know what will happen."

We left our room and made our way down the back stairs and into the kitchen. I asked the cook for some scraps of food. I thought if we brought her some food, she might tell us something. There was no one in the great hall. It was nice to know that everyone was feeling comfortable and going about doing their own things. I was sure that they were planning a huge event for Jared and I. It did not matter how big it was, or how small it was. He was finally going to marry me, and I could not have been happier. When we walked out into the court-yard, Charles and Jared were there with their horses. "What is this?"

"Well, we decided that we spend more time worrying about the two of you than we do being productive, so we thought that we would like to request permission to accompany you on whatever adventure you have planned."

"Well, Charles, whatever do you mean? Why would you presume we were going on an adventure?"

"Let us take a look at what we know to be truth. The two of you leave for a ride, which tells us you want to talk privately. You come flying through the village, to the castle, dismount your horses, and run into the house. You return with a sack full of food and your swords, and might I add, I know that look in Rebecca's eyes, and it can mean only one thing. Trouble," he said this in the kindest of ways and with tender loving care.

Rebecca stuck her tongue out at him and said, "Well, first of all, you will not like what we have planned, and second, you will not stop us from doing this."

Jared laughed. "In all of my days of loving you, Sabine, I would never think that stopping you was ever an option."

"I love only you," was all I said as I climbed on Raiden. I was not sure which way to go, but I knew that Raiden would remember, so I leaned into him and whispered, "Take me to the witch." He neighed and reared his head. I would imagine it was in protest, but he started walking. It was only a matter of moments before Charles realized where we were going.

"Do you really think this is wise, Sabine?"

"I do not know, Charles, but your lack of information concerning our future has led us to figure things out for ourselves. We are doing this, and I would appreciate it if you did not accompany us to the depths of the dungeons. Raiden and Spirit have already let us know that they are coming with us."

Jared chuckled. "I swear that horse is more human than he is animal."

The entrance to the dungeons was carved into the side of a cliff behind the barracks. Standing at the entrance were two guards. As we approached, I could see their faces, and they looked confused. I dismounted Raiden and walked up to the guards with Rebecca at my side and Raiden and Spirit close behind. "I am sorry, my lady, but I have orders not to allow anyone to pass."

Rebecca drew her sword. "I say this sword over rides your orders."

I laughed. "Rebecca, that will not be necessary, now will it?" I directed my gaze toward the guards.

"We are just obeying orders, my lady," he said with a nervous quiver in his voice.

Rebecca smiled at him as we walked past them. They both wanted to protest, but I think the fact that Raiden and Spirit were following left them a bit shocked. I was sure that the minute we descended the first stair case, one of them would be off to find Charles.

We made our way down and through the caverns of passage ways. I was not sure which direction we were to go, but Raiden knew, and he led us right to her.

As we approached the door, I heard her voice, "So what brings the chosen one to my door? Could it be the vision you had? Somehow, you know, Princess that it was not a vision at all, but the outcome of it all."

"What is this bile you spew forth old woman?" Rebecca was curt with her voice.

Devious just laughed. "Tis not bile but truth. You know, Princess, deep in your heart, that what you saw was the truth. The price you will pay is the death of all you love, and there is nothing you can do to stop it. Go on, Princess, and search your heart. You know I speak the truth."

"I know nothing of this truth. It was you putting your hateful thoughts in my head while I slept. I am here to tell you that it will not happen again, and if it does, then I am here to tell you that I will not honor the deal we made, and your life will end."

"It will not matter that my life will end. Your true love will do as you saw, and all will perish. It is your destiny now. You must end his life to stop it. Ending mine will do nothing."

I just stood there, looking in her eyes. I was frozen to the spot. I could see that she was speaking the truth. "Yes, Princess, you know it in your heart. You know that he must die. You waited too long to use the mist. Your love was in the darkness of death a moment longer than he should have been. It is just a matter of time before that mayhem begins to surface."

I remembered his outburst with his mother and the look in his eyes that day I took Raiden and went riding. Could what she be saying be truth? I looked out beyond my own thoughts to see deep into the witch's eyes, and the scene from the night before surfaced. Jared's eyes were colorless.

It was Raiden who brought me back to the moment. He had

nudged me with his nose. Rebecca was standing very close to me, her sword in her hand. "Let us finish her. What she speaks is untrue, Sabine. She must die."

"Death will not stop this, Princess, not my death anyway."

"SHUT UP, old woman!" Rebecca screamed at her.

Raiden nudged me again, this time harder. "What is it, boy?" His response was to push me away from the door and further down the hall. I heard the witch's voice mumble something. I could have sworn she said, "Yes, my old friend, keep her safe if you can."

He nudged me all the way through the hallways, up the stairs, and then out into the light of the day. Waiting, as I expected, were Jared and Charles. What I did not expect was Jared's reaction. "Have you completely lost your mind, Sabine? What were you thinking, going down there? She could have killed you!"

Even Charles was surprised at his tone and forcefulness toward me. "I have told you before, Jared that I can take care of myself. You are not my father, nor do you control what I do." I started to walk away, and he grabbed my arm. It was my natural reaction to defend myself, and I did. I grabbed his hand and removed it from my arm, throwing him to the ground. "DO NOT EVER believe that you can lay a hand on me!" I screamed at him.

Before he could recover, I was on Raiden, and we were moving. It was no time at all before we were on the top of the hill. He stopped, but I did not get off.

"Could what she said be true? Is Jared tainted? Why did she call you old friend? Do you know her, Raiden?" I did not really expect him to answer me. I just needed to speak these words, so I could hear how preposterous they sounded. Something deep inside of me, somehow, I knew that they were not at all preposterous, but held clarity. Jared had changed, and was changing still. Raiden moved me away from the witch before she could say anything more. Could the vision I had be the future for us all? Was I setting the path of destruction for all that I loved? The vision in my mind from the night before was still so very real; the smell of blood, the silence, the destruction.

I climbed off of Raiden, leaned into him, and whispered, "Please bring me Charles, no one else but Charles." Raiden nodded and was gone. I sat down and pondered my thoughts. Did I need to lock Jared up instead of marrying him, just until I could be sure he was all right? Could I risk everyone's life by not locking him up? I did not know how long I sat there thinking, but the light of the day had shifted in the sky. I looked down at Whispering Wind, at the people in the village, and the movement near the castle. The scene of what it once was, had been renewed, but it would always be shadowed by what had happened there. I could not let that happen again. As much as I loved him, I could not let it happen again.

Raiden came riding up with Charles on his back. "Is everything all right, Sabine?" he asked.

"Raiden, thank you. Would you please go back to the stables and leave us? Charles will whistle for you to return." He snorted and pounded his hoof into the ground in protest. "I need to speak alone with Charles. We will be all right." Raiden turned and made his way down the hill.

"Sabine, what is going..."

I held my hand up to silence him, watching Raiden. I waited until he turned to go into the village before I spoke. "No, Charles, nothing is right."

"Why did you send Raiden away?"

"I trust only you, Charles. Something is happening. It is not right. We need to talk, and we need to be alone." I sat down, never taking my eyes from the village. I just knew in my heart that Raiden would try to return. He could not hear this. No one could.

"Sabine, he is but a horse."

"Is he, Charles?"

"You are scaring me with this behavior, Sabine. Did that witch do something to you?"

"Not to me, Charles, but I fear she has to Juliana and to Jared. She channeled her thoughts through Juliana into me last night while I slept. The things she said to me today have given me great cause for fear, and the things she did not say to me have magnified them and filled me with terror."

"Then you must tell me everything, so I can help you."

I proceeded to tell Charles everything, never taking my eyes off the village. "When Raiden started to nudge me away from the door, I heard what the witch said to him, 'Yes, my old friend, keep her safe if you can.' I am not sure what it meant. I have been sitting here, thinking about what you told me concerning Raiden, about Merlin. Could Raiden be Merlin? Did Merlin really live at one time?"

"I am not sure, Sabine, but legend says that he did indeed."

"I suppose we will never know. Now, this is not the only reason I wanted to speak to you alone. Charles, I cannot marry Jared tomorrow. I cannot have a union if he is not himself. I will most assuredly be with child after, and if he is not whole, then I cannot do that. I think we need to restrain him someplace, perhaps in the dungeons. No, take him to the cottage, just until we are sure that he has not been changed because of the mist."

"Sabine, are you sure of this?"

"You have seen his behavior, Charles, his outbursts and his attempt to restrain me. You were not in my head last night. You did not see what he had done. You were all dead, and I would not be able to live if you were all dead. I killed him, and that is not my wish. I wish only to love him. Will you help me? I will have Rebecca stay with me tonight, and Jared with you."

"He will fight me, Sabine, and I cannot hurt my friend."

"Nor would I want you to hurt him. I love him, Charles. I am just afraid of him right now. Please help me. You say you are my guardian, but you cannot help me if you are dead."

"I will help you, Sabine. Somehow, I will do this for you."

"Thank you, Charles. Please, not a word of this again. No one must know. No one can hear us talking. Remove it from your thoughts. I know not what trickery or witchcraft is a bound. Trust no one, Charles, no one."

"I will not fail you, my lady."

"Thank you. Would you whistle for Raiden?"

I watched the dust fly as Raiden made his way through the village and into the fields. He was at my side in a matter of moments. Charles and I climbed on his back, and we made our way back to the castle. Charles went his way, and I went in to find Juliana.

She was playing in the great hall with Westin and Camille. When she saw me, she came running and jumped in my arms. "Where did you go, Sabine?"

"I went for a ride. Will you take a walk with me, my love?"

"Yes. Jared is looking for you." she leaned in and whispered to me, "I think he is mad at you."

I laughed a little. "Oh no, my love, he is not mad at me. He is mad at himself, but he will be fine, and we will find him when we get back from our walk, all right?"

She nodded, then wiggled around to speak to Westin, "Uncle, I am going with Sabine for a walk. Can we play when we return?"

"Of course we can."

Content with her answer, she assured me that she was ready. "Where are we to go, Sabine?"

I did not answer her. I just walked through the great hall and toward the kitchen. As we passed through, everyone was busy getting ready for tomorrow. I grabbed two apples out of a bowl, and we headed out the door and into the back garden. I put Juliana down and handed her an apple, and we walked to the edge of the garden, where the tall bushes were. I knew that no one was behind them because the cave was there. We sat on the ground and ate our apples, and when we were done, I began.

"My love, I want you to do something for me, all right?" She nodded her little head. "I do not know what the days are going to bring. There are still some people who are not happy with me, and I do not want anything to happen to you. Do you understand?" She nodded. "If anything bad happens, or starts to happen, I want you to go someplace for me. Behind me is a hedge. Do you see it?" She nodded. "Behind the hedge is a cave. You must never go there unless something bad is happening. No one must know that it is there. If something bad happens, Juliana, I want you to run to the end of the hedge over there." I pointed, and she looked then nodded. "You go around the hedge to the back of it, follow the wall all the way down to where we are sitting now, and directly behind me is the opening to the cave. You stay there until myself or Westin, or Raiden comes to get you. You do not leave it. Do you understand?" She nodded, this time with a smile. "You must not tell anyone. You just run and hide there. Raiden knows where it is, and so does Westin. No one but me and Blake knows that the cave is there. Do you understand me?"

"Yes, it is a secret. I will not tell anyone."

I smiled at her and scooped her in my arms. We giggled and rolled around on the ground. "I love you, Juliana."

"I love you, Sabine. I am glad that you found me."

"I am glad that I found you as well. Listen, tonight you are going to sleep with Camille and Westin. I am going to sleep with Rebecca."

"Where is Jared going to sleep?"

"He will sleep with Charles tonight. I am going to marry Jared tomorrow, and then Jared will sleep with me, and you will sleep with Rebecca after that. Is that all right?"

"I like Rebecca. She is my friend."

"Yes, she is, and she is like my sister. I love her very much." We lay on the ground, looking up at the sky, talking and laughing. She was only in her fourth year, but she had wisdom beyond her years.

It was Jared who found us, Juliana lying in my arms. "Will you ever forgive me, my love?"

"You are already forgiven. Come lay with us. The light of the day is leaving, and the sky is so beautiful at this time of the day."

We lay there on the ground until the light of the day was completely gone. It was Charles and Rebecca who came to find us for the evening meal.

"There you are. We have been looking all over for you. The meal is just about ready. Come on, sweetheart. Let us get you washed up," Rebecca said as she reached for Juliana. They walked hand in hand to the kitchen and disappeared inside.

"Well, brother," Charles referred to Jared as brother now. "I guess it is you and I bunking tonight. The guys have a little get together planned for you out in the barracks. You know, with it being your last night as a free man and all!" He laughed.

"Well, I have not been a free man in a long time, my friend, but I would not want to disappoint anyone."

We all chuckled and made our way to the dining hall. Charles and I did not let on that we had a plan. I needed to keep it out of my head, and so did Charles. I had no idea how far Devious' reach was, or what she was capable of. I wanted her dead, but I did not want to risk putting Juliana in harm's way.

We had our meal, and then Charles, Jared, Blake, and Westin all left. Rebecca, Juliana, Camille, and I all retired to my room. It was sweet that they had gotten me little gifts, but all I really wanted to do was sleep. I asked Camille to take Juliana. I kissed her goodnight and then changed into my sleeping gown. Rebecca sat in the chair by the fire and watched me with guarded eyes. She had something to say, but I was not sure she was going to say it. I climbed into the bed, fixed the blanket, and sighed. "Are you going to say what is on your mind, or just sit there and say nothing?"

"Something is going on with you and Charles. I just cannot figure out what it is."

I laughed. "I sure hope you do not mean that in a romantic way?"

"No, I know you, and I know him. I would never think that. I am talking about between the two of you. There are forced smiles, awkward movements, and a strange politeness between you both. I do not like it. I do not like that I feel as if you are keeping something from me."

"Oh, Rebecca, do not be silly. There is nothing about me, or Charles for that matter that you do not know. We are bound together, you and I."

"Perhaps, my lady, but I know you, and there is something you are not telling me."

I laughed again. "I am getting married tomorrow, that is all. I am a bit nervous about my wedding night. I know nothing of what to do."

That seemed to satisfy her, and we began to talk about all the things we thought were to be expected of us on our wedding nights. I did my best to not think about how I knew that night would never come. I felt as if I was being deceitful by not telling Rebecca of our plan, but I needed to be careful. I needed this to work. Soon, we were fast asleep, and thankfully, there were no visions like the night before. It was Juliana who woke me as she jumped onto the bed from Camille's arms.

"Wake up, Sabine. Today you are going to marry Jared. Camille and I made you your morning meal, so you do not have to go down stairs and see Jared."

I fast snuggled her up. "But what if I do not want to marry Jared?" Her face made me laugh. She scrunched up her nose and made a sour face. I laughed harder. "Of course I want to marry Jared, silly." She threw her arms around my neck and kissed me.

I got out of bed and played along. We ate, then we bathed, and I put on my gown. While Rebecca was lacing up my corset, a knock on the door made us all turn. "Sabine?" It was Charles. It was time to confess.

"Come in Charles."

He opened the door and stepped in. "Could I have a moment alone?"

We all looked at one another. "Of course. Would you all please excuse us?" Rebecca, Camille, and Juliana all left the room, and Rebecca gave us both her stare. She knew something was amiss. I just hoped she would forgive me.

"I did as you asked, Sabine. Jared is contained."

"Contained? What do you mean contained?"

"Last night we had some brew, and I put a powder for sleepless-ness in his glass. He fell hard, which is what I needed in order to remove him without question. I had to acquire the aid of Blake in order to remain here to pull off the rouse."

"Where did Blake take him?"

"He is on his way to the cottage, my lady, as well as Samuel and Gerald. We will keep him in the barracks there, where we detained Edward. You may go and see him anytime you would like. What shall we tell the others?"

"We tell them nothing. He will just be gone. You and I will not speak of this again in this house. The hill top is the only safe place." In a louder voice, I said, "Thank you, Charles. I am sure that he will be back in time." I smiled at him.

"I am sure you are right," he replied, and he walked to the door.

Waiting in the hall was Rebecca and Camille. "What is going on, Charles?"

"I am not sure, my love. I woke to find Jared has gone missing. His horse is gone from the stable, and no one has seen him. Sabine assured me that he is probably just riding before the ceremony. I am sure there is nothing to worry about." I felt bad for Charles as I listened to him lie to Rebecca. I knew she would forgive him. When Jared does not show up, I will ask her to ride with me, and then I shall tell her everything.

When they came back into my room, I could tell that Rebecca knew something was not right. "What is going on?" she whispered. I just smiled at her.

"The hour is upon us, Sabine. It is time to go downstairs." Camille was beaming. I was not sure if it was because she was so plump with child, or if she radiated happiness for me.

We made our way down the grand staircase and into the great hall. Everyone was there, all of Camille's brothers, all but Blake. As I approached, I had to make it look as if I was confused. "Where is Jared?"

"I am sorry, Sabine, but he has not returned yet."

"Has anyone gone looking for him?"

"Yes, I have several bands of men out looking for him. I have since rising this morning. I am sorry, but no one seems to be able to find him."

I sat down in a chair to play this charade out. I looked at all the faces of all those I had grown to love, and the guilt was more than I could bear. I ran out and headed straight for the stables. I found Raiden already saddled. I jumped on him and told him to ride. He took off, we reached the plain, and he really let his legs go. I closed my eyes and let the tears run. I could not believe that I had just lied to everyone I love. I banished my love to a distant land, and now I had to tell my best friend that I deceived her. I leaned into Raiden and whispered, "Take me to the hilltop." With that, he made his arch and headed toward Whispering Wind. Rebecca was on her way to find me. Raiden did not slow as we approached her, so she turned and followed us.

At the top of the hill, I dismounted Raiden and told him to go get Charles. He was already to the village when Rebecca caught up. "Would you mind explaining to me what is going on?"

I did not say a word. I just stood there, waiting for Charles. It did not take long for Raiden to return, the whole time with Rebecca questioning me. Charles got off of Raiden and reached for Rebecca. I looked at Raiden and said, "Go back to the stables and wait for Charles to whistle. Spirit, please go with him." Raiden snorted and stomped his hoof, making it known to all of us that he was not happy with my decision, but they went. I sat on the hill and watched as they made their way to the village. Rebecca kept asking me what this was about, but I would not speak until I knew they were back at the castle.

"Sabine, please tell me what is going on."

"Jared did not leave on his own accord."

"What do you mean?"

"Rebecca, come and sit with me." She sat on the ground in a huff. "The vision that I had was just that, a vision. The witch passed her thoughts through Juliana to me. She wanted me to see."

"You cannot possibly believe a word she says."

"I did not, not until we were leaving, and I heard what she said to Raiden."

"I did not hear anything, and why would she talk to a horse?"

Charles spoke, "Rebecca, Raiden is not just a horse. Have you ever noticed that they never tire? Have you noticed that they understand all that is said?"

"They? Are you to wanting me to believe that Raiden and Spirit are something other than horses? What did she say to Raiden?"

She said, "Yes, my old friend, keep her safe if you can."

"I am lost. I do not understand why that would cause you to believe that your vision is real."

"I have noticed some changes in Jared since we brought him back from death, and they seem to be coming more apparent. He has sudden outbursts of anger, random acts of physical contact with me, and not in a good way either. He seems to be confused a great deal of the time, and that is not him. He was the most alert, steel minded man I knew. Now, I am afraid for his life. I am afraid for all your lives. I have decided that I need to send Juliana away as well... her, Westin, Camille, and the baby. Charles, perhaps your parents should go as well."

"Sabine, this sounds so crazy. Are you sure you are not the one who has been affected by this witch?"

I giggled. "Rebecca, do you not see? You and I cannot be touched by her magic. That is why she is using Juliana to invade my thoughts. Nor can Charles or his bloodline, for they are the guardians. We are immune, but those that we love are not. Her connection to Juliana is great, so much so that she can transmit her thoughts through the child to others. I must get them as far away from here as possible."

"I agree with Sabine."

"Thank you, Charles, but we must tell no one, not even your parents, until the very last minute. Rebecca, you must keep these thoughts out of your head until everyone is safe, and then the witch will die. I believe that she can hear us through the others in our life. Jared is not a guardian, so she can manipulate him as well. She may think she is smarter than me, but she is not. I have her locked in the dungeons, and she will die soon enough."

"I need to process this, Sabine. What you are saying is beyond belief."

"I know it is, but everything that we have been through, Rebecca, everything that we are together is beyond belief. Why would this be so far out of reach that you cannot understand it?"

"You are right. I will believe only because you believe. You are my sister, and I stand with you no matter what." She embraced me.

"Thank you. Now, do not forget to not let this conversation into your thoughts. You must forget it and play along. Remember, Jared has run off and left me, so I am going to be devastated, and you will need to comfort me, but we must not speak of this until the ones we love are gone from here. Whispering Wind is not the home I used to know and love. Charles, would it be safe to take everyone back to the cottage? Will Jared be secure enough that he could not hurt anyone?"

"It is an option, yes. We are going to have to wait until Camille has her baby, of course, and that should be any day now. They will go in the dark of the night, just as Jared did. We will not speak of this again. I will just have it done. You do, however, Sabine, need to allow Juliana to spend as much time with Westin and Camille as possible. It will be easier for her. Not to mention, the bond you two share allows the witch access to your thoughts."

"Thank you, Charles. I will leave it all in your hands, and when it is done, Devious dies."

Charles whistled, Raiden and Spirit raced through the village and to the top of the hill to get us. Spirit carried both Rebecca and Charles back to the castle, where everyone waited for my return. There were condolences from everyone. I cried a bit and went on about how much I loved him and that I could not believe he left me like he had. I excused myself and asked to be alone. Everyone understood. I had to laugh to myself. I could not help but wonder what the witch thought of Westin's mind. I excused myself and went to my room.

CHAPTER THIRTY FOUR

Days passed, and I played my part. I stayed in my room pretty much alone. Rebecca came accordingly, and each time, I could hear her tell the others that I was the same. 'Poor child,' I heard Charles' mother say every time. I could not let the thoughts of what was happening invade my mind. I had only seen Juliana one time in seven days' time. She was adjusting well, and all she wanted to talk about was how much fun her, Westin, and Camille were having.

On the ninth day of my mourning for my lost love, Rebecca came running into my room. "It is time, Sabine. Camille is having her baby!"

We both rushed to her side, and it did not take long for her to give birth to a beautiful baby boy. Westin named him Stephan after our father. Now, it was time for Charles to put into play our plan. Camille needed a few days to recover, and then in the dark of the night, without any notice at all, they would be gone.

The days were long while we waited, but the dark of the night came, and when the light of the day returned, everyone was gone. I was not told where they went, and neither was Rebecca. They were just gone. The only ones that remained were Rebecca, Charles, Aidan, Edward, Joseph, Steven, and James. Blake had not returned, as he was to stay with Jared. We waited three days, and when the light of the day came on the fourth day, we stood in the courtyard. "Has everyone from the village been taken care of?"

"Yes, everyone is gone."

"It is time to end this, Charles."

All of us, including Raiden and Spirit, made our way to the dungeons. I unlocked the door for us to enter. Devious was sitting on the floor in some sort of trance. "It is time," I said to her.

"You think you have tricked me, Princess. I know what you did."

"You know what I did because your connection to me is gone. Your connection to Juliana is gone. You have no hold over me. It is time."

She looked passed me to Raiden. "You will not allow this, old friend. You know what will come of it if you allow her to kill me."

"He has no say in this old woman," Rebecca snapped.

"He knows more than you, Princess, and he will not allow this."

Rebecca laughed, and it was never a good thing when she laughed like that. "It is time." She drew her sword.

"We both need to do this, Rebecca, both of us." I drew mine, and together we struck her as she screamed. Her head rolled off into the corner, and the room filled with a greenish colored mist.

"What should we do with her body?" Adian asked as he backed up away from the mist.

"You need not worry about the mist or about her. You are the guardians, and she cannot touch you, not even in death. Her body shall remain here, locked in the belly of these dungeons forever." Raiden stood outside the door looking at her, and I swear he was smiling as I walked past him. Charles locked the door, and we made our way up and out of the dungeon. The mist seemed to filter its way up and out along with us. It filled the ground around our feet, and the light of the day seemed to go dull as it filtered out across the court-yards. I climbed on Raiden, and we proceeded to part Whispering Wind. As we made our way through the village, something fell to the ground in front of me. As I passed it by, I noticed that it was a bird.

A strange feeling filled my body. What was this mist? Was it the same mist that was in the vile I broke on Jared's chest to bring him back from the depths of death? I leaned into Raiden and told him to run, and we did, all the way to the hill top. We did not look back until we reached the top.

CHAPTER THIRTY FIVE

As I turned to look back at my home, the place of my birth, my mind flooded with the memories of my life there; the happiness, the love, and the death that once filled the halls of Whispering Wind. I closed my eyes to absorb it all, to hear the voices of those I loved, those who were now gone. My mother, my father, my brothers Ardes and Simon, and my sister Jenna, they all played a part in my training for what my future was to hold. They all died because of me. I could feel the tears as they fell on my cheeks. They were tears of gratitude for their sacrifice, tears of sorrow for my loss, and tears of exhaustion.

I opened my eyes to a horror far worse than that day I heard the thunder as I lay on this very hilltop. Whispering Wind was shrouded in a thick green mist. The castle, the village, the fields, it was the strangest thing. I swear you could almost feel it. The mist was death.

Look for
Whispering Wind The Mist

As I turned to look back at my home, the place of my birth, my mind flooded with the memories of my life there; the happiness, the love, and the death that once filled the halls of Whispering Wind. I closed my eyes to absorb it all, to hear the voices of those I loved and those who were now gone. My mother, my father, my brothers Ardes and Simon and my sister Jenna, they all played a part in my training for what my future was to hold. They all died because of me. I could feel the tears as they fell on my cheeks. They were tears of gratitude for their sacrifice, tears of sorrow for my loss, and tears of exhaustion.

I opened my eyes to a horror far worse than that day I heard the thunder as I lay on this very hilltop. Whispering Wind was shrouded in a thick green mist. The castle, the village, the fields, it was the strangest thing. I swear you could almost feel it. The mist was death.

The past three years had felt like a lifetime to me. My journey had been one that no princess should ever have to take. I should have been given in marriage to a man my father, King Stephan of Whispering Wind, had chosen for me at the age of just sixteen years. I should have a child or be ripe with one now, in a kingdom of my own. Instead, I watched as death rode across the plains that lay before me with the sound of thunder, taking all that was dear to me, and then set me on a journey filled with fear, determination, and the need to find those who murdered my family. I was driven by revenge. My heart wanted an adventure, but I think I got more than what I wished for.

My beloved Jared was brought back from the hands of death itself. My love, Juliana, lives with the passion of her parents, Jenna of Wellington and my beloved brother Ardes, in her heart. I sit surrounded by men who secretly in their youth swore to protect me, long before they knew who I was. It all seemed so far from the truth that it made me giggle.

I sensed their eyes upon me as I sit on my horse, Raiden, a horse who most believe is the spirits of those who have ridden him before me, possibly even the great Sorcerer Merlin himself, gazing out at the thick green mist that now engulfed my beloved Whispering Wind.

www.ingramcontent.com/pod-product-compliance
Lightning Source LLC
Chambersburg PA
CBHW030915050726
47498CB00003BA/759